# ICING IVY

Books by Evan Marshall

MISSING MARLENE

HANGING HANNAH

STABBING STEPHANIE

ICING IVY

Published by Kensington Publishing Corporation

A Jane Stuart and Winky Mystery

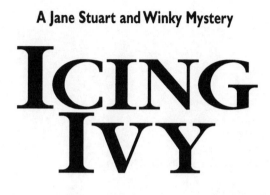

# ICING IVY

# EVAN MARSHALL

KENSINGTON BOOKS
http://www.kensingtonbooks.com

KENSINGTON BOOKS are published by

Kensington Publishing Corp.
850 Third Avenue
New York, NY 10022

All Kensington titles, imprints and distributed lines are available at special quantity discounts for bulk purchases for sales promotion, premiums, fund-raising, educational or institutional use.

Special book excerpts or customized printings can also be created to fit specific needs. For details, write or phone the office of the Kensington Special Sales Manager: Kensington Publishing Corp., 850 Third Avenue, New York, NY 10022, Attn. Special Sales Department. Phone: 1-800-221-2647.

Kensington and the K logo Reg. U.S. Pat. & TM Off.

Library of Congress Card Catalogue Number: 2002101746
ISBN 0-7582-0224-5

First Printing: November 2002
10   9   8   7   6   5   4   3   2   1

Printed in the United States of America

*To my mother,*
*Maxine Marshall,*
*with love*

*Let justice be done, though the heavens fall.*
—Legal maxim

# Acknowledgments

I would like to express my thanks and appreciation to the following people:

Frank Corso, Joseph M. Holtzman, Ph.D., and Warren Marshall for telling me about Trotsky and the ice pick. Or was it an ice ax . . . ?

John Baglieri, personal trainer extraordinaire, for lending me his name.

Ellen Reichert, for telling me about superfecundation.

Florence Phillip, for telling me about the cascadura.

John Scognamiglio, my editor, for his wisdom and encouragement.

Maureen Walters, for being the best agent an agent could ask for.

My family and friends, for their love and support.

# MT. MUNSEE LODGE

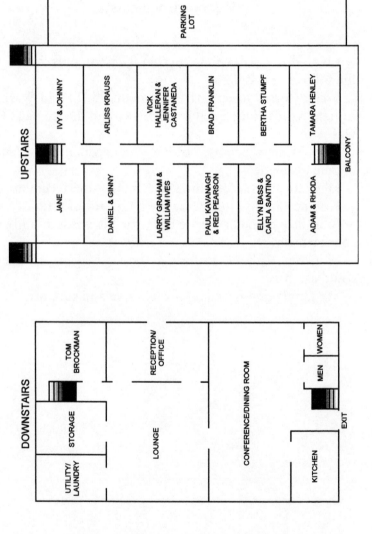

**DOWNSTAIRS**

| UTILITY/ LAUNDRY | STORAGE | TOM BROCKMAN |
|---|---|---|
| | LOUNGE | RECEPTION/ OFFICE |
| | CONFERENCE/DINING ROOM | |
| KITCHEN | | MEN / WOMEN |

EXIT

**UPSTAIRS**

| JANE | IVY & JOHNNY |
|---|---|
| DANIEL & GINNY | ARLISS KRAUSS |
| LARRY GRAHAM & WILLIAM IVES | VICK HALLERAN & JENNIFER CASTANEDA |
| PAUL KAVANAGH & RED PEARSON | BRAD FRANKLIN |
| ELLYN BASS & CARLA SANTINO | BERTHA STUMPF |
| ADAM & RHODA | TAMARA HENLEY |

BALCONY

PARKING LOT

# Chapter One

"Back soon," Jane called to Daniel, who smiled and waved from the office doorway. Then she turned and ran across Center Street onto the village green. Stanley, who had preceded Jane by less than a minute, was nowhere in sight.

She giggled. He must be hiding. A silly thrill building inside her, she started down one of the paths that transected the green, walking slowly and peering behind the trunks of the massive oaks that rose from the snow. "I know you're here somewhere."

But there was only silence, broken occasionally by the whoosh of cars passing on Packer Road, far to her right.

The ornate white Victorian bandstand came into view. Could Stanley be hiding in there? She squinted but saw no one.

*Wham.* Something hit the back of her coat, hit hard. "Ow." She spun around, not liking this game anymore. Stanley was laughing, his sand-colored hair blowing in the chill wind. Clapping his gloved hands together, he ran toward her, his camel coat hanging loose and open on his broad shoulders. When he saw her face, his smile vanished. "Sorry. Did that hurt you?"

"Yes," she said petulantly. "You didn't have to throw it so hard."

"I'm sorry." He put his hand on her shoulder and turned her toward him. His dark brown eyes were tearing in the cold. He kissed her on the lips. "Forgive me?"

She regarded him for a moment. Such a sweet man, so often like a boy. "Yes," she said at last. "Fine behavior for a police detective."

"Excuse me," he said with a disbelieving laugh. "You're the one who said she loved snowball fights at Christmas."

"True. I just don't like to be the one getting hit."

He shook his head. "Not exactly the kind of behavior one would expect from Shady Hills' own literary agent, either."

"I think this town knows me better than that." With a grin, she took his arm and cuddled against him, and they began to walk.

They were nearing the other side of the green, where Center Street continued in its U shape. Across the street, the window of Whipped Cream, the café where they planned to have lunch, twinkled red and green and blue. Ginny always insisted on colored lights, dismissing with a laugh the opinion of many Shady Hills residents that white lights were more appropriate for the upscale village.

"Pretty, isn't it?" Jane said as a black Mercedes passed in front of them and drove slowly around the green. She scanned the line of mock-Tudor shops that ran around Center Street—half-timbered, with steeply pitched roofs and a profusion of gables. With their coating of snow, they looked like something out of a fairy tale. "I do love this town."

From behind them came the sound of car brakes suddenly applied. Jane and Stanley turned. The black Mercedes had stopped in front of Jane's office, and now a man and a woman got out. From this distance, Jane couldn't tell if she knew them.

"Probably out-of-town shoppers," Stanley said, and they turned again toward lunch.

"Jane. Jane, is that you?"

It was a voice Jane had thought she'd never hear again.

Jane spun around. The woman who had gotten out of the car was waving broadly.

Jane squinted. Could it be? She drew in her breath sharply.

"Who is it?" Stanley asked.

A violent shiver ran through her. "It's Ivy," she said in a marveling tone. "Ivy Benson. You remember, Marlene's mother."

"Ivy Benson?" He looked shocked. "But I thought you two—I mean, didn't she—"

"Not want to be friends anymore?" she finished for him. "That's right. At least, that's what she said."

And Jane couldn't blame Ivy. A little over two years before, Ivy's daughter, Marlene, had come east to work as nanny to Jane's son, Nicholas—and wound up dead. Though Marlene had brought about her own demise by means of a chain of lies and deceptions, Ivy had blamed Jane for Marlene's death. And a friendship that had begun when the two women were college roommates had ended. At least, Jane had thought it had.

Ivy was running along the path toward Jane, waving frantically. As she approached, Jane could see that this was indeed the same old Ivy, compact but curvaceous, a thick mop of tightly waved blond hair crowning a round, sweet face with huge blue eyes. Even in her amazement at seeing Ivy, Jane couldn't help noticing that her old friend was looking exceptionally well. What had appeared to be her usual mass of hair was actually an artful cut, her once-untended brows appeared to have been professionally tamed, and the simple gold drop earrings and belted black cashmere coat were definitely several steps up from the old Kmart stuff that had once been her trademark.

Ivy, quick-stepping toward Jane in her high heels, was crying, and Jane found herself crying too as she welcomed Ivy into her arms.

"Ivy Benson," she said at last, drawing back. "What are you doing here?"

Ivy wiped away her tears with a black-gloved hand. "I was worried you wouldn't want to see me again. After what I said to you when . . . after what I said. But you're my best friend, Jane. I never felt right after what happened. And now that I'm living in New York—"

"You're living in New York?" Jane asked, incredulous. "Ivy Benson, who said she'd never leave Detroit?"

Ivy shrugged. "People change," she said brightly. "You wouldn't be*lieve* how I've changed. I've got my own *fabulous* apartment, a great job working for a newspaper, and . . ." She turned toward the man who had gotten out of the car and who was now strolling up the path. Jane turned to look at him, too, and found herself gaping. Good heavens, this man, whoever he was, was handsome. He was of medium height, lean, with an abundance of wavy black hair around a strong-boned face with refined, aristocratic features. He looked about thirty-five, vital and youthful against Ivy's forty. He reminded Jane of an updated Tyrone Power.

"Jane," Ivy said formally, gesturing for the man to come over, "I'd like you to meet my *boyfriend*"—she placed special emphasis on the word—"John Baglieri."

John came forward and took Jane's hand, his lips parting in a beautiful white-toothed smile. "Pleasure. Call me Johnny." There was nothing refined about the way he spoke, which was with an accent—Brooklyn? The Bronx? Jane couldn't be sure. It was what she would have called a New York "street" accent.

Stanley approached them, smiling politely.

"And this," Jane said, "is *my* boyfriend, Stanley Greenberg."

Stanley shook their hands enthusiastically. "I believe we've met, Mrs. Benson. At the police station, after your daughter . . ."

Ivy's face darkened. "Yes, of course we have."

"So," Jane said, eager to change the subject. "Ivy, you still haven't told me what you're doing here."

"Like I said, I've missed you, Jane. There I was in New York City—what, twenty-five miles away?—and you and I weren't even speaking. It was killing me. So I said to Johnny, 'Hey. It's four days before Christmas. I've got the day off. Let's go see Jane. Surprise her. If she won't see me, I'll understand, but at least I'll have tried.' So here we are. Johnny and I thought we'd take you to lunch." Ivy shot a quick glance at Stanley. "Both of you, of course."

"Actually, we were just on our way to have lunch," Stanley said, indicating Whipped Cream.

"Perfect," Ivy cried in a high squeak, and they all crossed the street and entered the shop. Jane's friend Ginny, Whipped Cream's only server, was clearing a table when they entered. With a curious smile she approached the small group, and Jane introduced Ivy and Johnny to her. Then they settled at a table near the café's great crackling fireplace.

"I can't believe it," Ivy said to herself as she perused her menu. "Here I am with my old friend Jane." She wiped a tear from her eye. "Can't believe it."

Jane watched her old friend. Hair, brows, jewelry, and clothing notwithstanding, she hadn't changed, not really. Though pretty, she still had a cheap edge to her, an indefinable . . . flooziness.

Ivy, who hadn't removed her coat, now let it slip from her shoulders to reveal a summer-weight ivory cotton blouse. She shivered, folding her arms and rubbing her upper arms for warmth. "Cold in here."

Inwardly Jane laughed. Ivy never dressed warmly enough.

"Would you like to sit here by the fire?" Stanley asked.

"Nah, thanks, Stan, I'm fine." Ivy gave Jane a fond look. "As Jane'll tell ya, I'm always cold." She opened her bag, stopped, and looked quickly around the table. "Is it okay to smoke in here?"

Ginny approached the table. "Forgive me for eavesdropping, but Charlie and George—they're the owners—don't allow smoking in here."

"Not a prob," Ivy cried, hands raised, then snapped her bag shut. Johnny was shaking his head. Jane's gaze was drawn to his white shirt, tight enough to reveal strong, smooth musculature. A few darks hairs curled at his open collar.

As if sensing her gaze, he looked up suddenly, and Jane felt herself blush. "So, Jane," he said, setting aside his menu, "Ivy was trying to explain what it is you do, but I still don't get it. Why don't you explain it to me?"

"Oh, Johnny," Ivy cooed.

"Of course," Jane said. "I'm a literary agent. I represent writers, sell their books to publishers, negotiate their contracts, manage their careers."

"I get it," Johnny said. He shot Ivy a look, as if to ask what was so complicated about that. "Pretty simple, really. And—if you don't mind my asking—does that make a nice living for you?"

Stanley looked up from his menu in surprise.

"I can't complain," Jane replied smoothly.

"What do you do, take a piece of the action?" Johnny asked.

Jane couldn't help making a little frown. Ivy saw it and nudged Johnny. "That's kind of *per*sonal . . ."

"Okay, sorry. Sorry, Jane." Johnny held up his hands.

Jane said, "No problem, I don't mind. I'm on commission, actually, so yes, I guess you could say I take a piece of the action. I've never quite thought of it that way." Laughing breezily, she turned to Stanley, who was not laughing at all, not even smiling, but watching Johnny in a most disconcerting way.

"Stanley," Jane said, a bit too loudly, and he snapped out of his stare. "Why don't you tell Ivy and Johnny what it is you do?"

"Sure," Stanley said, forcing a small smile, "sure. I'm a police detective. Right here in town. Shady Hills Police Department."

For the merest fraction of a second, Johnny's eyes widened. Then he appeared to collect himself. His mouth turned up at the corners, though Jane wouldn't have called it a smile exactly. "Now *that* must be interesting work," Johnny said.

Ivy turned to Johnny with a frown. "You knew that's what he does. He just said he met me after the whole thing with Marlene."

"Sure, right," Johnny said absently, and occupied himself once again with his menu.

"What about you, Johnny?" Jane said. "What kind of work do you do?"

"Huh? Me?" Johnny looked up with a blank expression, as if he'd never been part of the conversation. "I guess you could say I've got my irons in many fires. Kind of a jack of all trades."

"I see," Jane said, though she didn't see at all. She looked at Stanley. He was staring again.

Mercifully, Ginny appeared. "May I tell you about our specials?"

"Yes, please," Jane said, looking up attentively.

"*Def*initely," Ivy said, "and bring us some rolls or something when you get a chance, would you, hon? I swear I could eat a cow."

"Was that Ivy Benson?" Daniel asked, the minute Jane and Stanley entered the office. Sitting at his desk in the reception room, he had spun away from his computer, amazement on his handsome brown face.

"The one and only." Jane hung her coat in the closet, then took Stanley's.

"What did she want?"

"To see me again." They had exchanged phone numbers.

"Why?"

Jane frowned. "Because she's my oldest friend. She wanted to see me again. I think it was very brave of her."

Daniel shook his head and nibbled thoughtfully on the inside of his lower lip. "She wants something."

"Why do you say that?" Jane asked, finding herself becoming upset.

"Don't you remember the things she said to you? She *blamed* you for Marlene's death, when in truth—"

"I know what happened. You don't have to remind me, believe me." Jane shrugged. "As Ivy herself said, people change. She wants to be friends again. It was good to see her." She turned to Stanley, who sat in Daniel's visitor's chair, lost in thought. "All right, out with it."

Stanley looked up as if startled. "Hm? I was just thinking about that young fellow, Johnny. Bad news, if you ask me."

"Why?" Jane demanded, exasperated. "What is *with* you two?"

Stanley put up his hands defensively. "I could be wrong. It's just a feeling I got."

"Why, because he's a little rough around the edges?"

"No, it's not that. It was the way he was looking at me after he found out I was a cop. And—I don't know, the way he carries himself. I can just tell, Jane, the same way you can immediately tell a good manuscript from a bad one."

Jane didn't want to hear any of this. She wanted Ivy to be happy. Years ago, when Jane and Ivy were eighteen years old, freshman roommates in college, Ivy had confided to Jane that all she wanted was a good man and a good life. A man who loved her, asleep on the next lounge chair, while Ivy sipped extra-tall piña coladas served by beach boys in brightly colored shirts. Somewhere hot. With palm trees. That was how Ivy had envisioned the good life.

With a faraway smile, Jane turned to Daniel. "Speaking of bad manuscripts, have you had a chance to look at Bertha Stumpf's revised manuscript of *Shady Lady*?" It had taken every bit of Jane's skills of persuasion to get Bertha, who wrote historical romances under the pseudonym Rhonda Redmond, to revise her manuscript for her editor, Harriet Green at Bantam.

"Sure have," Daniel said lightly. "It still stinks."

"Really? Now what's wrong with it?"

"There's still absolutely no conflict between the hero and heroine. There's no reason why they shouldn't walk hand in hand into the sunset on page ten. Not only that, there's no plot. All they do is have sex."

"Sounds good to me," Stanley piped up.

Jane gave him an irritated look. "Don't you have some criminals to catch?"

He jumped up. "Well, I certainly know where I'm not wanted."

"Give me a break," Jane said, handing him his coat from the closet.

"I had to leave anyway," Stanley said.

"I know." Jane gave him a kiss as he opened the door to leave.

"Hello," Jane heard him say outside, and a moment later he was showing in Rhoda Kagan and her boyfriend, Adam Forrest. "Later," Stanley told Jane, and left.

Rhoda looked smashing, as always, in black slacks and a brilliant indigo sweater. Huge black bakelite earrings set off her sleekly cut dark brown hair.

"Hello, darling," she said, exchanging cheek kisses with Jane. "You remember Adam."

"Of course." Jane had last seen Adam at a local party about a month earlier. "How are you, Adam? You're looking well."

Adam, independently wealthy, always looked well— trim and tan and neat. Today he wore tan Dockers and an expensive-looking brown sweater. "Thanks, Jane." He seemed nervous, awkward somehow.

"So what's doing, guys?" Jane asked them. "You Christmas shopping?"

Rhoda shot Adam a look.

"Jane," he said, "Rhoda and I . . . well, *I* need to ask you a favor. . . ."

# Chapter Two

Florence's gaze was fixed on Winky, whose pregnant tortoiseshell belly swung from side to side as she padded across the family room and out into the foyer. "So what do you think, missus? Are you going to do it?"

Jane sipped her tea. She had just told Florence what Adam had asked her to do.

Adam had recently bought Mt. Munsee Lodge, located at the top of Mt. Munsee at the northernmost end of Shady Hills. The lodge was a popular spot for hikers and campers, except in the winter, when the lodge's previous owner had shut it down. But Adam had come up with an idea to make money in the off-season. He had been sponsoring five-day "theme retreats" on topics ranging from yoga to investing.

Adam had scheduled a retreat for would-be antiques dealers for the following week—the week between Christmas and New Year's—but had learned that morning that its leader would be unable to appear because his wife was quite ill.

It was Rhoda who had come up with the idea of organizing a fiction writers' retreat to take the place of the antiques one.

Florence said, "Why doesn't he forget about it and

enjoy the holidays?" A smile brightened her pretty coffee-colored face. "He doesn't need the money."

"Apparently he does," Jane said. "Or, to put it another way, it would help."

"I see . . ." Florence said thoughtfully. "But how can such a thing possibly be arranged on such short notice?"

"The lodge is small, so we wouldn't need many people. And Adam says he always has one-on-one instruction at these retreats—which is another reason why there can't be too many attendees. He said that if I can round up six instructors besides myself, he'll sign up six attendees from a writers' group here in town."

"What writers' group?"

"The Midnight Writers. I had no idea they even existed."

"Could you 'round up' six instructors?" Florence asked.

"I'm not sure. Probably, if I set my mind to it. I'd call editors, authors, other agents—nah, just editors and authors—and could probably come up with six."

"Don't you want to take the week between Christmas and New Year's off? You do that every year."

"True—which is why I'm available. I've been looking forward to spending the time with Nick, but I really do feel I should help Rhoda and Adam out with this. Besides, I've just had my vacation—I'm not in dire need of a rest." Less than a month earlier, Jane had spent two glorious weeks in Antigua. "And I'll make it up to Nick."

"You may miss the blessed event," Florence said, referring to Winky's imminent delivery. She rose from the sofa and took Jane's teacup. "Dinner in twenty minutes." She walked into the kitchen and stopped to glare at Nick's books and papers strewn all over the table. Jane heard her open the back door. "Master Nicholas," Florence called out into the garage. "Put down the snow shovel and come in here. Your homework is all over the table, and from the looks of it, none of it is done."

"Take it easy, I'm coming," came Nick's voice, followed by a giggle from Florence.

Laughing herself, Jane headed for her study off the living room to start making phone calls. The first would be to Adam, to tell him she'd decided to help him out.

It was a few minutes before nine that evening when Jane put down the phone, having successfully recruited six instructors for the fiction writers' retreat.

The phone rang. It was Ivy.

"I had to tell you how terrific it was to see you again, Jane. I hope we can be friends again, after everything that happened. I mean friends like the old days. I didn't get a chance to say that to you today, but I don't blame you at all for Marlene's death. I miss her terribly—she was all I had—but I know that none of it was your fault."

"Thank you, Ivy, I appreciate your saying that. Of course we can be friends again."

"I'm so glad. There was something else I forgot to ask you today. How is little Nicholas?"

"Not so little anymore—ten and a half years old."

"He can't be. I'd love to see him," Ivy said wistfully.

"I'm sure you will one day soon."

"Mmm. It must be nice for you to have him with you at Christmas. I mean, now that Kenneth is gone." Kenneth, Jane's late husband, had died a little over three years before.

"Yes." Jane felt uneasy. "Will you and Johnny be doing anything special for the holidays?"

"He'll be away. Business trip. He says he can't get out of it. You know how it is." Ivy let out a sigh. "This will be my second Christmas without Marlene. I suppose one day I'll get used to it." There was a long silence on the line.

Alone at Christmas . . .

"Ivy," Jane blurted out, "why don't you spend Christmas out here with us?"

"With you? Why, Jane, what an idea. But I couldn't—I'd be in the way."

"No, you wouldn't. We'd love to have you. You'll get to see Nick, and you'll love Florence—she's Nick's nanny, and a wonderful person."

"If you really think it would be all right . . ."

"Of course I do." Then Jane thought of something. "One thing, though. Right after Christmas—next Wednesday—I've got to go to a retreat I'm helping organize." She told Ivy all about it. "But we'd still be together during the holiday."

"True. Hey, Jane, do you think I could come on your retreat *with* you? I'm taking that week off from work. Wouldn't it be a gas?"

Jane frowned. "I don't think that would be possible, unfortunately."

"Yeah, I'd be in the way, I suppose."

"No, it's not that."

"I could help out," Ivy said eagerly. "Hand out paper and pencils, things like that. I'm very organized, as you know."

Jane had never thought of Ivy as being especially organized. She made no comment as to that. "I've never been to this lodge. I'm not sure there's room."

"I guess you'd have your own room, huh?"

"Yes, I imagine."

"Then we could room together. It would be like the old days at school. Wouldn't it be fun? Just you and me, hanging out in our jammies, eating Cheese Curls? What a way to spend the holidays. No chance I'd be lonely then."

Jane's heart went out to her old friend. How could Adam object if Jane shared her room with Ivy? "I guess it would be all right. . . ."

"You don't sound very sure."

"Yes, I'm sure," Jane said kindly. "I'd love to have you with me at the retreat."

"You and me and Cheese Curls. When should I come out to your house?"

The next day was Saturday. "Why not tomorrow? Then we can have the weekend to catch up, and Monday night is Christmas Eve."

"Perfect. Oh, Jane," Ivy said, tears coming into her voice, "I can't tell you how much I've missed you. I'm glad we're not letting what happened ruin our friendship. You're my oldest friend—my best friend."

Still feeling uneasy, Jane averred that she was glad, too. Then they made plans. Ivy, who had no car, would take a Lakeland bus the next morning from New York City's Port Authority Bus Terminal to Shady Hills. Jane would be waiting for her bus.

# Chapter Three

Florence entered the dining room bearing a platter of fish fillets covered with a rich brown sauce. Steam rose from the platter.

"That looks wonderful, Florence," Ivy said, craning her neck as Florence set it down.

Florence beamed. "Thank you. It is my very favorite recipe, from my mother—curried cascadura. I do hope you all like it. When I was growing up, we always had it on Christmas Eve—and many other times too. I had to go to my Afro-Caribbean market in Newark for the fish."

Ivy frowned. "Why'd you have to go all the way to Newark?"

"Because that is the only store that imports cascadura, or cascadoo as we call it back home. This fish is found only in Trinidad." Florence gazed across the dining room, a dreamy look in her eyes. "In my country they say,

*Those who eat the cascadura will,*
*The native legend says,*
*Wheresoever they may wander,*
*End in Trinidad their days.*"

Jane, her gazed fixed on Florence, said, "Why, that's lovely."

Nick, seated to Ivy's right, was gently petting Winky, who sat on the empty chair beside him. He stroked the cat's mottled orange-and-brown head but was careful not to touch her enlarged belly. "I've eaten this a zillion times," he declared nonchalantly, and Jane and Florence exchanged a smile.

"Indeed you have, little mister, indeed you have." Florence went back to the kitchen for platters of rice and green beans, which she set down on the table. Then she took up serving utensils. "If you'll pass me your plate," she said, reaching toward Ivy.

The telephone rang.

"Let it ring," Jane said breezily. "We're having dinner."

Ivy drew in a little breath and looked around anxiously.

"What's wrong, Ivy?" Jane asked.

The phone continued to ring.

"Nothing," Ivy replied, moving restlessly in her chair. "It's just that . . . maybe it's Johnny."

"Of course," Jane said. "Where is my head?" She jumped up, hurried into the kitchen, and grabbed the phone.

It was indeed Johnny. "Umm, yeah, is this, uh, Joan?"

"It's Jane," she replied, feeling uncomfortable.

"Right, Jane. Sorry. How's it goin'?"

"Fine, Johnny, and you? Ivy said you're away on business?"

"Well, I was—I mean, I was going to be." He sounded as if he didn't want to discuss this with her. "Is Ivy there?"

"Certainly. One moment."

Jane called Ivy, who hurried in. "Thanks, hon," Ivy said, and waited, apparently not wanting to begin her conversation until Jane had left the kitchen. Jane did and was aware of the door being closed quietly behind her.

Ivy and Johnny's conversation didn't last long. Florence

was still serving when Ivy returned to the dining room, an odd, preoccupied look on her face.

"Everything okay?" Jane asked.

"Yes," Ivy replied, smiling an uneasy little smile.

"No, it's not," Jane said with a laugh. "What's going on?"

Ivy picked up her fork and poked at a green bean. "Everything's fine, really. It's just that Johnny doesn't have to go away on business after all."

"Ah," Jane said. "And you want to be with him and are embarrassed to tell me. Ivy, don't worry about it. He's your boyfriend. I completely understand."

When Ivy looked up, her face bore no trace of the relieved smile Jane had expected. She still looked troubled. "Thanks, Jane, but he and I were wondering if maybe"— she winced, as if afraid to say the words—"he could come to your retreat too?"

Jane gave her a puzzled look. "Johnny? Why would *he* want to come?"

"It would be kind of a vacation, you know? It's so pretty here—Johnny kept saying so when we drove out on Friday."

Jane didn't know what to make of this. Ivy had always been a bit pushy, often inappropriate, and Jane's instinct was to simply say no. A fiction writers' retreat was no place for Johnny. Besides, if he came, he and Ivy would need a room of their own, and there probably wasn't one to spare. On the other hand, Jane thought, meeting Ivy's expectant gaze, she didn't know that for sure. She should call Adam and find out. Would it really be such a problem if Johnny did come? He and Ivy could take walks in the woods, do that sort of thing.

"Tell you what I'll do," Jane said. "Right after dinner, I'll call Adam—he owns the lodge. If he says he's got a room for you and Johnny, I have no objections."

Ivy looked apprehensive. "You think he might not have a room?"

"It's a possibility. I understand the lodge is small."

Ivy thought about this, then nodded. "Okay, thanks, Jane." She pressed her fork down on her cascadura fillet, crushing it. "I hope he says yes. It would be so good for Johnny and me."

Jane watched Ivy. It was suddenly clear to Jane that Johnny's coming to the retreat meant a lot to Ivy, that she saw it as more than just a fun getaway for the two of them. Why? Was their relationship somehow in trouble? Did Ivy hope this time away together would solve this trouble?

Dinner felt somehow strained to Jane, though the food was heavenly and they all talked and laughed. It was as if Ivy couldn't wait for the meal to end so that Jane could call Adam.

To Jane's surprise, Adam did have a spare room and was only too glad to let Ivy and Johnny have it. "You're doing me a tremendous favor, Jane. How could I say no? The room's on me."

"Thanks, Adam," Jane said, surprised to find herself disappointed by his response. Was it that she'd looked forward to just her and Ivy—jammies and Cheese Curls? Or was it Johnny? Somehow she couldn't imagine him at a writers' retreat. The idea made her uneasy. What would he and Ivy do all day? On further reflection, he hadn't struck Jane as the woods-walking type.

Lost in thought, Jane left her study and went in search of Ivy to tell her the news.

Later that evening, Jane, Ivy, Florence, and Nick sat together in the family room watching TV. Since Christmas vacation had officially begun, Nick was allowed to stay up late and had, in fact, chosen tonight's television viewing, a special Christmas episode of his favorite show, *Cyber-Warriors*. Jane was utterly bored, and it appeared that Ivy and Florence were as well. Nick sat at the edge of the sofa, jumping up and down every time a CyberWarrior laser-blasted a Vultron.

Jane let her gaze travel around the room. The Christmas tree had turned out especially well. Each year she added a new touch, and this year's was a collection of ornaments in the shape of tiny stacks of antique books wrapped with gold bows. Colored lights that reminded her of the window of Whipped Cream twinkled among the tree's branches. Beneath the tree, in a pleasing jumble, were a goodly number of presents. Jane had even run out the day before and bought something for Ivy—a bottle of Norell perfume, which had always been her favorite.

"Mom, look at this," Nick cried. Jane expected to see some especially exciting scene from *CyberWarriors*, but on the TV screen instead was a newscaster looking solemn.

"Good evening. We interrupt our scheduled broadcast to bring you an update on the bus hijacking . . ."

"What bus hijacking?" Jane said.

"Haven't you heard about this, missus? It's the big story right now."

"Shhh, listen," Ivy said, and they all watched the screen.

That morning, in the city of Paterson, New Jersey, a man described as heavily bearded and carrying a briefcase had boarded a New Jersey Transit bus bound ultimately for New York City. Approximately twenty minutes after boarding, as the bus sped eastward on Route 3, he brandished a gun and threatened to detonate a bomb in his briefcase if he did not receive full cooperation. Holding his gun to the driver's head, he commanded the driver to radio headquarters and relay his demands: a million dollars in unmarked twenty-dollar bills for the release of his hostages—the driver and thirty-one other passengers. This ransom was to be waiting for him at Gate B of Giants Stadium in East Rutherford within an hour.

An hour later, the commandeered bus pulled up at Gate B of the stadium, where police waited with the money. At gunpoint the driver opened the doors, and the money was thrown aboard. The gunman checked the money and, apparently satisfied, released the other passengers but not the driver, whom he ordered to shut the doors and take off. The bus then raced westward on Route 3, onto Route 46, then onto Interstate 80. It left I-80 at Shady Hills and sped north into Lincoln Park, where it finally stopped in a wooded area and the gunman disembarked. The authorities, who were interviewing the driver and the passengers, had as yet found no trace of him.

"Can you believe this?" Ivy said, wide-eyed.

The newscaster continued, "Police are combing the woods in the Lincoln Park/Shady Hills area for signs of this man. We now return to our regularly scheduled programming."

Once again, colorful CyberWarriors and Vultrons filled the screen.

"A million dollars," Ivy said. "Can you imagine?"

"That poor driver," Jane said. "And all those frightened people. I hope they catch him."

The credits for *CyberWarriors* had begun to roll.

"Well," Florence said, rising from the sofa. "It's time a certain young man got to bed, or else Santa Claus won't come with the rest of the presents."

"Come off it, Flo," Nick said. "There's no Santa Claus, and you know it. Besides, all the presents are there already."

"You never know." Florence grinned widely, eyebrows rising. She looked down at Winky. "And from the look of our little miss here, I think she's ready to give us a few presents anytime now."

# Chapter Four

Florence was right. The next day, Christmas Day, Winky gave birth to six kittens. She did so in a nest box that Jane (at the advice of Winky's veterinarian, Dr. Singh) had made for her in a corner of the laundry room by filling the bottom of a cardboard carton with old clean towels.

"A trouble-free birth," Florence, emerging from the laundry room, proclaimed to Jane, Ivy, and Nick. "I saw many cats give birth when I was growing up in Trinidad, and I can tell you, Winky is a natural."

"That's nice," Jane said, "but her birthing days are over. As soon as the kittens are weaned, I'm having her spayed."

"Oh, Mom," Nick whined. "I want Winky to have more kittens."

"Sorry. This is as large as her family gets. We have to find homes for these six, so start asking around."

"Will do, missus. I think my friend Noni would like one."

"What about you, Ivy? Know anyone who'd like a kitten?"

But Ivy, apparently having lost interest, was gone.

Early the next day, Jane and Ivy drove to the north end of town and, after passing through rutted fields of gray-brown stubble, entered the forest that covered Mt. Munsee and started upward.

Heavy snow had begun to fall. Jane switched on the windshield wipers, but they did little good. The road was steep and narrow, and the snowflakes that seemed to be falling straight at them made driving even more difficult.

Ivy seemed not to have noticed. "This is so exciting. Come on, Jane, step on it. We'll never get there at this rate."

Jane remained silent, concentrating on the road. Soon its angle became less acute, though the tree branches hung lower, nearly touching the car.

Then the woods cleared and they found themselves on a delicate suspension bridge. Glancing out the window and down, Jane saw a deep gorge filled with a dizzying swirl of snow.

"How beautiful," Ivy said.

"And scary. I hate that grinding noise the tires make on the bridge."

They made it safely to the other side and continued upward. Finally a sign appeared at the side of the road—MT. MUNSEE LODGE—and they emerged onto a narrow parking lot that ran the length of the lodge, a long, two-story rustic structure of dark wood.

The parking lot was nearly full. Jane had no sooner pulled into a space than she saw Adam in her rearview mirror, coatless, hurrying toward them from the lodge's entrance.

Jane rolled down her window.

"Welcome, welcome," Adam said, hopping from one foot to the other and rubbing his hands together. "You're just in time. We're all in the lounge having a get-acquainted breakfast."

Insisting on carrying their bags, he led the way into the lodge's reception area, a small room with a Formica counter.

At each end of the wall behind the counter was a doorway leading into what must have been the lounge, for through them came the sounds of talk and laughter.

"I'll show you your rooms," Adam said.

"I can wait," Jane said, feeling she should join the group as soon as possible. "Though I can't speak for Ivy."

"I'll wait too," Ivy said eagerly, and Adam, clearly pleased with this response, led them into the lounge, in which small groups of people chatted. Against the back wall stood a table bearing bagels, Danish, juice, coffee, and tea.

Jane was aware of someone standing beside her and turned to see Daniel. He had been the first person she'd asked to serve as an instructor. "You made it," he said. "Looks pretty bad out there."

"Not so bad," Ivy answered for Jane, looking around. At that moment Ginny appeared at Daniel's arm. Ivy looked confused to see her. "Don't I . . . ?"

"Know me?" Ginny laughed. "I waited on you at lunch last week. I'm also"—she put her arm lovingly around Daniel's waist—"this handsome man's girlfriend."

"Ah," Ivy said. "Will you be teaching too?"

"No," Ginny scoffed. "I'm just along for the ride."

"Like my Johnny," Ivy said.

Ginny looked surprised. "Your boyfriend? He's coming here?"

"Mm-hm," Ivy responded smugly. "Should be here any-time now."

"I'd better say hello to the others," Jane said. She spotted another of her instructors, Arliss Krauss, standing nearby, chatting with an older man. Jane approached them.

Arliss, a senior editor at Millennium House, a publisher with which Jane had done a good bit of business, seemed pleased to see Jane, though with the habitually dour, dead-pan Arliss, that wasn't saying much. She actually smiled a little as she greeted Jane, who noticed that Arliss was dressed for the lodge in brown wool slacks and a pretty tan corduroy shirt with the tails out.

"Good to see you, Arliss. Thanks so much for agreeing to do this at such short notice."

"No problem," Arliss said in her monotone voice. She turned to the man with whom she'd been chatting. He looked about sixty. He was tall and slim, with neatly trimmed graying brown hair. Jane saw kindness in the brown eyes behind wire-rimmed glasses. "Jane Stuart," Arliss said, "I'd like you to meet Brad Franklin."

So this was Brad Franklin. When Jane recruited Arliss, Arliss had recommended Brad, one of her authors, as an instructor. Brad, she told Jane, had written several novels under his own name but now made a handsome living ghostwriting novels for celebrities.

Brad said, "A pleasure, Jane," and shook her hand warmly. "Thanks for having me."

"Thank *you* for coming," Jane said, and excused herself to say hello to the others.

She decided to grab a bagel and a cup of coffee first, and made her way to the refreshment table, where Rhoda was straightening up.

"Morning, Jane darling. Glad you made it. Did you have any problems with the snow?"

"Nah. Piece of cake," Jane replied, smearing her bagel with cream cheese.

"Uh-uh-uh," came a whiny voice behind her, and forcing a smile, Jane turned.

"Hello, Bertha."

"Good to see you too, Jane." Chubby Bertha Stumpf pursed her lips and lightly fluffed her hair, which instead of its usual wrong shade of blond was now an odd assortment of blond and brown streaks. "How do you like the do?"

"Love it," Jane said. "How've you been, Bertha?"

Bertha tilted her head to one side and rolled her eyes heavenward. "Okay, I suppose. You know I finally persuaded that girl to accept *Shady Lady*."

"Oh? When was this?"

"Late Friday. She'll be calling you."

Jane guessed Bertha had done more bullying than persuading to get Harriet Green to accept her manuscript.

"Be a doll and see if you can get her to put a rush on my acceptance check, would you?" Bertha said.

Jane gave her a tight smile. "I'll see what I can do."

"We're going to have to have a serious talk about her, Jane. I can't go on with Bantam if they make me work with this girl."

"Stop calling her a girl, Bertha. She's a woman. She's also a very fine editor. And I'm afraid I won't be able to discuss your work here. We're here for the retreat, remember?"

Bertha clamped her mouth shut, as if a fury were building. "Of course I remember, Jane, I'm here because you asked me to be here. And let me tell you, getting out here from New York City was no easy game. Anyway, what I meant was that we could maybe discuss my career in our down moments—you know, when we're not teaching. Surely we won't be teaching every minute."

*My career* . . . If Bertha had used those words once since Jane had begun representing her five years earlier, she'd used them a hundred times. "You're right," Jane said placatingly. "I'm sure we'll find time to talk in our down moments. Oh," she said, pointing across the room. "There's Vick Halleran. Excuse me, I have to say hello to him."

"Okay," Bertha said, though her tone made it clear she felt it was not okay at all.

*Tough,* Jane thought, making her way toward Vick.

Though Jane had never represented V. Sam Halleran, they traveled in the same circles and she had known him for years. Kenneth had also known and liked Vick, as his friends called him. Soft-spoken and self-effacing, short and plump, he was considered a guru of fiction writing. He traveled around the country almost constantly, presenting seminars and workshops, and had also published several best-selling books for writers.

"Jane," he cried, smiling sweetly, and they embraced. "You're looking wonderful, as beautiful as always." He took in her flowing mane. "Love that red hair," he said with gusto.

"Thanks, but it's auburn," she replied with a laugh. "Where's Jennifer?"

"Not sure," he said, and he and Jane scanned the crowd.

To Jane's surprise, Vick's wife, Jennifer Castaneda, had also agreed to serve as an instructor. Jennifer was a writer of Latina romance novels. She was, in fact, the leading writer of these novels, with four back-to-back *New York Times* best-sellers to her credit.

"There she is," Vick said, spotting her by one of the doorways to the reception room. "Jen—"

Jennifer looked up and smiled at them both. Some said the olive-skinned beauty was worthy of Hollywood, perhaps to star in a film version of one of her own novels, and looking at her now, Jane had to agree. Jennifer's rich brown hair was pulled back from her flawless brow, accentuating her large dark eyes, slightly tiptilted nose, and over-full pink lips. A snug linen jumpsuit in a becoming shade of celery accentuated her ample curves.

"Jane," she said in her breathy little-girl voice, approaching them. She kissed Jane on the cheek and embraced her. She smelled of jasmine.

"You're looking as gorgeous as ever," Jane said.

"You too," Jennifer said with a modest laugh. She pointed toward the doorway where Vick had spotted her. "I was just talking to one of the students. Come on, I'll introduce you."

Jane followed Jennifer, who Jane realized hadn't involved her husband at all in the conversation. Glancing behind her, Jane saw him trailing along. Jennifer approached a good-looking black-haired man in his mid-twenties. Of medium height, he was exceptionally slight, with effete, almost feminine features.

"Jane Stuart," Jennifer said, "this is Paul Kavanagh."

Paul's face lit up at the mention of Jane's name. He took Jane's hand and brought it to his lips. "It is an honor."

"Oh, my," Jane said with an embarrassed giggle. "Thanks very much."

"No, I must thank you." He came closer—too close for Jane's comfort. "When Adam told our group you had agreed to run this retreat," he said softly, "I couldn't believe my good fortune. You know, I've submitted my work to you a number of times, only to have you reject it." He lowered his gaze in desolation.

Jane felt herself flush. "I'm terribly sorry . . ."

"No, no," he said, putting up his hand. "You were absolutely right in your assessment. This week, however, I think you'll be quite impressed with what I've got to offer."

Already Jane couldn't stand this little twerp. "I'm sure I will," she said, hating herself for being such a phony, "though I must warn you, as I'll warn all the others, I'm not currently taking on any new clients." A lie, but a necessary one if she was to avoid awkward situations like this one.

Paul gave her a conspiratorial wink. "You have to say that; I understand. But wait until you see my work."

Jane told him it was nice to have met him, and couldn't get away quickly enough.

Vick came close to speak to her. "You did the right thing, telling him you're not taking on new clients. Otherwise every one of these people would be after you at the end of the retreat."

"I think this one will be after me anyway."

"Don't worry," Vick said. "I'll make sure he understands."

She thanked him and, turning away, caught Jennifer rolling her eyes at what Vick had just said. Jane, pretending she hadn't seen this, looked briskly about her. "Now, who else should I meet?"

"You can meet me," came a husky, rather coarse female voice from behind her. Jane spun around.

A tall, willowy woman with long ash-blond hair parted in the middle and a large beak of a nose walked straight up to Jane and put out her hand. "I'm your next million-dollar client."

Before Jane could react, the woman burst into raucous laughter. "I'm kidding. I'll be some other agent's first million-dollar client. I just heard you say you're not taking on anybody new."

"Right," Jane said. "And you are . . . ?"

"Carla Santino." She put out her hand and held Jane's in a viselike grip. "Waitress by day, future best-selling novelist by night."

"Waitress . . . Don't you—"

"Look familiar? Probably. I work at the Shady Hills Diner on Route Forty-six. I've probably waited on the whole town as some point or another. But I don't intend to be there much longer."

"Well, good for you," Jane said, eager to get away from Carla. Carla herself provided the getaway, pointing to a petite, mousy-looking woman who stood a couple of yards away, her hands clasped demurely in front of her, watching them. "Ellyn, get over here."

The mousy woman walked in tiny steps toward them and stopped. She wore a plain black skirt and a pink stretch blouse. Her curly dark hair looked as if it hadn't had the benefit of a good haircut in years. She looked, it occurred to Jane, not unlike a brunette Harpo Marx.

"Here's my fellow best-seller," Carla said, slapping the woman on the back. "Ellyn Bass—Jane Stuart."

"Glad to meet you, Ellyn. You're also from Shady Hills?"

"Yes," Ellyn replied. Her voice was high and squeaky. "But I don't work like Carla. I'm only a housewife."

"Don't ever say that," Jane said with a smile. "You're setting back the women's movement by about thirty years. Say, 'I don't work outside the home.' Much more p.c."

Ellyn nodded solemnly, as if completely unaware that Jane was being funny, or trying to be.

"Right," Jane said. "Any children, Ellyn?" she asked brightly.

"Five-year-old twin girls."

"And a handful, let me tell you," Carla put in. "I've served them enough to know. I've also served that husband of hers," she added, rolling her eyes. "Nice-looking, but useless."

Ellyn made a little frown but said nothing.

"What kind of writing are you doing, Ellyn?" Jane asked, now eager to get off the subject of Ellyn's family.

"I write romance novels." A dreamy, faraway look came into Ellyn's eyes. "I *adore* romance novels."

"How wonderful. Do you know we have two romance stars with us as instructors this week? Bertha—I mean Rhonda—"

"I know." Ellyn rose up on her heels in excitement. "Rhonda Redmond and Jennifer Castaneda. I've read every book they've ever written."

At that moment another woman joined them. Jane was enveloped in a cloud of expensive perfume.

"Who's written?" the woman asked. She spoke with an aristocratic lockjaw drawl and was dressed to match in an expensive-looking tan silk pantsuit. Jane guessed her to be around fifty. Her hair was a subtle gold, swept back from her well-tanned face and turning up slightly at her shoulders. Jane was immediately reminded of the actress Dina Merrill.

Jane opened her mouth to answer her, but the woman smiled apologetically. "How frightfully rude of me. I apologize for interrupting." She put out her hand. "Tamara Henley. I assume you're Mrs. Stuart?"

"Yes. Please call me Jane. Ellyn was just saying she's read all of Jennifer Castaneda's and Rhonda Redmond's books."

Tamara's smile half vanished and she regarded Ellyn pityingly. "Romance. Yes, well, that's fine for some. I'm here to work on something a bit more . . . ambitious. I know you'll be able to help me, Jane."

Ellyn stared down at the floor, duly put in her place.

Jane said, "Don't sell romance short, Tamara. It brings a lot of women pleasure. Most of it is beautifully written, too. People who don't read it aren't aware of that. They have a certain prejudice."

"Mm," Tamara replied, clearly bored. "As I said, fine for some." Then she gave Ellyn and Carla an intense gaze, as if willing them to go away. When they didn't, she looked again at Jane and smiled. "So nice to have met you, Jane. I'm sure we'll have our chance to *really* talk." She swept off toward the refreshment table.

"Snotty bitch," Carla said, as if she were about to spit. "That one I've never waited on at the diner, I'm sure of that. She'd never set foot in it." She cast Tamara a resentful look. "She's not even a member of the Midnight Writers."

"Oh?" Jane said. "Then how did she know about the retreat?"

"She's friendly with Rhoda and Adam. He told her about it."

Carla was watching Tamara at the refreshment table with a resentful look that made Jane uneasy.

"On to meet the rest of the students," Jane said cheerfully, and spotted three men she hadn't met chatting together and laughing in a corner of the room near the refreshment table. Jane made her way over to them and said hello to a bald man with a pleasant round face.

"Hello," he said. He had a warm smile that crinkled the corners of his deep blue eyes.

"Jane Stuart," she said, putting out her hand.

"Oh, Mrs. Stuart," he said, and dried his palm on his trousers before taking her hand and shaking it energetically. "A pleasure to meet you. Red Pearson." Before Jane could speak, he touched his bare head and said, "When I had hair, it was red. Let me introduce you to my friends here." He gestured toward an unusually unattractive man with pasty features and thinning, wiry, ginger-colored hair. "This is Larry Graham, our resident electrician."

Jane shook his hand. "A pleasure."

"Mutual," Larry said. " 'Course, I'm not here as an electrician. I've got a book I'm working on."

"I would hope so," Jane said with manufactured fervor, and turned to the third man in the group, a tiny, shriveled creature who was eighty if he was a day. He was so thin and gaunt that it occurred to Jane that he would break if she touched him. But she put her hand out just the same and received a surprisingly firm handshake in return.

"William Ives," he said in a thin, wavering voice. "Pleasure to know you."

Jane noticed Adam gesturing to her from the edge of the room. "Excuse me," she said to the three men, and made her way through the crowd to him.

"Jane, I think we should get started. What I usually do—"

But he was interrupted by a man who had suddenly appeared, a hunched, sour-looking older man with a thatch of white hair. "Somebody spilled coffee all over the table," he said in a low, droning voice.

"Then clean it up," Adam told him impatiently. "What do you expect me to do about it?"

The man skulked away.

"Who was that?" Jane asked softly.

Rhoda appeared at Adam's side, wearing a look of distaste. "That's Tom Brockman, the caretaker," she told Jane. "He's hopeless—a carryover from the lodge's previous owner. I've told Adam to fire him, but he refuses."

"Let's not get into that now," Adam said to Rhoda. "I hardly think it's appropriate."

"No, but it's appropriate for Tom to stick his hand in the till when it pleases him."

"Rhoda," Adam whispered angrily. "Stop it. You have no proof that he's ever done that. Really, this is wrong."

"Such a prisser," Rhoda said with a dismissive wave of her hand, and walked away.

"Anyway," Adam went on, his face red, "after the icebreaker we usually meet in the conference room next door. We go over how the retreat works, that sort of thing."

"I'd be happy to tell them how the retreat works," Jane said, "if I knew."

"Oh, right, this is all new to you. Okay, then I'll do that, and if you hear anything you'd like to do differently, speak up." Jane nodded, and Adam stepped back to address the entire group. "Ladies and gentlemen, if we could all go into the conference room, right through that door, I'd like to go over how the retreat will work."

Everyone headed for the door. Passing Jane, tall blond Carla muttered, "Finally," then saw Jane and forced a phony smile, revealing long, horselike teeth.

This character wasn't going to be easy, Jane thought. But then, the others didn't look easy, either.

What on earth had she gotten herself into?

# Chapter Five

In her room, Jane took a stack of sweaters from her suitcase and placed them in the top drawer of the dresser. She reached for another stack of clothes, changed her mind, and went to the window.

The snow was still falling heavily. Through it Jane could make out the thick woods not far from the lodge. Through a break in the trees, she thought she saw a pond. If she had a chance, and if the weather allowed, she'd try to explore those woods while she was up here.

It was very quiet. The students were in their rooms, writing. In the conference room, Adam had announced the retreat's structure. Each morning, between breakfast and lunch, the students would write in their rooms. After lunch, during the first half of the afternoon, students would meet with their respective instructors (Jane had been assigned Larry Graham, the electrician) for their "one-on-ones," as Adam had put it. The second half of the afternoon students would have free, for socializing or whatever activities they chose. Then would come dinner, followed by an evening group session at which students would be encouraged to read from their works-in-progress.

She stepped from the window and, though she hadn't

finished unpacking, sat down at the foot of the bed and looked around the small room.

Right in front of her stood the dresser, long and low, with a mirror above. Atop the dresser was a vase containing an immense arrangement of fresh flowers. At the foot of the vase was the card she'd found attached: *Jane— Thank you so much for bailing me out. Your friend, Adam.* At the far left end of the dresser sat a Mr. Coffee machine—a nice touch, Jane thought.

Missing from the dresser—or from anywhere else in the room, for that matter—was a television set. How refreshing. Now if only there weren't a telephone on the bed stand, she thought, it would be perfect; but she knew, of course, that that wouldn't be possible.

The only other furniture was a small armchair to the left of the bed and a tiny desk and chair in one corner of the room. Nearby was the door to the bathroom.

Jane smiled. Rhoda had clearly added her own touches. In the bathroom Jane had found a basket of assorted scented soaps in the shape of pinecones and acorns. Here in the room itself Rhoda had added a holiday note: two large wreaths. A green one of fragrant eucalyptus and pine needles hung on the door to the corridor. On the wall to the right of the window hung a red one made of poinsettia flowers interwoven with cranberries.

She inhaled deeply, savoring the wreaths' mingled aromas. Then she was aware once again of the exquisite quiet. It really was quite lovely up here. She was surprised she hadn't been here before now. Rhoda had certainly mentioned Adam buying the lodge. Perhaps in the summer she and Stanley would come up for a night or two.

There was a boisterous knock on her door and Ivy burst in, face aglow. "He's on his way."

"Who?"

"Johnny, who do you think? He just called from his car. He should be here in about an hour."

But by lunchtime, two hours later, Johnny still hadn't arrived. Ivy sat glumly beside Jane at the large conference table that doubled as a dining table. Otherwise the chatter was lively and high-spirited, punctuated by laughter.

"Here you go, babe," Ginny said affectionately, setting down a plate of spaghetti and meatballs in front of Jane. Ginny had decided to make herself useful by helping to serve the meals—a job usually done by Adam and Rhoda alone. After all, Ginny had reasoned, she was a waitress. Jane watched Ginny set down a plate in front of Carla, who glanced at Ginny out of the corner of her eye but said nothing. Professional rivalry, Jane decided with an inward laugh, and started on a meatball.

The room grew quiet. Jane looked up. Johnny stood in the doorway, a thin coating of snow on his head and broad shoulders. In that brief moment, Jane happened to glance again at Carla and saw her lock glances with Johnny. It was as if, Jane thought, they had found each other by some sort of sonar. Quickly Jane looked at Ivy to see if she had noticed this exchange, but Ivy's eyes were also fixed only on Johnny. She jumped up with a joyful smile and ran to him, rising a little on her toes to give him a kiss. Then she turned around and giggled. "Everybody," she said, "this is Johnny, my boyfriend."

"Glad to know ya," Red called out, and tore into a roll.

Bertha, two seats down from Jane, leaned over Ivy's now empty chair and whispered ominously to Jane, "Sparks are flying . . . and I don't mean between Ivy and Johnny. She'd better watch out."

Jane felt a lurching in the pit of her stomach and decided not to respond to Bertha's comment. She simply smiled. As she did so, she noticed Red Pearson watching Ivy intently as she made her way back to her seat.

Jane looked back at the doorway. Johnny was gone.

"Where did he go?" she asked Ivy.

"Upstairs to shower and change."

"Doesn't he want lunch?"

Ivy shook her head.

At the other end of the table, Larry Graham appeared to be holding court, entertaining William Ives and Tamara Henley. "Not me," Graham said pompously. "I'm taking my book right from today's headlines—literally."

"What do you mean?" Tamara drawled, and now the whole table was listening.

"I'm using that hijacked-bus story. Except that in my book, the bomb in his briefcase is real."

This created a flurry of chatter.

"You might say that about my book, too," Red Pearson said loudly. Darting a glance at Jane, he touched his bald head self-consciously. "You remember that story a few weeks ago about that social club in East Harlem that burned down?"

"I remember that," Ellyn said softly. "The Boriken Social Club."

"That's right," Red said. "Some nut started a fire right outside the club's only exit."

"Why did he do that?" Tamara asked.

"To get back at his girlfriend for cheating on him. She was inside the club."

"But what about all the other people?" Carla asked.

"He didn't care about them, apparently. There were nearly a hundred of them. They all panicked. A stampede. Eighty-seven of 'em either got trampled to death or got asphyxiated by the smoke."

"How awful," said Ginny, who had sat down next to Daniel to have her lunch.

"Horrible," Rhoda agreed.

"Yeah," Red said with relish. "That's what my book's about."

"No happy ending there," Carla said on a mouthful of spaghetti.

"Well, I'm taking certain licenses with it," Red said. "You'll see."

"I can hardly wait," Carla said, looking bored, and grabbed a roll.

After lunch, Adam drew Jane into the lounge to speak to her. "How do you think it's going?"

"Too soon to tell, I think. We certainly have an interesting assortment of people."

"True," Adam said, looking troubled. Through the door into the reception room, they saw Tom Brockman go outside carrying a snow shovel.

"The snow is supposed to be real heavy," Adam said. "Could be an accumulation of three feet or more."

"Does it matter?" Jane asked. "We'll all be busy inside."

"True, but I need to get down into town for food and such."

"Of course. I didn't think of that."

"We're fine for a few days, anyway."

Larry Graham entered the lounge and hovered nearby, clearly waiting to speak to one of them.

"Do you need me, Larry?" Adam asked.

"I'm waiting for Mrs. Stuart. She's my instructor."

Jane noticed that he had a spiral notebook in his hand. "Oh, yes, of course. I'm sorry, Larry. Let's go up to my room and talk about your project."

# Chapter Six

Later that afternoon, as Jane left her room to go downstairs for dinner, Ivy emerged from her and Johnny's room directly across the hall.

"Johnny's changing. He'll be along in a few minutes." Ivy looked put out about something, her brow creased in a deep frown.

"Is something wrong, Ivy?"

Ivy sneezed.

"Bless you."

"Thanks. It's that awful man, Brockman."

"The caretaker? What about him?"

"He's impossible. Tell me something. Do you have wreaths in your room?"

"Wreaths? Yes, they're very pretty, aren't they? A nice holiday touch."

"I suppose they're pretty, but I'm allergic to them. I started sneezing the minute I got into my room. So after lunch I called down to ask that they be removed."

"And what happened?"

"Adam said he would send up this Brockman creature. About an hour later, he banged on the door. When I told him what I wanted, he said—I swear—that he was too busy to take them down and that I should do it myself. Can you believe that?"

They headed down the stairway to the left of Jane's door. "That is rather rude," Jane said, surprised. "But not the end of the world, right?" Reaching the bottom of the stairs, they crossed the lounge and entered the conference room, where it seemed most of the others had already gathered.

"I mean," Ivy went on, apparently unable to let go of this issue, "how much trouble is it to take down two wreaths?"

"True," Jane said reasonably. "Which means it wouldn't have been a lot of trouble for you."

"Jane, that is not the point, and you know it. I am *allergic,* first of all. Disturbing the wreaths would have set me off sneezing all over again. Second, guests shouldn't have to do things like that—at least, not in good hotels."

"We're in Mt. Munsee Lodge, Ivy, not The Plaza. Why didn't you ask Johnny to take the wreaths down?"

Ivy didn't answer.

They were passing Tamara Henley at this point. She looked up. "Did you say wreaths?" she drawled. "Have you got those awful things in your room, too?"

"Yes," Ivy burst out, clearly glad to have a sympathizer. "A red one on the closet door and a green one on the door to the bathroom. Stink to high heaven—I'm allergic to them. The green one has some of that smelly eucalyptus in it. What do I look like, a koala?"

"Well, to tell you the truth . . ." Jane said, and burst out laughing.

"Oh, Jane," Ivy said. "You used to say that to me in school. Remember? You were always teasing me like that." She pushed out her bottom lip. "I'm about to cry."

"Me too," Jane said with a sniff, remembering their carefree college days. They seemed a lifetime ago. The two women had been so full of hope then; it seemed they could have anything they put their minds to. Now, looking back, Jane reflected that she had achieved much of what she had wanted: a fulfilling career, a husband who loved her, a beautiful child. Ivy had none of that, none of her dreams. Tears came to Jane's eyes.

"You *are* crying," Ivy said.

Tamara threw down her napkin in disgust. "Oh, really. Please, ladies, not at dinner."

Jane laughed through her tears and nodded.

"My wreaths are both green," Tamara said. "Tackiest things I've ever seen. Like some hideous Christmas card or something."

Jane looked across the table and saw Adam, who had apparently overheard this exchange, frowning.

"I asked the caretaker to remove them," Ivy told Tamara, "and he wouldn't. He was already at my door, but he refused to take them down. Can you believe such insolence?"

"I suppose I can live with mine, bad as they are," Tamara said with a languid wave, but Ivy had turned away.

Johnny had entered the room. He looked extremely handsome in a charcoal sport jacket over black slacks and a black silk T-shirt. Ivy's face bloomed in an expectant smile as she watched him make his way around the table. When he reached Carla, he stopped and she looked up, the corners of her lips turned up in the tiniest of smirks. Ever so lightly, his hand brushed her shoulder. Then he moved on, heading for the side of the table where Ivy stood.

Ginny, bearing a platter of roast chicken, stopped and spoke softly to Jane: "Ivy had better watch out or she's going to lose him. If she hasn't already."

Taking her seat, Jane found herself deeply troubled by what she had seen and by Ginny's remark. Poor Ivy had been hurt or disappointed by men all her life, beginning with her father, who had walked out on her mother when Ivy was thirteen. Ira, Ivy's ex-husband, had had affair after affair during their marriage and then abandoned her as well, leaving Ivy to raise their daughter, Marlene, alone. Jane didn't want Ivy to be hurt again.

But Jane saw no way to prevent it if it was going to happen, especially when she saw Ivy watching Johnny make his way toward her, a hurt expression on her face.

Later, as dinner was ending, Tom Brockman appeared in the doorway from the lounge. He wore a bulky down parka that appeared soaked through. The room grew quiet.

"Snow's stopped," he droned. "But the bridge collapsed under the weight." There was a quick collective intake of breath. "Was tryin' to drive down into town for supplies. Nearly drove into the gorge."

Everyone broke into animated chatter.

"What are we going to do?" Arliss said in her droning voice that was not unlike Brockman's.

"Yes," Paul Kavanagh chimed in, "this is terrifying."

Adam rose from his chair. "People, people—please. There's nothing to worry about. There's another road. It's old and hasn't been used in a while, but it's there, and it goes down the other side of the mountain. I'll arrange for it to be plowed, but it will take a while. In the meantime, we've got plenty of food and supplies. So let's just enjoy our retreat, shall we?" He shot Tom Brockman a withering look.

"This is unacceptable," Ivy said to Jane a few minutes later in the lounge, where they sat side by side on a sofa.

Jane laughed. "Why, have you got someplace to go?"

"No, you know I haven't. It's just that we're . . . *stranded* here. What if there's an emergency and one of us needs to get down the mountain?" Ivy's eyes widened. "What if *you* need to get home because something has happened to Nick, heaven forbid."

"Calm down, all will be fine. Have a seat. The group reading is starting soon."

Ivy sat, twisting her fingers in her lap.

"Ivy," Jane said in a low voice, unsure how to begin. "Is Johnny . . . I mean, do you think he's really right for you?"

Ivy turned and looked at Jane as if she'd gone mad. "What are you talking about?"

"I don't know. It's just that he seems, well, interested in other women. Do you think he's really committed to you?"

"Oh, Jane," Ivy said solemnly, "absolutely. Johnny loves me as much as I love him. I know I haven't always had very good judgment in men, but of this I am sure. Johnny adores me. I do intend to have a heart-to-heart with him, though. I mean, he is a man," she said with a little laugh, rolling her eyes skyward. "I don't expect him to ignore a beautiful woman when he sees one, but he's got to be more discreet about it. Keep it to himself, you know?"

Jane nodded uneasily, her lower lip between her teeth. Looking around the lounge, she noted that Johnny was absent.

She directed her attention to Ellyn Bass, who stood at the front of the room, having bravely volunteered to be the first to read from her work-in-progress.

It was a historical romance set in eighteenth-century Scotland. In this scene, the hero was about to make love to a woman other than the book's heroine.

"Oh, no," Bertha suddenly blurted out, standing. "Cut. Unh-unh. No can do."

Ellyn gaped at her.

"You see," Bertha said, addressing the entire group, "in a historical romance, once the hero and heroine meet, they will fight, come together, be thrust apart—the natural rhythm of love—but the hero must *never, never* sleep with another woman."

"That's a crock," Jennifer Castaneda, sitting at the other end of the room, said matter-of-factly, and everyone grew very still. "Maybe in your books, Berth—"

"Rhonda," Bertha corrected her quickly. She never used her real name in public.

"*Rhon*da," Jennifer said, rolling her eyes. "But that's all so . . . eighties."

"Eighties!" Bertha's face grew red beneath its streaked blond crown. "I'll have you know that I am a bigger name now than I was in the eighties. To what do you attribute that?"

"People are ridiculously loyal to the oldies. I don't follow any of those silly rules in my books, and I think you'll find they're outselling yours."

Jane looked on, horrified, as if she were watching a car wreck.

"I think *you'll* find you're wrong," Bertha said viciously. "Besides, your books aren't even historicals, they're contemporaries—Hispanic contemporaries."

"*Latina. La-ti-na* contemporaries. That's the whole point. I'm writing what readers want today—a good story, without those foolish category rules."

"Category!"

Adam jumped up. "Now, now, ladies," he said with a laugh, his face an even deeper red than Bertha's, "I think everyone here agrees that you are both giant names in your field."

"Oh, she's a giant all right," Jennifer said.

Brad Franklin let out a guffaw, and Bertha turned livid eyes on him. His face grew instantly serious.

Adam cleared his throat loudly and addressed Ellyn with a wan smile. "You should be very proud that your book has been able to arouse such controversy already."

"That's right, Ellyn," Jennifer said, "you write 'em how you want. Your readers will love you for it. Before you know it, you'll be the next . . . Bertha Stumpf!"

William Ives, looking shrunken in the corner, said, "Who's Bertha Stumpf?"

Bertha surveyed the group in horror. "Well, I—I'm certainly not—" And she stomped out of the room.

"Good," Jennifer cried triumphantly. "Now we can continue without any more interruptions."

Ellyn chose not to read any further. Paul Kavanagh read next from his novel, an artsy coming-of-age story about a boy who, fearing he might be gay, went to see his priest.

"Ha," Ivy burst out.

"Ivy," Jane whispered fiercely.

"I'm sorry," Ivy called to Paul. "It just strikes me as funny."

Paul glared at her, openmouthed. "What's funny about it?"

"It's so obvious the boy is you."

Without a word, Paul turned and left the room.

Rhoda jumped up from her chair. "People, people, listen to me. We can't do this. We have to be considerate of one another's feelings or this isn't going to work. Constructive criticism only, please. Delivered . . . sensitively."

"Excu-u-use *me*," Ivy said.

Tom Brockman appeared at the side of the room and motioned to Adam, who got up and followed Tom into the reception room. As Carla Santino read from her mainstream women's novel, the sounds of Tom and Adam arguing heatedly could be clearly heard.

Forty-five minutes later, Jane, utterly exhausted, rose at the end of the group reading. Daniel and Ginny approached her.

"That was . . . interesting," Daniel said with a wicked grin. "Do you think Bertha will be all right?"

"Of course," Jane blustered. "She throws hissy fits like that all the time and forgets about them the next day. You two want to come up to my room for some coffee?"

"Sure," Ginny and Daniel said, and so did Ivy, suddenly standing at Jane's elbow. Jane would rather have taken a break from Ivy, but she saw no way to exclude her, so the four of them went to Jane's room, where she made coffee in the Mr. Coffee machine on the dresser.

Ivy took the chair behind the desk in the corner of the room, Jane dropped into the armchair, and Ginny and Daniel sat on the bed.

"This is all turning out pretty awful, isn't it?" Ivy said, and they all turned to look at her. "I mean, first the bridge collapsing, then that horrible reading just now. And then that repulsive Red Pearson made not one but two passes at me. What would ever make him think I'd be interested in *him?* Bald as a cue ball," she muttered.

Jane thought of suggesting that perhaps Red had noticed Johnny's interest in Carla and therefore deduced that Ivy was available, but of course Jane restrained herself.

"You know who's awfully sweet, though?" Ivy went on. "That little William Ives. Isn't he the cutest thing?"

Ginny looked aghast. "You mean that shriveled-up man with the skinny head?" She shuddered.

"Oh, come on, Ginny. Make believe he's your grandfather."

"My grandfather happens to be an exceptionally handsome man."

"You're being very . . . superficial—yes, that's the word. I think he's sweet, that's all. I also," Ivy went on, leaning forward a little, "had a very interesting chat with that Brad Franklin, the ghostwriter. *Very* interesting."

"How so?" Jane asked. "What did he say?"

"Never you mind," Ivy replied smugly.

Jane was about to object to Ivy's sudden discretion when there was a violent knock on the door. Jane hurried to open it and found Rhoda standing in the corridor. She bustled in, obviously disturbed about something.

"You're not going to believe this," she said. "You know Tom's room is downstairs next to the storage room?"

They all looked at her blankly.

"Well, it is. Anyway, Tom just told Adam that there are people *carrying on* in the storage room."

"Really?" Ivy asked avidly. "Who?"

"I don't know," Rhoda said, exasperated, and turned to Jane. "What should I do?"

Jane's eyes grew wide and she hunched her shoulders in a shrug. "Beats me. Let Adam handle it. It's his lodge. He can look into it if he likes." And she thought, *I've got a pretty good idea who's in there.*

For a moment Rhoda stood there, staring. Then she nodded resolutely, turned, and hurried out of the room and down the stairs.

"I'm not much in the mood for coffee after all," Ginny said, and Daniel nodded in agreement.

"I guess I'm about ready to turn in," Jane said, and was grateful when Ivy got the hint and left with them.

Jane took a long hot shower, put on her nightgown, brushed her teeth, combed her hair, and settled on the bed with a manuscript she'd brought from the office. Just as she turned over the title page, there was a knock on the door.

"Who is it?"

"Jane, it's me, Ivy."

Jane let out a great sigh. "Coming." Throwing on her robe, she went to the door and opened it. At the far end of the corridor, Tamara Henley emerged from her room, crossed to the room Carla and Ellyn were sharing, and knocked on their door.

Ivy walked into Jane's room and shut the door. "You know, that Tamara is totally cold and unfeeling. It's really bothering me. That nice William Ives can vouch for it."

"Vouch for what? What did she do?"

"Right after I left here before, I went downstairs to see if there was anything to eat in the kitchen. Tamara and William were in the conference room and we had some fruit together. Anyway, we got to chatting about this and that, and somehow I got on to how I lost Marlene. Well. Tamara made it abundantly clear that she didn't want to hear anything about it. Don't you think that's cold?"

"Yes, I do. I don't blame you for being hurt. Ivy, where's Johnny?"

"I think he's in the lounge, watching the news. Can you believe there are no TVs in these rooms? Speaking of the news," Ivy swept on, sitting on the bed, "have you heard anything more about that bus hijacking story?"

"No, why?"

Ivy shook her head, frowning, then yawned mightily. "I'm going to bed. Good night, Jane."

Bewildered, Jane let Ivy out and watched her enter her room across the hall. Then she resumed her position on the bed, took up her manuscript, and started to read.

Ten minutes later there was another knock.

"Oh, for goodness' sake." She went to the door. "Ivy, I thought you were going to bed."

"It's me, Daniel."

"Daniel?" She opened the door and he walked in.

"Sorry to bother you, Jane, but there's something I think you'd better know. A few minutes ago I was walking through the lounge. Ivy was there, sitting and talking with Larry Graham. Suddenly the door to the storage room opened and out came Johnny and Carla. You should have seen Ivy's face. Poor thing."

"Did Johnny see her?"

"Yes, he gave her a quick glance and walked past her as if she didn't matter in the least."

Poor Ivy. What would happen now?

"And as if that wasn't enough," Daniel went on, "as I was coming upstairs, I passed Tom Brockman. He had a real stormy look and I wondered what was bothering him. Then I bumped into Adam, who said he'd just repri-manded Tom for being rude to the guests."

She remembered Ivy's wreath incident.

"Adam told Tom that if he didn't lose his attitude fast, he'd have to leave as soon as the old road was plowed." Daniel looked troubled. "But it was the Carla and Johnny thing I felt you should know about."

"Thanks. I appreciate it. Not that I can do anything about it, but thanks."

She saw him out, took one look at the bed, and knew she was too tired to read now. She put the manuscript on the dresser, climbed under the covers, and switched off the lamp. A short time later, as she was drifting off to sleep, she was aware of the sound of people yelling. Slowly she came awake and realized they were Ivy and Johnny. She couldn't make out what they were saying, just that Ivy was crying, pleading.

This went on for some time. Finally it became quiet, and Jane drifted into an uneasy sleep.

# Chapter Seven

The atmosphere at breakfast was subdued, as if everyone had a hangover. Adam announced that the plowing of the old road had begun but would take a while.

As Jane sat down, Arliss took the seat beside her.

"Jane, what on earth was all that noise last night?"

"I don't know, Arliss."

"It was coming from that floozy's room—"

"Don't call my friend a floozy."

"It was coming from Ivy and Johnny's room, which is right next to mine and across the hall from yours. How could you not have heard it?"

"I didn't say I didn't hear it. I just said I didn't know what it was."

Arliss regarded her for a moment. "I see. Being discreet, are we? Well, it's unacceptable, Jane. I'm here as a favor to you, but this is my vacation and I expect certain standards to be met."

"All right, Arliss. If it will make you feel better, I'll ask Ivy to be more considerate. Couldn't you have done that?"

"Of course I could have. But it's not my job. You're the director of this thing, and it's your responsibility to make sure it goes smoothly. So far, I'm sorry to say, you've done a lousy job."

Before Jane could respond, Arliss got up and walked away, taking a seat at the far end of the table. Almost immediately, Daniel took her place. "Morning," he said brightly. "What was all that commotion last night?"

"None of your business," blurted Ivy, who sat directly across from them, glaring.

Daniel, shocked, took a quick bite of his croissant. Ivy got up and began to walk around the table. She stopped at the coffee urn, poured a cup, and headed back to her seat. As she passed behind Carla, she stopped, stepped closer to the table, and dropped the coffee right in front of Carla, who gasped and jumped up. "You bitch," she screamed. "You deliberately spilled that on me. I'm burned." She slapped Ivy hard across the face, then ran from the room.

Everyone was silent.

"Oops," Ivy said.

"Oh, Ivy," Jane said, throwing down her napkin, and hurried from the room to make sure Carla was all right. Upstairs, she knocked on Carla's door and Carla opened it. She had already removed her jeans, and she pointed to angry red marks on her thighs.

"Look at this. That bitch burned me. Can you believe it?"

Jane didn't know what to say.

"I know she hates me because she saw Johnny and me come out of the storage room last night, but that's too bad for her."

"You can't blame her for being upset," Jane said, then quickly added, "Not that I condone what she just did."

"It's not going to make any difference," Carla said, pulling on a fresh pair of jeans. "Stupid fool thinks Johnny cares about her. He was laughing at her when he was with me."

Jane felt a pang of hurt for her friend. Sadly she turned and left Carla's room.

Later, during writing time, Jane was in the lounge reading the manuscript she'd tried to read the night before, when Ellyn Bass timidly approached her. "Jane, could I talk to you for a minute?"

"Sure, Ellyn. What's up?"

"Something's bothering me. Last night Tamara came to my room and told me I have writing talent but that I shouldn't waste it on romance. Jane, I *love* romance. I love reading it and I love writing it. It really hurt my feelings when she said that to me."

"I don't blame you for feeling hurt," Jane said. "She shouldn't have said that to you—though I suppose she meant well, in her way."

"Aren't we all supposed to be encouraging? Supportive of each other's efforts, like Rhoda said?"

"Yes, definitely. I'm glad you mentioned this to me. I'll speak to Tamara."

Ellyn smiled. "Thanks, Jane. I'm really enjoying this retreat."

"Good, Ellyn, I'm glad." Jane smiled as she watched Ellyn leave the room.

Suddenly Ivy had taken Ellyn's place, and Jane felt her smile melt. Ivy looked miserable, her hair tousled, her clothes rumpled. She wore no makeup.

"Oh, Jane," she said on a little cry, sitting down beside her friend. "It's so awful."

"What is?" Jane asked, remembering the yelling coming from her and Johnny's room.

"I saw Johnny come out of that storage closet with Carla. I told him so last night, but he didn't care. He actually got mad at *me*." Carefully she raised her sweater to reveal an angry black-and-blue mark.

Jane sat up in alarm. "How did you get that?"

"He hit me," Ivy said, and started to cry. "He hits me a lot, Jane." She hung her head, staring into her lap. "He always hits me in places where it won't show."

Jane sat up, incensed. "Then you should have gotten rid of him a long time ago. How dare he hit you? You're well rid of him."

Ivy gave her head a little shake. "No, I'm not, Jane. He's all I have." She met Jane's gaze, her eyes brimming with tears. "Do you think it's that easy for me to find men?"

"But isn't no man better than one who hurts you?" Jane asked gently.

"No." Ivy paused, collecting her thoughts. "He got so furious at me for challenging him that he threatened to leave here with Carla the minute the road was clear."

"I don't know what to tell you, Ivy. If it were me, I'd let him go."

"But you're not me, Jane, don't you get it? You've never been me. You're beautiful and successful and funny and smart, and you got Kenneth, the man you wanted. The man who loved you and treated you like a queen. And if he hadn't been killed you'd still have him. Me, I got Ira, who constantly cheated and finally left me because I was 'stupid and boring.' You never met the men I dated after Ira. Each one was worse than the one before. Then I met Johnny. He's part of my new life in New York. I love him. He doesn't mean to hurt me, he just has a wicked temper. And he always says he's sorry afterward. I know he means it. I—I can't lose him, Jane. What am I going to do?" she asked miserably, and buried her face in her hands.

Jane simply shook her head. "I'm sorry, Ivy. I won't advise you about how to keep a monster like that."

Ivy looked again at Jane, this time as if she'd never seen her before. "You're not my friend, not really. You don't want me to be happy. I see that now. If I lose Johnny, you'll be glad, because you'd rather I had nobody than someone like him. You're a snob, Jane." She jumped up and ran from the room.

Jane sat very still. That last accusation had hit hard, and

hurt. It took all of her energy to rise and make her way through the empty conference room and into the kitchen for a much-needed cup of coffee. As she filled a cup, she heard people entering the conference room and realized they were Vick Halleran and Jennifer Castaneda. They seemed to be arguing about something.

"Vick, I came in here to get some writing done," came Jennifer's breathy girl-woman voice. "Do you think you could leave me alone for a little while?"

"You never want to spend any time with me," Vick whined. "You just wanted to get away from me. Maybe you wish you'd come to the retreat with *Henry.*"

Jane stood stock-still. If she emerged from the kitchen now, they would know she'd heard them, which would be too embarrassing to bear. So she stayed where she was, listening.

"Oh, shut up," Jennifer said. "I've told you a million times that's over."

Jane recalled that Jennifer's agent was Henry Silver, for whose agency, coincidentally, Jane and Kenneth had once worked.

There was the sudden sound of a chair scraping the floor. "I don't believe it's over, Jennifer. But whether it is or isn't," Vick said icily, "if you try to divorce me, I'll take you for all you're worth."

"Really?" Jennifer sounded amused. "And how would you justify that?"

"You'd be nothing if it weren't for me, if it weren't for all I've taught you about writing. You used me . . . and now I'll use you."

Then there was silence. Jane waited a good two minutes, then intentionally made some noise to signal her presence. Cup in hand, she bustled out, pretending to be surprised to find Jennifer typing away on her notebook computer.

"Hello," Jane said. Jennifer gave her a tight smile and returned her attention to her computer screen.

Feeling a headache coming on, Jane retrieved her manuscript from the lounge and took it up to her room. She had just finished reading chapter one when a loud *pop,* a sound she recognized immediately as a gunshot, exploded in the hall, just outside her door.

# Chapter Eight

Heart thumping, Jane hurried to her door, opened it a crack, and peeked out. A middle-aged man in a tan overcoat, sloppily obese and sweating profusely, ran past her room, holding a gun out in front of him. Jane peered down the length of the corridor in time to see Johnny run down the stairs. The man scrambled after him.

Across the corridor, Ivy's door opened and she stood there, looking badly shaken, her blue eyes huge.

"Ivy, what's going on?" Jane demanded.

Without responding, Ivy shut her door.

Other doors along the corridor were thrown open and alarmed faces peered out.

Adam came running up the stairway to the left of Jane's room. "Everyone stay in your rooms," he shouted down the corridor. He saw Jane and came into her room. "We've got to call the police."

"Yes. I'll call Stanley." She rang him at the station and found him in his office. She told him what had just happened, that a man with a gun had run through the lodge, chasing Johnny.

"Jane, I can't get up there until the road is plowed. I told you Johnny was no good. I'm sure there's nothing more to worry about. The two of them are probably far into the woods by now."

"But how could that man have gotten up here?"

"He must have hiked up one of the trails—there are lots of them. He was a heavyset man, you said?"

"Yes, that's right."

Stanley let out a little laugh. "He must have wanted Johnny pretty bad."

"I don't think this is funny," Jane said in alarm.

"No, of course not. Sorry, Jane. I'll see what I can do to hurry up the plowing and get up there."

Jane hung up the phone, an image of Johnny running through the snowy woods in her mind.

Adam said, "Jane, I want to talk to Ivy, see what she knows about this."

"Don't you think we should wait for Stanley?"

Adam ignored this, leaving Jane's room and crossing to Ivy's. He banged on her door.

"Go away," she shouted from inside.

"Ivy, open the door. We need to talk to you. Please."

After a few moments they heard her shuffling steps, and then the door opened. They walked past her, Jane closing the door.

"Ivy," Jane said, "who was that man chasing Johnny?"

"I don't know." Ivy sat down on the bed, the very picture of dejection.

"I think you do, Ivy."

"I don't know who he is, Jane. I only know that Johnny's been trying to get away from him. I don't know why." She looked up miserably into Jane's eyes. "Johnny was never really going away this weekend. I used you, Jane. I knew Johnny was looking for a place to hide from that man. When you told me about the retreat, I realized it would be perfect. So I got you to invite me, and then I convinced you to let Johnny come. I'm sorry."

"It doesn't matter, Ivy," Jane said sadly. "He's gone now."

The phone in Jane's room began to ring. Jane hurried across the hall and grabbed it.

"Hello, hello, missus," came Florence's lilting Trinidadian voice. "How are you holding up, all stranded?"

"Florence," Jane said, "you have no idea."

"I see . . ." Florence said, though she of course didn't. "I wanted to report in, tell you that Nicholas is fine, and so are Winky and the kittens. We're working on names, but no final decisions have been made. Is the old road clear yet? It seems everyone in town is talking about you all stuck up there."

"They're still working on the road." Jane thought of something. "Florence, has anyone come to the house looking for me or Ivy?"

"Why, yes, missus, as a matter of fact someone did. Yesterday. A man."

"What did he look like?"

"Kind of overweight, missus, in a light-colored coat, like a trench coat. Maybe in his forties. He asked for Ivy Benson. Why?"

"What did you tell him?"

"That she was at the retreat, of course. Why, missus? Did I do something wrong?"

"No, it's all right, Florence. I'd better go now. Give Nick a kiss for me, okay?"

"Will do."

As Jane hung up, Rhoda appeared in the doorway. She turned when Adam emerged from Ivy's room.

"Come on," Jane said to them both. "I want to see something."

"Where?" Adam asked.

"Outside."

Jane led the way along the corridor to the stairs down which Johnny and the gunman had run. They went out through the door at the end of the building and emerged onto the snow-covered lawn. Jane immediately spotted two sets of footprints. "This way."

The prints led into the woods, but there was no trail here, and they were quickly lost in the tangle of brush. Returning to the lodge, Jane wondered if the man with the gun had caught up with Johnny.

Not surprisingly, no one got any writing done that morning, and lunch was abuzz with speculation. Somehow Adam had found out it was Ellyn Bass's birthday, and after lunch he and Ginny brought out an Entenmann's coffee cake studded with candles, along with some fruit punch. Adam sent Tom into the kitchen for ice, but Tom reappeared a few moments later.

"Mr. Forrest, the icemaker is malfunctioning again. The ice cubes have melted together into a blob. Do you have the ice pick?"

"No," Adam replied impatiently, "what would I be doing with the ice pick?" He went into the kitchen himself, and they could hear him rummaging in drawers, then, "Damn."

He reappeared, looking frustrated. "I have no idea where it is. Tom, get a screwdriver from the supply closet."

Tom did, and soon Adam was hacking away at the cubes.

The cake and punch went a long way toward lifting the group's spirits. When it was time for the one-on-one sessions, everyone bustled off quite happily, almost as if nothing unusual had happened that morning at the lodge.

After lunch, Jane met with Larry Graham in her room for their one-on-one session.

"I didn't write anything this morning," he announced, falling into the armchair near the bed.

Jane sat behind the desk. There was something different

about him, Jane noticed, then realized it was his hair, that unruly mass of thinning orange fuzz. He appeared to have tried to part it in the middle—for what reason, she couldn't imagine—and had achieved a thoroughly unpleasant effect. He sat watching her.

"I suppose I can't blame you for not getting any writing done today," she said pleasantly, "what with all that's gone on."

"Yeah, that's it," he said, a smile breaking over his coarse features.

It was suddenly somehow clear to Jane that that hadn't actually been the reason, but that he was happy to use it as his excuse.

"What was that all about?" he asked. "With Johnny and that guy with the gun. Do you think Johnny is some kind of Mafia figure? Who was the other guy?"

Jane shook her head and tried to smile. "I'm sure I have no idea." She wanted him to stop talking about this.

"I intend to find out. I'm going to follow their footprints into the woods, figure out where they went."

"Already tried that," she said, and she could tell by his quick series of blinks that this had surprised him. "There's no trail where they ran into the woods, just sticks and underbrush. The prints get lost. Besides," she added, shivering, "I don't think we necessarily want to know what happened. That's one trail I've decided I don't want to follow."

"Mm," he said thoughtfully. "Trails . . . You know, there are some trails you can't see . . ."

What on earth was he talking about? "All righty, then," she said briskly, getting to her feet, "if you'll forgive me, I'll use the rest of our time for some reading—since you haven't written anything new for us to go over. You don't object, do you?"

"No, no, not at all," he said, still oddly preoccupied, and she showed him out, relieved to be rid of him.

She went to the window and gazed out into the woods, dark and forbidding on this bleak gray day. She glanced about her room and it seemed oppressive suddenly, shabby and depressing. She had to get out of there. Taking up her manuscript, she left the room and went down to the lounge, which was blessedly empty. She settled into a big leather chair near the built-in bookcases at the back of the room, sighed deeply, and resumed her reading.

She heard footsteps and, with a sense of dread, looked up into Bertha's pudgy face.

"Hello, Jane," Bertha said rather coolly.

Was she going to apologize for that scene with Jennifer? Hardly likely, knowing Bertha.

"Jane," she said, falling onto the sofa facing Jane's chair, "I think this is a good time to talk about my career."

Jane felt a kind of sinking nausea in the pit of her stomach. "Actually, this isn't a good time. I've got some work to do, and before you know it, it will be time for dinner."

Bertha looked at the watch on her chubby wrist. "It's hours till dinner. You just don't want to talk to me."

Bingo. "No, that's not it at all, Bertha. It's that I'm very busy, running the retreat and all. As I think I told you, there really isn't time to discuss your career during the retreat."

"That's not what you said at all," Bertha whined. "You agreed we'd find time to talk in our 'down moments.'"

Giving up, Jane set down the manuscript on the coffee table. "All right, let's talk about your career."

"Hello, ladies."

Jennifer Castaneda swept into the room. She wore a snowy white fisherman's knit sweater over black leggings. Jane reflected again on what a beauty this woman was, sleek and sinuous. She sat down beside Bertha and good-naturedly patted her knee. "I'm sorry about those things I said about your books."

Bertha looked amazed. "Why . . . thank you."

Would Bertha apologize back? Jane wondered. She doubted it.

She was right. Bertha just sat there, an expectant look on her face. Jane knew she was wishing Jennifer would leave.

But Jennifer crossed her legs and settled more comfortably on the sofa. "You've got to admit, though, that historical romances and contemporary romances are totally different."

Bertha drew in her breath to respond. Jane wasn't going to give her that chance. "I've been admiring that beautiful sweater, Jennifer. You know, I'm a knitter." When Jennifer looked surprised, Jane went on, "Mm-hm, I even belong to a knitting club. We call ourselves the Defarge Club. Cute, huh?"

Both Jennifer and Bertha had completely blank expressions.

"Madame Defarge was a character in *A Tale of Two Cities*."

Still the vacant looks.

"Surely you've both heard of Charles Dickens."

"Yes, of course," Bertha said, and shifted impatiently.

"Anyway," Jane hurried on, "I've made sweaters not unlike that. They're a lot of fun to do, all those cables and bobbles and things."

Jennifer gave Jane a wondering look. At that moment Tamara Henley entered the lounge from the stairs, passing through on her way to the conference room. "Hello," she drawled.

The three women smiled and returned the greeting, watching her pass through the room. The minute she was gone, Jennifer giggled and leaned closer to the two other women. "Speaking of clothes," she whispered cattily, "did you get a load of what Mrs. Gotrocks has got on? The woman does *not* know how to dress."

"Really?" Bertha said. "What was she wearing? I didn't notice."

"How could you not notice?" Jennifer said. "That gray skirt and lavender top. Clash city." She gave a little shrug. "I guess it just goes to show that money doesn't guarantee good taste."

Jane didn't like where this conversation was going. Sitting with these two was making her feel increasingly anxious. "Oh," she said suddenly, "I just remembered I've got to call my nanny about something. You'll both excuse me?"

Bertha, looking positively betrayed, stared at Jane as she rose from her chair.

Jennifer said, "Sure."

Jane hurried out of the lounge and up the stairs. She met Adam coming down.

"Hello, Jane. I've decided to throw another little party tonight. After that business with Johnny and the man with the gun, I figure everyone could use some special treatment."

"I think that's an excellent idea."

"Good. Rhoda and I will be hosting it in the conference room after the group reading."

She told him she'd see him later and made it to her room, where she actually managed to finish reading the manuscript.

# Chapter Nine

At dinner, Jane, sitting between William Ives and Daniel, glanced around the room, wondering where Ivy was. As if reading her thoughts, Daniel whispered, "Isn't Ivy coming to dinner?"

"I don't know," Jane replied, and at that moment Ivy appeared in the doorway.

She looked like hell, as if she hadn't bathed or changed her clothes since yesterday. She made her way over to Jane, William, and Daniel and took the empty seat next to William. Watching Ivy sit down a little too carefully, Jane wondered if she'd been drinking.

The atmosphere was subdued—Adam, Rhoda, and Ginny serving, everyone quietly eating. Adam, crossing the room with a tray, gave Jane an imploring look. She nodded.

"Well," she burst out sunnily. "How are everyone's stories coming along?"

They all looked at her, wary expressions on their faces.

Finally William looked up and smiled at Jane. "I think mine's a real humdinger," he said in his thready voice. "Maybe I'll get myself one of those movie deals. But I've got to executive produce."

Everyone laughed, the atmosphere loosening up.

"*I've* got a hell of a story," Ivy suddenly announced. The room grew silent again. Everyone watched her, waiting.

"Mm-hm," she continued matter-of-factly, spearing a piece of chicken and putting it in her mouth. "It's going to put someone in jail for years and years."

Again the uneasy silence. Jane didn't blame Ivy for feeling bitter toward Johnny and was happy that her friend was rid of him, but she didn't like the way this conversation was going.

"What about you, Carla?" Jane asked.

Carla looked up and scowled at Jane, who refused to be intimidated.

"How is your novel coming along?"

"Fine," Carla said brusquely, and looked away. "Pass the butter, please."

Jane gave up. The remainder of the meal was eaten in virtual silence.

The atmosphere of that evening's group session made Jane nervous, as if the air itself were charged.

Tamara read from her novel, about a woman dying of breast cancer. Red Pearson ripped it to shreds, calling it maudlin and melodramatic.

When he read from his own novel based on the Boriken Social Club tragedy, Tamara got him back by loudly scoffing at least three times.

William Ives, in his thin, shaky voice, read a passage from his novel about a lost woodsman. To Jane's surprise, it was extremely well written. She noticed Arliss, William's instructor, nodding approvingly at the other end of the room. Jane wondered, perhaps uncharitably, if Arliss had rewritten William's material. Brad Franklin, as if reading Jane's thoughts, called out, "Sounds like your teacher helped you with your homework."

"What is that supposed to mean?" William demanded.

Brad laughed, his shoulders rising and falling once. "It's obvious. Arliss rewrote your stuff. Or maybe she just wrote it, saved you the trouble of doing anything at all."

A hush descended upon the room. Arliss was watching Brad with a shocked, hateful look in her eyes. "That remark was totally uncalled for, Brad," she said, "and I resent it immensely."

Brad laughed again. "Sorry, sorry. I was only joking."

"You know," Ivy said, and everyone turned to her, "I think Brad is the last person who should object to someone's writing being 'ghosted,' since that's exactly what he does for a living."

Brad's face grew serious. "I just told you," he said tightly, "I was joking."

Ivy appeared to ignore this. "Damn cushy setup," she muttered. "Cushier than people think."

Brad gave her a surprised, murderous look.

Paul Kavanagh read more of his coming-of-age novel, a passage in which the protagonist experienced his first homosexual encounter. In the middle of the reading, Red yelled out that he hadn't come to this retreat to hear porno. This time Paul, who seemed to have girded himself for blows such as this, simply finished reading and took his seat.

Ellyn Bass read lovingly from her romance, dwelling on the heavy Scottish accents. Tamara rolled her eyes. To Jane's surprise, Jennifer criticized the passage, saying that dialect would make her book difficult to read. Bertha rushed to disagree, saying she thought the dialect was marvelously authentic. Listening to this exchange, Ellyn looked as if she would burst into tears at any moment. When Bertha reminded the group that her last Scottish historical romance, *Highland Rapture,* had been number 18 on *The New York Times* extended best-seller list and that she should know whereof she spoke, Jennifer rose a little in her chair and narrowed her eyes.

Eager to avert another battle, Jane stood and asked Larry if he would like to read. He gave her a puzzled look and reminded her that he hadn't written anything new. She apologized, moving on to Carla. Jane had succeeded in preventing another scene. Taking her seat, she glanced at Ivy, who was watching Larry closely.

When the session was over, Adam came in and reminded everyone of the reception he and Rhoda would be hosting in the conference room.

"That's one party I'll pass on," Ivy said softly to Jane.

Jane had no desire to attend either, though she knew she should. She decided to take a few minutes' break in her room first.

She took the back stairs to the second floor and made her way down the corridor. Passing Arliss's room, she heard Arliss speaking harshly to someone.

"If you want to keep this working," Arliss was saying, exasperation in her tone, "you've at least got to *read* them. Just how lazy are you? You should have told her you're not allowed to talk about them."

What was she talking about, Jane wondered, and to whom was she speaking?

Entering her room, Jane threw herself onto the bed and stared up at the ceiling. Her thoughts wandered to Ivy and Johnny, and she grew angry as she thought about how they had used and manipulated her. She was also certain that Ivy knew more about the gunman incident than she had let on.

Ivy hadn't gone to Adam and Rhoda's reception and must be in her room. Impulsively, Jane decided to speak to her, to confront her about what she'd done.

She crossed the hall and knocked on Ivy's door. There was no answer. Either Ivy had already gone to bed or she was still downstairs, in which case Jane wouldn't want to speak with her now anyway. The things Jane wanted to say could be said only in private. Besides, Jane had decided not to attend the reception; she didn't want to be spotted and buttonholed.

Deciding to speak to Ivy in the morning, she went to bed.

She was awakened by a knock on her door. Morning light shone between the curtains. "Who is it?"

"Jane, it's me, Stanley."

She jumped out of bed, made sure her hair looked all right, and threw open the door. He seemed surprised when she put her arms around him and kissed him. Then she noticed a man in uniform standing behind Stanley, who cleared his throat uncomfortably. "Jane, you remember Officer Raymond."

"Yes, of course," Jane said, serious now, grabbing her robe. "How are you?"

"Fine, ma'am, thank you."

Stanley said, "The road's finally clear, obviously. Now, can you tell me everything you saw relating to this gunman incident?"

"Yes, of course. Let me throw on some clothes."

She closed the door and quickly brushed her teeth and dressed. Then she asked both men to come in and told them what had happened.

"I'd like to speak to Ivy," Stanley said.

"Her room's right across the hall," Jane told him and led the way. Stanley knocked on the door. There was no answer.

"That's odd," Jane said, a shiver of fear running through her. "Where could she be?"

"In another room?" Stanley ventured.

"No . . ." she said thoughtfully. "There's nowhere else she would have spent the night. Stanley," she said suddenly, "I want Adam to let us into her room. What if she's done something—something to herself."

Stanley's eyes widened. "All right." He turned to Officer Raymond. "Dan, would you please go get Adam?"

Raymond nodded and ran down the stairs. A few moments later he and Adam appeared.

"What's going on?" Adam asked Jane.

"I want you to open Ivy's door. She wasn't in her room last night and she doesn't answer the door now."

"All right," Adam said. Taking a ring of keys from his pocket, he unlocked the door and led the way in.

The bed was neatly made, the room empty.

Stanley sighed ominously. "It's clear no one spent the night here."

"Where could she have gone?" Jane asked, though not expecting an answer.

"Jane, I want you to show me where Johnny and the man with the gun ran."

She led them along the corridor, down the stairs, and out the door of the building. It was still quite cold, a moistness in the air, the sky overcast and foreboding. Jane showed Stanley and Raymond the footprints leading into the woods. "But they peter out pretty quickly," she told them.

Stanley was moving slowly among the trees, deeper into the woods. "No, they don't," he said, taking one careful step after another. Raymond, Jane, and Adam followed him. Soon Stanley had led them onto a wide trail.

"Stay to the extreme right, please," he said, "so we don't mess up the prints." He turned to Adam. "Where does this trail lead?"

"To the pond."

"See this?" Stanley said, pointing to the ground. "The prints come out of the woods and onto the trail. And here," he said, pointing along the trail back in the direction of the lodge, "are two more sets of prints. They all merge here."

"But what does that mean?" Jane asked.

Stanley didn't answer, but followed the merged prints, the others close behind. "Ah," he said suddenly, pointing. "Two sets of prints veer off the trail again into the woods."

"Could Johnny and the other man have come this way?" Jane wondered aloud.

"It's possible," Adam said. "Eventually they would have come to another trail. There are so many of them in these woods, and many of them lead all the way down the mountain."

The remaining two sets of footprints continued along the trail, and Stanley, Raymond, Jane, and Adam followed them to the edge of the pond, which was larger than Jane had expected, its surface completely covered with snow.

Stanley walked to the pond's edge, his hands on his hips. He seemed to be staring at something. Jane walked up beside him.

"What?" she asked.

He pointed to an odd mound of snow about a foot from the shore.

"What is it?" she asked, wondering why he found it so interesting. "A rock?"

Wordlessly, Stanley approached the shape, knelt down, and brushed away some of the snow. To Jane's surprise, a bit of bright red was revealed. Puzzled, she frowned and moved closer. Stanley, intent on what he was doing, brushed away more snow.

Suddenly Ivy's face was looking out at them, her blue eyes open, staring, her cheeks bright red.

Jane gasped, stumbling, and clutched at Stanley with a clawed hand. "It's Ivy. Is she . . ."

"Dead."

Jane felt her face contorting and she began to cry. "It can't be. It can't."

Stanley had brushed away more snow. He stood and took Jane in his arms.

Through her tears Jane said, "She must have come down the trail for some reason, not realized she'd reached the pond, and fallen. She must have hit her head on the ice. Poor Ivy."

Gently, Stanley took Jane by the shoulders and looked into her eyes. "Jane, Ivy's death was no accident. I'm sorry, I don't want to have to tell you this, but you might as well know now. She's been stabbed."

Jane's breath caught in her throat. "Stabbed?"

"Yes. With a small, sharp instrument. If I'm not mistaken, an ice pick."

An ice pick . . .

The world began to spin. "Like Trotsky . . ." she said, and suddenly Adam and Rhoda were reaching out to her and calling her name and Stanley had his arms around her again, trying to hold her up, and everything went mercifully black. . . .

# Chapter Ten

Jane was aware of something cold and hard beneath her. She opened her eyes and saw Stanley's face against the gray sky. His own eyes grew wider, and he smiled with relief.

"Take it easy. Don't try to get up yet."

"What happened?"

"You fainted."

Then it all came rushing back to her—the mound of snow, Ivy's open eyes staring blankly—and she was overcome by a heavy wave of despair.

She felt a drop of water hit her forehead and flinched.

"It's starting to rain," Stanley said. "Do you think you can stand up?"

"I think so."

He took her by the arm, Raymond taking her other arm, and they helped her gently to her feet. "Easy does it," he said. "If you feel faint again, tell me."

"All right." She looked around and saw Adam and Rhoda standing nervously off to the side near a large rock. "Stanley," she said, turning to him imploringly, "what happened to Ivy?"

He paused, clearly reluctant to answer. "I told you, Jane," he said gently, "it looks as if she's been . . . killed."

He gave her a curious frowning look. "What was it you said about Trotsky?"

The ice pick. She shuddered. "That's how Leon Trotsky was killed. By an assassin in Mexico City."

Stanley gave her a strange look.

Officer Raymond stepped forward. "Actually, Mrs. Stuart, I believe it was an ice *ax* that was used to kill Trotsky—if you'll forgive my saying so." He gave a quick nervous smile and stepped back again.

Jane looked at him as if he'd lost his mind. "Who the hell cares how Trotsky was killed? My friend is lying there dead on the ice. Who did this to her?" She realized she was screaming. The three men looked alarmed. Rhoda had her index finger between her teeth, her eyes wet with tears.

Now the rain began coming down in earnest, fat plops of water hitting the crusted snow.

"Jane," Stanley said softly, stepping forward, "you've had a very bad shock. I'm going to have Dan here take you back up to the lodge, okay?"

Realizing there was nothing she could do there, that Stanley had to take care of his official business, she took Raymond's arm as he stepped up to her, and slowly he walked her back along the path toward the long wooden building looming ahead.

"Now what happens?" she asked him.

"Detective Greenberg will call dispatch for more officers. Also the Morris County medical examiner. They'll carry out the routine procedures—crime scene—and then," he said, hesitating, "the body will be taken to the autopsy facility."

Wordlessly, Jane nodded. She and Raymond entered the lodge through the door by which they had exited, at the end of the building. Entering the conference room, they stopped short at the sight of everyone sitting around the table, chatting as they ate. A hush descended on the group, puzzled gazes on Jane and the police officer whose arm she was holding.

Ginny stood up. She looked alarmed. "Jane, is something wrong? Where are Adam and Rhoda?"

"Here," came Adam's voice from behind Jane and Raymond. Jane turned. He was picking anxiously at the skin of his thumb. Rhoda stood beside him.

Daniel said, "What happened?"

"Bad news, folks," Raymond said gently, before Jane, Adam, or Rhoda could speak. "There's been a—"

"Ivy's dead," Jane said flatly. "Murdered."

Carla, about to take a bite of buttered poppy-seed bagel, stopped and grinned widely. "I'm loving it."

Everyone looked at her in horror. "Carla!" said Ellyn Bass, who sat beside her.

"Didn't like her," Carla said with a careless shrug, her mouth full of bagel. "That's what she gets for dumping that coffee on me."

"Oh, really," Tamara said.

Jane was aware of movement behind her and turned. Behind Adam and Rhoda were two more uniformed officers, standing side by side. Officer Raymond took a small step forward, taking charge.

"Sir," he said, addressing Adam, "is there a room we can use to interview everyone?"

"Certainly. Through there," Adam replied, pointing toward the lounge.

Raymond stepped to the doorway and took a look into the room. "That'll be fine. If you'll all come in here, please, and take a seat."

"But I'm still eating," Carla protested.

At the other end of the table, Bertha stood suddenly and threw down her crumpled napkin. "Oh, for pity's sake, woman, do as the officer says."

Carla rolled her eyes and flung the rest of her bagel onto

her plate. Poppy seeds flew onto the table. "Always so dramatic." But she stood and joined the others, who had already begun filing into the next room.

Bertha stopped when she reached Jane. "How was she killed?" Bertha asked solemnly.

Before Jane could answer, one of the officers stepped forward. "Ma'am, we'd appreciate it if you wouldn't discuss this amongst yourselves."

"Yes, of course," Bertha said with a sharp military nod, and eyed the officer up and down. Jane couldn't help thinking that he was quite handsome—tall, slim, dark-haired, with fine, regular features. Just Bertha's type.

Raymond, who stood close enough to have heard this exchange, spoke to the group. "That's right, folks, no discussion of any sort, please. Officers Bannon and Grady and I are going to take your statements, and then you can get on with your business."

"Get on with our business!" Arliss cried. "I really don't think so."

"Nor do I," Paul Kavanagh said, and there was a chatter of agreement from the others.

"Folks, folks, quiet, please," Raymond said, and turned to Adam. "We won't take up a lot of your time."

Adam said, "That's fine, but they're right. The retreat is over. I assume the old road is plowed, since you're here."

"That's right," Raymond said.

"Then when you're finished with everyone, they can leave?"

"Yes."

Tamara Henley shivered violently. "Then let's get this over with."

The three officers stationed themselves at different spots in the large room, notepads and pens in hand, and began their interviews. It was Officer Grady who spoke with Jane, asking her about her actions and whereabouts since the group reading the previous evening—the last time, it had been ascertained, Ivy had been seen alive. Jane told Grady she had gone directly to her room after the reading. She hadn't attended Adam and Rhoda's reception in the conference room. She had knocked on Ivy's door, wanting to speak to her, but there had been no answer. Then Jane had gone to bed.

When Officer Grady was finished with Jane, most of the others had already given their statements and left the lounge—presumably to pack and leave. Making for the stairway, she passed through the conference room and was suddenly face-to-face with Larry Graham. His skin was shiny with sweat, and there was an odd gleam in his eyes.

"I didn't expect the retreat to end like this."

She frowned. "No, of course not, none of us did. It's a horrible thing. . . ."

"I mean, we were supposed to go through Sunday. If you count today as lost, that's three days we're missing."

Anger welled up inside her, and she gave her head a little toss. "Exactly what is it you want, Mr. Graham? A woman has been killed. How can you be so insensitive?"

He shifted his weight from one leg to the other, opened his mouth, hesitated. Then he said, "I'm sorry about Ivy, but I just meant that because the retreat's been cut short, maybe you could . . . I mean, if I could be in touch with you later on about my manuscript . . ."

She rolled her eyes. "I'm not taking on any new clients at present. I thought I'd made that clear."

"But—"

She swept past him. As she reached the stairway, the outside door opened and Stanley entered. "Are you all right?" he asked.

"Yes, as all right as can be expected. I'm going upstairs to pack."

"I'll come with you."

In her room, she passed him her clothes and other belongings, which he placed in her suitcase on the bed.

"Stanley," she said suddenly, breaking the silence, "who would have wanted to kill Ivy?"

He shook his head. "That's what we're investigating."

"It had to be someone here at the retreat."

"Not necessarily. That fellow with the gun who chased Johnny into the woods managed to get up here."

"But it was most likely one of us. But who . . . and why?"

"We can rule some people out right away. It couldn't have been Adam or Rhoda, because they were hosting their reception in the conference room until after midnight—and it appears pretty certain Ivy died before then. We can also rule out Tom Brockman, because he was also in the conference room the whole time, helping out with the reception."

"What about the people who attended?"

"Can't rule them out. People were drifting in and out all evening, apparently." He took a deep breath. "The prime suspect, obviously, is Johnny."

"*Johnny?* Ivy would have been more likely to kill him." She told him about Johnny and Carla, and about Ivy's reaction. "On the other hand," she said thoughtfully, "they might have argued. The night before last I heard them screaming at each other in their room. What if they fought about Carla, and Johnny lost his temper and killed Ivy?"

"Possible, I suppose," Stanley agreed.

"Damn right it's possible. Ivy told me Johnny used to *hit* her. She showed me a black-and-blue mark on her side."

Stanley looked distressed at this revelation. He looked down, his face reddening, and finally shook his head. "You have to wonder why a woman would stay with a man like that."

"Because she was scared," she said simply. "Scared that if she lost Johnny, she'd have no one."

"And a man who hits you is better than no man at all?"

"To Ivy, yes. She said as much." Tears came to Jane's eyes. "After what happened to Ivy's daughter, Marlene, I'll never forgive myself if Ivy's killer isn't brought to justice."

Stanley's gaze met hers. "Now, Jane, don't you start playing detective again. You're a literary agent. This is a matter for us, the police."

She'd barely heard him. Lost in memories of her long friendship with Ivy Benson, she reached for the last of her clothes and dumped them in her suitcase.

# Chapter Eleven

"Missus, what are you doing here? We weren't expecting you and Ivy until Sunday."

Florence stood in the doorway between the foyer and the kitchen, a large bowl of chocolate-chip cookie dough in one arm.

"Hey, Mom—" Nick burst from the family room, his hands full of the miniature soldiers Jane had given him for Christmas. He rushed forward and gave her a tight hug.

She ruffled his clean brown hair, knelt, and planted a kiss on his cheek. "It's good to be home."

He gave her a shrewd look. "But you weren't supposed to be home yet. What's wrong?"

Jane's gaze shifted briefly to Florence, who must also have sensed something amiss and wrinkled her brow. "Is everything all right?" she asked.

"Yes, fine," Jane said brightly. "We ended early, that's all."

Florence was watching her. "Have you had your lunch, missus?"

"I'm not hungry, thanks, Florence. Maybe just some coffee."

"Of course," Florence said, and went into the kitchen. Jane hung up her coat and followed her. Nick had returned to the family room, from which came the sounds of *Home Alone*, one of his favorite videos.

Florence came up close to Jane. "What happened?" she whispered. "Where's Ivy?"

"Florence . . ." Jane began, and burst into tears.

"Missus! What is it?"

"Ivy is dead."

Florence's jaw dropped. She set down the bowl on the counter. "Dead?"

"Yes," Jane said, and sniffed.

Florence put a hand to her chest and drew in her breath. "Lord help us, no."

"Yes. Florence," Jane said, her voice breaking, "she was *murdered.*" She burst into fresh tears, and the two women embraced tightly.

"But who?" Florence said, patting her back. "Who would want to do that to her?"

"We don't know."

"Poor Ivy," Florence said softly. "I didn't know her very well, but it seems she never had much of a life."

From the center of the laundry room Jane, Florence, and Nick watched Winky care for her six three-day-old kittens.

"Mom, why can't I play with them?" Nick asked, his gaze fixed on the box in the corner.

"Dr. Singh says we should avoid handling the kittens for the first two weeks," Jane said. "Though I agree it's hard not to at least pet them," she admitted. "They are so cute."

"That they are, missus," Florence said. "But we can name them while we're waiting."

"I've already started on that," Nick said. "Now let's see . . . there are three that look like Winky."

"Right," Florence said. "Brown tortoiseshells. All females."

"Right. But they don't look exactly alike. One has funny dark marks above her eyes that look like another pair of eyes. So I've decided to call her . . . Four Eyes."

"Sounds good," Jane said, and she and Florence exchanged a smile.

"Then there's one with dark paws. I'm calling her Muddy, because it looks like she stepped in mud. And there's one that looks exactly like Winky. I haven't figured out what to call her yet."

"We'll work on that one," Florence said. "What about the other three?"

"There's that gorgeous one with the grayish white markings," Jane said.

"Also a tortoiseshell," Florence said. "I believe it's called a blue-cream."

"How do you know so much about cats?"

"I told you, missus, in Trinidad I saw a lot of kittens being born. Now this blue-cream tortoiseshell, it is also a girl."

"Let's call her Blue," Nick said.

"Okay," Jane said. "Now what about the other two?"

"Ah, the boys," Florence said. "And both orange tabbies."

"They're beautiful," Jane said, looking at the tiny orange-and-cream striped bodies. "What about these guys, Nick?"

"Well," he said thoughtfully, "one is more orange than the other, and I've noticed he keeps stomping on his brother and sisters. So I think we should call him Crush. Get it? Orange Crush."

"Love it. And the other one?"

"He's the smallest of the litter. He's Pee Wee."

"Very good, Master Nick," Florence said, and tossed back her head and laughed. "You still have to give some thought to the one that looks just like her mother."

"I will." Nick frowned in puzzlement. "Why are they all different?"

"Genetics," Jane said. "Not that I can explain it, but nature dictates that a certain mother and father will produce certain types of kittens."

"You know," Florence said thoughtfully, watching Winky, "I have read that a litter of kittens can have more than one father."

Jane looked at Florence in shock.

"It's true. While you were at the retreat, I thought about who the father might be—you know, tomcats in this neighborhood. And there are *two* I can think of who might be responsible for this bunch. I even called Dr. Singh, and she told me what this is called." Florence glanced upward, thinking. "Yes, I know. Superfecundation."

"Wow. You're smart, Flo."

Florence patted Nick's head. "No, just curious."

"Look what she's doing now."

Winky moved around the box, rubbing heads with each of her kittens in turn. Then she walked to a corner of the box and flopped onto her back. Immediately the kittens made their way over to her and began to nurse.

"You're a good mother, Miss Winky," Florence called softly, and she and Jane and Nick filed quietly out of the room.

"Hey, Mom," Nick said in the hallway. "Do you think Ivy would like to have one of the kittens?"

Jane's and Florence's smiles disappeared. Jane opened her mouth but was at a loss for words. Finally she said, "Nicholas, honey, I have something to tell you about Ivy. During the retreat"—she glanced quickly at Florence—"she had an accident."

"An accident? Is she all right?"

Jane put her hand on the back of Nick's head. "No, darling, she's not. I'm afraid she died."

Nick's face grew pale. "What happened?"

"She . . . fell on some ice and . . . hurt herself. I'm so sorry to have to tell you this news."

"Dead," Nick said hollowly, and caught his lower lip between his teeth, contemplating this idea. "And she was just here, having Christmas with us."

"Yes," Florence said, "that's right. And we had a lovely Christmas, didn't we? I'm sure Ivy left this world with happy thoughts in her head."

The two women watched Nick walk slowly down the hallway to the foyer and enter the family room; then they exchanged a sorrowful look. A tear rolled down Florence's cheek and she wiped it away, forcing a little smile.

Early that afternoon, Stanley called before dropping by. Jane made hot cocoa and served it with some of Florence's chocolate-chip cookies in her study off the living room.

"Are you sure you're all right?" he asked.

"I'm fine, really. It's just a terrible shock. She was my oldest friend."

"I know." He placed his hand on top of hers. "I want you to know we're working very hard on this, Jane. I'm sure we'll have some answers soon."

"Why do you say that? Have you got any leads?"

He looked uncomfortable. "No, not exactly. There were no fingerprints of any use at the crime scene, as you would probably have guessed. The ME says Ivy didn't put up a struggle. That means the killer sneaked up on her."

"No, not necessarily," Jane said impatiently. "She and the killer could have been chatting, and the killer could have whipped out that awful thing and stabbed her."

"I suppose," Stanley said, "but not very likely, in my opinion."

She shrugged. "Could the medical examiner tell from the wound whether the killer was right- or left-handed?"

He gave her an appraising look, lifting one brow. "Quite the detective, aren't you? Actually, I was going to tell you about that next. Unfortunately, in this case he wasn't able to tell."

She let out a sigh of discouragement. "Then I don't see why you're so confident about having answers soon. It looks as if this case may never be solved."

"Of course you're feeling negative about everything now. . . ."

"Someone needs to," she cried. "Poor Ivy, without a friend in the world."

"You were her friend," he pointed out softly.

"Not a very good friend. After Marlene died, I was happy to let the friendship be over. I should have gotten back in touch with her, tried to patch things up. It shouldn't have had to be Ivy who put our friendship back together. I feel so guilty about it all."

He sat silently for a moment, sipping his cocoa.

"I'm sorry," she said, smiling at him. "I don't mean to dump all this on you. What else can you tell me?"

"The footprints were pretty quickly washed away by the rain, but we did ascertain that there were *five* sets of prints, not four as we originally thought."

"Five?"

"Mm. Here's how we think it went down. Two people—presumable Johnny and his pursuer, the man with the gun—ran through the woods, onto the path for a short distance, then back into the woods. *Three* people, not two, followed the path from the lodge to the pond. Only two of these people, obviously, came back: the murderer and . . . someone else."

"Who could this other person have been?"

"Unfortunately, the prints were obliterated enough that trying to match them with the shoes of the people staying at the lodge was impossible." He set down his cup. "In the meantime, I've got some men searching the woods for signs of Johnny and the gunman."

Jane set down her cocoa and sat staring into the middle distance, contemplating this information. At this moment she felt that Johnny was the likeliest suspect in Ivy's murder, yet he himself had been another's quarry. Why had that man wanted Johnny? Where was Johnny now?

Aware of Stanley rising from his chair, she came out of her reverie.

"I should go," he said.

"I'm sorry, I haven't been very good company."

He bent and gave her a kiss on the cheek. "Don't worry about it. Try to get some rest. I'll be back tomorrow."

She saw him to the door and watched him back out of the driveway and head down Lilac Way.

# Chapter Twelve

After seeing Stanley off, Jane had returned to her study and tried to get through a stack of book proposals that had been submitted to the agency before Christmas. But it was hopeless. She couldn't concentrate. Letting a handful of pages drop to her lap, she gazed aimlessly out the window, which looked out on the left side of her small-ish front yard, the high holly hedge that enclosed it, and Lilac Way beyond.

As she watched, a car pulled slowly up the street and slowed when it reached Jane's house. The car was white, with familiar lettering on the side. It pulled into Jane's drive-way, and she realized it was a Shady Hills Taxi.

Frowning in bewilderment, she went to the front door, opened it, and looked out. Behind the wheel of the cab, eighty-something Erol, who had been driving for Shady Hills Taxi for more than thirty years, saw Jane, grinned, and saluted. She smiled and waved back, then squinted, straining to see who his passenger was. All she could make out were moving shadows as whoever it was in the back paid Erol, he handed back change, and the passenger handed back some money, presumably a tip. Erol looked at the bills he'd been handed and scowled.

The right rear door of the taxi opened, and an immense

bouquet—no, two bouquets—of red and yellow roses emerged first.

What on earth . . . ?

After the roses came a pair of pudgy legs.

No. It couldn't be.

It was.

With difficulty, Bertha Stumpf extricated herself from the cab. She pulled down her tight dress with a shimmying movement, then slammed the car door shut. Erol backed out and drove away up the street.

Bertha looked appraisingly up at the house, eyes narrowed. Then she saw Jane, her face bloomed into a solicitous smile, and she started up the path to the front door.

What was she doing here?

"Surprise!" Bertha cried, clip-clopping up the steps in her heels. "Bet I'm the last person you expected to see, huh?"

"That's for sure." Jane made herself smile. It occurred to her that she should have seen this visit coming. Over the course of their working together, Bertha had made several references to the possibility of their getting together sometime "in Jane's neck of the woods." Jane had found the idea repugnant. Not only did she find Bertha tiresome at the best of times, but she never socialized with the writers she represented. Even if she did, the last thing she would ever do would be to invite one to her home.

Years ago, when Jane and Kenneth had both worked at Silver and Payne, the large old literary agency where they had met, Beryl Patrice, the agency's president, had given Jane a piece of advice: "Don't ever wear your mink to lunch with a client, and whatever you do, don't ever let a client see where you live. Either the client will feel you live too lavishly and have achieved this affluence off her back, or else the client will feel you live shabbily and will decide you're a loser. Either way, it causes resentment. It's a no-win situation."

It was the only thing of any value Beryl had ever said to Jane. She wondered which category Bertha would fall into.

"Jane, darling!" Bertha cried dramatically, bearing the vivid bouquets up the steps like an Olympic torch, and threw her arms around Jane. "Please forgive my dropping in like this, but how could I leave town without knowing you were all right?"

"How did you know where I live?"

"You're in the book, Jane." Bertha trotted past Jane into the foyer. "What a fabulous house. So old-fashioned and cozy. And so big! What do you call this style?"

"Chalet, mock Tudor." Jane shrugged. Was this really happening?

"Well, it's adorable. Here," Bertha said, practically shoving the flowers in Jane's face. "These are for you, darling. I figured you could use some cheering up after what happened this morning. I'm so sorry." Jane took the flowers, and Bertha shrugged out of her coat.

Florence and Nick appeared from the kitchen and stood staring. "Bertha—oh, sorry," Jane said.

"No, my real name is fine here, silly," Bertha said with a wave of her hand. "This is family."

Family. Hanging up Bertha's coat, Jane felt as if she were going to be sick. "Bertha Stumpf, I'd like you to meet my son, Nicholas, and this is Florence."

Nick said a quick hi. Florence looked bewildered at this unexpected guest but stepped forward graciously and shook Bertha's hand. "A pleasure to meet you," she said.

Bertha gasped. "*Love* the accent," she said, as if it were something Florence had selected and purchased. She gave Florence and Nick an arch smile. "I've heard a lot about you two."

Still they both stood there, staring. Jane gave Florence a quick wave of her head that meant *Beat it*.

Florence relieved Jane of the roses, then took Nick by the hand and led him back toward the kitchen.

"My word," Bertha said, watching Nick nostalgically. "Such a handsome young man. The spitting image of Kenneth."

Bertha had known Kenneth in the early years when she and Jane worked together, but she was wrong about Nick's looks. In actuality, Nick looked mostly like Jane. But Jane felt no desire to point this out to Bertha, who now stood in the center of the foyer, looking around. "Well."

"Well is right," Jane said, able to bear it no longer. "Bertha, what are you doing here?"

Bertha turned to her, shock on her face. "I just told you. I wanted to make sure you were all right before I left town. How could I leave without seeing you?"

Easily, Jane thought.

"I mean," Bertha went on, "what's the difference whether I take a later bus? You matter most. So," she said, and turned a piercing look on Jane, "how're you holding up?"

"As well as can be expected." Anger welled in Jane and though she tried, she couldn't keep it tamped down. "Bertha, this really is the height of insensitivity. My oldest friend died last night—was murdered—and you use her death as an excuse to stop by here, at my home, to talk about your career."

Bertha opened her mouth as wide as it would go. "My *career?* What are you talking about? I've just told you twice—"

"Yeah, yeah, you told me twice. And you're full of it twice. I know you better than that."

"What are you saying? That I'm not a thoughtful person? Who was it who saved your life that time at the Waldorf when you were hurt so badly? Who told the police and the EMTs who you were? Who came to the hospital to make sure you were all right?" Bertha's eyes were moist with tears. "Really, Jane, I'm very hurt."

Jane rolled her eyes. "All right, I'm sorry. You want some coffee?"

"I'd love some," Bertha said, immediately back to business, and roamed into the family room. "Fabulous house," she marveled. "Fabulous."

"This way," Jane said, and led her into the living room.

"Even more beautiful," Bertha pronounced as she arranged herself comfortably on a sofa.

"I'll be right back," Jane said, and went to the kitchen.

"Missus," Florence whispered as soon as she saw Jane, "who is that woman?"

"Yeah, Mom," Nick said from the kitchen table. "She's so fat."

"Nicholas! That's a terrible, unkind thing to say."

Nick shrugged. "I can tell you don't like her."

She stared at him. "What do you mean by that?"

"I can tell, that's all. I can always tell. I think it's called body language."

"Oh, really?" Jane said, unable to suppress a smirk. "And what kind of body language was I using with her?"

"The kind that says, 'I don't like you, but I'm going to pretend I do.'"

Florence giggled. "Missus, can I make you and your friend some coffee?"

"Thank you, Florence, that would be lovely. And some of those cookies if there are any left." Jane glanced at Nick's crumb-covered plate. "And by the way, she's one of my clients. She writes romance novels under the pseudonym Rhonda Redmond."

"Ah," Florence said, her face lighting up, "the very successful Rhonda Redmond."

"Right," Jane said, "so behave yourselves, both of you."

Nick let out an evil little snicker, and Florence gave one solemn nod. Jane returned to the living room, where Bertha sat with her legs crossed. "Jane, I feel I'm intruding."

Very perceptive. "No, don't be silly, Bertha. It's a surprise, that's all. Perhaps if you had called first . . ." *I would have had a chance to tell you not to come.*

"You're right, I should have. But I didn't have your home number."

"Yes, you did. You just said I'm in the book."

"Oh, yes, right." Bertha shifted uneasily. "Anyway, I'm here now, and as soon as I'm sure you're all right and that there's nothing I can do for you, I'll be on my merry way."

"Very thoughtful," Jane said, sitting on the sofa perpendicular to Bertha's. "I'm fine, really."

"It's all such a shame. Not only about your friend, but about the retreat. It was going so well, don't you think?"

Jane frowned. "No, as a matter of fact, I don't. No one got along. Everyone was constantly sniping at one another. And the students' work itself was extremely disappointing—except, maybe, for William Ives's novel. I thought that was remarkably well written."

Bertha rolled her eyes and gave a lazy wave. "Please. Do you really think he wrote that? Gimme a break. Arliss wrote it for him."

"I know that's what Brad Franklin said, but do you really think so?"

"Absolutely. It was of publishable quality. How could that dried-up little raisin of a man have written that himself?"

"What does his appearance have to do with how he writes? You're not exactly—forgive me—Marilyn Monroe." *On the other hand, you're a lousy writer, so maybe you've got something there.*

"No, no, that's not what I meant. It's just that he came out of nowhere."

"You came out of nowhere once."

Bertha made an exasperated *tsk*ing sound. "Anyway, he wasn't the only student whose work had merit. My own Ellyn Bass is a lovely writer."

"You think?"

"Definitely. She writes with genuine passion. That's all that really matters. When you write with passion, your readers know it. Why do you think I'm so successful?"

"I don't know, why are you?"

Bertha placed the palms of her hands to each side of her on the sofa. "Jane, you are angry at me for coming here. Don't deny it. Instead of making these passive-aggressive little quips, why don't you speak your mind? I'll be happy to leave if you like. I'm not staying long anyway."

Jane lowered her gaze, duly abashed. "I apologize, Bertha. You're right. I was annoyed to see you. I never have clients in my home, and I'm not exactly in a visiting mood."

"All right, then. Thank you. Let's start again, shall we?"

Florence came in with the coffee and cookies. "Here we are," she said, and set them down on the cocktail table.

Bertha put milk and Equal in her coffee and grabbed two cookies, munching on one as she watched Florence leave the room. "She's a treasure, isn't she?"

"Yes, she is. She's like family."

"Like I said," Bertha cried in a high-pitched voice. "Me too. And what kind of relative would I be if I hadn't stopped by? So we were talking about the retreat and that sweet Ellyn Bass. You keep an eye on her, Jane. She may very well be the next me."

Heaven forbid. "Thanks for the tip. She is a member of the writers' group here in town, the Midnight Writers, so I can keep tabs on her."

"Good." Bertha started on her second cookie. "Have you heard from your friend Stanley?" she said with her mouth full. "Does he have any idea who did that awful thing to Ivy?"

"No. It's soon yet."

"True. But we all know who did it, don't we?"

"Who?"

"That Johnny, of course. I can imagine exactly what happened. I'm not a novelist for nothing, you know." Bertha closed her eyes and threw back her head theatrically. "Ivy was mad for the man," she began in a husky voice that reminded Jane of Norma Desmond in *Sunset Boulevard*. "And what happens? He and Carla take one look at each other and a fiery passion rages." She shook her head sadly. "Ivy had no hope of keeping him, poor little thing. But love doesn't die without a fight. On the path down by the pond, she confronted him, told him she loved him, demanded that he forget Carla . . ."

Jane remembered the sounds of shouting that came from Ivy and Johnny's room.

Bertha swept on, "But he would have none of it! He told her they were through. She slapped him. He hit her back. He has a furious temper—men like that always do. Enraged, she slapped him again. They struggled. She wouldn't let him go. And Johnny knew that the only way he could ever have Carla was to get Ivy out of the picture. So he whipped out the ice pick and—" She let her head fall. "Well. You know the rest."

Jane stared at her in amazement. "'He whipped out the ice pick'? What would he be doing carrying around an ice pick?"

"I don't know." Clearly Bertha felt this was a triviality. "He'd put it in his pocket earlier—you know, without thinking."

"Oh, Bertha," Jane said, "that's ridiculous. Whoever killed Ivy stole that ice pick with the express intention of using it on her later. This was no crime of passion."

"Hmm," Bertha said, considering, and shrugged. "Then I have no idea. *Unless,*" she burst out suddenly, "it was Carla! She wanted Johnny for herself and had to get Ivy out of the way. Now that would make more sense."

"Yes," Jane had to admit, "it would." Then she had another idea. "You know, I've just remembered something.

On Wednesday night Ivy told me Red Pearson had made two passes at her. She wasn't at all interested, of course. Maybe—"

"Maybe Red killed Ivy because she wouldn't have him? No way."

"How can you be so sure?"

Bertha blushed. "Because," she said, placing a hand delicately to her bosom, "Red Pearson was interested in *me*."

"In you?" Jane faltered.

Bertha stared at her coldly. "Is that so unbelievable?"

"No, no. It's just that I had no idea."

"*C'est vrai,*" Bertha said airily, then hunkered down. "I think he's dishy, don't you?"

"Red? Bald Red Pearson in the red flannel lumberjack shirts? Uh, no, I don't."

"Wait till you're a bit older, Jane. You won't be able to be so choosy."

"I won't need to be. I'll have Stanley."

"And if he loses his hair? Will you lose interest?"

"No."

"All right then. It may very well be that Red was interested in Ivy at the beginning of the retreat, but that was before he got to know me." Bertha wiggled her eyebrows. "And boy, did he get to know me."

"Bertha! There are some things I don't need to know." But Jane marveled that she hadn't been aware of this particular situation.

"And there *are* things you don't know," Bertha said, as if reading her mind. "Anyhoo, that's where I was after the police let us leave the lodge this morning—at Red's house. He's got a darling place way up at the north end of town—not terribly far from Mt. Munsee, actually—with the prettiest little yard—"

"You went to Red's?" Jane asked, scandalized.

"For *lunch*. We had a lovely time, and we're going to be getting together again, probably in New York. It was while I was at Red's house that I had the idea of stopping by to see you before I left town. Red wanted to drive me here, but I knew he was eager to start on some project in his house and told him I wouldn't dream of it. He had to get to some store called the Depot, or something like that."

"Home Depot."

"That's it. He said he hadn't expected to be home from the retreat so soon, but now that he was, he might as well get started. Your house would have been far out of his way. So he called me a taxi."

"I see," Jane said, growing bored. She wanted Bertha to leave now. She set down her coffee cup and stifled a yawn.

"You're exhausted, poor thing. I should go. Lord knows I need to get back to my desk. Lots to do."

"Oh?" Jane said, and the moment the word was out of her mouth she realized she'd fallen into Bertha's trap.

"Absolutely. Now that Harriet's accepted *Shady Lady*—you're checking on my money, don't forget—I've got to get started on a new proposal. The question is, who is it for?"

"What do you mean, who is it for? It's for Bantam, your publisher."

Bertha looked directly into Jane's eyes. "I can't stay there, Jane. As I've told you, I can't work with this girl they've assigned to me, and you said there's no one else there to work with."

"Whoa, hold it, whoa. What I said was that Harriet Green is a fine editor. I never said there's no one else at Bantam you could work with. What I said was that Harriet was as good an editor as any editor there."

"I find that difficult to believe. She's twelve!"

"Bertha, I've told you how that bothers me. It's ageist and disrespectful. She's a young woman. How would you like it if she called you a senior citizen? And what difference does it make how old she is? A good editor is a good editor."

"Jane, you have to understand about my writing, about me. I write romance from a worldly, experienced perspective. I bring my life wisdom to my writing. I can't communicate with a woman barely out of college. She doesn't understand where I'm coming from."

"Baloney."

Bertha stared at her. "I beg your pardon?"

"Baloney. Nonsense. Fact is, many of your readers are Harriet's age. If you think you're not getting through to them, you're in trouble."

"I take it, then, that you are not willing to ask that I be assigned to a new editor."

"You take it correctly. There would be no point."

"Then I must leave Bantam."

"Leave Bantam?" Jane cried. "You've been there most of your career."

"Exactly. Time for a change. My print runs are declining, and so are my sell-throughs. I don't make the printed *New York Times* list anymore. I don't even get a step-back cover anymore," she said, referring to a double paperback cover.

"Bertha," Jane said as gently as possible, "none of these problems have anything to do with Bantam. You won't reverse these trends unless you change what you're writing."

"Change what I'm writing! Rhonda Redmond?"

"Rhonda Redmond whose print runs and sell-throughs are dropping. We've talked about how the market for historical romances is changing. Why don't you try a Regency historical? That's what's hot right now."

"Regency," Bertha repeated distastefully. "So mannered and polite. Hardly a fitting backdrop for a Rhonda Redmond heroine."

"But that's just the point." Jane felt a headache coming

on. "A Rhonda Redmond heroine would be all the more shocking and scandalous in that society."

"Mm," Bertha said, though she was clearly uninterested. She brushed off her dress and rose. "I really should be going, Jane. Now that I know you're all right."

"And we've discussed your career."

"Oh, my goodness," Bertha said with a surprised little laugh. "We have, haven't we."

"But we've resolved nothing."

"True, but I do appreciate your thoughts, as always. You want me to write a Regency historical for Harriet at Bantam."

"Yes."

"Let me give it some thought." Bertha started toward the foyer. "Now if you'd be a doll and call me a cab to take me to the bus . . ."

"Don't be silly. I'll drive you," Jane said, taking their coats from the closet.

"You would? You're a sweetheart. Oh, and Jane . . ." Bertha said, buttoning her coat.

"Yes?"

"Please don't tell anyone about Red and me—not that you would, of course."

"Right. I wouldn't."

"Thanks. You know how people are."

Yes, Jane thought, putting on her scarf, she knew how people were. And as she headed for the kitchen to tell Florence and Nick she'd be right back, it occurred to Jane that she should be grateful to Bertha. She had, at least for a time, managed to take Jane's mind off poor Ivy.

Outside, Bertha paused and gazed up at the house. "Nice place," she said with a thoughtful frown, and started along the path to Jane's car.

# Chapter Thirteen

It was 9:30 P.M. Jane, Florence, and Nick had just checked on Winky and her brood—Winky had now taken to vigorously licking her young, which Nick found hilarious—and then Jane had gotten Nick into the shower and tucked into bed. Now, standing at her dresser and removing her earrings, she heard the doorbell ring.

Florence's steps sounded in the hall. "I'll get it, missus. I wonder who . . . ?" After a moment there came the sound of the front door opening, and Florence's voice again, "Why, Mr. Daniel. Are you okay?"

Daniel? Jane went out into the hall and to the edge of the stairs. Daniel, in jeans and coat, gazed up at her, a look of concern on his face, his brows drawn together.

"Hi, Jane. Sorry to bother you so late."

She descended the stairs. "What's wrong?" Reaching the foyer, she took him by the arm and led him through the living room into her study. It wasn't like him to simply show up, especially late in the evening.

"Jane," he said, taking the same seat Stanley had occupied earlier in the day, "something's been bothering me, something that happened yesterday at the lodge. I felt I should tell you about it, see if you thought it was worth mentioning to Stanley."

"Go on."

He shrugged off his jacket and laid it down on the small table between their chairs. "It was late yesterday morning, about eleven o'clock. Ginny had asked me to help set up for lunch. She realized the supply of napkins in the kitchen had run out, so she sent me to get some in that storage room off the lounge."

She nodded encouragingly.

He went on, "It took me a minute or two to find the napkins—it's quite a mess in there." He made a face. Messes always bothered Daniel. "Finally I found them and was about to leave the storage room, but as I was about to open the door, I heard voices in the lounge and realized they belonged to Larry Graham and Ivy."

Jane gave a bewildered little shrug. "So?"

"It was the *way* they were talking. I sensed something odd right away, and I confess"—he looked down in embarrassment—"I peeked out a crack in the door and watched them. They were sitting extremely close together on the sofa, and their heads were practically touching. Larry was smiling, and Ivy was leaning toward him, pressing her body against him. She said something like, '. . . down the path. It's safe there,' and Larry nodded, very serious."

"'Down the path'?" Jane sat up straight.

"Yes."

"Then what happened?"

"At that moment a noise came from the conference room beyond them—it sounded like someone bumping into a chair. Ivy and Larry both looked up sharply, and then Larry ran out to the conference room. He came back a few moments later. He told Ivy he'd heard footsteps on the stairs and had run up to see who it was, but that there was no one in the upstairs corridor, that whoever it was must have gone into his or her room." He stopped, watching her, waiting for her reaction.

"How positively odd," she said. "Were Ivy and Larry going to meet on the path? What could she have meant when she said it would be safe there?"

Daniel shook his head, at a loss.

Jane said, "Do you think Ivy and Larry could have been carrying on at the same time as Johnny and Carla?"

"Larry was hardly Ivy's type," Daniel pointed out.

"True, but she may have been using him to get back at Johnny." She suddenly remembered Ivy watching Larry so intently during the group reading Thursday evening. Could she have been planning her revenge on Johnny at that moment?

"I see why you thought this was so important," she told him. "What if Ivy and Larry did meet," she said thoughtfully, "Larry made clumsy advances toward Ivy—maybe wanted to go further than she wanted to—and she rebuffed him?"

"And he killed her in a rage?"

She shook her head. "Why would he have been carrying the ice pick?" She paused, thinking. "Our Larry theory doesn't really make sense, but I think we'd better tell Stanley about this. Why haven't you said something sooner?"

"I don't know. . . . In all the uproar, I guess I forgot. Then I remembered it, and it occurred to me that it might very well have significance."

"It may not, but the police have to know about it." She rose, picking up Daniel's coat and handing it to him. "Let's go."

Stanley lived on the top floor of a house on Christopher Street, not far from Hillmont Elementary, where Nick attended the fifth grade. From his La-Z-Boy in the corner of his small plant-filled living room, he listened to the end of Daniel's story and slowly nodded.

Jane said, "We don't know if it's significant, but we felt you should know about it."

"Absolutely. I know this Larry Graham character. The town had some trouble with him a couple of years ago."

"Trouble?" Daniel repeated.

"Mm. He bid on the electrical part of that big library renovation and got the job. But halfway into it, he claimed he'd been lied to about the original electrical work in the building and needed twice the money to do the job right. Not only did the library board feel that this was black-mail, but they couldn't understand why he hadn't in-spected the building carefully enough before he started to know this. They weren't even sure they believed him any-way."

"So what happened?"

"The board refused. They offered him a payment for what he'd done. He took it and stomped off, wouldn't co-operate with the new electrician they brought in. On top of that, it was discovered that he'd been cutting corners, and everything he did had to be ripped out. The board considered suing him, but in the end they decided not to throw good money after bad." Stanley shook his head. "Totally sleazy character."

"Are you going to speak to him about him and Ivy?" Jane asked.

"Absolutely. First thing in the morning." He shot Jane a warning look. "Now don't *you* get any ideas about play-ing detective and speaking to him."

Jane placed her fingers to her throat, affronted. "I wouldn't dream of it."

"Good," Stanley said, and gave a decisive nod. "I'll let you know what I come up with."

The next morning, Saturday, Stanley stopped by to see Jane. She was in the kitchen, making breakfast for Nick, who was in the laundry room watching Winky and her kittens. Stanley sat at the kitchen table and Jane gave him some coffee.

"I've just been to see Larry Graham," he said.

Jane turned, a bowl of beaten eggs in her hand. "And?"

"What a sleazy jerk."

She laughed. "Very professional."

"I'm not speaking as a police officer, of course."

"Of course."

"Anyway, he was shocked when I asked him about his intimate conversation with Ivy. He wanted to know how I knew about it. I didn't tell him, of course. He admitted to having the conversation and confirmed that Ivy said, '. . . down the path. It's safe there.' But guess what he said they were talking about."

She waited.

"Ice skating."

"Ice skating?"

"Mm-hm. You're not going to believe this, but fat, pasty-faced Larry is a former professional figure skater. Roughly twenty-five years ago, of course."

"You're right—I don't believe it."

"It's true. He says he had told Ivy all about it, and she wanted him to skate for her."

"How ridiculous. Even if he really was a skater, he wouldn't have had skates with him at the retreat. Besides, the pond was covered with snow."

"I put both those facts to him. He said they had agreed to borrow a snow shovel from the storage room and clear some of the pond. And he did have skates with him—at least he said he did."

"Why would he have brought skates?"

"Because he knew there was a pond near the lodge and thought he might skate there."

She poured the eggs into a hot frying pan and they sizzled. "He's full of it. I hope you didn't believe him."

"No, I didn't. Though I can't imagine why he wouldn't have just admitted that he and Ivy were planning to meet down the path to fool around."

"Because of Johnny, of course. He would have been afraid of what Johnny would do to him."

"Good point," he said. "I think they were planning to meet down the path because there was nowhere else they could meet—there weren't any rooms available, and they weren't going to use the storage room, after the fuss you said Tom Brockman made. I think Larry wanted more than Ivy was willing to give, and he got angry and killed her."

"With the ice pick he'd pilfered from the lodge's kitchen." She gave him a skeptical look. "Why would he have done that?"

He contemplated his coffee mug. "I have no idea," he said, deflated.

"Are you sure he's telling the truth about this skating stuff?"

"His mantel is lined with trophies and photos. I intend to check on it, of course—a search on the Internet should do it." He sipped his coffee. "But I'm not really interested in this Graham character. I don't intend to pursue him further at this point. It's Johnny Baglieri I'm after. I've still got men searching Mt. Munsee for signs of him and the guy who was chasing him. The ME says Ivy died between eight P.M. and midnight Thursday night. Johnny could have escaped his pursuer—or dealt with him in a worse way—and returned to the woods near the lodge to take care of Ivy."

"But why? What reason would he have had?"

"Maybe simply that she knew too much about his life, his dealings, his 'irons in the fire.' Who knows what he's involved in."

"But why would he have chosen to do it then?" She shook her head vehemently. "It doesn't make sense."

The eggs were ready. She scraped them from the pan onto a plate, which she placed at Nick's seat, then started making toast. "Nick," she called. "Breakfast."

He appeared in the doorway almost instantly, as if he'd been waiting in the next room.

"Mom," he said excitedly, slipping onto a chair. "I thought of a name for the kitten that looks just like Winky."

Jane and Stanley waited, watching him.

His face broke into a huge smile. "Twinky."

Stanley smiled. *"Twinky?"*

"Yup," Nick said solemnly. "It's short for 'tiny Winky.' Get it?"

Nodding, Jane threw Stanley a conspiratorial look.

"Know what else?" Nick said on a mouthful of scrambled eggs. "She's the one I'm keeping."

Stanley looked up in surprise. "You're keeping one of the kittens?"

"Yes, just one," Jane said, and looked at Nick. He was looking down sadly. She walked around the table and put her arm around his small shoulders. "We discussed it and agreed that one was as much as we can handle."

"Right," Nick agreed halfheartedly. "I hope Winky doesn't miss her other children too much."

Stanley gave him a kind smile. "I'm sure she knows your mom will find them good homes. Right, Jane?"

"Right," Jane said, looking down at her son, and squeezed him tight. "That's a promise."

After Stanley left, Jane went to her study to give the proposals another try. She rejected two and was halfway into her third when her thoughts drifted to what Stanley had told her about Larry Graham. She tried to picture him, obese and ungainly, spinning on ice, but the image was just too comical to take seriously. But, of course, as Stanley had pointed out, Graham had looked quite different in his skating years. . . .

The telephone rang. It was Daniel.

"Any news?"

She told him what Stanley had told her about Larry Graham.

"A skater? Him? That's the funniest thing I've ever heard."

"Mm, ludicrous, isn't it? But apparently it's true. . . ."

"Why do you say it like that?" he asked suspiciously.

"Because there's more there than what Stanley got; I'm sure of it. And I intend to find out what it is."

"Now, Jane . . . What are you going to do?"

"I'm going to go see Graham myself. And don't you dare tell Stanley. I'm sick of his lectures about not playing detective."

"I won't. But you don't know where Graham lives."

"Not a problem. Talk to you later."

"Jane—"

She hung up. Then she thought for a moment and took the phone off the hook.

She yanked out the telephone directory from the bottom drawer of her desk and checked the Yellow Pages under Electrical Contractors. Larry (not Lawrence) Graham was listed, but there was no street address, just "Shady Hills Area." His listing in the White Pages was the same.

Adam would know the address. She got his number from her address book and punched it out.

# Chapter Fourteen

Larry Graham lived at Hillside Gardens, a vast but down-at-the-heel apartment complex at the east end of town, across Route 46. Jane found a parking space not far from number 78, Graham's apartment. Graham opened the door before she could ring the bell. He wore jeans and a faded yellow T-shirt.

He looked her up and down in slack-jawed amazement. "What are you doing here?"

"I'm surprised to find you home," she said pleasantly. "Such a beautiful day." It was indeed a lovely day, sunny and unseasonably mild, the snow turning to slush. "I would have thought you'd have jobs to go to."

He laughed derisively. "Jobs! Why would I have any jobs today? I didn't line anything up. I was supposed to be at the retreat until tomorrow."

He actually sounded as if it was Jane's fault that Ivy had been murdered, spoiling his week.

"Good point," she said. "May I come in?"

He regarded her suspiciously. "What do you want?"

"I'd like to talk to you," she said, forcing her tone to remain gracious and keeping a mild smile on her face. She glanced into the apartment. "Well, may I?"

He shrugged indifferently. "I guess so."

She couldn't remember when she'd last been in an apartment like this. Everything about it was dingy, from the filthy gold-colored plush carpet that appeared to run through the entire place, to the scuffed off-white walls. The air had an oppressive animal stench, bringing to mind a large unwashed dog—which was exactly what appeared from the rear doorway of the living room. Jane didn't know much about dogs, but she knew this to be a collie. Its pale-gold-and-white coat was matted and dull; its eyes were a rheumy blue.

"Don't mind Alphonse," Graham said, flopping into a chair and indicating the sofa for Jane. It was as dirty as the carpet, but she made herself sit anyway, keeping her coat on. The dog hurried up to her and buried its nose in her lap.

"How sweet," she said, squirming. "But I'm afraid I may be allergic," she lied. "Could you call him off, please?"

"Alphonse!" Graham screamed, and Jane jumped. "Leave 'er alone."

The dog immediately withdrew its nose, slunk to the corner of the room, and fell onto its side, tucking its nose into its tail. It made a few snorting noises and closed its eyes for a nap.

Jane looked around the room. To her right was a fireplace, whose mantel was indeed lined with an assortment of skating trophies in various sizes. She spotted a picture of Larry skating in a pure white costume. He looked slim and athletic, not unattractive. Shifting her glance to Larry—pudgy, ungainly, the very picture of ungracefulness—she found it barely possible to believe.

He followed her gaze. "Yeah, it's true," he said. "I suppose your boyfriend told you about that part of my life."

"Why do you say he's my boyfriend?"

"Who?"

She felt herself blush. "Never mind."

"So let's cut the small talk, shall we? You're not here because you think I'm the next John Grisham. To what do I owe the honor?"

She realized she found him loathsome. Ivy couldn't possibly have been interested in him romantically. "I want to ask you about something."

He rolled his eyes. "My conversation with your friend? Listen, I'm sorry about what happened to her, I really am, but I don't know anything about it."

"What did she say to you?"

"Like I told Greenberg, she wanted me to skate for her. We agreed we'd meet down the path at the pond."

"At night."

"In the evening. It's never totally dark up there on the mountain. When else could I have skated for her?" he whined. "The retreat went all day."

"And you'd brought your skates with you to the retreat?"

"Yeah, *like I told Greenberg,* I knew there was a pond up there. I still skate a lot." His gaze shifted to Alphonse, now quietly snoring.

Graham was lying, Jane was sure of it. Though there was no way Ivy would have been interested in him, he might very well have been interested in Ivy, and Ivy might have intended to use that interest to her own advantage. "You can tell me if you and Ivy were going down the path for . . . to . . ."

"Make out?" His mouth opened wide in a mirthless laugh. His belly shook. "With her? Baby, I may not be what I once was, but I'm not that hard up."

"What's that supposed to mean?"

"Your friend, if you'll forgive me, wasn't exactly my type. Been around the block, if you know what I mean. Besides, she was Johnny's girlfriend. And nobody was going to cross Johnny—at least, nobody with any brains. And brains is somethin' I pride myself on havin'."

"Not your type, eh?" Defensiveness for her poor dead

friend rose in Jane like a tangible wave. "And what are you, Cary Grant?"

"Hey! You want to insult me, you can get outta here."

"I'm sorry, I'm sorry," she lied. "Please forgive me. I don't know if you're aware of this, but Ivy was my oldest friend. We went to college together; we were roommates. I'm trying to figure out what happened to her, who did that to her."

"Why don't you leave that to the police?"

He sounded like Stanley. "I'm . . . helping the police," she said evenly. "Now. You say Ivy wanted to see you skate. So she convinced you that it was safe—"

"On the ice," he said, nodding vigorously. "So we agreed to meet that night at the pond. Simple as that."

"Mm," she said, trying desperately to think of another tack. Then, all at once, she had it. "By the way, I've been thinking about your thriller idea—you know, about the bus hijacking."

He sat up a little. "Yeah?" He scowled suspiciously. "I thought you said you weren't takin' on any new clients *at present,*" he mimicked her.

"That's my standard line." She winked at him. "You understand. Otherwise I'd be inundated with submissions. But I've been thinking about your project, and I think you've got a smashing idea for a novel. You know, straight out of today's headlines." *Lord forgive me.*

His eyes widened and he raised his ginger-colored brows. "So you think it could go somewhere?"

*Yeah, right into the reject pile.* "Definitely. I have to tell you quite honestly that I was disappointed that you didn't write more during the retreat. I saw promise in your writing."

"You did?"

"Yes, I did."

He sat back and smiled. "Well, what do you know. Hey, that's great. So you think if I, you know, worked up more of the project, maybe you'd, like, work with me on it. Represent me?"

"Almost a certainty. Of course, I'd need a full outline of the story and at least the first three chapters. But I think I can say even at this point that it's a project I could really get behind."

His entire expression changed, growing warm and animated. "This is great news. You know, I always knew I had it in me, all these years I been sloggin' away as an electrician. I always knew I had what it takes. 'Larry boy,' I'd say, 'you did it with skating, you can do it with writing.' Hey, an artist is an artist, right?"

"Absolutely." She shifted on the dirty sofa. Then she waited, smiling at him.

He studied her for a moment, then leaned forward in his chair. "Uh, listen, Jane. Now that we're going to be working together, I guess I can be straight with you about what happened up there. Your friend Ivy—she was some kinky chick."

"What do you mean?"

"Well, she was playing some kind of weird game with me. Okay, I admit it, she had a thing for me, and I thought she was kind of foxy, in a slutty kind of way."

Jane forced her smile to remain in place.

He went on, "At first I didn't dare take her up on her advances because of Johnny. Finally I told her that. She laughed and said she and Johnny were finished, that Johnny was only interested in Carla. So I relaxed a little."

"What did you mean about a 'weird game'?"

"You're not going to believe this, but because I was writing a thriller about the bus hijacking, she thought *I* was the hijacker!"

"*You?*"

Alphonse jumped, then snuggled his nose back into his tail.

"Yeah. Funny, isn't it?" Graham said.

"But why did she think that?"

He smiled with only one side of his mouth. "Because she thought I knew that the hijacker's briefcase bomb wasn't real before it broke in the news. Fact is, I heard it on the radio like everybody else."

She remembered Ivy, sitting on her bed Wednesday night, asking if Jane had heard any more about the hijacking story.

"At least, she *pretended* to believe I was the hijacker," he continued. "So I went along with it, played her game. I figured, 'This babe is hot for me and gets off on this kind of make-believe stuff, so what do I care?' So anyway, that conversation in the lounge—it was about the money she thought I'd gotten in the hijacking."

"The money?"

"Yeah. She was pretending to blackmail me. She said she'd expose me if I didn't give her money. She wanted to meet me down by the pond to talk about it." He winked at her. "But I knew what she really wanted."

Jane winked back, feeling as if she might be sick at any moment. "Gotcha. And did you meet her?"

He looked down, embarrassed. "Nah. I thought about it all afternoon and decided it was a dumb idea. Not worth it, you know? She could *say* Johnny wasn't interested in her anymore, that he wanted Carla now, but how did I know if she was right about that? What if she was just using me to make Johnny jealous? Like I said, I wasn't about to make Mr. Johnny the Wiseguy mad."

"So if you didn't meet Ivy down the path, where were you that night?"

"In my room. I told that to your boyfriend."

Inwardly she winced. "Right. Did you tell him any of this?"

"No. Didn't think he'd understand." He sat up. "You believe me, right? I mean, you don't think I killed your friend? 'Cause I got an alibi."

"You do?"

"Sure. Ives."

"William Ives?"

"He was my roommate. He was in the room with me all Thursday night. You can ask him. He'll vouch for me."

"Of course he will. If you don't mind, I think I will speak with him, just as a formality. You wouldn't happen to know where he lives?"

"Sure I do. It's not far from here. He lives with his granddaughter. I'll get you the address. Ives and me, we got pretty chummy up there. Nice old guy. We promised we'd get together for a drink or somethin' once in a while, talk books." Laboriously he lifted himself from his chair and crossed the room to a console table next to where Alphonse still slept. He picked up a slip of paper from the table, grabbed another piece of paper and a pen, and jotted something down. "Here you go," he said, handing the paper to Jane. "Tell him I said hi. And you have my permission to tell him you and I'll be workin' together."

"Let's not jump the gun," she said hastily. "First things first."

"Oh, right. An outline and three chapters. Gimme a couple days."

"You got it," she said, rising, and was pursued all the way to the door by Alphonse, whose nose she could feel pressing into the back of her thigh.

William Ives lived about a quarter of a mile from Hillside Gardens, in one of the smallest houses Jane had ever seen. Getting out of the car, she reflected that it was barely more than a shack, a box covered with shingles shedding their coat of wine-colored paint, and topped with a deteriorating roof. A few scraggly juniper bushes lined a flagstone path up to the screen door, behind which stood shriveled William Ives himself, watching Jane with a puzzled look.

"Hello, Mr. Ives," she said cheerfully, approaching the door.

He made no response.

"Bet you're surprised to see me."

"My granddaughter's at work," he said, as a child might say his mommy's not home.

"Yes, I know you live with her. May I speak to you for a moment?"

"Sure," he said, but didn't invite her in. "That check I gave Adam for the retreat come back or something?" he asked, his thin voice rising nervously.

She laughed. "No, I'm sure it didn't. I just want to ask you a question. I'm terribly sorry to bother you and won't take up more than a minute of your time."

"A question?"

"Yes, an easy one. Was Larry Graham in your room with you on Thursday night?"

"Thursday night?" He frowned. "How am I supposed to remember that?"

"It would be extremely helpful if you could. Thursday night was, of course, the night before Ivy Benson's body was found."

The dry wrinkles between William's eyes drew together. "You think Larry did it?"

"I didn't say that," she responded evenly. "I'm just asking you a question. Was Larry with you the entire evening?"

His body shifted behind the screen door. "Why are you asking me about this? You're not the police. Unless your detective friend put you up to it."

"Actually," she said, feigning embarrassment, "he did. I help him out from time to time."

"I see," he said, and paused. Finally he said, "As a matter of fact, Larry was with me all that night. I know because we played blackjack the whole time. He beat me bad. I still owe him."

She regarded him through the door, tiny and shrunken in brown corduroy pants and a hooded red sweatshirt. He looked back at her, his thin lips set firmly. She believed he was lying. Why she believed this, she couldn't say.

"Mr. Ives, do you know it's a crime to lie to the police?"

"But you're *not* the police!" he said, and let out an ugly cackle. "Besides, I'm not lying. Why would I lie?"

He narrowed one eye. "Listen, if you're smart, you'll go talk to that vamp, Carla. Everyone saw how she and Johnny were carrying on. Carla and Ivy probably had an argument about him, and Carla killed Ivy. Simple. And you know that Carla has a mean temper. You saw how mad she got when Ivy dropped that coffee in her lap."

Suddenly he turned and looked back into the house. "I hear my great-granddaughter. She's up from her nap. Now leave us alone!"

And he shut the door in her face.

# Chapter Fifteen

It was noon when Jane pulled into the parking lot of the Shady Hills Diner on Route 46. It occurred to her that Florence, who had agreed to watch Nick, might be wondering where she was, so she called home on her cell phone. Nick answered. He and Florence were having lunch. The big news was that Winky, who hadn't ventured much out of the laundry room since giving birth, had just made a brief appearance in the kitchen.

Entering the diner, Jane found herself face-to-face with a glass case of revolving pies—Mississippi mud and lemon meringue and gooey, glistening pecan. It occurred to her that something sickeningly sweet would feel very good right now, after the upset of the past few days; but she fought this urge, knowing that such an indulgence would only succeed in putting back some of the weight she'd recently lost.

"One?" the hostess asked her.

"Yes," Jane replied, wrenching her gaze from the pies. "Is Carla here?"

"Carla? Sure, she's right over there." The hostess pointed.

Carla stood at a large table, taking an order. She wore a tight pale-blue uniform. Her ash-blond hair, still parted in the middle, was pulled back into a tight bun, accentuating her beak of a nose. At that moment she glanced up and saw Jane; she registered no emotion and immediately returned her gaze to her order pad.

"I need to speak with her," Jane said.

The woman frowned. "Well, as you can see, she's on duty. I can sit you at one of her tables if you like."

"Yes, that would work. Thank you."

The hostess seated Jane at a table for two only a few feet from where Carla stood. Carla was just finishing taking the orders from the occupants of the large table. Turning, she stepped directly over to Jane's table, as if she'd seen her sit down with eyes in the back of her head.

"Why do I get the feeling you're not here for a cheeseburger deluxe?"

"Hello, Carla."

Carla waited, pad and pen in hand.

"I would like a cheeseburger deluxe, actually. But cheddar, please, not American. With a Diet Coke. I'd also like to talk to you."

"Can't. I'm on duty."

"Carla, speak to me or speak to the cops. I'm told I should be speaking to you about Ivy's murder."

With a sudden smooth movement Carla slipped into the chair facing Jane's and leaned forward. "Listen, Jessica Fletcher, I know exactly what you're thinking. I would have liked nothing better than to kill Ivy when she spilled that coffee on me. But I'm no murderer." She gave a self-satisfied little smirk. "And I certainly don't need to commit murder to get the guys I want."

"Quite the mantrap, aren't you?" Jane said, moving her head suavely from side to side, mocking Carla's smug tone.

Carla sat up, embarrassed. "So are you gonna get out of here, or what?"

Jane frowned in shock. "Get out of here? You haven't

even brought me my lunch. Now, as I was saying, if you want to avoid getting a visit from a member of the Shady Hills Police Department, you'd better talk to me. It won't take long."

Carla waited.

Jane said, "All I want to know is what you were doing Thursday night—the night Ivy was killed."

Carla threw out her hands. "I was doing lots of stuff. I can't give you a minute-by-minute."

"Let me put it another way, then. Did you see Ivy that night?"

Carla pursed her lips, thought for a moment, then let out an exasperated sigh. "I saw Ivy twice, both times *inside* the lodge."

Jane waited.

Carla said, "The first time was in the lounge. I was blabbing with Vick Halleran, Tamara Henley, and that gross slob Larry Graham. Did you know he was once a figure skater?"

"Yes," Jane replied impatiently. "Go on."

"At the other end of the room, Ivy was talking to Bertha Stumpf—or Rhonda Redmond, I should say—and Jennifer Castaneda. I heard Jennifer say she was going outside for a cigarette, and Ivy said she'd join her. Jennifer was wearing this big thick sweater—you know, like a fisherman's knit—so she didn't need a coat or anything. But she told Ivy she'd freeze in the thin red sweater she was wearing. Ivy gave her a wave of her hand and said it didn't matter, she'd be fine, and they left together. I saw them go outside through the reception room door. Not too long after that, Vick excused himself to me, Tamara, and Larry, and left too."

Jane nodded encouragingly.

"I realized I was bored out of my mind talking with these people. Tamara is such a snob, and Larry—well, he gives the word *sleazy* new meaning. So I made up a reason to get out of there. Actually, I had a real reason. The room I was sharing with Ellyn had been freezing cold all day, so I went out to the reception room to complain to Adam about it.

"While I was talking to Adam, Ivy and Jennifer came back into the lodge. That was the second time I saw Ivy. Jennifer had been right about Ivy getting cold, because now Ivy was wearing Jennifer's white sweater. They were laughing about how much better the sweater had looked on Jennifer. Which is true—that broad's got some bod, let me tell ya.

"Ivy and Jennifer went into the lounge. I finished telling Adam to fix our heat and followed the two of them in. I was relieved to see that Larry was gone. Unfortunately, Tamara was still there, and Vick had come back."

"He'd come back?"

"Mm. And I noticed that he looked . . . kind of uncomfortable to see Jennifer come in. Everybody knew they were fighting a lot. Vick must have hoped he'd gotten rid of her for a while. Anyway, I didn't want to get stuck talking to him and Tamara again, so I grabbed some book from one of the shelves and sat down alone to read it. But wouldn't you know, Tamara came right over to me and asked me if I wanted to rejoin her and Vick. She said they were having a very interesting discussion about the public's current taste in literature. Can you imagine? I told her I'd rather read. I think I pissed her off, because she didn't answer and just turned, said good-bye to Vick, and walked out of the room."

"Then what did you do?"

"Nothing—I kept reading. The book wasn't bad, actually. Ivy and Jennifer had sat down together and were still joking around about how Ivy looked wearing Jennifer's sweater. Ivy took off the sweater and gave it back to Jennifer. Then Ivy said she was tired and was going up to her room. She left the lounge, and that was the last time I ever saw her."

"What did you do for the rest of the evening?"

Carla rolled her eyes in frustration. "After a while I went to my room, where I was stuck talking to the terminally boring Ellyn. But I didn't want to go out again. I stayed in the room for the rest of the night."

Carla stood. "Now get out."

"Probably a good idea," Jane said, casting a sickly look at a passing tray of food, "but one last question first."

Carla waited, shifting her weight from one hip to the other.

"Have you seen Johnny since he ran out of the lodge?"

Carla stared at her, poker-faced. "No."

"You're lying."

Carla leaned down close to Jane's face. "Listen, Mrs. Smarty Pants Literary Agent, I'm not answering any more of your questions. Now get out of here before I ask the owner to call the police."

"Call them," Jane said pleasantly.

"Oh, that's right, that Greenberg guy's your squeeze. Well I haven't seen Johnny, okay? I don't know what happened to him. Is that so hard to believe?"

"Yes."

"Why?"

"Because of how much you were attracted to each other."

"It happens." She shrugged. "You saw the guy with the gun. Johnny may be dead, for all I know."

"We can only hope," Jane said, rising, and walked out of the diner.

As soon as she had shut the car door, she whipped out a pad of paper and a pen and made notes about what Carla had told her. Then she drove home.

She found Florence and Nick in the laundry room, where they seemed to spend most of their time these days, watching Winky and her six kittens.

"Mom, look what Winky's doing," Nick said, pointing, a look of dismay on his face.

Winky had picked up Crush, the larger of the orange tabbies, by the scruff of his neck. She carried him across the box and set him down. Then she picked up Crush's younger brother, the other orange tabby named Pee Wee, and did the same to him.

"Ouch. Why is she doing that?"

"It doesn't hurt them," Florence assured him. "Mother cats do it all the time."

They watched as Winky flopped onto her side to nurse.

Florence turned to Jane. "And how are you doing, missus?" she asked quietly. "Are you all right?"

"Yes . . . just very sad. And curious."

Florence gave her an inquiring look.

"Thanks for watching Nick," Jane said, then went to her study, where she took out her notes from her conversation with Carla Santino.

One detail seemed relevant. Larry Graham was gone when Ivy returned to the lounge with Jennifer. What if, instead of going to his room as he'd told Stanley and Jane he'd done, Larry *had* gone down the path to meet Ivy after all. Ivy, obviously, had not gone to *her* room.

Jane stared pensively out the window.

Making a decision, she returned to the laundry room and asked Florence to keep an eye on Nick again. Then she hurried back to her car, pulled out of the garage, and drove quickly down Lilac Way.

# Chapter Sixteen

"You back already?" Graham said in surprise. "I'm already workin' on those chapters, but I'll need more time than this." He laughed, amused by his own joke.

"I'm not here about your book. May I come in, please?"

"Yeah, sure." He opened the screen door. Alphonse immediately appeared and pressed his cold nose against Jane's knee. She walked into the smelly living room, the dog in close pursuit. She turned to Graham with an imploring look.

"Alphonse," Graham shouted, "get outta here."

With a high-pitched whine, the dog turned and walked out of the room.

Jane sat down on the sofa. Graham stood in front of his chair. "Well?"

"Mr. Graham," she said, readying herself for her bluff, "someone saw you walking down the path to the pond on Thursday night. I know you didn't really go straight to your room. Why did you lie? What really happened?"

He sat down in the chair, watching her appraisingly. "Who says they saw me?"

"I can't tell you that."

He paused, eyeing her warily, and finally spoke. "I'm

not sure I believe you, but I'll tell you the truth anyway. I did go to my room from the lounge, and I stayed there for a little while, but I got to thinking about Ivy and . . . well, you know . . . she started lookin' better and better."

"Even though she might have been using you to make Johnny jealous?"

"I guess I was willing to take my chances. I was—"

"Horny?"

He looked horrified, embarrassed beyond words. "Anyway, like I was sayin', I decided to go meet her, play along with her weird game about me bein' that bus hijacker. She'd asked me to meet her down the path at nine o'clock, so a few minutes before nine I slipped out of the lodge and went down the path to the end, at the edge of the pond."

"And?"

"And she wasn't there. I waited a few minutes, no longer than that. Then I decided she wasn't coming. But as I was starting to leave, I saw her lying near the edge of the pond. I went close and saw she'd been stabbed with the ice pick." He wiped his hand across his glistening forehead. "I totally freaked out. I ran back to the lodge. I went in by the door to the kitchen and hurried up to my room."

He looked down. "I made a deal with old William. If he would say I was in our room the whole night, I'd do whatever electrical work needed to be done in that dumpy shack of a house he and his granddaughter live in."

"I see," Jane said slowly. "Did William want to know why you needed such an alibi?"

"Yeah, he asked. I told him Ivy and I had had a big fight, that Ivy was really upset, and that I didn't want to get in trouble with Johnny. He bought it. The old creep."

"Why do you call him that?"

Graham sat up straighter, frowning in outrage. "The next day, after they found Ivy's body, he came up to me and said now he knew the real reason why I needed him to

say I was in the room all night. He said electrical work
wasn't going to be enough, not by a long shot."

"What did he want?"

"I didn't give him a chance to get to that. I told him I
couldn't talk about it then, that I'd be in touch to work
things out."

"Then you intended to give him more?"

He threw out his hands. "Sure I intended to give him
more. What else was I supposed to do? How would it look
if the police knew I'd left my room the night Ivy was murdered? They'd pin it on me so fast your head would spin."

"But if you're innocent . . ."

"Are you for real? What does that have to do with it?
Lady, in this country, innocent people end up behind bars,
and guilty people walk. Happens every day. Ain't you
heard about O.J. Simpson, Claus von Bulow . . ."

"Von Bulow was acquitted."

This information appeared to make no difference to
him.

"I wasn't about to be part of that crowd."

"I see." She rose.

"What are you going to do now?"

"I'm going to tell Detective Greenberg what you've told
me. If you're innocent, as you say you are, then you have
nothing to worry about."

"So who saw me?"

"I'm sorry, I'm not at liberty to tell you that."

From her car she called Stanley on her cell phone and
told him what Graham had said. Stanley said he would be
right out to talk with Graham again, adding, "I'm still not
sure I believe a word he says."

Jane drove to the ramshackle little house where William
Ives lived with his granddaughter and great-granddaughter.
This time it was Ives's granddaughter who answered the

door. She was a tired-looking, big-boned blonde. She gave Jane a cautious once-over. "Yes?"

"My name is Jane Stuart. I'd like to speak to your grandfather, please."

"Gramps," the woman called back into the darkness of the house. "There's a woman named Jane Stuart here to talk to you."

For several moments the two women stood staring at each other. Finally Ives appeared, taking hold of the front door and letting out an irritated sigh when he saw her. "You back?"

"Yes. I want to ask you something. I've just been speaking to Larry Graham, and he told me about an interesting arrangement the two of you had."

The old man's eyes widened, then flashed to his granddaughter. "Roseanne, I'll be fine."

Roseanne shrugged and walked back into the house.

"What 'arrangement'?" Ives asked.

"I know about the payment you wanted for not telling anyone Larry Graham wasn't in the room with you all night Thursday. You know that's blackmail."

He bristled. "What business is this of yours?"

"Ivy was my best friend. How she died is my business."

"We don't know that Larry did it."

"No, but he's afraid the police will think he did, and you took advantage of that."

"So what?"

She shook her head. "I just wanted to verify that this 'arrangement' had taken place. Good-bye."

She walked back to her car, called Stanley again on her cell phone, and told him the part of Graham's story about the blackmail was true.

"Thank you, Jane. I appreciate your help," he said, but there was an odd stiffness in his tone. She decided to ignore it.

"Also," she went on, "I've been meaning to ask you. Is Johnny's car still parked up at the lodge?"

There was a brief silence. "Yes, actually, it is. We're going to impound it. If you must know, the car was stolen. It's been traced to a woman in New York City."

"Not surprising," she said. "He grabbed a car and got out of there."

"Mm," he said.

"Stanley, what's wrong? Why do you sound so odd?"

She heard him exhale, as if trying to control himself. "Jane, I appreciate your help, but you can stop playing cop now, stop interviewing people. In fact, I want you to stop. The chief said something to me today. Apparently William Ives called and complained about you bothering him."

*Why, that little weasel.*

Jane heaved a great sigh of impatience. "Look, Stanley. I've been running around getting you information you weren't able to get—information you've been only too happy to follow up on—and all of a sudden you want me to stop 'playing cop' because someone complains that I paid him a courteous visit. I never even went into his house, for Pete's sake."

"Jane, I'm only saying—"

"You can tell your chief that I will continue to try to find out who killed my friend Ivy. This is America; you can't control me like that. This is *my personal business*. Besides, judging from the way you and your colleagues have been handling the case, I don't have much confidence you'll solve it."

He was silent on the line.

"Good-bye, Stanley."

"Good-bye, Jane."

She snapped her cell phone shut and shook her head. Then, gazing out the window at Ives's shack of a house, she thought about the path, about the third person who went down to the pond Thursday night. The murderer. She decided that the likeliest suspects, after Johnny, were Larry and Carla.

Larry had wanted Ivy, that was clear. They might very well have fought. In a rage Larry might have stabbed her. But why would he have had the ice pick with him?

Carla had wanted Ivy's man. The two women might also have had a fight that culminated in murder. Jane thought Carla had been lying when she said she hadn't seen Johnny since he fled the lodge. How could Jane check up on Carla?

Of course. Ellyn Bass.

Jane called Adam. Rhoda answered.

"Hi, babe." Rhoda's tone was deeply sympathetic. "How are you holding up?"

"I'm okay, Rhoda, thanks. I still can't believe it."

"Has Stanley found out anything? Any leads?"

"No, not yet. Rhoda, is Adam there?"

"No, he had to run some errands. You want me to have him call you?"

"Maybe you can help me. I need Ellyn Bass's address."

"Sure, hold on." Rhoda put down the phone and came back on a moment later. "Here it is. Sixty-three McCoy Drive, Lincoln Park."

Jane thanked her and hung up. She started the car and headed north. Less than ten minutes later she had reached Lincoln Park. She pulled into a gas station and got directions to McCoy Drive.

It was a curving street in an affluent development consisting of large modern homes on smallish, carefully landscaped lots. Ellyn Bass's house was a taupe raised ranch. Jane approached the front door on a paving-stone path that ran between rows of low, bare azaleas. A few feet from the walk, near the front steps, a tricycle lay on its side. Not far from the tricycle was a small orange ball and a naked Barbie doll.

Jane rang the bell. From behind the door came the sound of a child running; then the knob jiggled. Finally the door opened, Ellyn Bass gently pulling away one of her twins, a pretty little girl with an abundance of dark hair.

"Mrs. Stuart!" Ellyn burst into a warm smile. "I can't believe you're here. How are you?"

"I'm fine, thank you, Ellyn. And please call me Jane. I hope you don't mind my stopping by like this."

"Don't be silly. It's wonderful to see you." Ellyn frowned sympathetically. "I'm so sorry about your friend."

"Thank you," Jane said graciously.

"Come in, come in." Ellen pulled the door all the way open, and Jane stepped into a spacious two-story foyer with a sweeping, curved staircase. In a corner of the foyer stood a magnificently decorated Christmas tree that reached the ceiling of the second floor.

Jane followed Ellyn into the living room. On a cream-colored carpet sat expensive cinnamon-colored leather furniture and glass-and-iron tables. "What a lovely home you have."

"Thanks. Coffee?"

"No, thanks. I can't stay long."

Looking curious, Ellyn sat down on the sectional sofa, and Jane sat too. At that moment the little girl who had come to the door raced into the room, followed by a second, identical little girl. Ellyn regarded them with dismay.

"Alyssa, Breanna, why don't you go back to the TV room and watch your *Little Mermaid* video?"

The girls ran out of the room. Ellyn dropped her shoulders in relief. "Now," she said, smiling sweetly, "what can I help you with?" She rolled her eyes upward in an expression of modesty. "I'm sure it's not about the romance I'm writing."

"No, I'm afraid it's not. Ellyn, I want to talk to you about Carla."

"Carla?" Ellyn's brow creased in puzzlement.

"I need to know if Carla was with you in your room the night Ivy Benson was killed—Thursday night."

Ellyn's eyes widened. "You think—you think Carla—"

"I don't think anything," Jane said hastily. "I'm asking this about everyone. I'm . . . helping the police, you might say."

"I see. Hmmm." Ellyn nibbled the inside of her lower lip, thinking. Suddenly her face reddened. "To be honest with you, she did kind of slip out at one point."

"'Kind of slip out'?"

"She left."

"When? Do you recall?"

"I'd say a little before nine o'clock. But I know where she went," Ellyn said quickly. "She went to see Johnny."

"Really?"

"Yes. The reason I know is that earlier that day, during writing time, Carla and I were in our room when suddenly Johnny knocked on the sliders from the balcony. I nearly had a heart attack."

"What did you and Carla do?"

"She let him in, of course. They acted as if I wasn't even there." Ellyn looked down, a hurt expression on her small face. "They arranged to meet that night. I promised Carla to keep their meeting a secret—she didn't want Ivy to find out about it and, you know, make a stink—but of course this was before poor Ivy got murdered. All bets are off, right?"

"Absolutely. Where were they going to meet?"

"They were going to 'meet' "—Ellyn made quotation marks in the air—"in Johnny's car. Pretty tacky, huh?"

"I'll say—though I'm not surprised."

"Me neither," Ellyn said. "I hate to say this, but Carla is not a nice person. In fact, I'd say she's downright vicious."

"Vicious?"

"Yes. Do you know, on Wednesday night she was undressing for bed and I happened to see that her thighs were burned from the coffee Ivy accidentally spilled on her. I said something about the burns, that maybe she should get a doctor to look at them. She completely ignored me. Her eyes turned into little slits, as if she was reliving the whole thing, and suddenly she blurted out—please pardon my French—'I'd like to kill that bitch!'"

"That certainly qualifies as vicious," Jane said. "Is there anything else you can remember that might be . . . pertinent?"

"No, I don't think so." Ellyn leaned forward. "Do you think Carla might actually have killed Ivy?"

"I don't think anything at this point. We're only gathering information." Jane stood. "Thank you, Ellyn, you've been extremely helpful."

"My pleasure," Ellyn said, walking Jane to the door. "I hope you'll think about doing another retreat. I had such a wonderful time. I honestly felt that someday I might achieve something with my writing."

"You will achieve something if you don't give up," Jane said sincerely. "As for another retreat, I can't say at this point."

"Of course you can't. I understand."

"Mommy, Mommy!" One of the twins appeared in the living room, her tights down around her ankles. "I had a mistake."

Ellyn threw her a weary look. It wasn't difficult to see why she had enjoyed the retreat.

"I'll let you get on with your day. Thanks again," Jane said to Ellyn, who was already tending to Alyssa/Breanna's mistake, and went out the door and made her way down the path to her car.

Heading back toward Shady Hills, Jane wondered if Ellyn's sleazy account of Carla and Johnny's tryst was true, or if Ellyn could possibly have been covering for Carla as William Ives had tried to cover for Larry Graham. Ellyn might even have added that last bit about Carla's rage to *appear* to be protecting her. Then Jane decided this was too far-fetched, that this theory didn't fit Ellyn's personality. What reason would she have had to protect Carla?

Ellyn was right: Carla was vicious. Jane was reluctant to approach her again, though of course she had to.

In the meantime, she wished she could find and speak to Johnny, who she now knew hadn't fled Mt. Munsee as early as everyone believed.

# Chapter Seventeen

As Saturday evening approached, Jane wondered if Stanley would call. They almost always went out for dinner and a movie on Saturday night.

But he was no doubt mad at her. Remembering what he'd said to her made her even angrier at him. She wasn't sure she wanted to see him. . . . No, she did want to see him, and decided to call. From her study, she punched out his home number.

He sounded deeply relieved to hear from her. "I'm sorry about what I said."

"Thank you, Stanley, but I believe I need to apologize to you."

"For what?"

"For embarrassing you in front of the chief. I'm sorry."

"So you've decided not to play detective anymore?"

"I didn't say that. What I mean is, I'm sorry I have to do what I'm doing."

"*Why* do you have to do this?" he said in a tone of forced patience.

"Because Ivy was my best friend, first of all. And because sometimes I think, well, that the police need some help."

"Okay, fair enough. So you're going to go on 'helping' us, but you regret that you have to do it."

"Yeah, that's about right."

He laughed. "Well, I know I couldn't stop you anyway. In fact, I don't believe I'd be able to stop you from doing anything you intended to do. But do me one favor?"

"Sure, name it."

"Keep me out of it."

"Really?" she asked, surprised. "In the past you've made good use of my help."

"And gotten in trouble for it."

"Stanley, you didn't get in trouble for solving cases with my help; you got in trouble for involving me in police business. What a bunch of hypocrites you all are."

"Yes, that we can be," he said brightly. "Now, what are our plans tonight?"

She smiled. "I'd love to see that new Russell Crowe movie. And we still haven't tried the new Greek place in Parsippany."

"It's a date."

It was strange to be with Stanley but not discuss Ivy or what Jane had learned that day. But Jane had a good time nevertheless. They talked about their plans for New Year's Eve, which was only two days away, and decided on a quiet evening at Jane's house—dinner with Nick (and Florence, if she didn't have other plans), a rented video, and champagne while they watched the ball drop in Times Square.

She knew for sure that she and Stanley were back on good terms when he kissed her deeply at the door before she went in.

Late Sunday morning Jane fortified herself and drove to the Shady Hills Diner. The hostess, the same woman who had seated Jane the day before, was puzzled to see her again. Perhaps she had witnessed the unfriendly exchange between the two women.

Carla, she said, was off today. Jane asked for Carla's home address.

"I'm sorry, I can't give you that," the woman said, no doubt curious as to why, if Jane was her friend, she didn't know it.

"No prob," Jane said, figuring she could always get it from Adam if she had to.

Then she got an idea. She went to the ladies' room, and on the way, stopped a waitress hurrying in the other direction. "Excuse me, I'm a friend of Carla Santino's from California. I didn't realize she wasn't working today. She doesn't know I'm here—I want to surprise her. I just found out she moved. Do you happen to know her new address?"

The woman, who wore a name tag that read *Jean*, frowned. "Carla didn't move. Hey, Bernie," she hollered to a man behind the counter. "Carla's still at Heather Gardens, right?"

"Far as I know."

"Oh, she's still there," Jane said. "I don't know where I got the idea she'd moved. Would you happen to know the apartment number offhand? I don't think I have it in my book."

"What number, Bernie?" Jean asked.

Bernie rolled his eyes, then turned and consulted a handwritten list on the wall. "Sixty-seven."

"Great," Jane said. "Thank you so much."

Heather Gardens was a condominium complex not far down the road from Hillside Gardens, where Larry Graham lived. In fact, the two complexes were practically identical. Jane parked in front of number 67, walked up to the scuffed tan front door, and rang the bell.

After a moment the door opened, and Carla stood there in a skimpy Hawaiian-print wrap, her ashy hair in a ponytail. Jane noticed that she wore no makeup. Her face had a dry, haggard look.

For the briefest moment Carla stared at Jane, her face expressionless. Then she slammed the door.

"Why, that—" Jane moved closer to the door. "Carla, I need to speak with you. Please. I know you met with Johnny on Thursday night. If you won't talk to me about it, I'll have no choice but to ask the police to do it."

After a moment the door swung slowly open. Carla regarded her furiously. "Well, come in."

Jane stepped into a tiny vestibule. Carla apparently had no intention of letting her go any farther into her home. "Well, what about it?" she demanded.

"Why didn't you tell me you'd met with Johnny?"

"What are you, stupid? Why do you think? Because I was afraid to."

"Afraid? Why?"

Carla nervously fingered a gold chain around her neck. "Because if you or the police knew Johnny was still around that night, you might think he killed Ivy—which he didn't. Or, if you knew I wasn't really in my room all night, you might think *I* did it." Through slitted eyes she gave Jane a sidelong glance. "How'd you find out I saw Johnny?"

Jane had no intention of putting Ellyn on Carla's bad side. "Let's just say you were seen. Are you still in touch with Johnny? Are you going to see him again?"

"I'm . . . in contact with him," Carla answered cagily. "I have no idea if we'll get together again." She cast her eyes heavenward, recalling pleasure. "Though I'd sure like to."

Jane regarded Carla thoughtfully. "Listen. I need to speak to Johnny. I'll make a deal with you. If you tell me how to reach him, I'll keep your meeting on Thursday night a secret."

"A little blackmail. Okay," Carla said slowly. "I guess he won't mind my giving you his number. He's a big boy. Wait here." She disappeared into the apartment for a few moments, then reappeared with a slip of paper on which a phone number was written. She handed the paper to Jane and smirked. "Tell him to call me."

It was a New York City number, area code 212. For a brief moment, Jane considered sharing it with Stanley, then remembered their conversation and decided against it. Besides, she always accomplished more on her own.

In her car, she called the number on her cell phone. The phone rang four times and was picked up by an answering machine. "Leave a message," came Johnny's rough-edged voice.

"Johnny, it's Jane, Jane Stuart. I need to see you. It's urgent." She left her cell phone number, not wanting him to call her at home.

She was back in her neighborhood, driving along Grange Road, when her cell phone rang. She pulled over and answered it.

"What do you want?" Johnny asked without preamble. He sounded different now—brusque, tougher.

"I know you were still around the lodge when Ivy was murdered."

"Murdered!"

Was he really surprised? Wouldn't Carla have told him?

"Yes, I'm afraid so," she replied, playing along. "The police are looking for you as the prime suspect. You can talk to them or me."

"You. Here in Manhattan. Tomorrow morning."

"Fine. Where?"

"In the park."

"Central Park?"

"Yeah. Uh . . . there's this playground. Go into the park at East Seventy-ninth Street."

"All right. What time?"

"I don't know, ten. And listen to me, Jane. You go to the cops about me, you're gonna be one very sorry lady."

# Chapter Eighteen

---

Jane got out of the cab at 79th and Madison and checked her watch. It was ten minutes before ten. She started walking the block to Fifth Avenue. The weather had turned fiercely cold—the temperature wasn't expected to rise above 23 degrees all day—and a relentless wind whipped between the stolid rows of townhouses, blowing back Jane's hair and finding its way up her sleeves and down the throat of her heavy wool coat.

Head lowered against the wind, she crossed Fifth Avenue and entered the park. Ahead lay the playground, deserted, as she'd expected it to be. To her right stood a row of benches, and she sat down on the one nearest to her, crossing her arms in front of her for warmth and surveying the icy gray landscape. At the horizon, black silhouettes of the skeletons of trees shook violently, as if they might break at any moment. As she watched, a dark figure detached itself from them and started down the slope toward her. It was a man, his hands plunged deep into his pockets. She realized it was Johnny. She rose, starting toward him.

The wind played with the glossy waves of his blue-black hair and reddened his smooth skin—succeeding, it occurred to Jane, in making him look even more handsome. A dangerous handsomeness. She felt a loathing for him rise up inside her. Keeping her face expressionless, she walked toward him.

He took her in with a glance, then looked all around, as if checking for observers. Apparently satisfied, he returned his gaze to Jane and said, "So Ivy got herself killed?"

She gave him a look of scornful disbelief. "You know she did. Carla must have told you." An especially strong gust of wind rattled them both, and she shivered. "Why did we have to meet here?"

"Why not? It's open, healthy . . ."

"Safe for you."

He shrugged. "So what do you want? Why do you want to talk to me? If it's about Ivy getting killed, I don't know nothin' about it."

"Johnny, who was the man with the gun?"

He smiled slyly. "Ah, the man with the gun. What's it to you?"

"Would you rather tell the police?"

His smile was gone. "I told you what would happen to you if you called the police. Don't try it, Jane. I mean it."

She was overwhelmed by a wave of revulsion for him. "What are you going to do, hit me?" She laughed in disgust. "Make sure you do it in a place that doesn't show. Coward. Bully."

He gave his head an uncaring toss and wet his lips. "That what you came here to say to me? I guess we're done, then."

"No, we're not. Ivy told me you only came to the retreat to get away from that man. She said you and he had had some 'business dealings.'"

"Business dealings," he repeated with a little laugh, "I like that. That's right."

"What happened to him?"

His face underwent a chilling change, as if behind those beautiful eyes he was reliving something cold and ugly. "Let's just say we . . . came to an understanding."

Staring at him, Jane swallowed. Then she shivered, but not from the cold. Pushing a lock of hair back out of her face, she said, "Johnny, why were you interested in Ivy in the first place? You know, good-looking guy like you."

"Why do you think?"

"I honestly can't imagine. I doubt it was for her looks."

He looked at her, saying nothing.

Jane said, "Her personality?"

"Oh, did she have one? No, it was because of her job. She worked at *Skyline*, remember? I was using her."

"In what way?"

"To find out if the newspaper had any information on one of my, uh, 'dealings.' I'd heard a rumor they did. I'd found out which editor was working on the story, figured out who his secretary was—Ivy—and 'accidentally' met her at some party I knew she'd be at."

He laughed, remembering. "She was wild about me. She agreed to help me right away. She kept saying she was trying to help me find out what I wanted to know, but she never did. Now I think she was stringing me along, stalling so I wouldn't dump her."

Poor Ivy. . . . Jane nodded sadly. "I'm sure that was true."

"And that's it," he said simply. "End of story. I got nothin' more to tell you." He stood waiting, his wind-reddened face nestled into his upturned collar.

She couldn't bear to look at him another minute. She turned and started back toward Fifth Avenue.

Jane hadn't originally planned to go to the office between Christmas and New Year's—she never did—but as she alighted from the bus in Shady Hills and made her way toward her car, she realized that some time there might lift her spirits, help restore a sense of normalcy.

As she drove around Center Street, she noticed a sign in the window of Whipped Cream that said: NEW YEAR'S EVE LUNCH SPECIALS. She'd completely forgotten it was the last day of the year. Stanley was coming over. She would have to find out if Florence would be staying in, plan dinner, pick up what she needed. She wouldn't stay long at the office.

She drove past her agency's front door and turned right into the narrow alley that led to the parking lot behind the building. Pulling into a space, she glanced up at the back door of the office, in the top half of which was a window. The lights were on. She frowned in puzzlement.

Entering the office, she found Daniel at his desk, typing away on his computer. He looked up, startled. "What are you doing here?"

"I might ask you the same thing."

He shrugged. "Just thought I'd grab the time to do some catching up. Ginny had to work today anyway."

She went up behind him and gave him an affectionate pat on the shoulder. "We're both nuts, I think. But thanks, Daniel."

Over his shoulder he gave her a sympathetic smile.

She said, "We'll make it . . . 'Work Lite' today, how's that? And I'll take you to lunch at Whipped Cream so we can see Ginny."

"Sounds great," he said, and glanced up at the wall clock above his monitor. It was nearly twelve-thirty. "Let me finish this letter and I'm ready."

She went into her office and smiled affectionately at the immense pile of work in the middle of her desk. She'd given up long ago trying to be organized. She was one of those people who got more done by staying messy. Early in their relationship, Daniel had tried valiantly several times to make sense of "The Heap," as he called it, but he only made things worse. She could never find anything. To others it looked like a heap, but to her it was comfortable and consistent, and it did have a loose sort of order to it. For instance, Daniel always placed her pink phone slips at the very center of the pile. There was one there now, and she frowned, surprised.

It said, "Please call Judy Monk, *Skyline*," and was followed by a New York City phone number.

"Daniel," she called, "who's this Judy Monk?"

He appeared in the doorway. "I meant to mention that to you. She called about twenty minutes ago. She said she works with Ivy. I could tell she didn't know about what happened. I didn't feel it was my place to tell her."

Jane sat down behind her desk and dialed the number. "Judy Monk."

"Yes, hello, this is Jane Stuart, returning your call."

"Oh, yes, thanks so much for getting back to me. I'm not sure you can help me. I work for a newspaper called *Skyline* in New York. One of my co-workers hasn't shown up for work today, and she doesn't answer the phone at her apartment. I'm concerned because she and her boss have an important meeting today. It's not like her to just not show up. Her name is Ivy Benson."

"Yes, I know," Jane said. "How did you get my number?"

"It was in Ivy's Rolodex. It was the only number that wasn't a business connection, if you know what I mean."

"Yes, I'm—I mean, I was her friend."

"Was? I . . . don't understand."

"Ms. Monk, I'm terribly sorry to tell you that Ivy is dead."

There was a sharp intake of breath. "Dead?"

"Yes. Were you and she close?"

"Well," Judy Monk said on an expulsion of breath, "I don't know that I'd say we were close, but we had a friendly relationship. I liked her. My cubicle is right next to hers. How did she die?"

"She . . . fell on some ice, hit her head. It happened last Thursday night. A terrible shock."

"Oh, my goodness gracious," Judy said in a low voice. "I can't believe it. Let me ask you—do you know who I should call about picking up Ivy's things? Her brother stopped by here on Friday, but I don't have his telephone number."

Jane sat very still. Ivy, like Jane, had been an only child. "What did her brother look like?"

"A heavy man, thinnish hair. Why? Don't you know him?"

"Uh—she had several brothers."

"I see. Well, he said he had her phone number, but not her address, so I gave it to him." Judy was silent a moment. "Odd that he didn't tell me about what happened to Ivy. He must not have known yet."

"What did he want?"

"He said Ivy had sent him for something in her desk. I let him look, but he didn't seem to find it."

Jane's thoughts spun. She realized she didn't have Ivy's address, either. She would need it, though.

"So do you know?" Judy asked.

"Know what?"

"Who can come for Ivy's things."

Jane reflected. Ivy had had no family. Marlene was gone, and Ivy had been long divorced from Ira. "I'll be happy to come," she said. "There's really no one else—since I don't know where her brothers are."

"You don't?"

"No. Ivy and they were . . . estranged."

"I'm not surprised. Ivy once mentioned to me that she had no one—no family, I mean. Come to think of it, I do remember her mentioning a Jane. She said you were her best friend."

Jane sat very still, a shiver of sadness moving over her. Her eyes welled with tears. With her free hand she played with the edge of a memo in the heap. "Yes, I was."

"Then I'm very sorry for you, too," Judy said. "If you could come, that would be most helpful."

"Not a problem. Tomorrow is New Year's Day. Would it be all right if I came on Wednesday?"

"Absolutely. Anytime convenient for you—I'm here from nine to five. Eight-fifty Third Avenue, between Fifty-first and Fifty-second, west side of the street."

Jane hung up. Judy Monk was obviously a trusting soul. She'd immediately accepted an impostor as Ivy's brother. Who was he? What was he looking for? Why did he want Ivy's address? On Wednesday Jane would need to get it from Judy, too. It shouldn't be difficult.

Returning from lunch, Jane and Daniel found a message on the answering machine.

"Yes, Tamara Henley here. Jane, if you could please give me a call as soon as possible, that would be marvelous." And she left her number.

Daniel frowned down at the machine. "What does *she* want?"

"Darned if I know. Probably wants me to read her manuscript."

She went into her office and called Tamara back.

"How are you, Jane? What an awful thing up there at that wretched place. And your friend, no less. In all the confusion I never got a chance to tell you how sorry I am."

"Thank you, Tamara, I appreciate that. Was that why you were calling?"

"Oh, good heavens no," Tamara said with a laugh. "I'm supremely embarrassed, but I must ask you. Foss and I are having some people over tonight for New Year's, and it suddenly occurred to me that it would be wonderful if you and your policeman friend could come. Around eight. I do hope you don't already have plans."

"Uh . . . I'm not sure, to be honest with you."

"Oh," Tamara said, flustered. "Well, if you'll check and let me know . . . Do come. I've invited Vick Halleran and Jennifer Castaneda from the retreat, and they've accepted. I'm also going to invite Daniel, that adorable assistant of yours, and his girlfriend. As far as I'm concerned, these are the only people at the retreat who had any class—except for you and your friend, of course."

"Thanks, Tamara." If she only knew the catty things Jennifer had said about her. "It's very kind of you to think of us. I'll get right back to you."

"Priceless," Tamara breathed, and rang off.

Jane called Stanley.

"Oh, I don't know, Jane," he whined. "I didn't like her much. Snob."

"Of course she's a snob. But think about it. This is a chance for us—for you, I mean"—oops!—"to chat with her, to find out if she saw or heard anything pertinent to Ivy's murder."

"We've already 'chatted' with her, Jane."

"Only perfunctorily. Come on, Stanley, we don't have any other plans, not really. Don't be such an old poop. I want to see her house," she blurted out.

He sighed. "All right. Tell her yes. If I'm not mistaken, she lives at the bottom of that new street off Magnolia Place."

"That's right. Those homes are *huge*. I want to see it. Come for me around a quarter to eight."

"Yes, ma'am."

"Please," she added. "And pick up a nice bottle of champagne on your way. Not too cheap."

She had no sooner hung up than Daniel appeared in her doorway. "Are you going?"

"Yup. I'm eager to see her place. Has Tamara called you yet?"

"Yes, I just hung up from her. I'm going to ask Ginny if she wants to go. We had planned to have a quiet evening . . ."

"What is it with you men? Of course Ginny will want to go."

Laughing to herself, she picked up the phone and called Tamara to accept.

# Chapter Nineteen

Tamara and Foss Henley lived in the bottommost of a string of contemporary mansions clinging to a cliffside on a street not far from where Jane lived. In fact, Jane reflected as Stanley parked behind a long line of cars, only a little over a year ago this spot had been a public dumping ground . . . the place where Ivy's daughter Marlene had died. Jane herself had nearly lost her life there.

It was a mild night and they decided to leave their coats in the car. Stanley made small talk as they approached the house, an enormous multiwinged structure of glass and stucco. "At the station we call this street 'Nouveau Row,'" he said.

"You don't know that all these people are nouveau," Jane said, gazing up the winding road at the other mansions dotting the cliffside. "The houses are new, that's all."

"Oh, these people are nouveau, all right. At least compared to people like Puffy and Oren Chapin," he said, referring to one of Shady Hills' matriarchs and her husband. "Now, this Foss Henley, he does something having to do with real estate. A developer, I think. Next door is Mark Radner, who's a top executive at Nabisco in East Hanover. I'm not sure about the next house, but the one above is

Gloria and Ian Ianelli, who—well, let's just say I wouldn't be surprised if they knew Johnny."

She looked at him, her eyes widening. "I *see.* Why didn't you ever tell me all this before?"

He shrugged uncomfortably. "There's a lot I don't tell you."

"For now," she said, shooting him an ominous sidelong glance, and he returned it with a look of mild alarm.

They were on the paving-stone path, approaching the front door, an immense slab of glass behind which they could see a two-story Christmas tree that reminded Jane of Ellyn's, and people in party dress milling around.

The bell was answered by Tamara herself, wearing a sleekly simple deep-cranberry dress and a magnificent necklace of diamonds set in either white gold or platinum. Her tawny gold hair was swept up becomingly from her aristocratic face.

"So glad you could make it," she said, kissing Jane, who formally introduced her to Stanley.

"Lovely to meet you under happier circumstances," Tamara said. "Now come in and make yourselves at home. We've got lots to eat and drink." She glided away.

"Does she ever," Jane said, eyeing a lavish hors d'oeuvres table and then spotting a busy bar at the back of the cavernous living room. Then Jane saw Daniel and Ginny standing not far away, chatting, drinks in hand.

"Yoo-hoo," Jane called softly. Ginny's face lit up, and she hurried over, Daniel in tow.

"Can you believe this?" Ginny said.

Jane shook her head in wonder. The left wall of the room consisted entirely of gargantuan blocks of rough stone. In the center of this wall was a fireplace, also enormous, with a raised hearth. To the right of the fireplace stood an odd, six-foot tangle of what appeared to be rusted wires in the approximate shape of the number six. A sculpture, Jane realized. "How odd . . ."

"My dad had a piece like that in his office," said Daniel, whose late father had owned one of the country's most successful magazines. Daniel had grown up in affluence and seemed never to be fazed by it. He was, in fact, quite wealthy himself since his father's death; yet he showed no signs of this literal change of fortune.

"My lucky number, six," came Tamara's voice behind Jane and Daniel, who turned to her.

"Oh?" Jane said.

"Mm. It's always been that way. I met Foss on the sixth of June. Our daughter was born on the sixth of December. It was on the sixth of August that our accountants told us we were officially millionaires. I could go on and on."

*I'll bet you could,* Jane thought. "Three sixes . . ." she said with a mischievous smirk. "The mark of the devil. Warner Books and Bantam Doubleday Dell were once at 666 Fifth Avenue."

"Of course they were," Daniel joined in, and they both laughed.

Tamara appeared to have heard none of this exchange. "Come," she said to Jane, "I want you to meet my husband."

Jane slid a glance at Daniel, who appeared not to care that Tamara hadn't included him. He winked at Jane and wandered away. Meanwhile, Tamara had fetched her husband and was leading him over, a man in a fawn cashmere jacket and black slacks. Around sixty, he was of medium height, balding, with a paunch. His features were coarse in comparison with Tamara's finely cut, aristocratic ones. As he took Jane's hand, his face bloomed into a handsome smile.

"Ah, our illustrious literary agent," he said. "Such a pleasure. Thank you for humoring my wife."

Tamara turned to him in feigned indignation. "Foss! Whatever do you mean?"

"Tell me honestly, Mrs. Stuart—"

"Please call me Jane."

"Jane. Is my wife the next Danielle Steel?"

"Maybe not yet," Jane said with good humor, "but she may very well be on her way." She laughed, and they all laughed with her.

"I never said I was the next Danielle Steel," Tamara pouted. "I said my books resembled hers." She gave him a dismissive flip of her hand. "What do you know anyway, wrapped up in your boring old buildings?"

He rolled his eyes good-naturedly. "Pleasure to have you with us," he said, gave them both a conspiratorial wink, and moved on.

Tamara positioned herself in front of Jane, as if the others were no longer there. "How are you doing, Jane?" she said with a sad little frown. "I mean, about your friend?"

"I'm doing all right, Tamara. Thank you for asking."

"Poor little thing," Tamara said, eyes unfocused, remembering. "She was so happy the last time I saw her."

"Where was that?" From the corner of her eye, Jane saw Stanley look away in exasperation.

Tamara caught it, too, and turned to him. "Is something wrong?"

Stanley laughed. "No, nothing, except that I wish Jane would realize she's a literary agent, not a police detective."

Jane feigned hurt surprise. "I've made *some* progress on this case, Stanley, you have to admit it. You know you want my help; you're just not allowed to say so. Besides, Ivy was very close to me. I've got a special stake in this."

"Of course you do," Tamara said.

Jane gave her a grateful smile. "Now, as I was saying, where was the last place you saw Ivy?"

"It was in the lounge," Tamara said. "Ivy was coming back inside with Jennifer. They'd gone out to have a cigarette. Ivy was laughing so hard, brushing the snow off her green sweater." Her face grew solemn and she turned to include Stanley in the conversation. "I'll tell you something I noticed, though. That despicable Larry Graham was watching Ivy and had an odd gleaming look in his eye, kind of . . . preoccupied. Then he left the room. What do you make of that?"

Stanley opened his mouth, but no words came out. Jane, too, was at a loss, but Jane was never at a loss for long. "It's so hard to say. Maybe he was attracted to her."

"Maybe. But of course Ivy was already seeing that Johnny character. Nasty doings," she cried, raising her index finger. Then she shrugged. "At any rate, my dear, you have my deepest sympathy. Now do relax and try to have a good time. There are some frightful people over there I must be nice to."

She walked off, leaving a heavy cloud of rose and violet in her wake.

"Let's mingle," Jane told Stanley, Daniel, and Ginny, and began drifting through the crowd. Near the bar she spotted Vick Halleran and Jennifer Castaneda, their heads close together, their expressions intense. She hurried over to them. "Good evening."

They both turned to her, huge smiles instantly appearing.

"How lovely to see you," Jane said, exchanging kisses with them both. Vick, wearing a blue blazer over a silk crew-neck T-shirt and gray slacks, looked as if he'd managed to gain at least ten pounds in the three days since Jane had last seen him. Jennifer, on the other hand, looked smashing in a gold lamé jumpsuit. "You both look fabulous."

"So do you," Jennifer squealed.

"You both remember Stanley Greenberg," Jane said, urging him forward.

For a moment they both stared at him, as if trying to place him. Then recognition dawned, and with it came puzzlement.

"Yes, of course," Vick said nervously. "How are you?"

"Fine, thank you," Stanley said stiffly.

"Don't worry," Jane said, "he's not here to interrogate you. He's . . . my date."

"Ah," Jennifer said, and giggled, looking Stanley up and down. Her gaze dropped to the empty glass in her hand. "Oops—empty. Excuse me."

Vick watched Jennifer walk away toward the bar, his expression uneasy. Jane remembered Carla saying he had looked "uncomfortable" when Jennifer entered the lounge the night of Ivy's murder. Why? Jane wondered. Could it have had something to do with Ivy? Did Vick know something he hadn't revealed? Jane yearned to bring it up but didn't dare do so with Stanley at her side. At any rate, Jennifer reappeared a moment later, holding a glass full of an amber drink. She seemed suddenly aware that Vick was still there, and her expression grew tense.

"I think I need a refill too," he said, and turned to Stanley and Jane. "See you both in a bit."

"Of course," Jane said, eyeing him curiously, and watched him walk, shoulders hunched, to the bar.

Jennifer, at ease again, focused on Jane. "Now. Let's talk about books, something we never got to do at the lodge."

Jane frowned in bafflement. "The entire retreat was about writing books."

"*My* books. You're an agent," Jennifer said, as if Jane didn't know. "What trends do you see? What should I be doing differently? There's always room for improvement."

"To be honest, Jennifer, I haven't read you."

Jennifer blinked hard. "You haven't read me? Nothing? Not even *Heat of the Night*?" This book, Jane knew, was her most recent hardcover, her biggest book yet.

"No," Jane said, wincing. "I'm sorry," she squeaked.

"No, no, don't be silly." Jennifer's gaze wandered. "Oh, I see someone I haven't said hello to. Will you excuse me?"

"Certainly," Jane said, and shot Stanley a look as the beautiful young woman slipped away through the crowd.

"Are *your* authors like that?" he asked.

"Eventually," she replied dryly and, taking his arm, propelled him through the crowd toward the food table.

They couldn't leave before midnight, of course, but once they had all shouted "Happy New Year!" and exchanged kisses and thrown black and white streamers across the room in every direction, Jane realized she was pooped.

"Let's go," she said softly to Stanley.

"Thank you," he said, raising his eyes heavenward.

"Oh, stop it. This wasn't so bad. We've met some interesting people, seen how the other half lives."

He shrugged. They said good night to Daniel and Ginny, then found Tamara, who was with her husband chatting with another couple, and told her they had to be going.

"We'll see you out," Tamara said, grabbing Foss and telling the other couple they would be back in a bit. When they reached the foyer, she turned to them. "Coats?"

"In the car," Jane said.

"Well, it's wonderful of you both to come," Tamara said. "We must get together again." She winked at Jane. "You're my kind of people."

Stanley said nothing, merely looked uncomfortable, and Jane, realizing she had to say something, blurted out, "Definitely. Well . . ." she said, kissing Tamara's cheek, and turned toward the door. As she did, she noticed a large sepia-toned photograph in an elaborate frame hanging on one of the foyer's stone walls.

"Pretty, isn't it?" Tamara said softly, coming up beside her. Jane was aware of Foss on her other side.

Jane studied the photograph. It was of a beautiful old neo-Gothic church with many pointed arches and a kind of interwoven tracery Jane had never seen before. "What church is that?"

Foss said, "It's St. Paul the Apostle Church in New York City. It was designed by a disciple of Cass Gilbert."

"The famous American architect," Tamara said.

"Yes, I know." Jane continued to study the picture.

"The photo itself is a work of art," Tamara said dramatically. "I simply had to have it. Foss and I paid a fortune for it at auction. We'll walk you out."

Outside, the air was refreshingly brisk. Jane breathed deeply, gazing up into a clear, starry sky. Then her gaze lowered and landed on a house across the street. She blinked. The structure could not have been more incongruous with the surrounding homes. It was a small, older home, quite shabby, and not much bigger than the house William Ives occupied with his granddaughter and great-granddaughter.

"The bane of our existence," Tamara said, glaring at it.

"It . . . needs some work," Jane said diplomatically.

"Oh, you don't have to worry about us," Tamara said. "You can be honest. It's a shack. It's in shockingly bad repair. You see, the people who live there are *renters*." She spoke the word as if she were saying *lepers*.

"I see," Stanley said, all seriousness.

"They don't do a thing to maintain the place. And ultimately," Tamara went on in a regretful tone, "the house's owner—a friend of ours, actually—will be blamed. Hardly fair."

She drew her gaze from the dilapidated house and returned it to Jane and Stanley. "Well, good night, my dears, and thank you again for coming. Jane, I'll call you about doing lunch."

Jane smiled, but behind her smile she was already composing a list of excuses.

# Chapter Twenty

Jane spent New Year's Day at home with Nick. Florence had gone to visit her friend Noni. Jane had given Florence a list of the kittens' names and descriptions, reminding her that Noni had said she wanted one.

Stanley had promised to spend the day with his younger sister, Linda, who was divorced and lived with her twelve-year-old daughter, Ashley, at the north end of town.

Winky and the kittens, whose eyes still had not opened, were a constant source of entertainment. Nick, stationed on a chair he had carried into the laundry room, looked up from a spiral notebook in which he'd started to record which kittens nursed at what times.

"Why are you doing that?" Jane asked, amused.

"Just keeping track of things," he replied, his expression intense as he watched the tiny creatures get their nourishment.

She looked over his shoulder and smiled. He glanced up, sensing her presence, and in his look, at that moment, she saw so much of Kenneth in his face that her breath caught in her throat. She still missed him terribly, even though he had died more than three years ago. She probably always would. Yet somehow the pain had lost its sharp edge. She guessed that was due to time, and to Stanley.

"Why are you wearing that apron?" Nick asked.

"Because I'm making New Year's dinner, remember? Florence is coming back in time for it."

"What are you making?" he asked warily.

"All kinds of good stuff. Caesar salad, rack of lamb—

"Blech. I hate those things. Can I have chicken fingers?"

"No, you may not have chicken fingers. You'll like what I'm making," she said, though she didn't necessarily believe that. "Besides, for dessert I bought a chocolate cream pie."

"Now, *that* I'll eat."

She turned to leave the room.

"Mom?"

"Mm?"

"Can we keep all the kittens? I'm afraid it will make Winky sad if we only let her keep one."

She gave him a kind smile. "I'm afraid we can't, honey. Two cats are enough for this household. And Winky knows we'll only give her babies to good homes."

His gaze dropped as he thought this over; then he nodded and returned to his recording. Jane headed back to the kitchen, from which came the tantalizing aroma of lamb roasting with garlic and rosemary.

At around eight o'clock that evening, Stanley called. He was home from Linda's. Would Jane like to come over for a drink? Jane had finished cleaning up after dinner, but felt funny leaving Nick.

"Don't you think twice about it, missus," said Florence, who had returned from Noni's earlier that day with a promise to take Crush. She gave Jane a mischievous wink. "In fact, if you need to be out for the night, that's okay, too."

Jane felt herself blush. "No, thank you, Florence— though I appreciate the offer."

That night, in Stanley's plant-filled apartment, they

sipped brandy and danced slowly to his collection of Frank Sinatra LPs, and Jane pressed her cheek softly against Stanley's and closed her eyes.

"Happy New Year!" Daniel greeted her at the office the next morning.

"Same to you. Hope you and Ginny had a nice day yesterday."

"Mm, a quiet day, the kind I like best."

"Did you enjoy Tamara's party Monday night?"

He smiled, wrinkled his straight nose a little. "Not very much, to be honest. I find her hard to take."

"I know what you mean."

"He seems very down to earth, though. The husband, I mean. What kind of name is Foss, do you know?"

"I believe it's short for Forrest."

He looked down thoughtfully at his keyboard, then resumed entering information into the database they used to record details of the book deals they made for their clients.

Later that morning, Jane took the Lakeland bus into New York and cabbed to Fifty-second and Third. On the seventeenth floor, a plump, prim-looking woman emerged into the reception area and introduced herself as Judy Monk.

"Let me say again how sorry I am about poor Ivy," she said in a low, solemn voice, her eyes full of kindness. "I'll show you where her office is—was." She led Jane back through a nondescript maze of cubicles and stopped at the entrance to one of them. "This is it."

She allowed Jane to go in first. A desk without much on it stood against the cubicle's back wall, so that Ivy would have had her back to the entrance when she was working. Above the desk was a bulletin board on which had been pinned what appeared to be several publication schedules. Then Jane noticed, at the extreme lower right corner, a photograph of Ivy and Jane herself, taken when they were freshman roommates at the University of Detroit twenty-one years earlier. "Oh, my goodness," Jane murmured, moving closer to the photo. The two young women—Ivy, chubby, with brown curly hair; Jane, reed thin, with straight reddish-brown hair—were smiling intently into the camera, their arms tightly around each other's waist.

Judy came up beside Jane. "My word. It's the two of you, isn't it? You *do* go way back."

"Yes, we do," Jane said sadly.

"Well." Judy surveyed the desk as if unsure where to direct her gaze. "I'm sure she was very lucky to have a good friend like you."

Jane met Judy Monk's gaze directly. "Thank you, but in all honesty, I'm not sure I was always a very good friend to her."

Judy's jaw dropped a little, and she gave a serious, bewildered nod. She gestured toward the desk. "I suppose I could have shipped her things to you, now that I think of it. There's not much here."

Jane regarded the desk, on which sat a keyboard and monitor, an uncluttered blotter, a telephone, a Rolodex, and a framed photograph of Ivy's late daughter, Marlene.

"That was her daughter," Judy said. "I know she passed away, but I don't know how." She kept her gaze on Jane, as if waiting for an answer.

"It was . . . an accident," Jane said, feeling for some reason that the truth was probably more than Ivy would have wanted Judy to know.

"How very sad," Judy said. "You know, I liked Ivy but never got to know her very well, even though she worked here for a good six months. She seemed that kind of person. Private. One thing we all knew, though. She had ambition." There was admiration in the statement.

"Really?" Jane said, turning to her. "Why do you say that?"

"She made no secret of the fact that she believed she

was better suited to the job of reporter, in spite of the fact that she'd been hired as a secretary. She told me once that she hated being a secretary and that a job like that was unworthy of her. She said that back in Detroit she held a much higher position."

Jane's heart went out to her poor dead friend, who'd needed to impress strangers with lies. In Detroit, Ivy had been a secretary at an insurance agency. "Yes, I believe she did."

Judy looked disappointed that this was all she was apparently going to get out of Jane. "I can believe it. She told me several times that she intended to be a reporter for this paper. In fact, there was one particular story she was after. Quite often she ran out of the office telling me she was following up on 'that story.'"

"Interesting. Did she tell you what the story was?"

"Oh, no. She wouldn't tell anyone. But she did say that when she was finished getting it, *Skyline* would promote her to reporter."

"Do you think that was true?"

"To tell you the truth," Judy replied, "I don't think she would have made it that far."

Jane frowned. "What do you mean?"

"Mr. Feingold was frustrated with her. He hired her to be his secretary, but she hated the work and was—I shouldn't say this—rather poor at it. I suppose I can say this now . . . I believe Ivy was about to get fired."

"I see," Jane said, and sat down in Ivy's chair.

"I'll leave you to it. I brought you a box." Judy indicated a smallish cardboard carton on the floor to the right of the desk and started out of the cubicle.

Jane thanked her and set to work. Judy was right; there wasn't much here. Clearly Ivy had kept her personal life out of the office, except for the two photographs. Otherwise, Jane found only some makeup, an extra pair of shoes in the bottom left-hand drawer, and a rose-colored pull-over sweater neatly folded in the drawer above it. There were no files in Ivy's desk, Jane noticed. The only papers were company-wide memos, takeout menus from local restaurants, photocopies of some not-very-important letters Ivy had typed for her boss, Andrew Feingold. Puzzled, Jane rose and went in search of Judy. She found her in the next cubicle, typing very fast. She gave a little jump, putting her hand to her breast, and turned. "Done already?"

"Not quite. A couple of questions, if you don't mind."

"Not at all," Judy said graciously.

"There aren't any files in Ivy's desk, and there's no file cabinet either. Do you find that odd?"

Judy drew her thick brows together. "I do find that odd. Mr. Feingold has asked me to gather up Ivy's files and deal with them, but I haven't had a chance to do it yet." She shook her head in bafflement. "I suppose she carried her files with her. Now that I think about it, she did carry a briefcase every day. It's the only explanation. As I told you, she was working on something she was keeping a secret, so it would make sense that she wouldn't leave the files lying around."

"What about her computer? Would there be files there?"

Judy gave Jane a strange look, as if wondering why Jane would want to know that. "Actually, no," she said slowly. "Everything is stored on the main server, nothing locally. These computers don't even have hard drives of their own."

"I see. Thanks."

With a chill at the memory of the man who had posed as Ivy's brother, Jane remembered she would have to check Ivy's apartment. Now that she thought about it, she was, as far as she knew, the only person Ivy had in the world who could dispose of her belongings at home, just as she was the only person who could take away Ivy's personal items here in the office.

Jane returned to Ivy's cubicle and finished up. The last

items she placed in the box were Ivy's two photos. Jane gazed wistfully at the one of both of them, then placed it atop the rest of Ivy's things. As she rose from the chair, something on Ivy's blotter caught her eye. Ivy had been a doodler. There were diamond patterns, sketches of girls with long, pretty hair, and a recurrent image of two palm trees, trunks crossed, six coconuts lined up at the base of their trunks. Yes, Jane remembered, this would have been just like Ivy—Ivy who never dressed warmly enough, Ivy who daydreamed about her happier, carefree someday life in the tropics. Ivy who had yearned for a better life, a better job, a good man.

Taking a deep breath, Jane picked up the box and went to tell Judy she was finished. She found Judy on the telephone, apparently with her boss. She gestured to Jane that she would be a moment. Hanging up, she said, "Thank you so much for doing this. Again, I'm so sorry about Ivy." She smiled kindly. "I'm sure you *were* a good friend to her."

"Thank you." Jane set down the box on the floor. "Judy, I wonder if you could give me Ivy's address." Ivy had never given it to Jane, nor had Jane found it among Ivy's things.

"Her address?" Judy frowned. "I don't understand. Wouldn't you have it? If you and she . . ." Now she eyed Jane with some alarm, as if wondering if she'd made a mistake giving this woman access to Ivy's cubicle.

Jane gave a little laugh. "I guess it does seem like an odd request. You see, Ivy and I had a falling-out. We didn't speak for over a year. Then she moved to New York and we patched things up, but that was only a few weeks ago. I hadn't been to her apartment yet, and I never got around to getting her address."

Judy lowered her gaze, considering. "Well," she said, looking up, "I suppose I could get it from Mr. Feingold's secretary."

"I'd be so grateful. I've got to take care of her things."

"Of course. One moment."

Judy went down the passage and disappeared into a cubicle at the end. She reemerged a moment later holding a slip of paper. "Here you are," she said, and glancing down at the writing on the paper before handing it to Jane, stopped and frowned. "That's odd."

"What?"

"This address. It couldn't be right."

Jane craned her neck to see it. "Why not?"

Judy showed it to her. It was an address on West 38th Street, with an apartment number. Jane looked at her, not understanding.

"This is Hell's Kitchen," Judy said.

"Right . . ." Jane still didn't understand.

Judy met her gaze. "But Ivy lived in Sutton Place."

Jane blinked. "Come again?"

"It's true," Judy said solemnly. "I was kind of shocked, too, when she told me. But she said she inherited an apartment there from her aunt. You don't think it's true?"

Gently, Jane took the slip of paper from Judy's hand. "I'll check out *this* address first," she said, avoiding the question.

Now Judy looked thoroughly stumped. "All right," she said softly. Her hand was limp when Jane shook it before picking up the box and saying good-bye.

# Chapter Twenty-one

Jane paid the cab driver and got out, then lifted out the box of Ivy's belongings. As the cab pulled away, she turned and looked up at the grimy five-story brownstone a few doors west of Eighth Avenue. Sutton Place it most definitely was not.

Carrying the box, she climbed the seven steps into the vestibule and consulted the address Judy Monk had given her. Apartment 5-C. On the wall to the right was a list of names next to buzzers. Beside 5-C was written JORDAN. Frowning in puzzlement, Jane pressed the buzzer. There was no answer. On an impulse she tried the door into the building, but it was locked tight. She rang the buzzer again. Nothing.

The door from the street opened, and a woman who appeared to be in her late sixties and carried a sack of groceries trudged in. She was quite heavy, her flesh straining against the pink sweater and skirt she wore under a man's oversized tan parka, its hood lined with ratty fake fur. Seeing Jane, she stopped and looked her up and down, her expression wary. "Who you lookin' for?"

"Ivy Benson," Jane replied.

"Not home. Ain't been home since before Christmas."

"You know her, then?" Jane said, brightening a little.

The woman let out a single high-pitched cackle. "Oughta know her. Rents a room from me." Jane noticed that the woman had no teeth, her mouth puckering in around her gums.

"Then you're the—superintendent here?" Jane asked doubtfully.

"No," the woman cried impatiently. "I just told you, she rents a room from me. In my apartment."

Then Ivy hadn't even had a place of her own. "I see."

"And who are you?"

"My name is Jane Stuart. I'm an old friend of Ivy's."

"So?"

"I'm here because—well, I'm afraid I have some bad news about Ivy. She's dead."

"Well, if she's dead," the woman replied without missing a beat, as if she'd just been told the toilet was leaking, "why are you looking for her?"

Jane forced a little smile. What a perfectly horrid woman. "You're right, of course. I'm here because Ivy had no family. I was pretty much the only person she had. I came to get her things."

"Damn straight you better take her things," the woman said, starting up the staircase that hugged the left wall of the corridor. "'Cause now I gotta rent that room again. Don't need all o' her junk in there."

Jane, still clutching the box, started up the stairs after her. The stairway smelled of unwashed bodies and disinfectant but most of all of garlic, a stench of garlic so strong that it seemed to come from the very walls, like sweat through the pores of skin.

Abruptly the woman stopped and looked down at Jane with a scowl. "Hey, how do I know you're really who you say you are?"

"I beg your pardon?" Jane said, confused.

"How do I know this isn't some trick to get into my apartment, to take my stuff?"

*Oh, for pity's sake.* "Look, Mrs.—"

"Jordan. It says it on the buzzer."

"Mrs. Jordan—"

"*Miss* Jordan."

"I'm sorry. Miss Jordan. If you need some kind of proof, I'm sure I could get it for you." Then Jane remembered the photo from Ivy's cubicle. "Wait, I do have something." She rummaged in the box and found the photo of herself with Ivy when they were freshmen. She held it out for Miss Jordan to see.

The older woman looked at the photo for a moment, then shifted her gaze to Jane. "Decided to go redhead in your old age, I see," she said, and chuckled at her own wit as she resumed her trudge up the stairs.

"Auburn," Jane said.

"What?" Miss Jordan squawked.

"My hair is auburn, not red."

Miss Jordan ignored her.

Jane was out of breath and her legs felt rubbery and weak by the time they reached the fifth floor and Miss Jordan put down her grocery bag to take out her key and open the door of apartment 5-C.

"Well, come on," Miss Jordan said impatiently, and Jane followed her inside. Miss Jordan crossed a small, shabbily furnished living room and entered a tiny kitchen, where she began putting away her groceries.

Jane said, "How long has Ivy been your, um, roommate?"

Miss Jordan slammed down a frozen half-gallon of Breyer's chocolate-chip ice cream onto the counter. "I *told* you, she rented a room from me. This is *my* apartment." She pointed down a short hallway leading off the living room to Jane's right. "Her room is the one on the left. I'd appreciate it if you'd hurry up with whatever you need to do. I've got plans tonight."

"Sure, no problem," Jane said, hating this woman, and

carrying the box she still held down the hallway, pushed open the door on the left. She gasped.

The room had been ransacked. The mattress of the single bed had been stripped of sheets and bedding and leaned against the wall. The box spring shot out at almost a right angle to the bed itself. The six drawers of a dresser on the other side of the room had all been yanked out, their contents rifled and dumped. A pale green oval chenille area rug had been tossed on top of a grimy white vinyl clothes hamper.

Miss Jordan's footsteps sounded in the hallway. "You know, I was just thinkin', there ain't no way you're gonna get all her stuff—" She appeared in the doorway and froze, shooting her gaze around the room. "What the hell d'you do in here?"

"It wasn't me and you know it," Jane said. "When was the last time you were in this room?"

Miss Jordan looked at Jane aghast. "What, you think *I* did this?"

"No," Jane said wearily. "I'm trying to figure out when this happened."

"I don't ever come in here. Why would I? It's Ivy's room, her privacy."

"Well, someone came in here, between the morning of Saturday, the twenty-second—that's the day Ivy came out to visit me in New Jersey—and now. No one broke into this apartment, apparently—"

Miss Jordan nodded in agreement.

"—which means it was someone with a key, or you let someone in."

"I didn't let nobody in," Miss Jordan cried defensively, gums flapping.

"Who else has a key to the apartment besides you and Ivy?"

"Just the super."

"You'd better call him."

"Damn straight I better." Miss Jordan stomped back down the hall to the kitchen. From the doorway of ivy's room Jane watched her dial the phone.

"Yeah, Rafael," Miss Jordan barked into the receiver, "it's Marie. Get up here. Now."

Jane glanced back into Ivy's room. There was no point in looking around. If there had been anything there to find, Johnny—for who else could it have been?—had no doubt found it. Ivy's briefcase, for instance.

Still carrying the box of Ivy's belongings from *Skyline*, Jane returned to the living room and waited awkwardly in the center of the room while Miss Jordan put away more groceries.

"You can sit," Miss Jordan said, more like an order than an offer.

Behind Jane was a sofa covered with a fluffy tan throw. She set down the box and approached the sofa.

"Hold it," Miss Jordan barked from the kitchen. "What do you think you're doin'?"

This woman really was too much. "I beg your pardon?"

"Flopsie. Mopsie. Cottontail. Vamoose!"

The fluffy tan throw stirred, and Jane realized now that it was, in fact, three Persian cats sleeping in a tight clump. At Miss Jordan's command they stood, stretched, and bounded off the sofa, leaving a matted thatch of shedded fur in their place.

Jane had second thoughts about the sofa and headed for a nice clean vinyl chair, when there was a knock on the door. Miss Jordan opened it to reveal a slight middle-aged man with thinning black hair and a full mustache. He wore jeans and a black hooded sweatshirt.

"What is it?" He spoke with a faint Hispanic accent.

"You let anybody into my apartment since—" Miss Jordan turned to Jane inquiringly.

Jane said, "Since the morning of the twenty-second."

He stared hard at Jane, as if she'd just materialized.

Then his gaze darted back to Miss Jordan, fear in his eyes. "Uh . . ." he said, as if trying to guess the right answer.

"Yes or no!" Miss Jordan shrieked, stomping her foot.

He jumped. "Um, yes!" He smiled, almost triumphantly, as if now he would win the prize. "The roach man!"

Miss Jordan scowled. "The roach man?"

"*Sí.* It was . . ." His gaze wandered. "Last Friday. You were not home."

"Just one problem, bozo," Miss Jordan said. "I don't got no roaches." Before he could respond, she took him by the wrist like a little boy, snapped, "Come," and led him down the hallway to Ivy's room. "Take a look at what you did."

He peered into the room. "*Dios mio!* Who did this?"

"Your roach man, that's who!" Miss Jordan moved close to Rafael, right in his face. "Why'd you let a stranger into my apartment without asking for no ID? What kind of super are you? I'm gonna call the police."

"Wait," Jane said, and they both turned to look at her. "Rafael, tell me, please, what did the man look like?"

"What did he look like?" He waved his hands frantically. "I don't know, like a man," he cried, his voice breaking.

Jane said, "Tall, short, fat, thin, blond hair, brown hair . . . ?"

"What's the difference?" Miss Jordan demanded.

"Because I need to find out who searched Ivy's room," Jane said, as if speaking to a cretin.

Miss Jordan looked as if she were about to clobber Jane. Her shoulders slowly rose. Jane wouldn't have been surprised to see steam shoot from her ears. "You're crazy, you know that?" she said in an ominously low voice. "I knew I shouldn't'a let you into my apartment." She poked her finger hard into Jane's chest. "Get the hell outta here."

"No, wait, please," Jane said, turning to Rafael. "This man. Was he young, dark-haired, good-looking?"

Rafael slid a scared look at Miss Jordan, afraid to

speak, but finally he dared to shake his head. "No," he replied in a low voice. "No, that was not him. This man, he was balding, heavy."

Jane nodded, remembering how Judy Monk had described Ivy's "brother."

"I said *get out,*" Miss Jordan screamed. "Get out! Crazy rich broads playing police," she muttered, and marched back to the phone, where quite distinctly Jane could see her dialing 911.

Jane looked back at Rafael. He shook his head and gave a helpless shrug of apology. Shaking her head, Jane picked up the box of Ivy's belongings, walked out of the apartment, and headed down the garlic-scented stairs.

"Miss?"

Jane turned. Rafael stood at the landing.

"Was Miss Ivy upset about her room?" He smiled sweetly. "She's a nice lady."

She went back up the stairs to the landing. "I'm sorry to tell you this," she said gently, "but Ivy . . . Ivy died."

His eyes grew wide. "Died? How?"

"She was at a retreat with me in New Jersey. Someone— she was murdered."

He slapped his hand over his mouth, as if he himself had uttered the word. Jane gave a sad little nod.

Miss Jordan appeared in the doorway of her apartment. "You want to get arrested, lady?" she said in a vicious, piercing voice, " 'cause if you do, stick around. The cops are on their way."

They ignored her.

"Very nice lady," Rafael said, looking down. "She told me her story—about her daughter dying, about her marriage that didn't work. Not a happy life. But now . . . now things were better for her. A good job. It was taking her places, she said. And a new man who loved her." Jane made no response to this. "A man," Rafael continued, "who wanted to marry her."

Pity for her old friend pierced Jane's heart. "Did you meet him?" she asked.

"No, but Miss Ivy told me about him. He knows what happened to her?"

"Yes, he knows."

"He must have been very upset. Heartbroken."

Jane touched his hand resting on the banister, said good-bye, and shot Miss Jordan a cold look before starting down the stairs.

Rafael called after her, "Oh, there is someone else who should know about this."

She turned, waited.

"Her very best friend. They go way back, Miss Ivy said, all the way to college. Jane, her name is. Yes—Jane, that's it."

She stood very still. "Ivy told you about her?"

"*Sí.* The only person she had left in the world, she said—besides her boyfriend, of course. Miss Ivy said this friend Jane was always there for her, a true friend." His eyes narrowed, a thought occurring to him. "But you must know her, if you are also Miss Ivy's friend."

"Yes," she said softly, "I know her." Very slowly, she turned and started down the stairs.

"Miss?" Rafael called, and she turned again. He looked puzzled. "Who are *you?*"

She opened her mouth to speak, hesitated, closed it, and shook her head in quick apology. Turning again, she hurried down the stairs, the box of Ivy's belongings in her arms.

Outside, walking toward Eighth Avenue, she found she was crying. As she reached the avenue, a police cruiser passed her, turning onto 38th Street. She turned and watched it stop in front of Ivy's building.

# Chapter Twenty-two

She walked, preoccupied, the box in her arms, up Eighth Avenue toward the Port Authority Bus Terminal.

Ivy hadn't changed at all. Still as competitive and insecure as ever, she had lied to Jane about her apartment and the kind of job she had. At *Skyline*, she had lied to Judy Monk, saying she lived at Sutton Place. Jane laughed out loud. She had to hand it to Ivy; she must have figured if she was going to lie, she might as well go all the way. Ivy had even felt compelled to lie to the slovenly Miss Jordan, who had referred to Jane and Ivy as "rich broads," and to Rafael, the superintendent, who believed Johnny wanted to marry Ivy.

Ivy's dreams, all lies.

Like her and Jane's friendship?

"You okay, ma'am?"

Startled, she looked up. A young police officer had approached her, his expression solicitous.

"Yes, I'm fine," she said. "Why?"

"I saw you crying . . . lugging that box and all."

"I'm fine," she repeated, "but thank you." She gave him a grateful smile, and he gave her a curt nod back. Then she crossed 40th Street and entered the bus terminal.

She checked her watch and realized she'd just missed

the 3:00 P.M. Lakeland bus to Shady Hills. She decided a cup of coffee would taste very good right now, and went into a sandwhich shop, settling at a small table with a large cappuccino and a chocolate almond biscotti.

As she sipped, the rush of commuters outside the café blurred and Ivy's ransacked room came into sharp focus.

Johnny had done that, of course. Not himself—he was too smart for that. The day after he killed Ivy, he hired some thug to pose as Ivy's brother to get her address out of Judy Monk, then as "the roach man," to do Johnny's ransacking for him. Obviously Johnny had decided that whatever he had told Ivy in confidence about his shady dealings was no longer safe. It made perfect sense: If he and Ivy had broken up because of Johnny's indiscretions with Carla Santino, Ivy would no longer feel any obligation to keep Johnny's secrets.

And so he had murdered her.

Then he had sent his man to search Ivy's room for any incriminating notes, papers, files.

Jane frowned. One thing didn't make sense, though. Rafael had said he'd never met Johnny. In that case, Miss Jordan probably never had, either. Ivy wouldn't have wanted Johnny to see how she lived—her reason not to have given him her address.

Then if neither Rafael nor Miss Jordan knew Johnny, why did he feel a need to send someone else to search Ivy's room?

Jane shrugged. Perhaps the reason had nothing to do with whether Rafael and Miss Jordan knew Johnny. Perhaps Johnny had simply been unable to do it himself because of another commitment; perhaps he was somewhere too far away to get to the room as fast as he would have wanted to, and so he sent someone else. Perhaps it was simply that Johnny didn't want to run the risk of being identified later.

Had the searcher found what he was looking for? Jane

wondered. If yes, then Johnny's job was done; he was safe; his secrets had died with Ivy. If no—the likelier scenario, for even Ivy would have been smart enough not to leave such information in such an insecure place—then he would keep looking, for Ivy must have made notes, written something about her story, somewhere. But where had she kept them?

Jane sat up sharply. But of course. *With her.* In her purse. *In her luggage.*

She frowned. What had happened to Ivy's handbag? To the big suitcase she'd brought with her from New York? Jane whipped out her cell phone and called Stanley. Buzzi at the desk said he was out, so she called his cell.

"And how is your new year so far?" he asked jovially.

"Fine."

"You don't sound very convincing."

After his demands that she stop playing detective, she was hesitant to ask him even one question about Ivy's case. But the worst that could happen was that he would say no. She hoped he still remembered what a good time they'd had at his apartment Tuesday night. Then, taking no chances, she decided to remind him. "You're a very good dancer, do you know that?"

"What?"

"I loved dancing to your Sinatra albums. Can we do that again soon?"

"Of course," he said, his voice relaxing. "But that's not why you called, is it?"

"Well, no, not exactly. Stanley, what happened to Ivy's purse and suitcase?"

"Her what?"

"Her things. The stuff she had with her at the retreat."

"Oh. Why?" he asked suspiciously.

Where to begin? She'd done so much without him to reach this point. "Stanley," she said, mustering her courage, "I have good reason to believe Ivy was murdered because of a story she was pursuing for the newspaper she worked for, *Skyline*."

"I'm listening."

"Last Friday—the day we found Ivy's body—someone got into Ivy's apartment pretending to be the exterminator and trashed it. I think whoever it was was looking for Ivy's notes, files, whatever she had written down about this story."

"And did this person find these notes et cetera?" he asked, sounding interested.

"We have no way of knowing. There's a chance he didn't. In which case, there's only one place those notes could be. In her handbag, in her suitcase—among the things she carried with her."

"So you're saying that if we go through Ivy's things and find out what story she was after, we'll know who killed her."

"Right. So." Energized, she sat up and shook back her hair. "Where are her bag and suitcase?"

"Here at the station, of course."

"And can we have a look through them?"

"Sure, but it won't do us any good. We've already looked. Nothing in there but clothes, makeup, toiletries, and so on. Oh, I almost forgot, three issues of *The National Enquirer*. Jane," he said, a note of impatience coming into his voice, "do you really believe we didn't think of that?"

"Well . . . I didn't know if you knew about her job at the newspaper."

"Of course we did. Jane, when someone is killed—when we're conducting a murder investigation—we make it our business to find out all we can about the victim. Because it's true that, as you point out, clues from the victim's life almost always point to the identity of the killer."

She slumped back into her seat, toying with her coffee stirrer. "I see."

"Listen, if you want to look, come look."

"I don't see the point," she said lifelessly.

"But you can if you want. I certainly won't stop you."

She said, "Why are you being so cooperative? I thought you wanted me to stop playing detective?"

"I do. But it's no skin off my nose to show you something like a suitcase and a pocketbook. Besides, these things will probably go to you eventually anyway. As far as we've been able to tell, Ivy had nobody. No relatives and few friends. You were the best friend she had."

That deep despair swept over her again and she saw Rafael's serious face before her, the big mustache moving as he said, *Miss Ivy said this friend Jane was always there for her, a true friend.*

"Are you there?"

"Yes. Sorry."

"You want to look, then?"

"No . . . On second thought, yes. I'll come by in the morning."

"Jane, are you all right? You sound odd. Sad or something."

"Sad or something?" she said, faintly amused. Really, were all men like Stanley? He really was a dear, but sometimes he could be so utterly clueless. "My best friend is gone, Stanley. Yes, I'm sad."

"Right," he said, abashed. "I'm sorry, Jane."

"It's all right," she said softly. "See you tomorrow."

Snapping her cell phone shut, she put on her coat. Then, with a deep sigh, she grabbed the box and headed through the crowd toward the escalator and Platform 405.

She passed the newsstand, which featured racks of books among the magazines. She spotted a paperback edition of Jennifer Castaneda's second-to-latest novel, *Mojito.*

She stopped and took down a copy. The cover depicted a beautiful golden-skinned Latina woman peering seductively out from under a huge straw hat in vivid circular stripes of fuchsia, canary, and lime. The hat reminded Jane of hats and bags she had seen at the straw markets in Antigua on her vacation the month before. In the woman's hand was a tall, wet highball glass of pale green liquid full of bubbles and ice cubes, a mint sprig on top—presumably the drink called the Mojito.

Then Jane realized that the woman under the hat was Jennifer Castaneda herself. Jane flipped the book over and gazed down at Jennifer's author photo, in which she was gazing out from under a much smaller hat. In all other respects the photograph was strikingly similar to the cover illustration.

An ambitious woman. Poor Vick Halleran. Had he had any idea of what he was getting himself into when he fell in love with Jennifer Castaneda?

Shaking her head, Jane replaced the book on the rack. She thought about Vick again, and realized all at once that while she was in New York, she really ought to see him. She moved to the edge of the crowd, set the box against the wall, found Vick's home number in her address book, and dialed it on her cell phone. It rang quite a few times, and she had almost decided to hang up when he answered.

"Hello, Jane. This is a pleasant surprise," he said, though he sounded puzzled and perhaps a bit uncomfortable to hear from her.

"Vick, I'm here in the city and wondered if I could take you to lunch. You busy?"

"Not anymore. I've just finished teaching my writing workshop at The New School—I had my home calls forwarded to my cell phone."

"Then you can do it?"

"I'd love to."

They arranged to meet at the school and go to lunch from there. Jane took a taxi to Twelfth and Sixth. Vick was waiting for her on the corner, a big smile on his round face.

"What a treat," he said, taking the box, which he insisted on carrying for her. "I can't remember when I've seen you so many times in such a short period."

He led the way to a diner two blocks from the school and they took a booth. "So how are you, Vick?" she asked. "I'm sorry the retreat ended the way it did."

"It's certainly not your fault. What a horrible thing. That poor woman. Have the police got any leads?"

"No."

He lowered his gaze to his placemat, which bore a map of Greece. "The retreat wasn't going well for me anyway, Jane. I might as well tell you this now. Jennifer and I are getting a divorce."

"Oh, Vick," she said, putting her hand on his. "I'm so sorry."

He gave his head an uncaring little toss, though he still wouldn't look at her. "Last night Jennifer finally confessed she's still having an affair with her agent, Henry Silver. She's moving in with him." Finally he met her gaze. "I suppose it was pretty clear at the retreat that things weren't exactly right between Jennifer and me."

"Yes, I have to admit it was. I'm terribly sorry."

"Thanks, Jane, I appreciate that."

"Vick," she said, shifting in her seat. "There was something I wanted to talk to you about at Tamara's party Monday night, but I never got the chance."

"Oh?"

"Last Thursday night—the night before Ivy was found murdered—when Ivy and Jennifer came back into the lounge after they had their cigarettes, why did you look so uncomfortable?"

He blinked, brows lowered. "You weren't there, were you?"

"No."

"Then how do you know about it?"

"Carla told me."

He eyed her warily. He was quiet for a long moment, his

face deeply troubled, his gaze fixed on the window beside their booth. The waiter arrived, and they ordered sandwiches.

Jane waited. Vick met her gaze, watched her for a brief moment, and seemed to make a decision. "It was because of something that had just happened," he said.

"Yes?" she prompted.

"In our room, before we went down to the lounge, Jennifer and I had a hideous fight. I accused her of continuing her affair with Henry. I said I would leave her if she didn't end it. She told me she was planning to leave me anyway; she just hadn't wanted to leave before her book was done."

He shook his head in wonder. "That's what she's like. A cold, calculating, ambitious monster. I've never met anyone like her. I loved her once, you know. I think I still do. But I never imagined that she was this kind of person."

Jane nodded sympathetically.

"There's more," he said. "Jennifer left our room, and I went downstairs a short time afterward. I went to the lounge and found her there. It was extremely uncomfortable for us both. After a short time, Jennifer announced she was going outside to have a cigarette. I'm positive she did this just to get away from me."

Jane said, "And Ivy went with her."

"That's right. As Jennifer walked out of the lounge, she tossed me a look"—his hands clenched—"this smug, self-satisfied expression that made my blood boil. It was like she was saying, 'I win.' I don't know. All I do know is that at that moment I decided to confront her again. I left the lounge and went outside. I saw Jennifer and Ivy standing together in the parking lot, a good distance away. They were smoking. As I made my way toward them, they separated. Ivy walked to the edge of the path that led to the pond and started down it . . ."

At this, Jane sat up straighter, listening intently.

". . . and I saw my chance to have it out with Jennifer. I hurried up to her. It was dim; the parking lot lights aren't very bright. I was furious as I approached her, got angrier and angrier the closer I got. I was so mad I thought I'd— I'd have a heart attack or something. Anyway, I walked right up to her and said, 'Listen, you ice bitch. If you leave me I'll sue you for everything you're worth. I'll ruin your career.' Then I grabbed her shoulder and spun her around—to discover, to my horror, that it wasn't Jennifer but Ivy. She was wearing Jennifer's white fisherman's knit sweater. Jennifer must have lent it to her."

"What did Ivy do?"

"She just stared at me. I was mortified, of course. I apologized to her, asked her to please forget it, and hurried back to the lodge.

"*That's* why I looked so uncomfortable when Jennifer and Ivy came back into the lounge. I was wondering if Ivy had told Jennifer what I said to her. I can't see how she wouldn't have."

"No," Jane agreed, "neither can I."

Their lunch arrived and they began to eat, but neither of them was particularly hungry. They made awkward small talk about the publishing business, about the course Vick was teaching.

After lunch, outside on the sidewalk, she gave him a kiss and a tight hug and told him again how sorry she was and not to be a stranger. Then she watched him walk away, a sad, middle-aged man with lowered head and slumped shoulders.

# Chapter Twenty-three

It was dark as Jane stared out the bus window at the buildings of Weehawken, thinking about what Vick had told her. Was that really all there was to it? Perhaps he was telling the truth as far as it went; perhaps he really had mistaken Ivy for Jennifer. But had he only spoken to her?

What if it had actually been Ivy who went down the path, and Vick followed her, thinking he was following Jennifer? What if Vick, in his fury toward Jennifer, had grabbed Ivy, mistaking her for his wife, and killed her?

Vick had always struck Jane as the sweetest, most gentle of men, but it was common knowledge that very often when this kind of person blew, he blew big-time.

But why would Vick had been carrying the ice pick?

Moreover, why would *Jennifer* have left Ivy and started down the path? What was she doing there? Back at her office, Jane decided simply to ask her. She finally tracked her down at Henry Silver's office.

"Jane," Jennifer said, as if speaking to a child, "you can't call me here."

"Why not?"

"Because I'm—I'm busy. I'm in a meeting. What is it you want?"

"I just want to ask you a question." When Jennifer

made no response, Jane went on, "Last Thursday night, when you and Ivy went outside to smoke your cigarettes, why did you leave Ivy and go down the path that leads to the pond?"

"How do you know I did that?"

Jane hesitated, then said, "Vick told me. He also told me about his mistaking Ivy for you."

"I know all about that," Jennifer said impatiently. "Ivy told me everything."

"So? Why did you go down the path?"

"Um . . . hold on," Jennifer said; then, muffling the phone, "Henry, baby, I'm going to take this call in that empty office, okay?" She came back on the line. "Wait a minute, Jane."

After a few moments Jennifer picked up again. "All right. When Ivy and I were having our cigarettes, Ivy told me that that sleazeburger, Larry Graham, had the hots for her and wanted her to meet him on the path at nine. I started teasing Ivy about it. Then, just as a goof, I ran over to the path to see if Larry was already there waiting for her. I did start down the path, but it was so dark I couldn't see three steps in front of me. I got creeped out and turned around and came back out of the woods. Any more questions?"

"No," Jane said, thanked her, and rang off.

It was almost time to go home. She tried to concentrate on the first draft of a manuscript she had recently received from Carol Freund, one of her biggest clients, but it was no use. She stared out her office window at the village green, dark gray and winter-gloomy. It had begun to snow, the flakes drifting toward her window and melting when they hit the glass.

Drifting . . . A conversation with Stanley came back to her, about the reception Adam and Rhoda had hosted, about people drifting in and out. Then she remembered passing Arliss's room and hearing her berating someone.

Whom had Arliss been berating, and about what? It might be totally irrelevant . . . or it might not. She decided to call Arliss and ask her to lunch.

"Why, Jane?" Arliss asked with characteristic bluntness. "I just saw you last week."

"I know, but there's something I want to discuss with you."

"Go ahead."

"I'd prefer to do it in person."

Arliss let out an impatient groan. "Now you've got me all nervous, like you're going to tell me something bad about one of your clients I'm publishing." One client Jane had with Arliss was Carol Freund, whose manuscript sat before her on the heap.

"No, it's nothing like that. That much I can tell you."

"I see," Arliss said, though she clearly didn't. "Are you free tomorrow?"

"Absolutely," Jane replied, and they made arrangements.

The following morning, Jane stopped at the Shady Hills Police Station. Stanley was waiting for her in his office doorway. They stepped inside and briefly kissed.

"I've been thinking about our conversation yesterday afternoon," he said, dropping into the seat behind his desk as she sat down in his visitor's chair. "I shouldn't ask you this, because I already know the answer, but you never did stop playing detective, did you?"

"Nope. Haven't gotten much of anywhere, though," she added ruefully.

"Neither have we," he admitted. "Though one of the men I had searching the woods did find a flashlight Adam has identified as one he kept in the storage room. It was under a bush near the beginning of the path down to the pond."

"Interesting," she said. "Now. Do you want to know what I've learned?"

"You know I do."

"Good," she said, hunkering down, and carefully told him what she'd learned so far from all the people she'd talked to. It took a good half hour.

"That's a lot," he said when she was finished, his tone full of admiration.

"Thanks. Only problem is, any and all of them could have killed Ivy. Every single one had both motive and opportunity. The only ones in the clear are Adam and Rhoda and the people at their reception. Actually," she corrected herself, "the people at the reception aren't even in the clear. You told me everyone was drifting in and out."

"That's right." He grinned mischievously. "What if together the people at the reception planned Ivy's murder, one of them carried it out, and then they all covered for each other? Like that Agatha Christie novel."

"Stanley," Jane said in annoyance, "this is no joke."

"I'm not joking."

"Yes, you are, and it's not funny. This is my oldest friend we're talking about." She gazed dejectedly at her fingernails, which she realized she needed to have done. "I'm very frustrated—"

"Of course you are."

"—that you don't understand how important it is to me to discover the truth behind what happened to her. You're treating this like all your other cases." Tears came to her eyes.

"I'm sorry, Jane. I didn't mean it to sound that way. I do know how important she was to you."

She sniffed. "Apology accepted. Now where's the bag and the suitcase?"

"Oh, right. Just a minute." He left the office and returned a moment later with Ivy's red leather drawstring handbag and a large black suitcase on wheels. He handed the bag to Jane.

She opened it, peered inside, and rummaged about.

Stanley had been right. She found nothing but everyday items like keys, chewing gum, cigarettes, a lighter, some makeup, a nail file, a purse containing a few bills and some change, a Visa card, an ATM card, Ivy's driver's license, and photos of Marlene and Jane. No notes, no paper, not even a small notepad.

She pulled the bag shut and placed it on Stanley's desk. "All right, how about the suitcase?"

He placed it on his desk and unzipped it. In it lay a messy assortment of clothes, more makeup, a pair of running shoes, a small blow-dryer, and, as Stanley had said, three issues of *The Enquirer*. Idly Jane lifted out the tabloids and regarded them. On the top copy, someone—presumably Ivy—had drawn a mustache on Cher. With a little laugh Jane flipped to the next newspaper. The headline read HOLLYWOOD STARS' INCOGNITO TRICK—NO MAKEUP! Below it was a quiz titled *Guess Who?* consisting of a row of women's unmade-up faces, labeled only A, B, C, and D. Beneath each picture Ivy had penciled in her guesses: Demi Moore, Kelly McGillis, Roseanne, Mary Tyler Moore.

"Ever the intellectual," Stanley quipped, and Jane shot him an icy look. Shaking her head, she placed the newspapers back into the suitcase.

"Wait, missed something," Stanley said, and pulled out the third tabloid, whose left margin was crammed with messy ballpoint doodles.

She glanced at them and shrugged. A French poodle with exaggerated pom-pom fur. The word *Johnny*, written three or four times in different sizes. A snowman. A banana. Dollar signs. Two palm trees—

Jane pulled the paper closer.

"What is it?" Stanley asked.

"Nothing," she said, though unsure why. Ivy had drawn the same image four times: two palm trees, trunks crossed, with six coconuts at the base of their trunks.

"What?" he asked insistently. "Hieroglyphics?"

"Mm, that's it," she said, dropped the papers into the suitcase, and zipped it shut. "You're right," she said with a sad little smile. "Nothing here."

He zipped the suitcase shut. At the door of his office he gave her a kiss. "I'll call you later."

"Well, what is it?" Arliss said before her bottom had even settled in her chair. They were at Dig, Jane's least favorite restaurant.

"Take it easy," Jane said. "Why are you still wearing your coat?"

"I'm not," Arliss said, and shrugged it off, letting it fall onto the back of her chair.

"Why don't you check it?"

"I never check my coat. Why should I pay somebody a dollar to hang up my coat and then take it off the hanger for me?"

"Wow. I guess publishing salaries are as bad as ever."

"Easy for you, Jane Stuart. Big-shot agent with hotsy-totsy clients. I'm a single woman—yes, making a not-gigantic salary—and I have to be careful."

Jane had never considered herself either a big shot or hotsy-totsy, but did not respond to this comment. Nor did she remind Arliss that she, too, was a single woman who had to be careful. Of one thing, however, she was reasonably certain: She earned more money than Arliss.

Arliss flipped the napkin off the bread basket and tore two thick slices off the French bread. She began slathering one of them with strawberry butter. "Even the way I eat," she went on in her annoying monotone. "I make lunch my big meal of the day so that Millennium can foot the bill."

"All right, Arliss," Jane said, rolling her eyes, "I get the point."

Arliss made an unattractive pouting expression with her mouth. "Fine. So," she said, meeting Jane's gaze, "what is it you couldn't discuss with me on the telephone?"

"It's about the retreat."

Arliss looked at her in frank surprise. "What about it? Did they find out who killed your friend?"

"No, that's not it. It's about something I heard you say."

"What?" Arliss threw down her slice of bread. "What did I say?"

The waiter arrived. "Would you like to hear our specials today?"

"No!" Arliss barked at him, and he turned and fled. "Now what's this all about, Jane? Stop pussyfooting around. What were you doing, eavesdropping on me or something?"

"Not intentionally. It was last Thursday night, after the group reading. I was heading down the corridor to my room when I passed your room and heard you, well, yelling at someone."

Arliss eyed Jane coldly. "What was I saying?"

"Now let me see if I can remember. It was something like, 'If you want to keep this working, you have to read them.' Then you called whoever it was you were talking to lazy and said something like, 'You should have told her you can't talk about them.' Who were you talking to? What were you talking about?"

Arliss looked at her as if she were crazy. "Why should I tell you that? What business is it of yours? What does it have to do with anything?"

"Now calm down. My guess is that it was Brad Franklin you were talking to, and that the 'her' you were referring to was Ivy. If I'm right, your conversation could have something to do with Ivy's murder."

Arliss pondered this, rubbing a few strands of her lank brown hair between her thumb and forefinger. At last she said, "You're right, it was Brad I was talking to. I remember it now. We were talking about his work as an instructor at the retreat. He was complaining to me that it was turning out to be more work than he'd expected and he didn't want to do it. I told him he had to read Red Pearson's work more carefully. You remember that Red was Brad's student."

"Yes, I remember," Jane said flatly, staring at Arliss. "What about when you said, 'You should have told her you can't talk about them'? Who were you referring to? Shouldn't have told *whom* about *what?*"

Arliss pursed her lips and shrugged.

Jane said, "Know what I think?"

"No, what?"

"That you're lying."

Arliss slammed her hand down on the table, drawing the attention of the couples to either side. "How dare you call me a liar!"

"Knock it off, Arliss." Jane checked her watch. "I haven't got all day. Either you tell me the truth or I sic Detective Greenberg on you."

Arliss calmed down somewhat. "Supposing—just supposing—I'm not telling you the truth about what I was saying and who I was saying it to, what makes you think I was talking about Ivy?"

"Well, were you? You still haven't told me who 'her' was. If you were talking about Ivy, it's important. Everything Ivy did and said is important in this investigation. So . . . were you talking about Ivy?" Jane peered at her shrewdly. "Did it have anything to do with Ivy's saying Brad had a cushy setup?"

Arliss tossed her head from side to side. "Oh, all right— yes!"

"Okay," Jane said with a note of triumph, "now we're getting somewhere. Let's start again." But suddenly the truth came to her, like a light being switched on in her head. Her mouth fell open, and she stared at Arliss in wonder.

"What is it?" Arliss asked suspiciously.

"It's *you.*"

"What's me?"

"*You* ghost all those celebrity novels, not Brad. I'm right, aren't I?"

Arliss's gaze dropped to her menu. "Yes," she said in a tiny, cracking voice. Jane wondered if she was about to cry.

"Why?" Jane asked.

Arliss looked up. "Because I love him!" she blurted out, again drawing stares from each side of the table.

"It makes perfect sense."

"Does it?" Arliss asked nastily. "Or are you going to start judging me? I can't openly be the ghostwriter on the celebrity books Millennium publishes, because I'm an editor there. It would be a conflict of interest. But I have the talent for it, Jane. So Brad and I worked out an arrangement. We've been doing it for years. He—"

"He's your front, your beard."

Arliss simply nodded. "After the group reading Thursday night, Brad came to my room. He was upset. He told me he and Ivy had been chatting, and he had accidentally revealed the name of one of the celebrities he ghosts for. As it happened, Ivy had read all of that celebrity's books. She got all excited and wanted to discuss them with Brad. But of course Brad couldn't discuss them, because not only does he not really write them, but he never even bothers to read what I write. *That's* what I was saying to him—that he can't be so lazy, he has to at least read the books if we're going to keep making this setup work. Then I asked him why he didn't simply tell Ivy he wasn't allowed to talk about the books he ghostwrites.

"Brad finally managed to change the subject, but he could tell that Ivy was suspicious." Arliss threw back her head defiantly. "So now you know our dirty secret. If you've got any decency, you'll *keep* it a secret."

"I will," Jane said sadly.

"Thank you, Jane," Arliss said, surprised. "May I ask why you would do that for us?"

"Because although what you're doing is not only immoral but also illegal, it's not my place to spill the beans. I feel sorry for you, Arliss. I only hope you're getting a big enough kickback from Brad that you're not really as poor as you make yourself out to be."

"I do all right. As for your pity, you can stuff it." Arliss closed her menu. The waiter returned. "We're not eating after all," she snapped at him. He scurried off, and Arliss started squirming into her coat.

"I'm not feeling very hungry either," Jane said, rising from her chair.

Arliss started away from the table, then stopped and turned to Jane. "So tell me. Was our conversation really something you needed to know about? Are you happy now?"

"I'm not happy, Arliss, but yes, it was definitely something I needed to know about."

Arliss narrowed her eyes. "How so?"

"Because it implicates both you and Brad as suspects in Ivy's murder. Ivy had figured out your scam, or was on the verge of doing so. You and Brad would have had a strong financial incentive to keep her quiet."

There was an odd silence. Jane and Arliss looked down to see that the couples at each side were watching them in fascination. "Mind your own business!" Arliss snapped at them, then turned on her heel and stomped from the restaurant.

Jane wasn't far behind.

# Chapter Twenty-four

"You haven't touched your dinner, missus," Florence said, her face full of concern. "Did I overcook the meat?"

"No, Florence, it's delicious," Jane said. "I'm just thinking."

Nick turned to her, chewing on a piece of meat with his mouth wide open.

"No see food, please," Jane said absently.

Nick clamped his mouth shut. "What are you thinking about, Mom?"

"Ivy," she replied, her tone despondent.

"I'm done," he said. "May I please be excused?"

"Sure."

He ran off.

"Has Detective Greenberg made any progress?" Florence asked.

"Not really. It's not as if we don't know anything. We know a lot. In fact, the lodge was positively jumping the night Ivy was killed, and my guess is that we know about virtually all of it. And yet . . ."

"And yet, missus?" Florence paused, her fork in midair.

"And yet there's one thing that keeps troubling me."

"Yes?"

"Okay," Jane said. "You're smart. Let's see what you make of this. Ivy was going after a big story for the newspaper where she worked. A story so big that I don't think she would have risked leaving her notes in her apartment." She hadn't told Florence about Ivy's room having been searched. "She must have had notes, a few words, something. Where would she have put them?"

"That's easy," Florence said. "She would have kept them with her at all times. That's what I would do."

"I thought the same thing. But nothing was found on Ivy, in her room, or in her handbag or suitcase. Where else could these notes possibly be? It would have had to be someplace she knew was safe."

"Easy again," Florence said with a smile. "Right here."

Jane frowned at her. "Here?"

"Sure. In this house. She would have left the notes here and then picked them up after the retreat. Don't forget, Ivy didn't know she wasn't coming back here."

For a moment Jane stared at her. Then she slowly rose. "You know, I think you may have something. Excuse me."

She hurried out to the foyer, up the stairs, and along the hallway to the guest room. Her gaze went immediately to the nightstand to the left of the bed. Rushing over to it, she pulled open its one drawer and gazed down upon a small spiral-bound notebook. She flipped it open. On the first page were several notes:

> hiding
> corporate layers—have to pierce them to top
> speak to club owner, manager—other employees
> speak to neighbors
> city records—public?

The second page, the only other page in the notebook that had been used, bore only a drawing:

"Find anything, missus?" Florence poked her head into the room.

Jane slipped the notebook into the pocket of her skirt and went out to the hallway. "Yes. You were right. Ivy did leave a notebook in the night table. But I'm afraid there's not much in it."

Florence looked disheartened.

"But thank you for the tip," Jane said, descending the stairs. "Now let's finish that delicious dinner you made."

# Chapter Twenty-five

That evening, Jane sat in the laundry room, staring unseeing at Winky and the six kittens while Nick moved excitedly around the box, jotting in his notebook.

She was thinking again about Arliss and Brad. Were they really suspects? Would either or both of them have committed murder to protect this secret? People had been known to murder for far less, though Jane didn't feel it was likely in this case. And Arliss had confessed to her arrangement with Brad without putting up much of a fight; why would she have done so, if this was a secret worth killing for?

She remembered life with Ivy all those years before in the dorm at college. Ivy, always full of energy, eager to participate, but never really one of the crowd . . . a person people often laughed at behind her back.

Jane frowned at this memory. She recalled that sometimes she was aware that she was Ivy's friend simply because she pitied her.

A sad, unfair end to an empty, unfulfilled life. Would her murderer escape justice? Perhaps. Neither the police nor Jane had made any real, meaningful progress.

Vaguely she was aware that Nick was leaning into the

nest box, busily doing something with his hands. Focusing on him, she rose a little in her chair to see what he was doing, and frowned. He appeared to be tying small lengths of ribbon around the kittens' fluffy middles. They squirmed and squealed in protest.

"Nick! What are you doing? Stop that."

He looked up at her, wide-eyed. "But I have to, Mom."

"Have to what?"

He straightened, lengths of colored ribbon in one hand. "I'm color-coding the kittens. It makes tracking easier."

She frowned. "Color-coding? Tracking? What are you talking about?"

He tapped his notebook. "I was looking over my notes last night, and I noticed that when the kittens nurse, some get more time than others. I'm sure Winky would want to know this, so I'm tying these different colored ribbons around the kittens so she can keep them all straight and give them equal time."

Jane laughed. "Oh, Nicholas. That's very considerate, but Winky doesn't need colored ribbons to keep her kittens straight."

As if in agreement, Winky looked up at Jane and let out a loud meow.

Florence strolled into the room, carrying a bottle of laundry detergent. "Your mother is correct, Master Nick," she said, placing the bottle in the cupboard above the clothes dryer. "Besides which," she added with a light-hearted laugh, "cats are color-blind. The ribbons will all look the same to Miss Winky."

Jane's eyes popped open and she checked the clock on the nightstand: 6:23. She hadn't slept all night, not really. Her mind was too full of clues, images, numbers, bits and pieces, all swirling maddeningly.

Numbers . . .

Colors . . .

She sat bolt upright in the bed, threw aside the covers, quickly showered and dressed.

By seven o'clock she was at her office. She called Stanley, who had just arrived at the police station.

"Don't you see?" she said. "This case has been all about the senses—and we've been blind. Meet me at Larry Graham's apartment. I hope we're not too late."

Entering the parking lot in front of Hillside Gardens, Jane scanned the cars for Stanley's cruiser but didn't see it.

She got out and ran up to Larry Graham's door. Raising her arm to knock, she realized that it was ajar. She knocked anyway, then rang the bell. There was no answer.

"Larry—" she called through the crack. Still nothing.

Something pressed against her leg and she jumped. Looking down, she saw a long furry nose. She pushed the door open and knelt to pat Alphonse, who responded with a high whimper.

She walked in past the dog, who didn't seem to want to move. The living room was empty.

"Larry—" she called again.

She went out the rear door of the living room, along a narrow corridor, and into the kitchen.

A hand roughly grabbed the left side of Jane's neck at the same time that something sharp and cold jabbed the right side. She gasped.

"Don't move, unless you want a screwdriver through that pretty neck."

She slid her gaze sideways to look at Larry. On his colorless face was a look of fierce determination, as if he was afraid of doing this wrong. A drop of sweat ran from his upper lip into his mouth.

"I expected to find you dead," she said, not moving.

"Did you now? That's very interesting, since it's going to be the other way around." He tightened his grip on her neck, pushing the screwdriver harder against her.

"Ow."

"Shut up. Now here's what we're going to do. You're going to walk in front of me to my truck. It's parked right outside. If you try anything funny, this screwdriver goes right into your back. You got it?"

"Yes. Where are we going?"

"For a ride. Go."

She walked toward the front door.

"Not that way. We're going out the back door."

Alphonse appeared in front of her and stuck his nose between her legs.

"Alphonse!" Graham shouted. "Go lie down."

With a whimper the dog retreated to the corner of the kitchen and fell onto his side, watching them with big sad brown eyes.

They reached the apartment's back door.

"Open it," Graham commanded, and she pulled it inward and started out.

"That's my truck over there," he said in a low voice right behind her, and pointed to a beat-up dark gray pickup parked to the right. "Let's go."

She considered making a break and running for it. Surely she was in better condition than he was. If she was going to do it, the time was now.

"Don't try running or anything," he said, as if reading her mind, and she felt the screwdriver jab hard into her coat, right in the middle of her back. "It would be so easy."

Her heart sank. She walked slowly to the passenger door of the pickup truck and he opened it. "Get in and roll down the window."

"What?"

"Just do it."

She got in. The truck's cab was littered with greasy hamburger wrappers, empty paper and Styrofoam cups, and yellow carbon copies of invoices headed *LARRY GRA-*

*HAM, ELECTRICAL CONTRACTOR.* The air in the cramped space had a stale, sweaty smell.

"Roll down the window," Graham said.

She'd forgotten. She rolled it down. As soon as she did, he reached in and unscrewed the pop-up-style door lock, removed it, and dropped it into his shirt pocket. In its place in the door was merely an empty hole.

"In case you decided to get adventurous," he said, and made his way around to the other side and got in. He started the truck, shifted it into gear, backed out, and started around the parking lot toward the exit.

"So you did kill Ivy," she said, turning to him with a look of loathing, as they left Hillside Gardens.

In response he picked up the screwdriver from where he had set it beside him on the seat and brandished the tool in the air. She saw now that it was huge, at least a foot long.

"Where are we going?"

"It doesn't matter." He laughed, his fat shoulders shaking. "You certainly won't care."

He turned onto Route 46, heading east.

In her bag, her cell phone rang.

He turned to her sharply. "Give it to me. *Don't answer it.*"

She found the phone in her bag and handed it to Graham. He flipped it open and immediately terminated the call. Then he dialed a number. After a few moments he said, "We're on our way there. . . . Yeah, me and her. . . ." He snapped the phone shut and it immediately started to ring again. He rolled down his window and tossed the phone out. Jane heard it hit the pavement with a clatter, and the ringing abruptly stop. Had it been Stanley? she wondered. Florence or Nick? Daniel?

"Sorry, wrong number," he muttered.

"That was an expensive cell phone," she said quietly.

"You won't be needing it."

"Who did you just call?"

"None of your beeswax," he shouted. "Now sit back, relax." Suddenly he thought of something, and his face lit up. "Hey, my manuscript's in the backseat if you want to read it. I wrote some more."

"No, thanks, I'll pass."

He gave her a hateful look through slitted eyes. "You didn't really think my writing had promise, did you?"

"No."

"You were just, like, manipulating me to get me to talk?"

"Yes."

"Phony bitch."

"Murderer." She sat up in renewed anger. "Where are you taking me?" she demanded.

"None of your business," he snapped back. "Now keep your mouth shut. It's a long way and I don't think I can take much more of you. Pushy broad."

He switched on the radio and found the news. The police had captured the bus hijacker in a wooded section of Kinnelon, New Jersey, and identified him as Gary Larkin, twenty-nine, of Lyndhurst. Apparently he had been distraught after his wife left him and he lost his job in the same week.

Graham laughed a wheezing laugh. "See! I still can't believe your bubble-brained friend thought it was me."

Jane opened her mouth to protest.

His laughter died instantly. "I said keep your mouth shut, and I meant it." He turned up the radio.

Jane gazed out the window as the Willowbrook Mall swept by. She slid a glance at Graham and saw that he had moved the massive screwdriver to his lap. It occurred to her to grab the steering wheel and make him lose control of the truck, but what good would it do her? She couldn't throw open her door, because he had the lock in his shirt pocket. She considered grabbing for the screwdriver, using it on him, somehow getting the truck to stop. No, he was bigger and stronger than she was, and she would undoubtedly end up being the one impaled. She'd have to wait until they got wherever he was taking her to make her break.

He was heading for New York City. He had driven from Route 46 to Route 3, through the Meadowlands. Now they were on 495, stuck in the Lincoln Tunnel traffic at rush hour.

The truck was at a near standstill. If only she could get her door open . . . She glanced around at the surrounding cars. Could she somehow get the attention of another driver? No, everyone had his gaze fixed on the road, jockeying for that next inch forward.

As they approached the Lincoln Tunnel toll booths, she considered screaming to the toll collector. But at the last moment Larry veered into an E-ZPass lane and drove right through.

Emerging from the tunnel, Graham went west on 42nd Street and continued on it all the way to the West Side Highway, onto which he turned north.

"Where are we going?" she demanded again, glancing to the left across the Hudson River at New Jersey.

He ignored her. He remained on the West Side Highway for some time, finally getting off at West 96th Street. He took this east all the way to Park Avenue, onto which he turned left. They were in East Harlem, passing bodegas, tiny coffee shops and pizzerias, apartment buildings.

Abruptly he turned right onto East 116th Street, drove halfway down the block, and pulled into a space on the right side of the street beside a massive stone building.

Jane looked around. "You can't park here. There's a fire hydrant."

With a grunt of exasperation he held the screwdriver aloft. "Don't you ever shut up? Roll down your window."

She did, as he got out and came around the front of the

truck toward her door. She considered scrambling to his side and bursting out his door, but in the next instant he was looking in at her through the window. Maybe she could make a run for it once she was on the sidewalk.

"Okay, here's what's gonna happen," he said in a low voice, though the street was deserted. He took her door lock from his shirt pocket and screwed it back into the hole. Then he pulled it up. "We're going into this building here."

She glanced up at it. "Why?"

"Because I said so. Don't you worry about it. Like I told you, pretty soon it won't matter."

So he would murder her, too. She saw that there was no escape now. She was going to die, just like Ivy. She thought of Nicholas and a great dread rose in her—dread of his losing his mother at ten years old, dread of not being around to watch him grow up, get married, have children.

She got out of the truck and walked ahead of him. Once again she felt the screwdriver press into her back.

She gazed up at the building. She knew what it was now. A car sped past them on the street, and was gone.

"In here," he said. "Stop."

She halted and peered into a small courtyard in the building's side. "Where?"

"Come on," he said impatiently, and gave her a sharp shove toward the building. Now she could see steps leading up to a door. "That's right, up there," he said, and when they had climbed the steps, he took a bunch of keys from his pocket, reached in front of her, unlocked the door, and pushed it open. Beyond it was a gloomy dimness. She could see a wall streaked with black. A smell suddenly reached her—a sour, acrid odor that made her gag. The smell of burning, of charred wood . . . and flesh.

"Oh," she said, holding her coat over her mouth.

"You get used to it," he said, and pushed her inside. Graham produced a large flashlight that he must have brought from the truck and switched it on. They stood in a long corridor off which a number of doors opened on both sides. "Go to the end," he said, shoving the screwdriver at her back with his other hand. When she had reached the second-to-last door on the right, he said, "This door. Go."

She pushed it open and took a cautious step inside. Graham swept his flashlight slowly around a vast, cavernous room that had clearly been ravaged by fire. The walls and high ceiling were charred black. Cracks ran up and down and from side to side like alligator skin, indicating to Jane that the fire that had raged here had reached an extraordinarily high temperature.

Strewn among black pillars were the charred remains of tables and chairs, merely blackened boards and sticks now. The center of the great room was oddly clear. A dance floor, Jane realized.

"Why have you brought me here?" she asked, though she knew.

He didn't answer, instead continued to sweep his flashlight around the immense room.

At that moment they heard rhythmic footsteps, the sound of a woman's high-heeled shoes. Graham fixed the beam on a doorway exactly opposite the one through which they had come. A woman stepped into the bright yellow circle of light and started toward them, strolling between the bits of burned furniture, her hands plunged deep in the pockets of a full-length fur coat the exact same blond color as her hair.

# Chapter Twenty-six

Her scent reached Jane first—roses and violets, sickly sweet against the stench of rotting ashes. Then Tamara Henley stopped a few feet from Jane and Graham, looked Jane up and down, and smiled ruefully. "And to think I once wanted to have lunch with you."

"I can't make it," Jane said, her voice brimming with contempt.

Tamara threw back her head and laughed. "Oh, you definitely will not be able to make it." Her coat was of luscious beige chinchilla. Not a strand of her hair was out of place, and she was heavily made up. A small cascade of diamonds hung from each ear.

"All dressed up . . ." Jane said.

"And so many places to go. I've got another of our buildings to go to this morning, then a luncheon and board-of-directors meeting at the Frick. I certainly don't have time for your nonsense."

"*Nonsense?* You murdered my best friend."

Tamara shrugged indifferently. "She should have minded her own business."

"She was about to discover that you and your husband own this place. The Boriken Social Club, once St. Paul the Apostle Church."

"Now you see," Tamara broke in peevishly. "That was exactly the problem with your cheap little friend. She failed to make a very important distinction. Foss and I own this *building*. We *rented* it to the people who ran the Boriken Social Club. There's a world of difference."

Jane looked at her as if she were mad, which Jane realized she undoubtedly was. "No, there isn't. As the owners, you were responsible for meeting the building code, for installing a sprinkler system, making sure there were enough exits. Because of you and your husband, eighty-seven people died in this room."

"It wasn't our fault some lunatic decided to start a fire outside the exit to get back at his cheating girlfriend!" Tamara shouted.

"No, but it was your fault there was only one exit—that one. Those poor people had nowhere to go."

"Actually, there were two exits: the front door and the one you two just came through. Is it our fault that idiot started his fire in front of one of them? Besides, the club owner could have renovated at anytime." Tamara shook her head impatiently. "We're going in circles, and I'm getting extremely bored." She turned to Graham. "Thank you for bringing her here."

Graham stood up a little straighter, as if Tamara were his general. "My pleasure, Tammy."

Tamara approached him and patted him on the back. He smiled and nodded modestly. As Jane watched, something popped out of his Adam's apple—the sharp tip of a thin metal rod. Graham's eyes bugged out, and he put his hands to his throat and turned and stared at Tamara. She raised one leg and with an elegant gold high-heeled pump gave him a firm kick in the side. He crashed to the floor, landing on his back. Blood spurted from his throat, getting on his hands, which now merely fluttered in the vicinity of his neck. As Jane watched in horror, his eyes grew glassy and lifeless.

Jane recoiled in horror.

"I told him not to call me that," Tamara said. She bent and grabbed the flashlight from where it had fallen beside him. Shining it on Graham's face, she watched him dispassionately for a moment. Then she bent again, roughly turned Graham's head to the side, and yanked out the ice pick she had used to kill him. Its tip shone reddish-black, as if it had been dipped in paint.

Straightening, Tamara noticed a large splotch of blood on her coat. "Oh, pooh!" she cried. "Look at my coat. And I've got my luncheon and board meeting."

Jane, heart banging, short of breath, regarded this monster, then looked down at Graham. "Why did you do that?" she asked, though she knew the answer.

"Oh, he deserved it," Tamara tossed off. "He tried to blackmail me. Me!"

Of course, Jane thought. And he'd gotten the idea from William Ives, who had blackmailed him. Jane said, "Graham knew you'd heard him and Ivy making plans to meet on the path. He knew you knew she would be there. Then he arrived at the pond and found her dead."

"Mm," Tamara said, regarding the ice pick thoughtfully.

Jane continued, "While Larry and Ivy were talking in the lounge, he heard you in the conference room. He hurried out to see who might have overheard them, but you were gone. But he did smell your distinctive perfume." She thought back. "That's what he meant when he made an odd comment to me about there being some trails you couldn't see. *Scent.*"

Tamara's mouth dropped open, and she glared in annoyance at the corpse of Larry Graham. "*That's* how he knew I'd been there? Ooh, that stinking liar. He told me he'd seen me. I *do* have to stop wearing so much scent."

"The point is, he must later have put two and two together. He knew you had known Ivy would be on that path. He knew *he* hadn't killed Ivy. So he took a flyer, blackmailed you, and hit the jackpot. What did he want?"

Tamara laughed. "Work!"

"Work?"

"Yes, he knew Foss was a developer. Graham wanted the job doing the electrical work in our next building. I told him he could have it, with a few conditions. First, that he go to Ivy's office and get hold of any files she had on her 'big story.' He found nothing. So I told him to get into Ivy's apartment and look there. Nothing again. I figured she must have had her notes with her, but I couldn't very well search her room at the lodge—the police would have taken anything they'd found anyway—and I couldn't get into the police station to search her luggage. I could only pray that nothing had been found.

"Then," Tamara went on, glancing at Graham's body, "last Saturday night, he called me. He said you'd been to see him twice asking questions, that you'd found out a lot. I had to find out how much you knew. Why do you think I invited you to my New Year's party—because I *like* you?" She shuddered. "I had to invite all those other dreadful people from the retreat to sort of—camouflage you, if you know what I mean. At my party, you said you'd made progress in finding Ivy's murderer. Well, I couldn't have that, could I? So this was my last condition for Mr. Graham—to bring you here."

*And I walked right into your hands,* Jane thought.

Tamara gazed down again at Graham's lifeless form and shook her head. "He wanted us to have an ongoing 'relationship,'" she said distastefully. "Can you imagine? He said he was 'growing' his business, that all he wanted to keep quiet was one big job a year."

Jane looked around, took in the charred surroundings. "I take it this was the next building."

"Not precisely. Our next building will be the one we'll

build here after we tear this one down. That moron who started the fire outside the club had no idea what a favor he was doing us. Foss and I will collect the insurance and put up a magnificent fifty-story office building on this site—this *historic* site, I should say."

"An office building?"

"Absolutely," Tamara replied, regarding Jane as if she were intellectually deficient. "Harlem is hot now; don't you know that? The second Harlem renaissance. We have an ex-president here. Commercial rents are doubling. On 125th Street they're tripling. We'll have this building rented well before it's finished." She looked around in disgust. "But first we have to tear down this mess. Little will anyone know that you and your friend here will be in the rubble. I'll burn your bodies first, of course. I'll do that before I leave here this morning. I've brought some gasoline." With her free hand she vaguely indicated the dimness behind her.

She frowned. "I've got one question for you, Jane. Had you yet figured out that it was I who killed Ivy?"

"Yes."

"May I ask how? Was it my perfume?"

"Scent? No. It was color."

Tamara frowned. "Color?"

"You made a mistake about Ivy's sweater."

Tamara eyed Jane shrewdly. "What mistake?"

"The key to solving this case," Jane said thoughtfully, "was a comment made by my son's nanny, Florence, about cats being color-blind. Suddenly several details I'd ignored became extremely important—and made sense of everything."

"So," Tamara said petulantly, "cats are color-blind. Big deal. What does that have to do with anything?"

"So are you." Tamara made no response, just watched Jane, who went on, "That's why your clothes sometimes clash. That's why you said both of the wreaths in your room at the lodge were the same color. People with color blindness can't tell the difference between red and green.

"In the conference room, when you were talking about the wreaths, I saw Adam frown. But he didn't frown because you'd said they were tacky and offended him. He frowned because you'd said they were both the same color. He knew they weren't and was puzzled by your remark."

Jane's eyes unfocused as she cast her thoughts back to the night Ivy died. "Red and green . . . Ivy was wearing a red sweater on the night she died. You said the last time you'd seen Ivy was in the lounge, and that she was brushing snow from her green sweater. But when Ivy came into the lounge, she was still wearing the white fisherman's knit sweater Jennifer had lent her.

"In truth, when you last saw Ivy—on the path, by the light of the flashlight you'd stolen from the lodge's storage room—she had already given the sweater back to Jennifer. Ivy's own sweater was red, but you remembered it as green because you can't tell the difference between the two colors. But it didn't matter whether you remembered the sweater as red or green. What mattered was that you didn't remember it as white, and thereby gave yourself away."

Tamara shook her golden-coiffed head in amazement. "You are a marvel." Then her face grew pensive. "I wonder if I'll need to take care of Adam. If he 'puts two and two together,' as you put it . . ."

"Monster," Jane spat. "Cold-blooded murderer. You stole the ice pick from the kitchen at the lodge, went down the path, and waited for Ivy, who planned to meet Larry, who she must have believed was the bus hijacker." She shook her head sadly. "She thought she was black-mailing him. He thought she was into some kind of kinky foreplay.

"So what did you do when Ivy got to the end of the path? Talk to her a little? Just jump out and stab her?"

"Does it matter? Yes, we talked a little. I pretended I'd come out for some fresh air. I got her onto the subject of the story she was pursuing about the Boriken Social Club. She told me she'd discovered that the company that owned this building was Coconut Grove Development. The irony was, she hadn't the slightest idea Coconut Grove was Foss and me."

"But you knew it was only a matter of time before she discovered that . . . before she pierced the many corporate layers you and your husband had placed between you and your tenants to protect yourselves, to keep you anonymous. Ivy's story would have ruined you both, would have put you in jail for a very long time. How did you know she was working on that story?"

"She simply started bragging about it the first night we were at the lodge. That shriveled little old man, William, and I were sitting in the conference room, having some fruit we'd scrounged up in the kitchen. Ivy came in and began chattering about her 'big story' behind the Boriken Social Club fire, about how the company that owned the building would be in major trouble when she was through. Not to mention the big promotion she'd get at *Skyline*."

Tamara looked irritated. "I kept trying to press her for more details, to find out how much she knew. But then she changed the subject, and all she wanted to talk about was her daughter who died." She shrugged. "It didn't matter. I knew enough."

Jane gave an ironic laugh. "Ivy thought you didn't want to hear about Marlene because you were cold and unfeeling."

"I *didn't* want to hear about Marlene. Who cares about her foolish daughter?"

Jane ignored this last remark. "I found palm trees and

coconuts on Ivy's desk blotter in her office at *Skyline* and elsewhere among her things. The palm and coconuts are, of course, your company's logo. The name *Tamara* means 'palm.' *Foss* is short for 'Forrest.' A palm forest . . ."

"Is a coconut grove," Tamara finished, looking endlessly bored.

"And in the center of the logo, of course, is a six, quite prominent. And at the bottom, *six* coconuts. Six, your lucky number. Very clever, really."

"No, you're very clever, Jane. You must be a whiz at *The New York Times* crossword puzzle."

Jane said, "At dinner the night Ivy was killed, when she said she had a story that would put someone in jail for years, we all naturally assumed she was talking about Johnny. But she was actually referring to whoever owned Coconut Grove Development.

"You and your husband are slumlords of the worst kind." Jane's voice was full of contempt. "You let this magnificent building—St. Paul the Apostle Church—become a firetrap. Yes, Ivy would have had one hell of a story. About your neglect that turned this place into a death box. About its lack of a sprinkler system, its inadequate exits. Your blatant building-code violations led to eighty-seven people getting trampled to death in a panicked stampede or dying from smoke asphyxiation." She looked around her, almost expecting the ghosts of those poor souls to appear, their screams to resound in the dimness.

"I told you," Tamara said through clenched teeth, "this club was owned by our *tenants*. Foss and I had nothing to do with it."

"You and your husband still feel no responsibility for what you've done—or not done," Jane marveled. "Slumlords rarely do. The way you look at it, you and Foss are the victims, am I correct?"

"Yes, for once you are."

Jane nodded. "You made this attitude quite clear when you said the owner of the house across the street from yours would be blamed for the negligence of his tenants. And when you scoffed when Red Pearson read from his novel based on the club fire: It wasn't to get back at him for criticizing your story; it was because his telling of the club fire tragedy was, to your way of thinking, inaccurate.

"Everyone had it wrong, you thought. Everyone was making you and your husband the culprits. So—in order to protect yourselves—you killed the woman who would make it all public."

"You bet I did," Tamara said resentfully. "I wasn't going to let some tacky little slut playing Lois Lane ruin everything Foss and I have built. Cause some huge scandal, turn Foss and me into another Harry and Leona Helmsley. No, thank you."

Tamara turned down the corners of her mouth disdainfully. "Ivy was an idiot. She started telling me this slob"— she gestured toward Graham's corpse—"was once a figure skater. She said Larry was going to skate for her, and turned around to look at the pond. That's when I stabbed her. She made the funniest little squeaking sound." She giggled.

Jane winced.

"It was quite easy, really," Tamara said. "Killing her, I mean." She held up the ice pick, admiring it. "I liked it so much that as soon as I'd decided I was going to get rid of you, I drove over to Fortunoff in Wayne and picked this up." She smiled. "Fortunoff. The Source."

She checked her slimly elegant watch. "Oh, dear, getting late. You've wasted enough of my time." Suddenly she lunged forward, like a fencer, thrusting the pick at Jane, jabbing her right hand. Hot pain seared the center of Jane's palm. She looked quickly and saw blood seeping from the wound.

She had no sooner looked up again than Tamara rushed forward with a cry, throwing her whole weight at Jane. Jane managed to grab the arm holding the pick and put all her strength into forcing it away. Tamara was surprisingly strong. For a moment, as they pushed at each other, their faces were only inches apart, and Jane saw unadulterated hatred—and madness—in the other woman's eyes.

Jane drew back her right foot and kicked Tamara as hard as she could in the shin. Tamara let out a grunt of pain, the flashlight went flying from her hand, yet the pressure of her arm against Jane's barely lessened, and her hand still clutched the ice pick, its bloody tip now only inches from Jane's face.

With a great mustering of strength, Jane surged forward, and the two women toppled to the floor, Jane on top. The ice pick's handle hit the floor and was knocked out of Tamara's hand, landing a few inches from Larry Graham's inert body. Jane scrambled for it, grabbed it, and swiftly stood. Tamara had also gotten up and stood a few yards away, watching.

Jane clutched the handle of the ice pick with both hands, pointing its tip straight out before her. She waited. Tamara took a step closer.

"Stay back," Jane warned, but Tamara took another step. Jane broke out in a sweat, wondering if she could stab someone—even Tamara—even if it was to save her own life. Then a great rage overtook her and she realized that of course she could—could and would.

Tamara's foot came flying toward Jane, knocking the ice pick out of her hands. Tamara quickly retrieved it. Jane turned and ran.

She went back out the door through which she and Larry had come, and to the left down the long corridor. She ducked into one of the rooms toward the end on the left, unsure if Tamara had seen her.

Silently she slid behind the door, then stood as still as a statue, waiting, peering into the gloom through the crack of the door, between its hinges.

There was absolute quiet . . . then a crunch, followed by the faint creak of a floorboard not far away. Jane held her breath. She realized her hands were shaking.

And in the next instant Tamara was there, looking straight at her through the crack of the door. With all her might, Jane slammed the door into Tamara's face.

Tamara made an odd choking-gurgling sound, then collapsed.

Slowly Jane walked around the door. Tamara lay in a chinchilla sprawl, on her back, the ice pick having pierced her throat and emerged from the back of her neck. Her eyes were open, still full of gleaming hatred.

Jane gasped, turning quickly away.

Then Tamara moved and Jane returned her gaze to her in horror. Tamara's lips were moving. Cautiously Jane leaned over her, straining to make out what she was trying to say.

"Not . . . our fault," Tamara whispered. In a flash her hand flew up and grabbed Jane's face. Jane drew back, pulling at Tamara's arm, but couldn't loosen the clawlike grip, the fingernails digging into her cheeks.

And then, in the next moment, the grip was released as Tamara's hand went limp and her arm fell to her side.

Jane began to cry. Stepping over Tamara's body, she walked slowly down the corridor and found the door to the courtyard. There was Graham's pickup at the curb. She made her way toward it. As she reached it, her legs suddenly weakened and she faltered, grabbing at the truck for support.

"Lady, you okay?"

She looked up. A petite young woman came toward her wheeling a wire shopping basket full of groceries.

"I'm fine, thank you," Jane said, but her legs betrayed her again and she fell to the sidewalk.

The young woman rushed to her and helped her gently lie down.

"Help! Somebody help me!" Jane heard the woman cry.

"What's the problem?" came a young man's voice.

"I don't know what's the matter with her. Maybe drunk."

Through partially closed eyes Jane saw the young man's dark face—shrewd, serious—come near hers. "Lady," he said softly, "you okay?" Then she felt him touch her coat.

"Look at this," she heard him say.

"Oh, Lord. What is that?"

"What do you think it is? It's blood."

"Blood? Whose? Hers?"

"Hell, I don't know. Get a cop."

# Chapter Twenty-seven

That afternoon, Jane sat at her favorite table at Whipped Cream, staring into a magnificent fire in the brick hearth. Stanley sat beside her, gently holding her bandaged right hand.

"Ivy, my poor old friend, was a tragic figure, really," Jane said. "She had poor judgment and was of weak moral character—she tried to blackmail Larry Graham, though for something he hadn't done—yet in the end she was killed because, for once in her life, she was trying to do something good—expose a terrible evil." Tears rolled down her cheeks.

Ginny, who had been behind the counter preparing hot cocoa for the three of them, appeared carrying a tray holding the three mugs. She, too, was crying. She set down the mugs on the table, then sat down beside Jane and took her other hand. Stanley put his arm around Jane's shoulders, and they all gazed at the holiday decorations surrounding the fireplace. Brilliant lights, like the ones in the café's window. Red and green . . .

"It's not fair," Jane said.

"No," Stanley agreed, "it's not fair." He gave her arm a soft, comforting squeeze. "Not fair at all."

\* \* \*

"And so you see," Jane finished, smiling across the dinner table at Nick and Florence, "your comment, Florence, about cats being color-blind was the key to solving this case."

Nick, to whom Jane had finally revealed the truth about Ivy's death, sat very still, his gaze lowered to the table.

"A wreath of poinsettias and cranberries," Florence said thoughtfully. "You know, missus, at home in Trinidad, our national flower is the wild poinsettia—the chaconia."

Jane and Nick looked at her. She went on, "It is a very beautiful, deep-red flower and grows in the forests. To the people of Trinidad and Tobago, it represents the imperishability of life."

She shook her head, remembering, eyes unfocusing. "When I was a little girl of nine, my older brother Charles died. It was a terrible time. As the months passed, everyone in my family seemed to get back to normal except me. I could not rid myself of my deep sadness. One day my mother took me by the hand to our kitchen. On the table, in a vase, she had placed a glorious long spray of chaconia. It was early September, when this flower starts to bloom. It was so very red and lovely.

"'Florence,' my mother said to me, 'look at the flower and think of Charles. And whenever you think of Charles, think of the flower and remember, he is still with us. In our hearts, he is still with us. He never went away.'"

"That's sad, Flo," Nick said, gazing solemnly across the table at her.

"No, Master Nicholas," Florence said with a laugh, "it is happy! Our friends never leave us, even when we cannot see them. What's important," she said, looking at Jane, "is that while our friends are still here on earth, we do our best to be kind to them. To be a good friend."

She gave Jane a reassuring nod.

"Thank you, Florence," Jane said softly.

"For what?" Nick asked.

Winky leapt onto the table with a joyous rumbling cry.

"Hey, Wink!" Nick cried happily. "You haven't done that in weeks." He turned to Florence. "I guess she knows life goes on, huh? That even though most of her babies are going away and she'll never see them again, she'll still have them, like you said."

"Yes, Master Nick," Florence said, gently removing Winky from the table. "She knows."

# Author's Note

I hope you enjoyed reading *Icing Ivy*, my fourth Jane Stuart and Winky mystery. By now Jane, Nicholas, Florence, Stanley, Daniel, and all the other residents of Shady Hills are family to me, as I hope they are to you.

One of the reasons this book was such fun to write was that Winky became a mother, an event long in the planning. Though Jane, Nick, and Florence made it their business to find good homes for all of Winky's kittens, this is not always the case.

## *The Best Thing You Can Do for Your Cat*

The fact is, there are too many kittens and too few good homes. Animal shelters are overburdened with unwanted animals. Each day tens of thousands of cats are born in the United States alone. At this rate, there are not enough homes for these animals, and millions of healthy cats and kittens are euthanized. Others are abandoned to fend for themselves against automobiles, cruel humans, the elements, and other animals.

Please spay or neuter your cat. Not only will you be stopping this unnecessary suffering, but you will also be doing something good for you and your pet.

Spayed and neutered cats are better, more affectionate companions because they focus their attention on their human families. They are less likely to bite. Unaltered cats often show more behavior and temperament problems than cats that have been spayed or neutered.

Spayed and neutered cats live longer, healthier lives.

Spaying a female eliminates its heat cycle; females in heat often cry incessantly, urinate frequently (sometimes all over the house), exhibit nervous behavior, and attract unwanted male cats. Spaying females eliminates the chance of uterine or ovarian cancer, and significantly reduces the likelihood of breast cancer and of a disease called pyometra.

Neutered males are less likely to spray and mark territory, and to roam in search of a mate, risking injury in traffic and fights with other males. Neutering males reduces the incidence of hernias, perianal tumors, and prostate disease, and eliminates the possibility of testicular cancer.

If you have reservations about spaying or neutering your cat, it may be because you believe one or more of the myths surrounding this practice. Spaying or neutering will not change your cat's personality. Nor will it make your cat fat and lazy—only a poor diet and lack of exercise will do that. Spaying and neutering are neither dangerous nor painful. These low-cost procedures are the most common surgeries performed on cats. With a minimal amount of home care, your pet will resume normal behavior in a few days.

If your cat gives birth, don't wait too long to have her spayed. Wait until two weeks after her kittens start to be weaned—in other words, six to eight weeks after she gives birth. Remember that a surgery appointment may need to be made several weeks ahead.

Remember also that kittens don't need to wait too long to be spayed or neutered. Veterinary societies and shelters have accepted early sterilization as safe. It can be done on cats as young as eight weeks old.

For more information, visit the Web site of The Ameri-

can Society for the Prevention of Cruelty to Animals at
http://www.aspca.org.

## The Story of the Ice Pick

Some of the best history is what we don't learn in
school. When Jane learns that her friend Ivy has been
stabbed with an ice pick, she says, "Like Trotsky . . ." and
faints. What's the story behind that?

In 1940, the exiled Bolshevik leader Leon Trotsky was
living in Mexico City. His greatest enemy, Joseph Stalin,
had pursued him across continents via his murderous
agents in an effort to assassinate him, but had thus far
been unsuccessful.

Ultimately Trotsky's murder would be accomplished by
a man named Ramon Mercader. Though Trotsky was protected by bodyguards, Mercader penetrated his defenses
by means of a clever ruse. After ingratiating himself with
the members of Trotsky's household and gaining their
trust and acceptance, he arranged to meet personally with
Trotsky on the pretext of discussing an article he had written. They did meet, and Trotsky dismissed the article as
banal and without interest.

On the morning of August 20, Mercader showed up at
Trotsky's villa and was again allowed to visit with Trotsky
alone to discuss the article Mercader had written.
Trotsky's wife, Natalia Sedova, later related: "I was in the
room next door. There was a terrible piercing cry . . . Lev
Davidovich [Trotsky's birth name] appeared, leaning
against the door frame. His face was covered with blood,
his blue eyes glistening without spectacles and his arms
hung limply by his side. . . ."

Mercader had struck Trotsky in the back of the head
with an ice pick he had hidden in the pocket of his khaki
raincoat. According to Mercader himself, "I put my rain-

coat on the table so that I could take out the *piolet* [ice pick] in the pocket. When Trotsky started to read my article, I took the ax and, closing my eyes, gave him a tremendous blow on the head. The man screamed in a way that I will never forget—Aaaaaa! . . . very long, infinitely long. He got up like a madman, threw himself at me, and bit my hand—look, you can still see the marks of his teeth. Then I pushed him, so that he fell to the floor."

Trotsky's bodyguards rushed into the room and began to beat Mercader, who, having never killed before, was stunned at the sight of Trotsky on the floor. The guards wanted to kill Mercader on the spot, but Trotsky intervened: "He must be forced to talk."

Trotsky was rushed to the hospital. "The doctor declared that the injury was not very serious," Natalia said. "Lev Davidovich listened to him without emotion, as one would a conventional message of comfort. Pointing to his heart, he said, 'I feel . . . here . . . that this is the end . . . this time . . . they've succeeded.' "

He underwent surgery and survived more than a day. He died 26 hours after being attacked, on August 22, 1940.

On some points of this legendary story, people disagree. Some say it was an ice *ax,* not an ice pick.

I immediately found this story fascinating. What mystery writer wouldn't? For my purposes in icing poor Ivy, an ice pick worked best.

### *Wheresoever You May Wander . . .*

Curious about Florence's Curried Cascadura? The cascadura fish—or cascadoo, as it is commonly called—is about as Trinidadian a creature as one could find. This small, primeval fish from the Silurian age, with a scaly, armor-plated shell resembling that of the catfish, lives embedded in the freshwater mudflats of Trinidad's southern coast, as well as in sluggish rivers, ponds, and swamps. Though this strange fish is served in Caribbean restaurants around the world, most of us do not have access to this delicacy. The following recipe, therefore, substitutes snapper for cascadura.

If you *are* fortunate enough to have real cascadura, remember that it must be washed thoroughly and meticulously in fresh water until all the mud on the fish is removed.

### Florence's Curried "Cascadoo"

#### 4 Servings

1 large shallot, finely chopped
1 piece of fresh thyme, finely chopped
1 piece of fresh parsley, finely chopped
1 leaf cilantro, finely chopped
½ teaspoon vinegar
¼ teaspoon salt
¼ teaspoon pepper
4 fresh snapper (or cascadura) fillets
¼ cup (60 milliliters) lime juice
1 tablespoon vegetable oil
1 large onion, chopped
3 tomatoes, chopped
3 cloves garlic, chopped
2 tablespoons curry paste
1 cup (250 milliliters) coconut milk
1 whole hot pepper wrapped in cheesecloth and tied securely

Combine shallot, thyme, parsley, and cilantro in a cup with vinegar. Add salt and pepper. Marinate 4 snapper fillets in herb seasoning and lime juice for at least 2 hours.

Heat oil in a large pot. Add onion, tomatoes, and garlic and sauté for 2 minutes. Add curry paste and cook for another minute. Add coconut milk and simmer for 5 minutes. Add the marinated fish fillets and coat thoroughly with the curry sauce. Add the pepper, cover, and simmer until fillets are flaky—about 10 to 15 minutes.

Remove fillets and serve on a platter covered with the curry sauce. Serve with rice and vegetables.

### *From Havana With Love*

Intrigued by the drink after which Jennifer Castaneda named her novel? I was. The *Mojito* (pronounced "moe-HEE-toe"), born in Cuba in the 1910s, is a refreshing rum drink popularized by the patrons of Havana's most famous bar, La Bodeguita del Medio—most notably Ernest Hemingway. It's currently making a big comeback. Great with barbecue. Come to think of it, a *Mojito* would be a nice accompaniment to Florence's Curried Cascadura. Here's how to make one just the way "Papa" liked them. ¡*Salud!*

### Mojito Cocktail

½ teaspoon sugar
½ lime, juiced
1 sprig fresh mint, crushed
½ cup crushed ice (use ice pick? never mind)
2 fluid ounces (60 milliliters) light dry rum
4 fluid ounces (120 milliliters) soda water
1 sprig fresh mint for garnish

In a highball glass, stir together the sugar and lime juice. Bruise the mint leaves and drop them into the glass. Fill glass with crushed ice and pour in rum. Pour in soda water to fill the glass. Garnish with a sprig of mint.

I love hearing from readers. If you have a comment about *Icing Ivy* or any of my books, I invite you to e-mail me at evanmarshall@TheNovelist.com, or write to me at Six Tristam Place, Pine Brook, NJ 07058-9445. I always respond to reader mail. For a free bookmark, please send a self-addressed stamped envelope. Please visit my Web site at http://www.TheNovelist.com.

Evan Marshall

Jayne Mansfield

# Jayne Mansfield

## A Biography

## by May Mann

Drake Publishers Inc. New York

LCCN    72–10488

ISBN 0-87749-415-0


Published in 1973 by
Drake Publishers Inc.
381 Park Avenue South
New York, N.Y. 10016

# PREFACE

Many people of repute today testify to psychic experiences. Some report visitations from people who have passed on. I had never had any interest nor any communication with the dead, until Jayne Mansfield's tragic death.

I can only report the facts which are witnessed and duly sworn to as the truth. It is my belief that one's mind should be free to accept the truth as it is, and not as it is *wanted* to be. That is the why and wherefore of Jayne Mansfield and this book. And why Jayne came back in her spiritual state to my house. For here in my home and garden Jayne had known some of the happiest times of her life: her bridal shower, baby showers, birthday parties and all of the holidays we had celebrated together.

For several years Jayne and I had been compiling a book on her complex, sometimes torrid, even spiritual and fantastic life. "I want the truth told, all of it," she'd insist. "I'm three different

women. I know there's one of me I admire and there's the perverse
other me I despise. And then there's the glamourous, manufactured me on the screen and in the night clubs. Why am I so driven
with wildness?"

The book was nearing completion when she was killed, her head
severed from her body by the broken windshield of a speeding car
in the early morning hours outside New Orleans.

I now had the task of writing the Jayne Book myself. Delving
even more closely into the intimacies of Jayne's life, I became so
appalled, and later so despondent. that I finally put my Jayne Book
away. I had no intention of completing it. I had my own life to
live—and the behind-the-scenes aspects of Jayne's life were too
awful.

Then came her call from the spirit world asking me, holding me
to my work and my honor, to complete the Jayne Book!

Jayne Mansfield, the voluptuous super sex symbol, and I were
close friends and intimate confidants for twelve years until she was
killed in the automobile accident June 29, 1967. I was to discover
that even after her death, she still needed me in may ways.

During 1966 and 1967 Jayne had been hounded relentlessly by
damaging front-page headlines proclaiming: "Jayne Sued As Unfit
Mother," "Jayne Mansfield Asked To Leave Film Festival," etc.
On television she was maliciously reported, "Jayne—unwed but
pregnant."

"Why such vicious lies?" Jayne would demand, her longlashed
brown eyes filling with tears. "Why is everyone persecuting me?
It's like a devil is trying to destroy me—murder me." Indignation,
wrath and bewilderment claimed the curvy blonde sensuous girl as
she'd pace the floor of her Pink Palace or my home—trying to think
of ways to combat the evils that were clearly pursuing her. The
diamond rings on her slim fingers would crush into the suntanned
flesh as she clenched her fists with frustration. "Why me? Why
me?" she'd ask over and over. "Why me?"

"My only recourse is clear—your book to tell the truth behind those headlines! I know the truth will vindicate me. I'm not a whore. I'm a lady, and I am a good mother!"

"Who else do I have to turn to?" she sobbed to me the last night of her life in Hollywood. Did she sense that fate had decreed a horrible death for her within a few hours on a lonely road between Biloxi and New Orleans?

"You're the only one who has never wanted anything from me," she said during our last heart to heart girl talk. "All the rest, everyone whose professed to love me all wanted money, used me, even Jayne Marie my own daughter tried to destroy me." The dam of her emotions finally burst loose. "Oh, May, I don't know," her chin trembled. "Even my own mother hasn't spoken to me in months. I guess she also believes all of those evil headlines!" Jayne began to cry again releasing more of the long pent-up anguish within her.

I had never seen Jayne sob hysterically like this before. Jayne was too resolute, too independent. too proud to show tears, or to ever admit defeat in anything. She was too determined to secure her "image" intact at all times. She was "The International Movie Star Sex Goddess!" That spelled glamour Jayne had worked hard, long hours for it. She had no intention of losing it.

Jayne and I spent all night getting the intimate pictures that had never been published and the last chapters ready for me to complete the Jayne Book. By four in the morning I insisted I had to go home. Jayne walked out to the electrically controlled gates with me. We stood for some time. talking in the moonlight. She was so disturbed, so unhappy, so beside herself, so forlorn, that I put my arms around her to comfort her.

The next morning Jayne left for Biloxi, never to return. She sent me a letter expressing her delight with the chapter I'd sent her. She had posted it at midnight. Less than an hour later her car crashed into a deserted spray truck. Jayne's beautiful head had been sliced off on the windshield. Sam Brody, her lawyer-lover, and the driver had also been killed. Three of her small children, badly injured, had somehow survived pinned under the the back seat of the car.

The book, as far as I was concerned, was finished.

My conscience bothered me as time passed because I knew how much Jayne wanted her defense—the true inside story of her life told. I began having dreams in which Jayne would appear. "May, I want the truth told, the whole truth about me." she would repeat. "All everyone knows about me is the publicity. Some people even hate me for it. Let people judge me as I am." She'd say this over and over in my dreams just as she had said it that last night at the Pink Palace!

"Above all I want my children to know the real me! They must not believe, when they grow up, what is not true. I depend on you. You promised?"

I'd awaken and Jayne would be gone. But they didn't seem like dreams. Each time she'd say the same words. "Finish the book! Please! Please! Please!"

Jayne, I remembered, often quoted some phrase of philosophy she had memorized. She delighted surprising people who did not suspect that she had an I.Q. of 163 in college. "Anyone who composes an autobiography should be inspired by a burning devotion to truth!" Jayne would say. "Regardless of personal feelings, or pride, or even of dignity and social decency, she has to write the truth, or not at all!

Some of the intimate details of her life I considered too daring, too revealing, and far beyond the dictates of privacy. "I've lived it and paid the price fully in both pleasure, success, heartbreak, pain and notoriety," she'd insist. "I am entitled to say it all. That's what I want, all of it as it is!".

Jayne continued coming to me in dreams. It was always always "Please! Please Please! You promised!" For my own peace of mind I began praying that she would stop. It was frightening. I wanted no dealings with the supernatural, although I loved Jayne.

Writing about the last two years of her life had proved to be too morbid. I could not keep on reliving Jayne's life every day by writing about it. It was too depressing.

The Jayne Book material was in a file in the garage. Suddenly a succession of strange events began . For eight consecutive days world famous psychics tried to see me. The first day Lee Atkinson and Cobina Wright invited me to their salon to meet psychic Richard Ireland who would answer any questions. I was unable to accept. The second day mutual friends insisted I attend a party at Peter Hurkos' home. "Sit next to me," said Mr. Hurkos. "You are the only one I'll read for. I feel I have something important for you." I declined, not wanting any romantic part of my love life, which I presumed it would be discussed before the other guests.

I was a little surprised on the third successive day when a friend unexpectedly telephoned introducing Louise H., a famed self-pro-claimed witch with amazing psychic powers. Miss H. called me twice to give me a reading, but for one reason or another I was unable to schedule time to see her. Maria Graciette, the author of a psychic book, called on the fourth day—and again I had no time to talk to her.

By now, however, I was beginning to wonder what this was all about. Baroness Lotta von Strahl, a well-known sensitive who works with the psychology department of UCLA, made an unex-pected social call on the fifth day - just as I was leaving for an urgent appointment. On the sixth day Mr. George Dareos, the world-famous psychic came to see me from his home in San Bernardino. Mr. Dareos said he felt compelled to see me and he only had twenty minutes to stay. At the same instant, both an electrician and a plumber, due for repairs on my house, arrived. By the time I had explained the emergencies to them. Mr. Dareos had left.

I was now extremely puzzled by all of these psychic powers converging upon me for no apparent reason, and day after day! When would it all stop?

Mr. Andre, a Hindu E.S.P. lecturer, was the seventh to call and on the seventh day. I could not make an appointment for him, since my schedule as a columnist was filled for two weeks ahead.

On the eighth day a long time friend, Yvonne Avery, telephoned. Her tone was urgent. "I have to see you tonight at 7:30," she said. I apologized but said that was impossible. I had a previous engagement. "Break it, " she insisted. "I must see you." Yvonne was adamant.

"I was one of the world's foremost psychics as a child," she revealed. "I toured the world in the theater and concert halls with my gift. When I grew up I went into business. I retired from it. But I still have it and I feel that I must see you at once, tonight! For some reason, it cannot wait!"

Since I'd never known Yvonne was psychic in all the years I'd known her, I was secretly amused, polite and by now very curious too, although I actually could not take her professed power seriously. Would she see a new man—a new love—coming into my life? I didn't want to appear rude to her, but my greeting was purely tongue in cheek! Also I was slightly annoyed at her for practically forcing me to change my plans for that evening.

Yvonne and I sat down in comparative quiet, alone in my bedroom. Yvonne began to concentrate. As she began to talk to me about myself and some of the men in my life, I noticed that Princess, my pink point white Siamese cat suddenly sat up alert. She was staring with big eyes in wonder, looking just past Yvonne and I remarked on it.

Instead of relaxing, as a cat usually does, Princess remained rigid, sitting at attention, and staring with fascination at some object I could not see. Again I interrupted Yvonne to remark, "Look at Princess! I have never seen her so interested! She is so tense! Isn't it strange the way she stares. But she isn't looking at you, Yvonne?" I was laughing.

Yvonne's face suddenly turned white. I thought she was going to faint. She stammered something like, "No, it isn't!" And then she sort of slumped down by the bed, like she was kneeling and leaning against it for support.

Yvonne had become very quiet!

"What's the matter?" I asked. Suddenly I felt the smile leave my face. I looked at Yvonne and then at Princess, who both seemed transfixed, staring in the direction. "What is the matter, Yvonne?"

"No, I can't tell you. I'd better not say," she replied.

"Go ahead, you can tell me anything," I insisted. At the same time I was looking at Princess again, who was still sitting alert, tense and transfixed, looking at something in the room which I could not see.

"Well," Yvonne almost gasped, "I don't know how to say this. It has never happened to me before in my life! But Jayne Mansfield is here. She is standing right here in this room next to me."

A distinct chill went over me. I now realized that Yvonne was completely serious.

I glanced again at Princess. Jayne had adored my pussycat so much that she had declared herself "Princess's godmother." Princess was still looking saucer-eyed at something or someone I didn't see, but the cat did see!

"I feel Jayne Mansfield very strongly!" Yvonne said almost shaking and visibly moved. "She has taken over completely. She says you were sisters in her former life."

Before Yvonne had begun my reading, she had told me to take a pen and paper and write down anything important she might say. Now I began writing down every word. I transcribed it exactly as it happened, as follows:

"Jayne says you were very close in another life, and you were together in many experiences. That is why you had such a great rapport in this life.

"She is standing right here. She is in white and more beautiful than I ever saw her. There is a blue light which fades into a white and pink light about her. On earth she says she was very spiritual. She was a true psychic and had deep intuition about things and people. She says her trouble came when she didn't listen to her first intuitions, that's when she'd get into trouble. She had feelings about things.

"She says, 'Tell the truth, May!' Tell May to tell the truth in the book. Don't stop the book. Tell her that I am really here. I am very busy and I am deeply concerned over my children. She says she is with you a good deal and she laughs a good deal with you. She says she wants you to know she was in an immediate plane of transition at the fatal car crash. She gazed at her body in horror that anyone should see it like that. She says you and she have been very close, very close, and you are sisters and your destiny has been intertwined. 'When May passes to this plane we will be together and will seek adventure and life here and will come back together.'

"She says she is and has always been the seeker of truth. 'This will tell May, so she will know I am here talking to her. Tell May to spare nothing, to tell the truth in the book, and it must be finished.'

"She says she came tonight to give evidence and not to grieve, for 'this life is unbelieveably beautiful. Grief is a waste of time and keeps people earthbound.

"'I came tonight because this woman is a psychic. I have been trying and trying to get through to you. This is the first channel through which I have been able to get to you. My teenage daughter suffered great emotional trauma. I am so sorry about it. It grieves me even now. The things that happened will leave scars on her for a long time.

"'We both wanted the same things, May and I. Her happiness is yet to come, in the kind of a man we both wanted. I feel pure happiness.

"'I regret that I took Mickey so lightly in life. I realize that he loved me for me, and not for gain, when we were married.'"

At this point I asked Yvonne to describe Jayne to me again. She said, "She is ten times more beautiful. Her hair is still long and pale golden blonde.

"But listen," Yvonne said, "Jayne is talking. She says, 'It is a mistake when people think you don't have a love in another life. You are much more aware. You are not alone. You meet love but there is no sex. It's completion, much more beautiful and more satisfying. It has not happened to me yet. One day I will have this here. I have not seen your mother (whom she knew well and who had died in 1958) as she is on a higher spiritual plane.

"'Passing over was quick and beautiful except when I looked to see my body. I thought if only I could have stopped people from seeing me like that!

"'Clarify the truth of everything in the book. Explain that there was nothing selfish in Mickey's motives toward me, and I look back and realize that now. Tell him to see Maria gets a father's unselfish love.

"'Tell all of the conversations we had the night before my death and everything I confided to you at all times during the years.'"

Yvonne was drained emotionally and slumped to the floor. I looked at Princess, who was alert and staring for the entire time. Now she relaxed and cuddled down to take a nap.

It all seemed incredible.

I thought of the eight psychics who had been making themselves known to me during the last eight days. This had never happened to me before. Then Yvonne came and here was Jayne!

I suddenly felt compelled to return to the book. I bought a ream of standard white typewriter paper. Opening it, to my amazement, it was "Jayne Mansfield pink," the color of the Pink Palace and her highly publicized, favorite color. Was this coincidence?

I sat down and wrote this preface just as it happened. I gave a copy to Yvonne and asked her to take it to her lawyer and sign it. "People will think this is publicity for the book, and that we manufactured this," I said. Yvonne signed and her attorney approved.

I put this preface safely away for awhile. When I next took the material out to start working, I glanced at the front pages of this "preface" to find them marked with drops of thin red blood! I screamed in horror! Subsequent pages were dripped with this strange kind of thin blood. Absolutely no one had access to the manuscript which had been securely locked away. How? Why? Where? When? By what? By whom?

This book is written with neither malice nor bias for anyone concerned. It is simply reporting the truth as Jayne had insisted and as she requested it after death. Yvonne and I were both completely without previous experience of such phenomena. I have never delved into such phenomena—nor do I wish to do so in the future.

I went to London to do further research on material Jayne had told me was there and that was pertinent to the book. It's all here.

May Mann
Hollywood, Calif.

# CHAPTER I

A tourist bus loaded with sightseers slowed down on Sunset Blvd. as it approached Carolwood. It was early July 1967. The driver began his spiel into the mike. "At the right folks, is the heavily shrubbed and tree-ed estate rented by Elizabeth Taylor and Richard Burton, when they were filming *Virginia Wolff* in Hollywood!

"We are now driving half way between Bel Air and Beverly Hills. Hollywood is a few miles east straight ahead.

"But here's where all the millionaires and super movie stars live. We're in the heart of it all.

"At your left, see the famous Pink Palace of Jayne Mansfield, who was killed in that great tragedy in Mississippi!" The bus idled almost to a stop. The passengers craned their necks out of the windows to gape at the imposing two-story pink stucco mansion with its tiled roof. It was partially hidden by the tall palm trees whose fronds hung dry and dreary in the breeze behind a twelve-foot high, black iron fence. The huge front gate was decorated with hearts and emblazoned with three foot high initials "J.M."!

June grass and weeds had taken over the driveway between the fence and the road. However by humping your shoulders, you could look directly through the iron bars of the gate and see the massive carved wooden front door. It was closed and somewhat shielded by a ten foot span of brick and sprouting vines. This was a replica, as every Jayne Mansfield fan well knew, of the Appian Way outside of Rome. Mickey Hargitay, in the last days of his marriage to Jayne, had constructed it to please Jayne.

Women, men, and children carefully and curiously scrutinized the scene, and then the windows of the house, in the hope of seeing someone or something. The bus pulled slightly off the road and came to a full stop.

"Yes, many a time Miss Mansfield herself would stand on that grass. She'd wave and smile friendly like at everyone here on the bus," recounted the driver. "See that balcony up there at the left? Well, I've often seen her in a bikini with her long yellow hair flowing down to her backside, sunning her famous curves up there. Many a time," he drawled. "Jayne Mansfield loved folks. She is the only movie star who never tried to hide from people. She was a lovely girl!"

The passengers suddenly riveted their attention on two figures coming out of the pink mansion. One was a black woman in a maid's uniform, the other, a young girl with dark hair and dark glasses. The girl kissed the black woman, walked down the drive-way, through the iron gates and past the busload of sightseers. She stopped once and turned to look back at the house and then went on, oblivious of the curious onlookers.

Jayne Marie Mansfield, Jayne Mansfield's oldest daughter, now just a little more than 16, was leaving the Pink Palace for the last time. It was no longer the happy, gay home of which her mother had dreamed, and it hadn't been for a long time.

Any hopes of reviving the lost gaiety were destroyed by the tragic death of Hollywood's super-star, Jayne Mansfield.

# CHAPTER II

It was the grim thirties and America was picking herself up by the bootstraps from the crash of 1929. Men were no longer standing in soup lines. Franklin Delano Roosevelt used the radio for his weekly fireside chats with Mr. and Mrs. America. Prohibition was repealed. Unemployed men could join C. C. camps to be fed, clothed and earn a living wage.

People who grew up in the roaring twenties like Zelda and Scott Fitzgerald, the Duke of Windsor, Fatty Arbuckle, Flo Ziegfeld, Jimmy Walker, Olive Thomas, the Morgan twins, and elite, rah rah men and women, whose unrestrained pleasure-bent lives were deplored by the preceding generation, now had their own children. How they would mold and shape the lives of this new generation was the question asked throughout the country.

The Legion of Decency was inaugurated by a committee of Catholic bishops. Its purpose was to arouse public opinion against "morally objectional" pictures, and to urge people not to patronize them.

John Dillinger, bank robber, made headlines; the Philippines were granted independence, the Dionne Quintuplets arrived; Engelbert Dolfuss, chancellor of Austria, was shot presumably by Nazi conspirators, and Italy threatened Ethopia; Will Rogers was killed in a plane crash.

In Hollywood, Darryl Zanuck, who would one day make Jayne a star at 20th Century Fox, became production chief of Warner Brothers. Gangster films were the vogue. Marlene Dietrich began wearing pants. Gretta Garbo, John Gilbert, Mae West, Sonja Henie, Norma Shearer, Tyrone Power, Alice Faye, Constance Bennett, Jean Harlow, Clark Gable, Joan Crawford, Katherine Hepburn, and Spencer Tracy were the film idols.

It was into this generation that Jayne Mansfield was born. She would grow up fascinated with the movies, would avidly read the movie fan magazines, and would, one day, be a film idol in her own right.

Jayne was born Vera Jane Palmer on April 19th, 1933, in Bryn Mawr, Pennsylvania on the Philadelphia Main Line. Her father was a lawyer. Jayne tells it: "My father wanted a son to carry on the family name and tradition, because Daddy always said he was going to be President some day. He was brilliant and he had that kind of determination and strength. I have inherited this determination and drive from him.

"I also know how to handle people. I had to develop unusual diplomacy—right from the beginning to get people to like me. All of my childhood I was criticized by Momma and all of her relatives. I wanted to please people and hear them compliment me instead of shaking their heads and saying 'Oh, Jayne, No!'

"We had an average small white frame house in an average middle class neighborhood in Phillipsburg, New Jersey. My mother was very strict, too strict! She had taught elementary school, and rules and regulations were natural to her. I know she loved me, but she expected perfection from a little child. I admit I was a handful right from the beginning. I had such an imagination and was always telling fabulous stories. I looked out at the hot dusty roads in the summer. I imagined they were beautiful winding roads in some far away place like the French Riviera, or in Italy. There was always a tall, dark, handsome knight coming to rescue me on his white horse. Later he came in a big white Cadillac!

"Since I had such an unusual imagination, I saw everything differently than most people. They said I told lies. I did not. I have always had the guts to be truthful. I just saw things more spectacularly. Momma was always after me with, 'Is that the truth, Jayne? Are you telling the truth, Jayne? Are you sure, Jayne? If you are not telling the truth you know you will get a spanking! It used to ring in my ears.'

"I had few playmates. The ones I had seemed childish. I was restless and I grew bored easily. At the University of Texas it was discovered I had an I.Q. of 163. Everyone laughed when I'd mention it. I cooled it. In Hollywood, I realized it would ruin my feminine, sexy 'image.' Who wants a brainy blonde?

"I was always dancing to the radio and play-acting. I wasn't quite sure what I wanted to be. Sometimes I thought I'd become another Shirley Temple! I loved her. Later I played that I was like Lana Turner. I liked the sexy sweet way she looked. In Hollywood, I was accused of trying to imitate Marilyn Monroe. Actually, I was completely different. But Jackie Kennedy imitated my voice on T.V. when she was in the White House.

"I loved to sit on Daddy's lap and have him hold me, hug me, caress me, and kiss me. I could never get enough love to feel secure. My mother would often scold both of us. She said it wasn't lady-like to be sitting on a man's lap, even Daddy's, all of the time. She'd say that I got his trousers wrinkled. Many times as he told me bed-time stories he'd pinch my cheek and whisper in my ear, 'I'm glad you are a girl Jaynie . . . I love you so much—we are not going to have any more babies—just you!' I loved him. I'd get him to tell me over and over and over that he loved me.

"I was my mother's pride—and her pain in the neck. I could never please her for long. I used to try so hard when I was little—but we simply didn't relate. When I grew older, I gave up trying.

"Momma had me taking piano and violin lessons. I worked hard because I was a little afraid of her and I wanted her approval. I never fully got it.

"Everything in her house had to be in perfect order at all times. No one could relax and just let go and have a good time for fear of getting something out of place. 'This is *my* home,' she'd remind me. I promised myself that someday I'd grow up and have a home of my own, a pink palace, pink because it's such a happy color—- and everyone could do just as they pleased. Everyone would enjoy themselves in my home.

"One day we were driving up a hill and I was sitting on Momma's lap. I was only three. My father laughed at something I said, and in that second, he slumped over the wheel with a heart attack!

"I shall never forget seeing his head fall back. Momma jabbed the brake with her foot and grabbed the wheel, to get control of the car.

"We sat there for quite awhile—but my father was dead.

"My father's death made a great impression on me. I was always asking to go to the cemetery to visit his grave. I'd sit there and talk to him. I'd cry and cry. 'Daddy you understand me and Momma doesn't,' I'd sob. I'd lay on the grass of his grave and kiss the grass over him. He'd know I was kissing him. He was the only man I ever knew who really loved me unselfishly—who never used me for personal gain.

"I had a tremendous, sometimes overpowering need for love and affection. Momma probably felt it inside of her heart, but she was never demonstrative. I picked up all the stray dogs and cats I could find, and brought them home. I had to have something in my arms to love, or I felt terribly lonely.

"Momma wouldn't let me keep the strays. I shall never forget when I sneaked a cute fluff-ball of a kitten into bed with me one night. It made a wet spot on the sheets! Momma was enraged!

"I promised myself that when I grew up with a home of my own, I'd have all of the dogs and cats I wanted. They would run through the home and enjoy it with me. I have never forgotten when one little cat got emotional, and messed on the front room carpet. Momma, to my horror, rubbed its nose in the mess! She said she was doing it to teach it a lesson! I gathered the poor little cat to my bosom to comfort it. Of course I got some of the mess on my clean dress. Momma was furious! I ran outside and hid with the cat, cleaning it off and comforting it as best I could. Of course I got a spanking.

"I didn't hate Momma. Instead I felt sorry for her—for her narrow outlook and lack of compassion. She couldn't help it."

Jayne and I compiled this chapter on her childhood over several months. We'd meet for lunch at 20th Century Fox Studios and I'd jot down what she remembered pre-Hollywood.

Jayne saw her first motion picture when she was six years old. She told me how it affected her. "I came home and imitated the stars in some of the scenes. I knew then I was going to be a movie star some day. When Momma saw me acting in front of the mirror in the bedroom I told her that I was going to be a movie star. 'I am going to be famous like Daddy was going to be famous,' I said. 'I'll be famous for both of us.' Momma laughed.

"By now Momma had married Harry Peers, a nice man who was a traveling sales engineer and we lived in Dallas.

"One day I borrowed Momma's high-heeled slippers, and some lipstick. I was bent on making myself look like a movie star. 'The only trouble is my name,' I thought. 'I should have one like "Rosebud" or "Juliet" or something special to be a movie star! I can't be just plain "Jane"!'

"Momma, oddly enough, decided to humor me. She agreed.

'Well, if it will make you happy, you can put a "Y" in the middle of your name, and be "Jayne." That will be different'.

"I liked that. Then I overheard her talking to one of her bridge club ladies, and she said 'Imagine Jayne wanting to be a movie star.' She made it sound sinful! 'She'll outgrow it,' she said. 'She'll go to college and become a school teacher—she does have a good mind!' How often Momma ridiculed my dreams of becoming an actress.

"I read all of the movie magazines. I read about Joan Crawford who was a waitress and she made her dreams come true. I knew I could do it too.

"I looked at the little kid in the mirror with the mousey brown hair, and horn-rimmed glasses and I vowed that I would be beautiful some day. And I would be a movie star. A Big Star!

"I continued with my lessons. I played in violin and piano recitals. And when Momma entertained her bridge club, I always played a solo or two when she asked me.

"Momma was the important woman of our house. She never let me forget she was boss. I was always in her shadow. Every time I tried to step out on my own, I was in trouble with her. I began to realize that when I became a star—some day—and eclipsed her, she would be very jealous of me. There was nothing I could do about it. I was always sorry that my mother and I could not have had a close relationship. I promised myself that when I had children they would be my confidantes, and we would always be close and affectionate. I'd give them all of the love I never had when I was growing up. Momma probably had it for me—but she didn't show it.

"I suddenly changed when I became twelve years old. I changed overnight from the skinny little girl to one with curves popping out all over. One of the school teachers, a man, started finding excuses to put his arms around me when he talked to me. And the boys began to whistle. My dresses became tighter, and I loved the attention. Momma kept trying to get me to wear a size larger dress or sweater or skirt to grow into. But I liked the tight feel of clothes on my body. It was like a caress.

"A lady teacher sent a note home to Momma to call her. She suggested that Momma put a brassiere on me. Momma called her and apologized. She hadn't realized the need, since I was only past eleven. But now she did. I wore brassieres until I was fourteen and then I abandoned them forever to be free. I like to feel my body free as though I am floating in air. I hate underthings. I loved to sleep nude. This shocked my mother, who insisted I wear a nightgown.

"I always said if I could ever get out of Dallas, I would. I'd start the day looking pretty, and then the perspiration would pour down my face and ruin my make-up. Momma thoroughly disapproved of make-up. I would put it on in the ladies room or at a rest room of the nearest service station. Before going home, I'd retrace my steps and wash it off.

"When I was fourteen, the boys were hanging around our house. Momma said it was disgusting and I wasn't to date until I was at least over sixteen. She couldn't get rid of the boys and I didn't want to. I loved their admiration and the candy bars they'd bring me.

"One night, I told my mother I was going to a girl's party. I didn't mention there would be boys there.

The kids were all older than I was. I was given a glass of what I thought was lemonade. Actually it was a vodka collins.

"Drinking was something I always said would never affect me. I wouldn't waste so much time being crocked. I loved life. I wanted to live and not watch it from the side lines. It was a hot night. I had my third 'lemonade' and passed out. The next thing I knew someone was pouring black coffee down me and I was throwing up. We were out on a porch and I was leaning over the bannisters. Suddenly I fell, unconscious.

"One of the boys put me in his car and drove to a parking place so the fresh air blowing into the car would make me come to. I can't remember the details, but I was raped. I couldn't tell my mother.

"When my period didn't arrive on schedule, my worst fear was confirmed. I was pregnant! What should I do? Even if I could,—I would never have an abortion. To me that is murder! I'd have my baby. But what about Momma?

"I felt I should get married right away. It wasn't difficult to select a husband at school. Paul J. Mansfield was one of the best looking students in school.

"I saw him at church. I made it a point to walk out when he did. He had to notice me. I smiled and we became acquainted. Two months later we were married. Since I was fourteen we had to lie about my age for the license. But I looked easily eighteen.

"It all seemed so easy to get married, but when I got home, I didn't have the courage to tell my mother! I just couldn't take one of her scenes. Paul would see me every day, and take me home every night. I had an eleven o'clock curfew, and if I didn't make it there would be a big uproar, so I always made it on time.

"I was over three months pregnant, and I was beginning to show. I had to tell my mother. She suddenly was very suspicious and so the scene came anyway. Except I told her I was already married and showed her my marriage license.

"Momma said that I had ruined my life and her life! And what would all of her friends be saying if I had had to get married! It was awful, and I was glad I could walk out of the door to Paul's comforting arms.

"Momma said I had made my bed and I would have to lie in it, and to expect no help from her. I assured her I wouldn't bother her again. Then she relented and she bought me a pretty white wedding dress and we had a wedding of sorts. But I always remembered her telling me never to expect help from her.

"I continued going to school until the time Jayne Marie was born. I became used to the snide remarks and the other kids giggles and whispers behind my back. I didn't care.

"Paul and I had a rough time. I peddled photo albums door-to-door and he took odd jobs, swept floors and sold magazines. We took turns taking care of Jayne Marie so we could both attend classes. Many times I would have to take Jayne Marie and her diapers and nursing bottles to class with me.

"Paul fully knew of my ambition to become a movie star. He had to go to summer camp for ROTC Training. His parents agreed to take care of Jayne Marie. And I went off to U.C.L.A. with Hollywood next door, for a tri-mester course in dramatics.

"I was registered in a woman's dormitory and I worked hard. I was lonely, even though it was fine in the daytime! Paul and I wrote letters every day and I hounded the mailbox. But nights were the loneliest. When I saw two hamsters in a pet shop window, I couldn't resist them. I bought them and skipped lunch, which was good for my figure anyway. I didn't think they'd multiply so fast. Certainly I have never believed in birth control. Soon I had two dozen hamsters running around. Worse still, two of them made a mistake and snuggled into the house mother's bed one night instead of mine. The dorm made me give the poor little babies away. After that, I'd visit the animal shelters and the pounds and pet the animals. They needed love as badly as I did.

"Paul had agreed that I would be known as *Miss* Jayne Mansfield when I went to college. This would save me a lot of questions and embarrassment. Everyone began insisting that I enter the 'Miss America contest.' I realized this was an opportunity, so I agreed. I was so excited when I was chosen in the local final twenty. I made the mistake of telling Paul, and he demanded that I either drop out or else! So I had to resign. I never knew whether I would have won or not.

"Paul and I made a compromise. I would go with him through his two years training on active duty as an army officer. Then he would spend two years with me in Hollywood to give me my chance to be a film star. We both knew that some day I was to come into a big inheritance from my grandfather. I vowed I would spend every cent of it becoming a film star. I could never be happy again unless I at least tried. Paul agreed. He also agreed that if I made a hit he would become my manager."

"The Army life," Jayne said, "wasn't a drag." "I was constantly reading Shakespeare and practicing acting. I also exercised daily to attain the most feminine figure in the world. I still had my mind on winning a contest for this was the quick way to get a studio contract.

"My exercising had to be on the lawn in front of our house on the Army base—where else? I couldn't go to a gymnasium because I couldn't afford baby-sitters for Jayne Marie. I simply put on a bathing suit or some leotards and I'd go out in the sunshine and go to work for a couple of hours.

"The only trouble I had was that I always gathered an audience. That was alright because being watched gave me poise and self assurance.

"The Colonel's wife, however, got upset at all of the attention I was receiving. She told her husband and her husband told Paul that I had to stop. It seemed my daily exercise was upsetting the whole army base. Some of Paul's fellow officers or superiors would always drop by. I could have been a regular Mati-Hari. As it was, two or three officers were shipped out because their wives thought they were becoming too attached to me.

"Paul became more and more jealous and less and less attentive. When I tried to be affectionate with him, he didn't always respond. Then Paul was sent to Korea. Jayne Marie and I went back to Dallas, and I enrolled at Southern Methodist University.

"Now I had Paul's army allotment and life wasn't so difficult. I didn't have to peddle things door-to-door to make a living. I enjoyed my studies and I made straight A's.

"When Paul came back I was already packed to go to Hollywood before he even set foot in the house. He thought I might have changed my mind about Hollywood by then. But he was stuck with his promises.

"During the time Paul was gone, I had collected quite a few

animals: two dogs, three cats, four birds, a beautiful white rabbit for Easter, a duck and a Gila Monster. The Gila never bit me, but when I learned he could be fatal, I had to take him out to the swamps and let him go free.

"We found an apartment in Westwood, after a long hot drive from Dallas. Even while Paul was unpacking the car, I went to a telephone booth and began putting dimes in, making calls to agents listed in the Hollywood directory. I didn't have any luck until I decided to call Paramount Studios direct.

"I was put through to Mr. Milt Lewis, the talent Chief. I told his secretary I was a beauty contest winner from Dallas, and had newly arrived to become a movie star. She was so surprised, she gave me an appointment.

"I worked hard to impress them. I looked like a sexpot but I could read Shakespeare. I prepared some lines from *Romeo and Juliet* and Shaw's *Saint Joan.* Everyone was impressed and surprised! I thought I had a contract when they gave me a screen test. But I was never called back, Every time I called I was told, 'Don't call us, we'll call you when we have something.'

"It was the Hollywood run-around. But it didn't discourage me.

"I realized Paul's army savings wouldn't last forever. I started selling cooking ware door to door. I applied at Grauman's Chinese Theater for an ushers job. I was thrilled when I got it. This would enable me to see and be seen in Hollywood."

# CHAPTER III

Paul was disgusted. Every day he'd say to Jayne, "Haven't you had enough?" He wanted to cut out for back home in Dallas. Jayne's mother wrote warning letters that she would lose her husband. Even Paul's parents were losing patience. The red, flashy Buick convertible that the young Mansfields had driven to Hollywood, which Jayne said, "announces we're going places big," was requiring repairs. "We just weren't making a regular salary selling kitchen ware."

Paul argued, "Forget it Jayne! We are college trained. Why starve in Hollywood for nothing? Your chances, Jaynie, are so slim!"

"I knew he didn't like to sit home and baby-sit Jayne Marie, so I took her along with me almost everywhere. And when I managed to get some money together, I made a down payment on a used Jaguar, and had it painted pink! Paul was furious. We needed the money for food, to go to the dentist, for new tires for the Buick. I was building 'My Image,' " Jayne explained.

"It was really rough by now—our marriage. Our communication was gone. Paul forgot our bargain—Hollywood for two years! I only managed to hang on by having the guts to stay myself—to be all woman! I refused to quarrel, or say, 'Go to Hell. I'll do it on my own!' I have always used the power of complete femininity: speak softly, tenderly under all circumstances. Even when I was in complete disagreement with Paul I'd pull my claws in. I based my whole life and career on being sweet and very feminine! No matter what was happening, I refused to become a nervous, high-strung woman with a high voice, excitable, hard, harsh. So, what could Paul do, but stay on. A bargain is a bargain!

"We were living up in Benedict Canyon in a little house on stilts. We were on the poor side of the road. Big mansions dotted the other side. 'Some day we'll have one of those,' I'd tell Jayne Marie. She was too little to understand, but she'd nod her head.

"I discovered one day the big movie star Steve Cochran lived in a house much like ours down the road on Yokum Avenue. I dressed like Daisy Mae and went to his Lil Abner party on Sadie Hawkins Day. Steve lived the informal, open house life always with a couple of pretty starlets to keep his place clean. When I went there, I always took Jayne Marie along as my chaperone. But it was exciting for me to have a real movie star for my next door neighbor.  ·

"Paul complained that I wasn't being a good wife. I was too intent on my career. These were the months of misery, despair, unrest, always trying to please Paul, to take care of Jayne Marie, and to keep on trying against unforeseen day-to-day disappointments. There were so many girls in Hollywood trying too. Most of them were single. They didn't have a baby to take care of, or a house to clean and meals to get, or a husband who was getting angrier and angrier. I couldn't blame him. But that was what we were in Hollywood for—my big try. I had waited 6 years for it. I'd keep reminding Paul that it was now or never at all!

"I went to the modeling agencies—all of them. Some gave me jobs. But not enough. I was the sexy type, and I could pose in bikinis. But I soon learned that movie starlets would pose in them free, to get their pictures in the papers. And when you did get a job, you had to fight for your honor. Whoever hired you always had sex on his mind. I was a married woman, although I never said so. I had no intention of becoming an adultress. My religious training from home was still strongly with me.

"I had a body yes, but I also had brains and an in-born stubborness. I was determined to work things out and make it—my way.

"I hadn't had any luck house-to-house selling with the aluminum ware for a whole week. I had to have money to buy food. And not only food, but gas for my little, pink Jag. By now I had a gimmick. Pink was my color because, 'It makes me happy. It is bright and gay. "Mansfield pink" will become famous,' I'd tell anyone who'd listen. I put pink curtains up in our little canyon house. I called it 'Mansfield's Madness.' Now I had something to intrigue the photographers. 'Come up for a drink and paint me pink.' I'd invite anyone who had a camera. I'd add I would be happy to pose for any layouts they'd like. I was desperate. I was running out of time.

"Paul set a time limit on my career. He now hated the idea of my being a movie star. He only wanted me as a wife. My place was at home. He was sick of the whole thing. But I had to be more. I would have died with all of my energy and mind going a mile a minute if I had had to stay home. I could have the children, yes! I was equipped for children and a full-time career, too.

"One night when things were really hopeless I applied at a model studio on Santa Monica Blvd. They are still there dingy little places. A man would come in and be shown the photos of the models. He would select which one he wanted. For twenty dollars a half hour he could photograph the model. I didn't realize what kind of place this one was. I was told I had to pose nude. I said, 'Not entirely?' The manager said, Of course. And there is a customer waiting. He pushed me into a room. I held my robe around me, frightened. And I looked into the face of a middle-aged man. He smiled.

"I stood there, while he got his camera ready. I knew I was supposed to drop my robe, but I couldn't do it. I just couldn't do it! I didn't know what to do. I began to cry.

"'I didn't know I was to pose in the all-together,' I told him. 'I need the money so badly. I have a little girl waiting for me at home, and we are out of food. I don't know what to do.'

"The man looked so surprised. He asked me a few questions. Finally he said, 'Here put your clothes on. I'll take you home.' He paid the fee anyway and he gave me ten dollars too. He drove me to a supermarket and bought a bag of groceries for me. He never even asked to kiss me.

"I have always had a good effect on men. Few of them have tried too hard to take advantage of me. They see I am honest and I am trying to do my best. Very often they turn around and help me.

"Every day I would set out on a new plan to become a movie star. Every night I'd come home more discouraged. There was no one to keep up my morale, only me. My mother thought Hollywood was sinful. My husband hated it. I wasn't being fair to my child nor to him, I was constantly reminded. I knew I could make it up to them in every way, if they'd just help me get the chance.

"It was a very hot summer day and I started out again, wondering what to do, where to go next. One of the photographers I had met at Grauman's Chinese Theatre had told me, 'You are a sexy broad. But you need big apples!' Before he could explain what he meant, he was off to shoot a picture of Loretta Young arriving! I kept thinking about the big apple bit. I was so naive. I thought maybe, it meant that if I carried a big apple that would give me the appearance of Eve in the Garden of Eden.

"On this day, as I passed a market, I bought a red apple, for luck. I was walking along shining it with my hanky when I heard a whistle! A news boy had whistled! 'You are a dish,' he said admiringly. The apple had done it. I was so happy that someone thought I was pretty and sexy! It was the only encouragement I had received in days. I wanted to give him something. Before I knew it, I had handed him the apple. 'Are you the Apple Queen?' he asked.

"I explained to him that I had been told I needed big apples for luck or something. He was only fifteen, but how he laughed! 'They meant you need to put some falsies under your bra,' he said. 'All the starlets do,' he explained.

"But I'm pretty good as I am," I told him.

"All the dolls with the big boobs get photographed," he said with candid honesty. "Yours could be bigger, lady!"

"As I walked along I looked into the store windows at my reflection. I would do something about that too, I decided. My measurements then were 38-21-35.

"One of the photographers introduced me to Frank Worth who was with INP, a wire service photo syndicate. Frank was a big, friendly guy, like a Newfoundland puppy. I liked him. I asked if there was any way he could help me. He said he had lots of connections and he'd see.

"One day Frank called to tell me a friend of his, Bert Kaiser, was making a movie. He had Lawrence Tierney and John Carradine signed. He was looking for a sexy girl to play the feminine lead. Maybe she would be me!

"Frank told me that he and his friend would be up to Mansfield's Madness that night and he'd make the introduction. This meant I'd have to ask Paul to stay in the other room or suggest he go out so no one would suspect I was married. That would kill any interest in me as a young, glamorous starlet!

"But the plans got changed for lack of finances, and Frank said I'd have to wait.

"I had bleached my hair blonde from my natural brunette. Paul hated it. He was still terribly possessive, and he kept referring to me as 'my wife,' when we had made the pact that I was to be

"Miss" as far as my career was concerned.

"He'd keep saying, 'When I married you, you had brown hair and you weighed 138 pounds. That's the way I married you, and that's the way I love you.'

"By then I had dieted and was svelte in the movie star tradition.

"One night when I got in very late after appearing at the Palladium for a charity benefit, I found Paul who'd stayed home to baby-sit Jayne Marie, more disgruntled than ever. There wasn't anything I did that pleased him by then. He also hated my pets—-my great dane and my poodles. He was furious when they let go on the carpets and blamed me. I wouldn't give them up.

"'Man-like,' he said on this night, 'It's either me or your career. Choose right now.' I didn't want to quarrel so I just walked into the bedroom and shut the door. He packed and left for Dallas. Actually I was relieved. But now I had to face it. I was terribly alone. It was like being put out to sea: sink or swim!

"Many days Jayne Marie and I lived on pork and beans, and less. At least she was always fed. When there wasn't enough food for both of us, it was good for my figure. By now, I had an eighteen inch waist—through going hungry!

"I saw a poster, one day after Paul left, on a light pole on Sunset Blvd. that read, 'Enter Miss California Contest. Entrants should register with the *Los Angeles Daily News.*' There was no gas or money now for my car. I hopped the first bus and went to the newspaper office. I asked the first man I saw outside the building where to go to enter the contest. 'Better take off that wedding band,' he advised, 'if you're going to be "Miss California." Beauty contests are for single girls!'

"I put my wedding rig in my purse. I never wore it after that.

"I found the desk where I was to sign in an as entrant. I have been 'Miss Texas Tomato' and 'Miss July Fourth' and . . . I went on happily and really enthused.

"'Where are your pictures in a bathing suit?' the editor asked. I told him I didn't have any.

"'Well,' he paused, then decided, 'Stand over against that back-drop. I'll have a Daily News man shoot you. You can go into the washroom and put on your bathing suit.'

"'I don't have one,' I told him sadly. 'And I don't have any money to go and buy one. Can't you just take me in my dress, if I raise the skirt high?'

"The man sighed and said, 'Okay. Here take this five bucks and go out and get a suit. Com back and we'll take your picture! I have a hunch you'll win.'

"I was afraid to take the money. I hesitated. He got mad.

"'Take the god-damn money,' he swore. 'I don't want your body. Can't you recognize a decent guy when you see one?'

"I realized he meant it. I took the money and went out and bought a pink bikini. I came back and put it on in the washroom. As my picture was being snapped, the cameraman grinned. 'That's the best five dollars he ever spent. You're a honey. I know you're going to win. You can at least give me a kiss.' I did happily!

"I was so excited. The next morning I was up early and to the news stands. Sure enough, there I was on Page 8 with the heading 'Miss California Contestant Jayne Mansfield.' The newsman saw the animation on my face. 'That you?' he asked. I said happily, 'Yes.' I bought twenty copies. I would send them to all of my family and friends in Texas. I just knew that now I was on my way!

"I sent a copy, special delivery, to Paul in Texas. I sent one to my mother, my grandmother and everyone I knew. They didn't believe in me, but I wanted to share my first success with them.

"Now everyone began calling me up; the photographers boys I had met! They were all so encouraging. They just knew I would win. If I did, they said I could go into the National Miss America contest, and win fifty thousand dollars! My chances were very good because I could play the piano and violin. If I won, I was sure to wind up with a movie contract.

"As usual came the big let-down. I was always building up to them. I received a wire back from Paul. I opened it so happily, knowing how happy he was for *my* success—'the star,' for *our* success. The wire read: Forbid you to enter Miss California Contest. You are a married woman with a child. If you don't disqualify yourself, I will take steps to see that the judges know the truth.

"I cried all night. Jayne Marie, who didn't know what it was all about, tried to comfort me. My whole world had ended. The next morning, I realized that reverses need only be temporary. I wired back to Paul, 'You win.' I realized now that he didn't love me really. He only wanted what he wanted, or he would have wanted me to be happy. He could have the money I'd make if only I could be a movie star! Meanwhile, there was no money in my purse. I was flat broke again and I had to get food for Jayne Marie. Whenever there was not enough to eat for me, I'd say to myself, 'Good Jayne. Now you'll have a real tiny waist.'

"I put up little cards on the nearby supermarket bulletin board saying, 'Piano and violin lessons at your home. Expert teacher. One dollar half hour.' I added my telephone number. I didn't have a piano. But I did at least have my violin with me. If I could get pupils, Jayne Marie and I wouldn't have to apply for County aid! I couldn't write home to Paul or to Momma for money.

"It was with real humility that I went back to the Daily News and looked up my editorial friend who had bought me the bikini. I confessed to him why I had to resign. Then I began crying my heart out. Some newsmen gathered around me. They were all sympathetic. 'I have wasted your five dollars,' I told my benefactor. 'But some day I'll try to pay you back when I earn money. If you have any children, I can give them music lessons,' I offered.

"'Just give me a smile, and let me see you in the bathing suit sometime,' he said. 'That will be fine with me.'

"The very next day I received a call from Frank Worth. He said the picture deal was now on. The film was entitled *Hangover*. He and the producer drove up to Mansfield's Madness, and we celebrated my contract for $100 a week to make the picture. Frank advanced me five dollars but I didn't tell him it was for food. I just said I hadn't been able to get a check cashed and could he loan me five.

"I was to play a sexy girl of the streets, sensual and bad. It was a quick picture, made in ten days. I didn't even get two hundred dollars. But I loved every minute of being in makeup; even when I had to lay on the hot sidewalk playing my own dead body for an hour at a time; the budget didn't allow stand-ins or a dummy corpse.

"'Now you can say you have starred in your first picture!' Frank told me.

"The night the picture wound up Jayne Marie, Frank and I celebrated with the corned beef hash plate and cokes at Coffee Dan's on Hollywood Blvd. Then we went to a movie at a little theater. Said Frank, 'I'll come in here a year from now and see you, a big movie star on this screen!' A year later, he actually went into that same theater to see me co-starring with Cary Grant in a 20th Century Fox movie.

"Now I had many opportunities for picture layouts. Everyone tried to help me with any contacts they had.

"I should have an agent, I was told. I called several of them, but no one wanted me unless I had film footage, pictures, a scrap book and proven experience. It always came to, 'Call back after you have done something more.' I went to all of the studio casting offices. I couldn't even get inside. I never heard any more from Paramount. I was getting desperate again.

"I was lonely inside now that my five-year marriage with Paul was over. I realized I hadn't made him happy. Half of the time the dishes weren't washed and the kitchen was dirty, for each morning I started out in full pursuit of my dream. I'd pray for help and for inspiration. I guess a lot of people think that a girl who shows her bosom and wears tight dresses can't be close to God. God has always been close to me. Only he knew what was in my heart.

"When it seemed there was no place else for me to go, except back to Texas with Paul, my telephone rang and it was Frank

Worth. 'The picture's going to be run tonight. You can see yourself up there on the screen!'

"I was beside myself with joy. At last a foot in the door and as a star too! I loved me up there on the screen. Being an actress. And a star! 'I love you Jayne Mansfield,' I told "my image." 'I'll work hard for you! Nothing, or no one, could ever make me let you down!'

"'I'll celebrate my next picture in champagne,' I told Frank. Now it was cokes all around. Jayne Marie went to sleep in Frank's lap during the showing. He was not a romance—just a pal. The title of the picture, *Hangover*, was changed to 'The Female Jungle.' Nothing happened for weeks after that.

"I finally got a job at Ciro's, the most famous night club in town as a photographer's assistant. I'd snap pictures, even of Errol Flynn and one time of Joan Crawford. I'd take them to the dark-room, develop and print them and return them to the customers. I met quite a few stars that way. One night, my benefactor from the *Daily News* was there.

"Newspaper people are very important and I have always believed in the power of the press and publicity. I learned quickly how to use that power and to cooperate with the press fully at all times. It became a love affair. I have never let the press down, even at times when I have been greatly criticized for my publicity.

"My *Daily News* benefactor said to call a producer, Mr. Jacobs, at Warner Brothers in the morning. Next day I was ushered into Mr. Jacobs' office in time to go to lunch with him in the studio commissary. I was walking on air. I only wished I had some marvelous clothes to wear. I knew mine left much to be desired. I had to make do with what I had.

"During lunch I stole glances at Doris Day and James Garner sitting nearby giving press interviews. Someday this would be happening to me. Maybe next week even, if I signed a contract. James Garner was lunching with the columnist, May Mann. 'I'd love to have her for a friend,' I thought. Well, someday maybe, although girls never liked me. But men did—and men were more important.

"Mr Jacobs told me the odds. Over 10,000 beautiful girls come from all parts of the world to Hollywood each year, he said, to become movie stars! He suggested I give up and get married and have a family. I told him I had already tried that. Now I was determined to have a career. He took me on a courtesy visit to the sets. He said, 'If anything comes up, I'll call you.'

"I met important men at Ciro's. Some offered to help me. Usually they'd ask me to their apartment for dinner. I knew what the price tag was. I declined. I wasn't a whore. I was a nice girl, trying honestly to establish a career.

"I was a swinger after Paul left. I began dating lots of men. Often they'd have to include Jayne Marie on our dates, since I had no money for babysitters. Some didn't mind. Some did. Some tried to make it with me, even when she was asleep on the back seat of the car."

# CHAPTER IV

Jayne was now at a loss for money for clothes. She desperately needed new clothes. Most of the time she wore skirts and sweaters or blue jeans. And it was in this rather forlorn and shabby ensemble that she walked into Emeson's, a chic gown emporium in Studio City, a suburb of Hollywood. In hand was her smiling three-year old daughter, Jayne Marie, who also looked as though she could be refurbished.

"She laid it straight on the line to me," said Walter Emeson, the designer and proprietor. "This was late 1955. She said in an ultra-soft, little girl, breathy voice, 'Mr. Emeson, I came to town to become a movie star. You have no idea how I have worked and struggled.'"

"I'm well aware of girls trying to crash movies," he replied. In the next breath she told him she had no clothes except what was on her back!

"You see, we have sort of been locked out of the house," she explained. "And tomorrow I am going to have my first screen test at Warner Brothers. And I haven't anything except what I have on. Can you help me?"

Mr. Emeson explained that he was in business to make money, and he could not give away clothes.

"This is probably a lot of nerve," she persisted. "I have no money, but I have tomorrow afternoon for the test. My whole future depends on it. You have no idea how difficult it is to get a screen test! It has taken me months!"

Then she smiled and Mr. Emeson began melting. "You have made such fabulous gowns for Alice Faye, Vivian Blaine and Mary Healy who are all at Fox," she enthused. "I have managed to visit that studio, and I have seen their clothes. That is how I know all about you, Mr. Emeson. I saw those marvelous dresses in the window. Could you please do something for me? Could I have an outfit on credit? If I get a contract, I'll pay you back with my first pay check!"

Mr. Emeson later told me, "I took Miss Mansfield to the bookeeper and asked her to fill out a credit card.

"She filled out the application for credit as 'Mrs. Paul Mansfield!'

"I took her into a dressing room, where she removed the man's white shirt and torn, old blue jeans and thongs she was wearing. I took her measurements. She was smaller then. She was either 21 or 22 years of age. Her bust was 40 and her waist 23 and her hips measured 37. She had practically no underwear on at all. 'I don't wear them,' she said naively, and in such an innocent manner, that I would have been the embarrassed one, had I taken exception.

"I chose a sexy, fitted black jersey with a high turtle neck collar and long sleeves with the whole back bare. Otherwise, it had a fully covered effect. She was delighted. Then she said, 'But what can I do for shoes and gloves and a bag?' I honestly don't have anything except what I wore in here.'

"'A knock-out,' I thought. I decided I'd have to go all of the way.

I took her down the street and bought her shoes and black hose, gloves, a purse, some appropriate costume jewelry and a pair of panties. The latter, I insisted she had to wear. The bill came to $75.

"Five days later, she called very excited. 'I got the job! I have signed a contract at Warner Brothers! I'll get my first pay check in ten days. It is $75 and I'll bring it right in!'

" 'This is my first movie money. I told you I'd pay you,' she said, handing me her Warner Brothers studio check when she came into the shop. Then she said, with her eyes sparkling and radiating a marvelous glow and vibrant femininity that was to take her to the top, 'No matter how big I get, you'll always do my clothes!' And she did, to the very end!

"She then explained she had another problem. She couldn't go on the street wearing the black, sexy, backless jersey every day. So we sold her a little wardrobe. About four or five dresses. From then on, it seemed like every time I opened the newspaper there was Jayne Mansfield's picture in some pose or another. The columns were filled with news items, many of which, I assumed, she manufactured herself. She'd come in for a new dress for a big date with Greg Bautzer. 'He dated Joan Crawford,' she'd enthuse, 'and now it's *me*!' Each new dress meant a new, important man was taking her out. She lived in a whirl of excitement!"

Jayne tells it: "My Warner Brothers' salary was $250 a week, which was two and a half times my first movie salary. I grabbed it before they changed their minds. I hugged and kissed both the producer and the director. I worked in the picture for two weeks. Actually, I worked more for the camera boys and news photographers than I did for the movie camera. They put a tight sweater on me and shot loads of pictures for publicity.

"Solly Biano, head of casting and talent, called me in to a projection room to see myself on the screen. I fell in love with the girl up there. I said, 'I'll work even harder for you now!'

At Will Wright's one day over a soda, Jayne met Jim Byron, a press agent. He told her, "You can become a big star with the right kind of promotion and publicity." He outlined some stunts and ideas that could make front pages and the fan magazines. She was all for it, but she had no money. He said okay, he'd take five per cent of her salary, which was so little. It was agreed. He also introduced her to Bill Shiffrin, who became her agent. In one day, Jayne had acquired a top press agent, a top agent, a top lawyer Greg Bautzer, and Charles Goldring, a business manager. "I now have the necessary staff for a big star," said Jayne with delight. "For the first time I have help and backing—lots of it."

The career stunts began immediately. "Jim sent me to take his Christmas presents to the city desks of the newspaper men and the columnists." Jayne said, "I wore a red velvet, tight, scoop-necked dress. I would go up behind each man, kiss him on the cheek and present his gift. It worked. I made friends with everyone.

"Jim Byron told me he was sending me on a movie press junket being given by RKO for Jane Russell's new picture, *Underwater.*

Many versions have been given of Jayne's advent on this junket, which was the turning point in her career. Her photographer friend, Frank Worth, tells how it happened this way: Jim Byron had already fixed it so Jayne could go. Jane Russell was delayed a day. The camera boys were ready to start shooting, but, of course Jane Russell, the big star hadn't arrived. We went outside and there were Mala Powers, Debbie Reynolds, and Lori Nelson lined up for pictures. They were all nice girls working at RKO. Then, out walked Jayne Mansfield and everyone gasped. It wasn't just her red bikini. She was spectacular, with the biggest bosom in a decade. I marveled at her. She was quick to learn. When I first knew Jayne she was too normal in that department. I showed her how to push them up under a special kind of bra, to make them appear big for the quickie movie she'd made for my friend. Jayne learned fast. Now she was super. The guys shot a few of the other girls, Debbie, Lori and Mala, and then concentrated on Jayne.

"I asked Jayne if she could swim under water, and manage to let her bra strap break. She said yes and dove in. We got magnificent shots and then, sure enough, she burst the button holding her bra. The guys kept shooting like crazy. Jayne came up for air, modestly clasped herself in front and managed to climb out of the pool, running for the nearest bath house.

"The next day Jane Russell arrived. She came out to be photographed, but most of us had run out of film!"

Jayne tells it: "When I got back to Los Angeles the newspapers were full of my pictures. In the next few weeks, the magazines, many with outside covers of me carried the pictures. It was easy then for Jim to arrange all sorts of titles for me like 'Miss Cotton Queen,' 'Miss Freeway,' 'Miss Negligee,' and dozens more.

"Bill Shiffrin concluded a contract with an independent Producer for me to co-star with Dan Duryea in a film, *The Burglar*, to be made in Philadelphia. Jim Byron had all of the press out to see me off on the plane. Everything I did was news—even more than Elizabeth Taylor!

"I had quietly begun my divorce suit from Paul. He was now back in Texas, working for a railroad. He was also threatening to ask custody of Jayne Marie. Naturally, I took her with me.

"In Philadelphia I thought the world was mine now. I knew that when I returned from this loan-out I'd be put into big pictures, with no less than leading lady billing.

"On the set in Philly, everyone was gathered around to read the trade papers which had been air mailed from Hollywood. Some one exclaimed, 'There's a big story here on you, Jayne.' Smiling, I picked it up to read, "Warner Bros. Drops Jayne Mansfield."

"I couldn't believe it. I called Bill. He was out. I got Jim. He said it was true. 'But why?' I demanded. 'I am a star! I am making money right now for this studio. Why?'

"Jim told me that it happened to many contract players. 'There will be something better,' he said. 'I'll fix it with the press. I'll say you asked out of your contract to do a Broadway play!'

"'But I don't want to do a Broadway play,' I told him. 'I only want to be a Hollywood star in films.' I was crying. I was heartbroken. I felt this was the end.

"Bill Shiffrin got on the telephone that night. He said, 'I've got an idea. They want a brassy, sexy, dumb blonde for *Will Success Spoil Rock Hunter* on Broadway. You are only ninety miles from New York. Take your scrapbook and your stills and go in and convince them you are the girl they are looking for!'"

"Jayne had called to say she was leaving for Philadelphia, 'on loan-out to make a picture with a big star, Dan Duryea,'" Walter Emeson recalled. "She exclaimed breathlessly, which was the natural inflection of her voice, 'I am playing the feminine star lead.'"

She was still driving her old, clicky clack pink convertible. Jayne Marie, now 3 1/2, was always with her.

Walter Emeson recalled this time in Jayne's life. "I got a frantic call from Jayne from Philadelphia. 'You were so lucky for my first audition. Could you get me a dress for my next big one? It is going to be the big, super moment of my whole life!' She was elated. 'I am to be discovered on Broadway! ! !'

"She absolutely believed it. There was never a thought of failure. She was almost childlike in her statements—all positive fact. At times you had to stifle a laugh at her self-assurance. But everything would come about as she anticipated.

"Jayne's call came on Friday. I arranged to take off until Tuesday and flew to New York for her audition.

"Jayne had driven up from Philly in a little, black second-hand Jag she had now acquired. I had made a form-fitting, black satin dress that fit her like spray paint. It had the built-in brassiere for support, for she didn't need extra size.

"Jayne had taken a room, a very small one, at a little hotel called The Rockingham, across from Penn Station. First thing, we tried the dress. It needed a little bit of fitting. We got a maid at the hotel to do it. At the same time, she made arrangements with the maid to take care of Jayne Marie and her two dogs. Then we went to the little restaurant which was next door to the theater. We had orange juice. We got to talking and instead of being promptly on time, with the theater only next door, we walked in a half hour late.

"About eighty per cent of the girls auditioning were blonde. They were all in theater seats studying a one-page script. I ran backstage to get one for Jayne and to sign her name in with the casting director. Each girl was told to walk up on the stage, go center, do a full turn and read a paragraph. Since Jayne was so late, we sat in the last row.

"When Jayne's turn came, unlike the others who walked rapidly up to the stage, and read fast, as though they were afraid of taking too much time, Jayne sauntered and slithered to center stage. When she reached front center, she did a sensuous turn, taking three times as long as anyone else. Then she began reading the paragraph. She had only read four or five words when Julie Styne jumped up with great excitement! 'Don't read any more! You'll spoil the illusion! You look the part! You are perfect! We'll train you. You're hired—if Mr. George Axelrod agrees!'

"He told Jayne to call Mr. Axelrod at four that afternoon. I took her to Lindy's to celebrate with champagne, hamburgers and scrambled eggs.

"Jayne was so nervous she couldn't sit still. We went back to the hotel, and I showed her another dress I had brought. 'That will be my lucky dress!' she exclaimed. It was a mandarin type with a round, raised collar and a very high slit on one side. The simulated fronts looked like the front was open. And it was very tight!

"Jayne couldn't sit still. 'I'm so nervous. Let's go to a movie to kill time,' she suggested. We went out and walked along Broadway for a while, window shopping. We went into a movie, but she couldn't sit still. 'Everything depends on this!' she said. Then it was about four o'clock!

"Jayne stopped at the first telephone booth. It was connected with a Nathan's hot dog stand, and there was little privacy. She kept saying over and over, 'so much depends on this!' She seemed to be saying silent prayers as she dialed. Each time the line was busy! She dialed repeatedly for a half hour before she finally got through.

"She was able to confirm her appointment and we rushed to Mr. Axelrod's office. When he gave her the role, she grabbed him and hugged and kissed him. 'I promise you, you won't be sorry,' she said.

"She was like a little kid, grabbing my hand and running me out of the office to find another telephone booth. She dialed her agent, Bill Shiffrin, in Hollywood, and told him the glad news. As quickly, she dialed Jim Byron, her press agent, and then Greg Bautzer.

"'They are the only ones I have to tell, Walter,' she was suddenly forlorn. 'They are the only ones who care. I no longer send my little success stories home to Dallas. They don't want to hear them.'

"She returned to the hotel, collected Jayne Marie and the two dogs, and ordered some dinner and a bottle of champagne sent up to her modest little room and we celebrated. Then she drove back to Philadelphia—Broadway's glamorous, about-to-be toast of New York—in her shabby little car!

"There was just time for her to drive back to California after completing the film in Philly. She sold her few possessions including the car and closed up the little house she had rented. Then it was on to New York for her big try on Broadway."

Walt Emeson was in New York for Jayne's Broadway debut. "Opening night was like nothing I have ever experienced in the theater. Jayne, wore a smile and a big bath towel on stage! And she wriggled and squirmed under it on a massage table. That night, Jayne Mansfield became the big star of the year—Broadway's new, big baby!

"The critics who had come to eat up this presumptious little nobody loved her! The reviews were great. She made the play a hit. It was in for a long run just because of Jayne Mansfield. She made the cover of *Life Magazine* and all the others.

"After the show opening night, we went to Sardi's. Wires came from all over and certainly from everyone in Hollywood. An offer came from 20th Century Fox for a contract!

"Jayne had now managed to take a suite at the Gramercy Park Hotel, befitting a new star. 'I don't know how long I can stay there,' she confided. 'Because I have some debts.' We had champagne, the works, and Jayne recalled, a year ago I celebrated my first movie at Coffee Dan's on Hollywood Blvd. with cokes.

"Jayne ordered more and more clothes. She began buying furs, and expensive fake jewels. She would wear costumes that were created for her theater appearances as part of her everyday wardrobe. 'I have to look like a star twenty-four hours a day. I'm always on,' she'd explain.

"To her credit, she never sold her clothes to thrifty gown shops. Instead she'd send them to the Good Will shops. 'Maybe some girl trying for a career, who has no clothes—like me, when I first came to Hollywood—will find these lucky for her,' she'd say generously."

Jayne was fast becoming the toast of Broadway. Buddy Adler, production chief at 20th Century Fox, was going to screen test Jayne for a long-term contract at Fox. Jayne, however, in her first enthusiasm and gratitude for getting the Broadway role, had signed with Jules Styne for the run of the play which threatened to run for years. Styne wanted to produce the movie version of the play and star Jayne. Since Adler now had her under contract, Styne's agent, Irving Lazar, asked Adler to buy the play and produce the movie. Adler said he didn't want to make a picture out of a play that made fun of Hollywood and movies.

Lazar argued with Adler for weeks, saying "if you will release Mansfield, we can make the picture and make the girl a star!" Adler replied, "We are making her a star. When she reaches Hollywood, she's going to be as big as Marilyn Monroe. If she ever gets out of the play we are going to star her in Steinbeck's *Wayward Bus.*"

# CHAPTER V

It was 1956. Grace Metalious' book *Peyton Place*, revealing the scandals of a small New England town, shocked the nation. Floyd Patterson had become the new heavyweight champion of the world, Civil Rights shook the south. Martin Luther King, Jr. organized a bus boycott in Montgomery. People were taking tranquilizers, called Miltown, to calm their nerves. Maria Callas was heckled at the Metropolitan. Nikita Khruschev told representatives of the western world, "We will bury you." Hollywood movie star Grace Kelly announced her engagement to Prince Rainier III of Monaco. And Jayne Mansfield became the darling of Broadway, the glittery, gay white way and the neon night clubs.

This sudden burst of Jayne Mansfieldism on Metropolitan New York resulted in a natural controversy of acclaim and disclaim that surrounds people who are constantly in the news. "What is Jayne Mansfield really like?"

It was obvious that Jayne loved being a star. In person, it was widely reported that she was a very sweet, appreciative young woman with tremendous enthusiasm and energy. She wore her dresses skin tight—without any evidence of underthings. In exploiting her obvious physical appeal, she had hidden an unsuspected talent which was a highly important facet of her personality. It was discovered that this sex goddess, who wrapped herself in her imagination and a bath towel on the stage of the Belasco Theater in *Will Success Spoil Rock Hunter*, had much more than a forty-inch bust and a twenty-two-inch waist! She had attended both the University of Texas and the University of California at Los Angeles. "A girl has to have brains to get somewhere in this world," she'd daintily sigh with a delicate heave of bosom. "Brains are a handicap for a woman if shown. I only use mine secretly."

Jayne was introduced as the belle of five of New York's elegant society balls and countless civic affairs. She was a distinguished guest on the dias of the City of Hope's $100-a-plate dinner at the Waldorf. Not one of the honorable congressmen, judges and dignitaries, who spoke at these events, could refrain from including Jayne in their remarks.

If the pace of events slackened, Jayne would go to Danny's Hideaway, a favorite gathering place for celebrities, to get into the action. She would always telephone the columns before show time to give each one something new and exclusive. She said she couldn't waste a single minute for she was already going on 23 and this was it for her career. "It's now or never," she'd say a dozen times a day.

At El Morroco, Manhattan's plush night club, Jayne was seen repeatedly with such popular escorts as Oleg Cassini, George Jessel, Greg Bautzer as well as highly eligible young bachelors in the social register.

Robby Robertson, a pilot of American Airlines, was her favorite date. "I'd probably go steady with Robby," said Jayne, "if he were here." Robby had to leave her four days a week to fill the obligations of his job. He was considering remedying that absence with a change of position.

Every night there were not only stage door johnnies and fans at the stage door for Jayne, but loads of pink flowers arrived from numerous admirers. "Jayne has the world in the palm of her little pink hand," wrote Walter Winchell.

Jayne tells it: "Walter Winchell adopted me in his column. I coined words like 'D/voon.' A song, 'It's D/voon,' with my picture on the cover of the sheet music, became a hit. My picture was on the covers of music albums like 'Music for Bachelors to Dream By,' and on candy boxes and a candy bar. Almost every store window in New York City had my picture in front, and those that didn't—I would go in personally and hand them one. Then I got the idea of blow-ups, five-feet-by-three. I'd autograph them to a respective shop or store and walk in with one and give it to the owner. I had many different poses, so each would have an exclusive. No one refused me. And there I was, block after block, smiling out at the public."

Soon Manhattan windows were completely covered. Jayne then enlisted the help of a young college admirer. Almost every late afternoon they'd drive into the surrounding suburbs and "place" Jayne Mansfield pictures in windows. It was like a campaign. And it worked!

"I became the most highly publicized star on Broadway. One wire service said over a million lines of copy had appeared about me the first six months. I had become 'The World's New Sex Symbol.' In the beginning, they began comparing me with Marilyn Monroe! That would never do. I dreamed up my own distinct image. I could hear Poppa approving from way up there. I was using my head like he would do. I announced that pink was my favorite color. I wore only pink and I had my poodles dyed pink. It was all just marvelous! I was the toast of El Morroco. Walter Winchell singled me out to mambo every time! A dance was named 'The Jayne Mansfield Mambo.' A day didn't pass that my picture wasn't in the newspapers and items about me in the columns.

"My career was taking all of my time. But I managed to date men after the show. Men whom I felt would be good for me. There was no sex in my life—I was too busy being my sex-pot image. Besides, in a one-room apartment with Jayne Marie, there was no place for it had I been so inclined and, I was still married.

"The world was mine at last. My dreams were now realities. Even though some people knew I had a little girl, five-year-old Jayne Marie, they didn't want to hurt my sex symbol image. She was never mentioned in my publicity.

"Then, as always, just as everything I had worked so hard for was being realized, the past reached out to pull me back again. Paul, and my mother were now determined, that I quit and return to Dallas and be a dutiful housewife. 'You've had your fling warned Paul, now come home or I'll tell the world you are a married woman with a child that you're hiding! You are riding high under false colors!'

"I pled—I argued—I did everything. He was determined to stop my career. I begged him not to ruin me. He was adamant. I told him he could be my manager and take all of the money, only please let me continue long enough to get into pictures. It was like sitting on a powder keg. Any minute it would blow up in my face! Everything began to go against me.

"Paul Mansfield sued me for divorce and, just as he had planned, it hit the papers big! On advice of my lawyer, I filed for separate maintenance, hoping to stall a divorce. I really didn't want a divorce. Paul counter-filed, demanding custody of Jayne Marie. He said he wanted to put himself in a bargaining position to renew our marriage. But now I realized that it was long over. If someone loves you, they want your happiness. His love was completely selfish. I felt sorry for Paul, but we now lived in two different worlds. I said to him, 'I'm 23. I'm past my youth. I'm getting old. I gave you the best six years of my life—now I want my own.'

"Being a mother was not an asset for a sex symbol. Being one who had tried to hide it and Paul's declaration that I was an unfit one, was worse. The columnists began to turn against me. I was suddenly referred to as a publicity hound. Meantime, I was going to high school proms to award trophies, place crowns on prom queens' heads, attend lodges and civic events. People loved me anyway. More important, I was still doing great in the theater every night. I was a hit in a hit. But with so much trying to destroy me, how long could it last?

"Marilyn Monroe was fighting with 20th Century Fox. She wanted out on her contract. She was refusing pictures. I asked their New York talent scout for a screen test and got it.

"It was nail-biting time again. I called and called to ask if the studio had made a decision. Always, I received that same reply: 'We'll call you, don't call us.'

"New York City which had folded me in its arms six months before with adulation was suddenly becoming more and more unfriendly. I didn't quite know what to do. I hadn't done anything differently than I had at the beginning. I could feel it and I read it. Everyone began saying I'd overdone my publicity. But if I stopped—I'd be dead!

"I called 20th Century Fox in New York and asked Joe Hyams, their publicity man, if he would mind if I attended the premiere of the new Richard Burton picture, *Alexander*. 'I'll just walk in through the lobby and go out the side door,' I said. 'I have to be in my own theater at eight, so I won't need tickets.' I wore a ravishing, new, white satin evening gown sparkling with sequins that took my Broadway play salary for a whole week! I took another week's salary for a luxurious white fox stole. I often skipped meals to afford the clothes I needed to look like a star. I had no real jewelry. I wore all kinds of flashing rhinestones.

"I arrived at the premiere, stepped out of a chauffered limousine, which I had paid $25 to rent for twenty minutes! I walked into the theater lobby, pausing to smile for the cameramen, knowing that my fake diamonds were blazing in the lights. I looked like what everyone thought a Hollywood movie star should look like—exciting, dressed glamorously and extravagantly; my white fox stole trailed on the ground behind me, with as much casual elegance and disregard for luxurious furs, as I could muster.

"Richard Burton and some of the stars of the picture walked in unnoticed. The show was all mine! As I slipped out the side door inside the theater to make my 8:30 curtain, I saw press agents arguing with Mr. Burton. 'Please go out and come in again so the press will know you're here,' they said. Richard was not exactly for it. But they were telling him, 'You didn't fly all the way over from London for nothing!'

"The next day I heard from a friend at Fox, the studio was furious with me. One of the studio men was as ungentlemanly as to rage and pace the floor of his office, actually screaming, 'I could kill that Jayne Mansfield broad! Here we give a premiere for the stars of our picture, go to the expense of flying our stars in from Europe, and this simpering, so-called sex-pot, half-naked dame gets all the press. Tell her, in these exact words, she'll never come to any event I ever arrange!'

"That's why he was so mad at me. I had captured ninety-nine per cent of the picture's publicity at the premiere. It wasn't even my picture, and I wasn't even their star! I was told again that in New York, they were going to start banning me from attending premieres.

"That was when May Mann came into the picture. Every time, when the whole world was against me, and my career, seemed finished, God always sent me help. This time it was a kind friend, who was a very powerful columnist on the *New York Herald Tribune*.

"May was young and new in New York. She was not embittered. She had no frustrations to take out on anyone. She was pretty and popular. She looked like a movie star herself. I always told her she was the prettiest gal of them all.

"I recalled meeting her at the Wilshire Ebell Theater in Hollywood only six months before. Steve Cochran had taken me to the opening of the Ice Follies. Enroute he said he had to go to the Wilshire Ebell Theater for May Mann who was officiating as mistress of ceremonies and chairman of The Annual Oscarette Awards. Steve said he would be on stage for just a moment. I waited in the wings and watched while May introduced, Natalie Wood, Jimmy Dean and others. I stood, backstage wishing I was a star and could go out to be introduced. I mentioned it to someone and they said, 'Only stars are introduced.' I felt like such a nobody, which I was at that moment. Then I saw Miss Mann glancing back to me. I smiled at her. And suddenly she called and beckoned me on stage. She introduced me graciously. She said, 'I always predict the new star for next year. I believe she will be Miss Jayne Mansfield.' I was thrilled. Nobody, of course, took that very seriously.

"Then, in New York, when it seemed everything I did was gaining criticism and I was being called a publicity hound, May called me. She said she wanted to see me, see where I lived, and see if she could do a constructive story on me. She said that we Hollywood people had to stick together, now that we were in the Big City.

"The next afternoon she came to my crowded and littered apartment at the Gorham. My maid was there. So was Jayne Marie and the four dogs. Two of the dogs had just messed the floor. Before we could get it cleaned, May walked in. There wasn't any place clean enough to sit down, as I had just finished a picture lay-out in Central Park, and I hadn't had time to get things ready at home. In spite of her chic dress and white gloves, May helped me clean up. Then she said, 'Jayne, the reason I am here is I want to write a big piece on your being a good mother. Not just the sex-pot that lives on publicity, but the truth, and the real you I see here. Few glamour girls, and especially a star in a Broadway hit play, would live like this to keep their children with them. Stars put them in boarding schools and see them on a night off, if they can't afford a suitable home.'

"I argued with May's thinking. 'If you write the truth as you see me in this mess and establish me as the mother of a five-year-old girl, it will take away all of the glamour I have so carefully built. My sex goddess image will be destroyed!

"May told me of a wire story that had reached her desk from Paul Mansfield in Texas, claiming I was an unfit mother. This, she said, could be disastrous while the truth that I was a good and devoted mother would win the public's admiration. We debated the point, and finally I decided to take the gamble. How a sex-pot image could be also a mother image, I didn't know! Either way, by Paul or May, I might be ruined!

"The next day on the front page of the *New York Herald Tribune* there was a picture of Jayne Marie in my arms with May's column headed, 'Jayne Is A Good Mother.' I had been so afraid all of these years that the mother image would hurt me, and date me out of my sex symbol image. Instead, congratulatory wires, reaffirmed friends, and even sympathy poured in. The press wrote their approval of my now-disclosed struggles. The P.T.A. began inviting me to attend their social gatherings. May was and is an exceptionally bright girl. She, too, had been a national beauty contest winner. She had a quick mind. We compared IQ's. We had so much in common, including sincerity, honesty and guts. Best of all, there was nothing phoney in our friendship. We became friends without trying. We will always be friends. That's the one thing I can be sure of."

# CHAPTER VI

The "Good Mother Image" proved the turning point in Jayne's career. It paid off and became part of her Sex Goddess build-up.

"Miss Photo Flash of 1952," woke up one morning to find herself for the second time on the cover of *Life Magazine*. The magazine had summed Jayne up correctly with their initial cover photo blurb, "Broadway's Smartest Dumb Blonde." The inside story had reported, "Her manner is warm and simple and candid. She answers honestly and without offense many questions that other actresses would consider intrusion of privacy. But it is interesting to note that she always 'presents' herself."

Others reported: "She is never seen in the same dress twice—due to her canny consideration to always look new and different for the flashbulb boys. A west coast dressmaker, Walter Emeson, sends her a steady supply of clothes from California. In New York, Oleg Cassini is dressing her. She has purchased an $18,000 white mink coat on the installment plan. She is invariably well-groomed in public, but she never wears hose. She thinks it is more sexy for her toes and legs to be bare; it's also less expensive."

Others now commented that Jayne Marie, her little daughter, was always in tow. "It is not uncommon to see Jayne Mansfield sweeping into El Morocco where she deposits her child with the maid in the Ladies Room, and then sips champagne with an admirer at a banquette for ten minutes. Then, she smilingly departs to collect her child and go home." More and more, the little girl was in Jayne's publicity pictures. It was a contrast—the shapely Jayne in her sex-symbol clothes snuggling the child on her lap in affectionate, motherly poses. This was unique. It aroused even greater interest than Jayne photographed with men she dated. However, with her usual impetuosity she managed both.

When Grace Kelly announced that she was going to become a princess when she married Prince Rainier, Jayne Mansfield began openly speculating. "I want to marry royalty and have a crest on all of my nightgowns and on my fleet of Rolls Royces. I want to live in a big palatial palace." Eligible, if impoverished, nobility were constantly brought to Jayne's attention by the columnists. Some gallant, if threadbare members of Russian nobility sought her out at the stage door.

With the divorce in the works she bagan dating in the news. Before she had been a little afraid of Paul Mansfield's publicly denouncing her. Even though she was photographed at El Morocco and various events, she was careful not to say anything that Paul could use against her as his wife.

Danny's Hideaway now gave a big celebration party for Jayne. All of the prominent people in town came to pay her homage; the men—not the women. Women were either envious or not willing to bask in Jayne's light, so they ignored the invitations. Robby Robertson was pressing marriage, even though her divorce would not finalize until January 9, 1958, several months away. Jayne still had a royal prince in mind like Grace Kelly's.

In naming her ten most fascinating bachelors for Leap Year in the *Herald Tribune's* May Mann Column, Jayne disclosed some revealing facets of the men she preferred:

"Robby Robertson, thirty-six , has to be first. He's six feet tall with dark brown eyes and charcoal gray hair. I feel so companionable and safe with him. He's so sympathetic and understanding.

"Greg Bautzer, forty-one, an attorney, is tall, dark and so smartly dressed. He is like a regular standby. He's always there to take a girl to the most elegant parties. Even though he dates the most famous women in the world, he makes a girl feel like she is the only one. He is extremely solicitous. Greg will dash across the room, tripping over people, just to light a woman's cigarette!

"Adlai Stevenson is a strong, powerful man and so sure of himself. I admire such strength of character. I don't know him but I'd like to.

"Nick Ray, the movie director, is forty-one, tall and attractive. He directed *Rebel Without a Cause*. He has that rare combination of brawn, brains and achievement. I like that.

"George Nader, thirty-five, is tall, dark, handsome and single. Women everywhere have a crush on George. I am no exception; although we have met, we have never dated.

"Richard Egan, thirty-six, is tall, dark and handsome too. I like his religious background and his deeply spiritual side. Also his extra good manners. He has the polish and quality of a real gentleman.

"Oleg Cassini, the designer, is around forty. I love the clothes he makes for women. He is a gentleman, and such a man of the world, with his poise and self-assurance. Greg and Oleg Cassini are the romantic types who send great boxes of flowers. I like that.

"Steve Cochran, thirty-six, tall, dark and handsome in a rugged sort of way, was one of my first dates in Hollywood. Steve is casual at all times. If a girl proposed to him, he could say 'no' so easily that no one would be embarrassed or feel frustrated. He has the he-man charm that women fall for. He doesn't rely on techniques.

"Johnny Ray has a voice that goes right through me. I can't even think what he looks like or does, or what makes him so appealing. I just know I want to listen to him and get caught up in that old little white cloud.

"George Jessel is so witty, so amusing. Such fun to date. He is very popular and knows everyone. I also like his suave ways. The closest way to my heart is through intelligence.

"A woman loves to think of herself as a little kitten to be pampered and adored," sighed Jayne. "I do. I'm twenty-three, alert and eligible! I'd like to meet Bob Wagner, Bob Stack, Tyrone Power, Marlon Brando and Liberace, bless his heart. And somewhere, I hope there is a real prince for me.

"I want lots of babies. I'm good and I'm healthy. I want to become a princess—or even a queen—if there is a king for me. There's Clark Gable!" she sighed.

Jayne's dream of a real royal prince, like Rainier, evaporated one night when she went to see the Mae West show at the Latin Quarter. In Miss West's chorus of muscle men there was one who smiled down at Jayne's table, and intrigued her. After the show, this tall, handsome muscle man, who had been a "Mr. Universe" asked to meet her. He was Mickey Hargitay, a Hungarian refugee.

From that first meeting Jayne could envision no one in her future except Mickey. "Ooooooh, he's so gorgeous and so big!" she exclaimed like a little girl with a new toy. "And in bed—he's so great! He has the biggest pectorals this side of the world. You can't believe him, he's so good!" she ecstacized.

Sexual attraction was now suddenly uppermost on her mind. For the first time it exceeded her career. When the Mae West show moved on to Washington, D. C., Jayne and Mickey were constantly on the telephone, or they were flying back and forth to see each other. Miss West, objected to the Mansfield publicity infringing on her act and her name. Mae West publicity was strictly Mae West. There were press conferences by Miss West and others by Jayne and Mickey with all sorts of allegations. Mickey left the Mae West troupe to devote his time to Jayne in New York.

This did not set well with 20th Century Fox which had already weathered Jayne's headlined divorce from Paul Mansfield. The studio had tested Jayne in New York and had offered her a contract. She could not accept, however, because she still had a run of the play contract. Buddy Adler, production vice president of Fox Studio, announced he had already signed Jayne to a fabulous exclusive contract. It would become operative when Jayne became available. Jayne's popularity was a major factor in sustaining the play's run on Broadway. Adler and Fox became impatient. Since the play presented some problems for translation to the screen, Frank Tashlin tailored it for Jayne Mansfield and Hollywood. After he had succeeded and the screen play was completed, Jayne and the play were still very big in New York. In desperation, 20th Century Fox paid $100,000 to spring Jayne from the play and return to Hollywood. She was immediately set to co-star opposite Tom Ewell and Edmond O'Brien in *The Girl Can't Help It*.

The title of Jayne's first film was appropos of the woman herself. Strongly advised to dismiss and forget Mickey Hargitay, Jayne refused. She loved him. She couldn't go on without him. She would marry him as soon as her divorce was final. The studio believed that in those six months they could find a prince somewhere in Europe to divert her interest in Mickey and build a more suitable romance for Jayne's image.

"I knew I wanted Mickey ten minutes after we were introduced at the Latin Quarter," Jayne said. "We have been so close ever since. I've had to go it alone, with my family and Paul putting obstacles in my path all the way. Mickey wants to devote himself to helping my career. It's like I've been pulling a huge wagon alone. Now there will be two of us.

"As for being royal and having a royal palace, Mickey is a builder. He can lathe and plaster and lay marble and he is going to build me a big palace in Hollywood. I have an inheritance of $90,000 when my paternal grandfather's estate is settled. We are going to put it all in a house. Mickey will build it—more magnificent than Pickfair."

The studio pointed to the fact that the more famous Jayne became, the more proposals she would get. She'd have a greater choice. Besides, all her life she had wanted to become a "big star." Now was her chance. A marriage to a mere muscle man would spoil it all.

"It took Mickey to put my feet on the ground," she told Buddy Adler in conference in his New York office. "I was like a negative before it is dipped into developer and comes out a picture. Mickey has made me realize that I want to be a happily married woman more than anything else in the world. I want to be successful Mr. Adler. But I do not want to forfeit my life—a wonderful life, the sharing of a clean, beautiful spiritual life together."

Mr. Adler protested vigorously. The studio was inclined to drop all interest.

"Even though you've already paid a hundred thousand dollars to get me out of the play?" Jayne was incredulous.

"Mr. Zanuck doesn't think much of you now as an investment the way things are with you and Mr. Hargitay," Mr. Adler replied.

"So he wants me to date lots of men?" Jayne asked. "All for publicity?"

"That's the formula. It will be done in a more conservative manner; in good taste."

"All right," Jayne capitulated. "On studio hours you can arrange all sorts of romances for print. But just know, Mr. Adler, that Mr. Hargitay will be in my bed waiting for me at night. And no other man ever will be. Because I am going to marry Mickey."

Mr. Adler, long experienced with the emotional explosions of actresses, smiled. He had won.

The next day's papers, to the studio's embarrassment, stated Jayne's side.

"Is nothing private or personal with that dame!" ranted Mr. Adler. He read: "What can a girl receive dating a dozen different

men, but ten dozen different, mixed-up situations. And men who
expect a girl to go to bed after a first date. Champagne for breakfast
may sound great, but it gives you a hangover. Men who go with
you because you are a sex symbol get draggy. I've been actually
miserable when I was fantastically happy.' Now I feel clean, wholesome, poised with just one man who loves me. Mickey and I have
made no promises. It isn't necessary. Our outlook on life runs
parallel in every way. In fact, we never had to talk about getting
married. In our hearts we knew it would be. Mickey feels that I'm
the only woman in the world for him and I know he's the only man
in the world for me."

"Ye gods!" exclaimed a publicist assigned to Jayne. "Will the
broad stop talking to the press about unmentionable things. She's
cooperative and sweet—but she does her own P.A."

"The girl can't help it," a columnist rejoined.

Fox Studio had no choice but to go along with Jayne who
continued, in spite of many warnings, to be her own, outspoken
press agent. She left Broadway for Hollywood to star in her second
movie. But no one remembered her first, *Female Jungle*, for which
she was paid $100. Her starting salary now at Fox was $2500 a
week!

# CHAPTER VII

Twentieth Century Fox had recently weathered the unexpected expose of Marilyn Monroe's nude calendar and the fact that she wasn't the highly publicized orphan, but had a mother in a mental institution. The studio was now wary of new talent that might plague the press department with such alarming reversals in its publicity releases. As if that wasn't enough for a studio who had just paid a fortune to obtain a new star by buying her Broadway hit play, then came headlines that there was a Mrs. Mickey Hargitay in the picture seeking a divorce, "So that my husband might be seen around with actress Jayne Mansfield, who will make a motion picture star out of him." Further, Mary Hargitay divulged the fact Mickey was a father and asked for monthly support for their daughter, Tina, age seven!

"How in the hell can you build an exciting, fresh, young, glamorous sex symbol out of a divorced woman with a child, who is announcing she is going to marry a divorced man with a child? Is that young love?" A publicity man wrung his hands. Higher-ups agreed. There was nothing to do, however, but make the best of what the studio now considered looked like a bad bargain. Further, Hollywood was well aware that Jayne, in her constant quest for publicity in New York, had over-sold herself. Some New York editors and one photo agency had "banned any more pictures or puff on Jayne Mansfield unless it is a matter of legitimate news!"

Fox would try to overcome all obstacles with a well thought out publicity build-up, and Miss Mansfield would have to be carefully molded into a new, more sympathetic image, to make her acceptable to the public. "She'll not make a move or speak a word without me," a unit man assured. But they did not know Jayne.

In New York Jayne had given more time to her publicity than to her role on Broadway. The press agents took her in shifts. Jack Toohey, with the show, scheduled Jayne from 6:00 A.M. to 1:00 P.M. Then her own press agent took over until show time. Jayne accepted any and all requests—over the protests of her galaxy of press agents. When they'd explain to her that posing for some of the scandal sheet magazines was bad taste, and that posing in a bikini on a beach and posing in a bikini in a bedroom were two different things, she would agree. "You're right. I'll watch it and only do what you approve." But she'd go right on doing it anyway. No one could tone her down. Not even when the papers and the press were tiring of her innovations and publicity tricks. Jayne was like one addicted. She couldn't stop.

Arriving in Hollywood, secure with the knowledge of a signed, seven-year contract with 20th Century Fox, Jayne stepped off the plane with her daughter, Jayne Marie, four dogs and Mickey Hargitay. Jayne's press agent, Jim Byron, had the photographers and press out to greet her. The studio, had not yet resigned itself to the fact that Jayne would be unmanageable. During a studio publicity conference, Jayne agreed on all points of the campaign the studio had in mind. And, as usual, she went right on doing what she thought best for her career on her own.

The red carpet and the glamorous plush star treatment was rolled out for 20th Century Fox's new glittering star, however, on order of Harry Brand, vice president and publicity director. "Jayne is a very intelligent girl," he defended. "Jayne Mansfield, alone, accounted for more than 450 performances of the play, *Rock Hunter* and that's an enviable mark for any Broadway new star!"

Jules Styne had said in New York, "She has a certain wonderful quality of naive bouncing enthusiasm, a very feminine and sweet girl. If she would forget her dogs and her publicity for one year, she'd become a big film star!" But where she had been using publicity in the beginning as a means towards an end, now the means and the end had alarmingly become inseparable!

Frank Tashlin had already been assigned to direct Jayne in her first major motion picture.

"I knew Jayne was perfect for a picture I had ready," said Mr. Tashlin. "I had only seen pictures of her, but I knew she would be perfect. When I met Jayne it was love at first sight. She was adaptable, marvelous and eager. She was an instant hit here in the press, with newspaper and magazine interviews scheduled around the clock. Our picture was a big success. Then I was handed *Rock Hunter*. It was anything but what a movie studio would want, for it lampooned Hollywood. I rewrote it, replacing the movies with a T.V. background. In fact, I used only one speech from the play—one of Jayne's.

"Jayne was so in love with Mickey, and I believed in her sincerity. She was so child-like, so refreshingly honest and enthused. She arrived on the set on time, letter perfect in her lines. She always knew every bit of business in the script, even to the timing of picking up a cup of tea or whatever. I was amazed at her complete professionalism.

"When she anxiously asked me to find a part in the picture for Mickey, I acquiesced. I put Mickey in the film, playing a T.V. jungleman. Jayne was so appreciative. She told me, 'You know

Mickey had to give up his job with Mae West when he fell in love with me. I have to make it up to him.'

"It was one of my most colorful experiences in filmmaking. Mickey would carry Jayne in his arms from the dressing room onto the set. There was always romantic by-play between them. They exuded happiness and it touched everyone.

"She confided that she had dated the director, Nick Ray, and she seemed a little flustered when he first came on the set. Everyone had the feeling that there had been something powerful between them, but her enthusiasm for Mickey overcame any uneasiness she had felt momentarily.

"Jayne had everything—beauty, talent and drive—but she blew her career at Fox with too much publicity. No one could get through to her that she was hurting herself with this constant barrage of daily publicity in the papers and press. She would call her own press conferences for the most minute detail or happening. The photographers would turn out in droves to photograph Jayne, scantily attired as they knew she would be. They could always sell the pictures of Jayne's cleavage somewhere."

Jayne had put a $4,000 down payment on a two bedroom house in Benedict Canyon on the outskirts of Beverly Hills. It was furnished in Modern Sears. It became a part-time photo studio and animal shelter. Interviewers and lensmen had to step carefully to avoid dog manure on the carpets. There were also several cats and some had litters of kittens. Jayne Marie and her playmates ran in and out. Mickey was constructing a swim pool and seemed in charge. "It was like seeing two beautiful, big animals at play," one reporter declared. Jayne's Mad House was like nothing Hollywood had ever seen.

"Jayne was possessed with her cleavage—her big breasts. They seemed to be her security," Frank Tashlin disclosed. The screen test George Axelrod had made of her in New York had made the party circuit in Bel Air long before Jayne arrived at Fox. Josh Logan said it was the first time he had ever seen a film in which the actress rubbed her bosom against the camera lens.

Sophia Loren came to Hollywood for the film, *Boy and the Dolphin*, with Alan Ladd. A welcome party was given for Sophia at Romanoff's. "Jayne came to me and said, 'They want me to go,'" said Mr. Tashlin. "I told her: 'Don't go. You will be more there by your absence.' But she went. She managed to bend down to Sophia as the photographers caught pictures of Sophia's eyes looking at Jayne's all-but-bare cleavage popping out! Since Loren was known for her's, the picture made front pages all over the world. 'If only you'll have more confidence in your ability!' I told Jayne.

"Both of our two pictures made big money and Jayne was set for her third. 'It is to be with Cary Grant!' she ecstasized. Her eyes were wide with excitement. 'Imagine me in a movie with Cary Grant as my leading man!' She was walking on air! I begged her, 'Don't do it! Don't do it Jayne! Don't play second fiddle to Suzy Parker,' who was in the picture too. I pointed to the fact that Suzy gets Cary in the film. But Jayne made the picture. And when she was assigned *The Wayward Bus*, again, I advised her against it. 'What can you do sitting in a bus for a half hour?' She had a child-like quality of faith andi irrepressible enthusiasm. She couldn't understand what could possibly hurt her.

"One day she came into my office wearing a striped, tight sweater. 'Jayne!' I exclaimed with a slight impatience. 'Why do you wear a tight sweater like that with stripes? Don't! It looks so phoney.' She protruded out like she had her old laundry packed inside her bra. 'But, it's all me!' she protested innocently, and started to pull up her sweater. 'It's all me!' 'Stop. I take your word for it,' I said.

"She had some happy news to impart. She had just inherited $90,000 from her grandfather's estate. 'I am going to have a big palace—a movie star palace,' she said. 'Mickey is a builder. He learned the trade in Budapest, I think. With this money, we can have a real movie star house with rooms and rooms and rooms!' I tried to tell Jayne that it would be better for her to invest her money and get seven per cent interest. With that you will always have $7000 a year income for life. You'd never have to want for anything.

"But Jayne—well, the title of my first picture with her, *The Girl Can't Help It*, was really her. Getting herself before the public consumed her. Publicity opened it's arms and beckoned, and that's the path she chose."

"Just think of all of the publicity I can get with a pink movie star palace!" she said sweetly to Harry Brand, her studio mentor. "It will not only be a wonderful home, but a good investment in my career. I can dress and act glamorously like a movie star should. I walked my new pet leopard on a leash down Hollywood Boulevard yesterday," she giggled. "I had a big, pink satin bow tied around his neck! And I wore a pink jumpsuit and a big, pink picture hat. It was really divoone! The newsreels turned and three T.V. stations turned out for it. Aren't you proud of me? And I didn't bother you at all. And I plugged the picture! When I have a gorgeous movie star palace for a setting! You see the possibilities!" Mr. Brand smiled acknowledgment.

While Jayne may have upset the publicists at Fox from time to time, she was the delight of production and makeup and wardrobe. Everyone was excited about the new sex-pot. Unlike Marilyn Monroe, she was punctual and cooperative. "The only problem with Jayne," said Helen Turpin, head of hairdressing, "was that she always arrived with a couple of her dogs and sometimes a child or two. That we didn't mind so much, but she was always on the telephone every second, or calls were coming in for her. It was constant interruption and bedlam. While she gave people the impression she was an exhibitionist, that was actually a professional thing with her. Actually, she was a wonderful mother who loved her children and animals but she always had a thousand things going at once.

"She never wore underpants and sometimes when she wore a short dress, I'd say, 'Jayne!' She'd smile and pull her dress down over her knees. She had a great naivete and shamelessness that comes with real decency. Once you accepted that fact, Jayne was for real."

By coincidence, Jayne and I both returned to Hollywood at the same time, although for different reasons. My mother was ill and I was given a leave of absence from the New York *Herald Tribune*. Jayne was always on the telephone, relating the happenings of the day. She was publicity-dating some of the contract players at Fox, "but I always get home in time to see Mickey!" she'd tell anyone and everyone including the press.

Mickey had dug out the backyard of Jayne's small place and had put in a swimming pool. For respectability's sake, Jayne told me, "Mickey has a room in a house a block away. But he's here every day. He takes Jayne Marie to school and he does so many things for me and my career. I don't know what I'd do without him."

"But," she sighed, "the studio doesn't want me to marry Mickey. Marrying him can end my contract. But I can't help it. The studio keeps telling me it will spoil everything if I marry him. Mickey's so in love with me," she rapturized. "He's so physically exciting. I just have to marry him, career or no career."

"I want to have a baby, Mickey's baby, right away when we get married," she confided to me. "I know that is all wrong for my career, but maybe I can make the world know that I am a woman first and an actress second. I'm too much woman to be career-minded now that I'm in love. Oh May, it's so wonderful to have a man all my own!"

Meanwhile the studio publicists paced the floor wondering just what to do about Jayne Mansfield. In what direction could they build her image when every day she was threatening to tear it down. The studio had never made such a big investment to get a star. $120,000 was on the Fox books to buy the screen rights to the play, *Rock Hunter*, which they couldn't use except the title—just to bring Jayne to Hollywood. In the beginning, she had been compared to Marilyn Monroe. But Jayne Mansfield had turned out to be nothing like Marilyn. Jayne was a complete original with new problems by the hour!

# CHAPTER VIII

The thing to do with Jayne, the studio decided was to get her away from Mickey. Let her see the world and the potential by sending her on a personal appearance tour with her pictures. This would give her an international star image and create a demand for her films on the foreign market. She would meet important, attractive men, and experience first-hand the thrill, excitement and rewards of being a big film star. Mindful of Jayne's earlier statement in New York that she hoped to meet a royal prince charming as Princess Grace of Monaco had, a few eligible noblemen were invited to meet Jayne at various scheduled parties on her itinerary. Royalty was eager to meet the glamorous new star!

The tour was scheduled for forty days starting in New York and hitting all of the big cities in Europe. The studio prepared a lavish new wardrobe for Jayne. It was replete with luxurious furs and rented jewels. She was assigned a publicist and a beautician. She would look every inch the STAR!

Jayne was tearful at leaving Mickey behind. The studio was adamant. This was her assignment alone, no Mickey Hargitay! Mickey resigned himself to taking care of Jayne Marie and completing the swimming pool.

The studio had arranged for Jayne's appearance at a command performance for the Queen of England. Marilyn Monroe's dress and cleavage had been widely criticized at her presentation to Queen Elizabeth at a similar affair years previously. To avoid any such mishaps that could be construed as disrespect to England's conservative and gracious queen, the studio thoughtfully created a proper dress for Jayne to wear to the royal presentation.

Jayne and her entourage arrived at the New York airport to find the red carpet rolled out. The year before there had been no cameramen to record the propitious moment of Jayne's arrival. Only Jayne with Jayne Marie, two chichuahuas and a poodle. Now the crowds had to be held back by police while extra security guards were posted. Jayne stepped out of the plane smiled and waved to her subjects like a queen. Armsful of red roses were handed to her as she walked through roped off paths to her waiting limousine. Airport, studio and civic authorities were solicitous of her every whim. "This is the star treatment," she squealed happily. "Last time I had to take my own baggage. I had to get my own cab."

New York loved her all over again. The press waited in lines outside her door. The same press that had banned her, had been bored with her, had poked fun at her as a publicity hound, was now eager to write of her triumphs: "Broadway's own has become a big movie star!"

Even the members of the cast of *Will Success Spoil Rock Hunter* had mellowed. Some who had resented her for upstaging them, or stepping on their lines, now only remembered that, "she never made a mistake, was letter perfect on stage. She was always sweet and kind to everyone."

Ed Sullivan had her on his show. Jayne had worked incessantly for a year to get on the Ed Murrow person to person show. "Now I am really national," she sighed. "Momma and Dallas see the Ed Sullivan show!"

In London, Jayne's publicized arrival found thousands of people at the airport to see "America's Queen of Sex." London bobbies turned out in triple files to handle the crowds. Jayne was floating on air, she said, with happiness. There was no mention of Mickey Hargitay in her press interviews, but every night she called him at an appointed hour.

Doris Durkus, one of the studio's leading hair stylists, accompanied Jayne on the 40 day international tour. "Although like almost everyone else, I loved Jayne," said Doris, "I only agreed to accompany her if she agreed to no dogs." Jayne agreed, but as soon as we were in London she forgot her promise. She bribed the chauffeur assigned to us to find her a Pekingese puppy. I told her, 'I won't carry it.' She said, 'I will.' It seemed her breasts and something little and cuddley to love were her security. She had the little puppy with her everywhere, hugging him to her. He was very cute and I quickly forgave her. The only trouble with Jayne and her dogs was that she had no time to walk them, and no time to house train them. They were always a real problem."

A photographer caught Jayne going up a stairway and shot her from below and rear. The picture of only her fanny came out front page in all of the European papers. Most stars would have been furious at the unflattering pose. Jayne only giggled. "There's an old adage I learned in Hollywood; as long as they spell your name right!" she said.

A London columnist wrote, "Jayne is too FAT. We love our Diana Dors who is svelte." "Okay, so I won't eat," Jayne said.

The day of Jayne's presentation to the queen, her dress by Charles LeMaire arrived from 20th Century Fox by air. When she went to put the dress on, just before leaving for the Command

Performance, the zipper wouldn't work. Jayne squealed, "What will I do? I ate an egg for breakfast, that's what is wrong. I can't eat anything or I gain weight." She was almost in tears because she wanted to wear the dress so much. Doris finally sewed her into it.

A rope with security guards kept Jayne and Cecil B. DeMille on the red carpet awaiting the Queen. On the other side, Doris stood behind Jayne with needle and thread due for any emergency. The Queen was interested in Jayne, and stopped to chat with her. Jayne had been practicing her courtesies, and the dress miraculously held while she bowed low to Her Majesty. Jayne was enthralled with the Queen. "How beautiful she is. Her pink and white complexion," she marveled. Then, "Oh I'm so glad my dress was high in the neck. A queen like Queen Elizabeth deserves that respect."

From then on through the entire tour it was lightening changes of clothes, press conferences at crowded airports, lines of people on the streets to glimpse Jayne as she swept by in her limousine. It was also T.V. and radio appearances, luncheons, cocktail parties, dinners, homage, admiration and adulation, all for Jayne the movie queen. Men with titles, wealthy and poor, men in government and in the theater and films all sought Jayne. Some called her and some even followed her from country to country. One she liked, was Tony Castello, a rich young nobleman and big landowner in Rome. He pursued her from city to city. He sent flowers and gifts. Jayne had to admit, were it not for her nightly calls back home to Mickey "who keeps my head on and my feet on the ground," with all of the heady excitement, she just might have been swept away with it all.

"Oh if Momma could only have come along and seen all of this," she would exclaim at times. "Momma never believed it could happen big for me. If she could only see now. She'll never believe all of this," Jayne would say. Momma, back in Dallas, Texas had to believe, for the wire services and 20th Century Fox were keeping all America posted on their newest star's phenomenal strides to world acclaim. By the time Jayne had completed her tour, she had enough film offers to work in Europe alone for the next six years. It was a great success. Fox was tremendously proud and happy. Jayne had fulfilled their expectations fully. Now if she has only put marrying Mickey Hargitay out of her mind.

In spite of the tremendous success of Jayne's European personal appearance tour and the press headlines: "Hollywood's Queen meets England's Queen," a proposal from handsome young Duke Amoalli in Rome, and numerous film offers in Europe, Jayne could hardly wait to get home to Mickey's arms.

The night Jayne returned she announced she was going to marry Mickey Hargitary at once.

"20th Century Fox arranged the most exciting schedule in each capital city," Jayne said. "I know the studio doesn't want me to marry Mickey, but I'm too much woman. I've already told the studio my decision. They were very gracious about it. But I don't blame Fox for being bitterly disappointed. I would be too—if I had a Jayne on my hands. I'm sharp enough to know good business. With Mickey and love I'll become even a bigger star."

The first night of her return home Jayne called me to rush over for girl talk. We sat by the new swimming pool with a 12 foot figure of Jayne Mansfield painted on the bottom. Mickey had the ten foot painting of Jayne in a bikini done as a surprise.

"Career-wise, I know I shouldn't marry. But he has the biggest—and I'm not going to let go of it," Jayne confided.

"The studio has again told me it will spoil everything if I marry him," she said, as we sat in the damp chill. It grew to be eight, nine, ten and eleven o'clock, as we talked things out.

"Mickey's so in love with me," she rapturized. "He's so physically exciting. I am so turned on by him. I wouldn't trade him for any of the millionaires or the titled men I met in London or anywhere. All I could think about was getting back here to Mickey. Where do you think we should marry?"

I asked Jayne if they'd set the date. She said, "No. I have thought of holding a big wedding in the Rodeo Room of the

Beverly Hills Hotel and making it one big exciting wedding."

I disagreed. "They hold so many press parties and cocktail parties there," I said. "A wedding would seem like another party. A wedding, Jayne," I advised, "should be intimate, beautiful and sacred—not a publicity thing. Why don't you make it private and simple? Remember "when people accused you in New York of doing everything for publicity? You've got to show that your wedding is real. Remember, a lot of people besides the studio are opposed to Mickey."

"You're so right," she agreed thoughtfully, hugging the white mink tighter around her and slumping deeper in the cold iron pool chair. "They think he is an opportunist. I read that he thinks I am a younger Mae West and all. But I don't believe it. I know he loves me," she said. Then, "You always do everything so beautifully. What do you suggest for the wedding? Help me plan."

"I have to be in New York no later than January fifteenth to report back to the *New York Herald Tribune*," I said.

Jayne began to count. "I can't be married before January 11th, because that is the day my divorce from Paul Mansfield will be final."

"If we hurry and have the wedding on that date then you can be here with me. I'll do it," she announced with a squeal of delight. "Where shall we have it?"

"I have a brilliant idea," I beamed. "There is a beautiful little all glass church set in the hills overlooking the Pacific Ocean at Palos Verdes. It's called the Wayfarer Chapel. It would be perfect. Not only is it romantic and picturesque, but it is far enough away from Hollywood, about twenty five miles, so it would be private. No publicity. It would be beautiful."

"I think I've seen it at a distance—from the road," Jayne said. "I'll call the church tomorrow and see what happens."

"I'll give you a bridal shower at my house," I offered, caught up in Jayne's enthusiasm. On second thought I added, "But no photographers, Jayne. And no publicity. This should be just for you and Mickey. You've got to prove that this is real love and that your marriage is sacred. No publicity!"

"Would Don Maloof sing at our wedding?" Jayne asked. Don was a tall handsome young man of 24 whom I was dating at the time. Often he and I, Jayne and Mickey dated as a foursome. "I am sure Don would be delighted," I assured her.

Jayne and I sat there until midnight planning the wedding. Finally Mickey walked out and exclaimed, "You two girls are going to have great big colds in your noses. Better come inside!"

"Oh Mickey," Jayne giggled, "We are planning our wedding. It is going to be beautiful. Absolutely beautiful!"

The next day Jayne telephoned Reverend Kenneth W. Knox of the Wayfarers Memorial Chapel.

"I was surprised at her call," Reverend Knox said. "I expressed mixed feelings about such a highly publicized sex symbol as Jayne Mansfield getting married in my chapel. I told her I could not consent until she and Mr. Hargitay came down to talk about it. I was quite hesitant, especially when she said, 'but your church will get so much publicity out of it.' I assured her that was what I did not want, and why I hesitated.

"When they came to see me, my wife said she did not want to meet Jayne Mansfield. She did not like the Mansfield image at all. She found it revolting blatant sex. I found Jayne and Mickey however, to be completely different people than I had assumed they would be. They were not at all like their publicity. She was ladylike, sweet, kind and exceptionally attentive. I told her I hesitated in having movie stars march in on our chapel, and I was always on my guard. I would not let the chapel be used for anything that smacked of commercialism.

"They both promised there would not be any publicity. As I looked at both of them, I thought how much good these two can do, if they let the public see them and their complete dedication to each other, as I saw them. 'If I marry you in this chapel and you are using the chapel, I warn you, it is a very dangerous thing. These are real things. These are the concepts of God here, that you will be working with.' They seemed very impressed.

"I had them sit down for a long time. I told them the most important thing in life is the relationship between two people. No matter what you, Jayne or Mickey, attain separately, no matter what fame and fortune, if you fail in this love and respect you have found for each other, you will fail to attain the best life has to offer.

"Jayne volunteered in a subdued voice, 'I know. The love of a man and a woman is a rare precious thing; a direct concept of God. The more you relate to an individual in a close relationship, the more you become aware of what life is all about and the broader your base for living becomes,' she said to my surprise. She was very intelligent. 'If you can find everything in one person, the search is ended and you keep developing. Ours is a real marriage, born of real love and union. It takes place within, and there our heaven is. She explained, 'you develop it, you keep experiencing more and more. You arrive at the top of one hill, and you see there are more. It has been confirmed and validated in every area of life. You develop an ideal and a quality in this personal belief. It is a spiritual basis of togetherness and fulfillment in every level of expression, creative, physical, emotional and spiritual. That's why we want our marriage over anything else in the world.'

"Jayne and Mickey sat with their eyes glistening with unwashed tears. I urged them to hang on to what they had. 'You have God's rare gift of love for each other. This happens once in a lifetime. You are going into this with your eyes wide open. God help you, if you have used this chapel's concept. Here is a trust. If you betray it, it is at your own risk. If you lie to yourself or to each other, I won't take the responsibility of judging what the results and the rewards can be.'

"I justified myself further after they had gone that even though they were two divorced people, they were sincere. And that it was now their responsibility. I had also told them further, that we would have to talk again. As time progressed, and as we talked prior to the wedding, I was convinced that they had everything going for them."

"You have built this marriage up into something wonderful", I told them happily. "You can prove that it can be done." Jayne reassured me that it would be a quiet dignified wedding. And right up until three days before the ceremony, I believed it would be. "For there was no publicity, as agreed upon," concluded Reverend Knox.

Meanwhile, back in Hollywood, Jayne and I became very busy together planning the bridal shower and the wedding. "I wish I could wear white. I have a really lovely wedding gown from my picture with a veil and a train," Jayne sighed. "I guess it wouldn't be proper for a second wedding."

"You can wear pink," I offered. "Since pink is your favorite color, a soft pale pink would be pretty." Jayne agreed. Pink it would be.

We made out a list of guests to be invited for the bridal shower. Jayne's mother and step-father, the Harry Peers, were to arrive from Dallas for the event. I was to wear a pale pink lace bridesmaid's dress for the ceremony. Don agreed to sing the songs Jayne selected for the wedding. He would wear black tie and tux. It was an exciting time for everyone concerned.

Jayne held her own press conference to announce her marriage date.

"I want my wedding to be sacred and very intimate," she said. "This is one thing that is for me and Mickey alone. And," she added, "for those closest to us, who love us and want to share our happiness! It will be a small private ceremony."

We kept talking about Jayne's small intimate wedding right up to when it happened. Unexpectedly, Jayne, Mickey and I were caught up in the exciting whirl of ecstacy and surprise, which was propelled with the good wishes of a rosary of friends, all of whom wanted to be a part of Jayne's wedding.

"The girl just can't help it." Sybil Brand, the wife of Harry

Brand said. She had taken a genuine interest in Jayne, and championed her when criticism became strong. "Everywhere she goes, every move she makes—photographers appear, writers arrive, and Jayne is delighted."

"I decided," Jayne told me, "the press is so wonderful to me. I love them all. I love everyone and I am truly so grateful." She did and she was. "I've decided I have to invite them. Maybe just a few. I can't be happy and disappoint the press." I readily agreed.

With all of the anticipated privacy, Jayne, however, kept holding press conferences on her wedding plans.

"Of course, we go to our own church, the All Saints in Beverly Hills, but this little glass church at Palos Verdes is away from Hollywood," she said at one. "There we can have a quiet ceremony. One I have always dreamed of. At first I visualized a big church wedding—walking down the aisle on the arm of my father to 'my own prince charming.' But now I want my wedding simple and small and sweet. This little chapel holds only a few people. And at night we will have candlelight and moonlight. The moon will show through the glass spires for the whole church is glass. It is just everything I want," she declared happily. "Oh, I'm so in love, so happy!"

Six days before the wedding, a finely engraved pink invitation arrived which read: "Mr. and Mrs. Harry L. Peers request the honor of your presence at the marriage of their daughter, Jayne Mansfield, to Mr. Miklos Hargitay on Monday, the thirteenth of January at eight o'clock in the evening. The Wayfarers Chapel. Palos Verdes Drive South, Portugese Bend, Palos Verdes."

"May, I am wearing the pink lace as you suggested for my wedding," Jayne telephoned me that very night. "I thought it over, and I decided to have a very special dress. It is going to be a dream. And May, listen to this," Jayne said excitedly, "Mickey and I are going to move into a beautiful big new home in Holmby Hills. It is Mickey's wedding present to me. Except I'm paying for it with my $90,000 inheritance. It will have a heart shaped pool! We'll move in March 1st. But Mickey is going to remodel it and make it into a pink palace for me!"

Then Mickey was on the telephone. "We could only make the down payment on it," he laughingly explained. "You know I'd give Jayne the world, if I had it," he added seriously. "Sometimes," he said in a low voice, "I can't believe my good fortune in having such a wonderful girl, and that she is going to be my wife. I don't think I deserve her, but I'll try."

Then Jayne was back on the telephone. "I don't know what I ever did before Mickey came along," she said. "I want to be the best wife in the world for him. May, you don't know how wonderful he is in so many ways. He never steps into the house that he doesn't take over the whole responsibility. If there is a leaky faucet, or something that he can do, he does it. He helps Jayne Marie with her lessons, and reads to her. When I try to get him to sit down for dinner, he won't unless I sit down with him."

Jayne revealed that they had just finished dinner and were still at the table. Jayne had cooked the dinner herself. "I often cook dinner now for Mickey," Jayne said. "Of course, I do. Any woman who can't cook for her man isn't all woman," she disclosed. "And Mickey's best friend, Ross Christina, who is to be our best man, arrived tonight from Indianapolis. You'll have to meet him, May," Jayne enthused. "I thought of him for you. He's very nice. He's six feet four inches tall, and dark, handsome and twenty-five. I have to get you two together."

"I always had to go it alone with my career, and take care of Jayne Marie right along with it," she chatted. "Now Mickey has come into my life. He's taken the load of responsibility off my shoulders. He's a real man.

"I never knew a man like Mickey, a man who has authority in his voice, and at the same time is so considerate and gentle and understanding. I adore him. There is not a single bit of jealousy or impatience about the demands of my career. He is all for it—for me—whatever makes me happy. We haven't had one misunderstanding—not even one quarrel. He makes every hardship a pleasure. I have the hardest time trying to do something for him. I don't know how I ever lived without Mickey."

# CHAPTER IX

Jayne Mansfield was the only celebrity in Hollywood known to have a press secretary. He sent me the guest list for the bridal shower. I had mentioned I would like to keep it to twelve to fifteen close friends, at the very most. The list named sixty. Jayne never thought in small terms on anything; always big. Daily, she'd have her press secretary call to add more names to the list. I was overwhelmed when the list had grown to seventy-five. I began to protest! My home was not a hotel!

One hundred invitations duly went out in the mail for the bridal shower. Fifty replys of regrets speedily returned. Jayne had named Marilyn Monroe, Elizabeth Taylor, Debbie Reynolds, Marlene Dietrich and practically all of Hollywood's top feminine stars. Some she knew—most she knew of, but had never met personally. She was blissfully unaware that few actresses would want to play secondary roles to Jayne, even at her bridal shower. They were either envious, uncaring or just cautious. All were fully aware that wherever Jayne would be, they were sure to emerge as backdrops for her aura of exhibitionism—whether intentional or not.

To stabilize this event, I invited a few name friends of my own, so Jayne wouldn't be embarrassed by a complete absence of actresses. Maureen O'Hara, Patti Moore, Margaret O'Brien, Marilyn Maxwell, Vera Ellen, Pat Wymore and Terry Moore accepted even though, at the time, they had never met the guest of honor. They, too, wanted it to be a happy time for Jayne with no disclaimers.

"It would be nice to have the husbands and boyfriends come in later for a supper," Jayne suggested. Jayne had no conception of the work or apparently of the time and money such a big party demanded. Jayne had never been a hostess. Each day she or her press secretary would call with another name to be invited. She had invited mahy more without informing me.

I repeatedly demurred, "It's getting way to big Jayne! My house won't hold one hundred and twenty people at once!"

"Oh, put them anyplace. You have that huge, big drawing room," she purred. "Everyone can scatter through the rooms."

"You can't do that to the wives of studio executives and directors and producers," I implored. "Besides, I want to give you a beautiful party—not a haphazard jamboree!"

I realized I had better put my foot down once and for all! "Not one more guest," I said. I was adamant! "And no photographers! This is not a publicity affair. It is an intimate, personal bridal shower and I intend, since it is my house, it is to be done in good taste. I refuse "to let this be turned into a circus. Remember, It's strictly private. No publicity! "Remember you've been heavily criticized as a 'publicity hound.' Now everyone loves you, so don't start the 'wrong image' all over again!"

Jayne meekly agreed. She realized I meant it!

It was now four days before Jayne's wedding, and the newspapers were filled with the attending excitement of the nuptials. The studio was hounded with requests for press coverage from all over the world. The wire services were installing special wires at Marineland, a resort a few miles removed from the little glass chapel.

Jayne professed that she was bewildered at all of the big hullabaloo over her modest, intimate little wedding!

As the hours progressed towards my bridal shower for Jayne and Jayne's "quiet, little, personal wedding," it was amazing how the columns and the radio and the television kept blurbing new facts about both! Jayne, I learned, kept giving press conferences to divulge the latest details. Her enthusiasm was unquenchable. I was not, I decided with resignation, about to turn her off in fear of spoiling her happiness.

Photographers and press media from all parts of the world were rushing in and out of Jayne's house at all hours of the day and night. Wedding presents were arriving and so were curiosity seekers who stood out in the road.

Squeals of delight emanated from her tiny bedroom at the back of the house. Photographers, sitting outside around the pool, swiveled their necks at the gleeful squeals inside, hoping the window would open, and Jayne would reveal what was going on!

The lens boys were rewarded when, unannounced, Jayne walked out to model a sheer yellow negligee that was part of her bridal trosseau. A tiny pair of panties and her hands clasped on her breasts assured her modesty, to some extent, was intact.

Mickey Hargitay arrived. On seeing his future bride in such disarray he swore a soft oath, swooped her up in his arms and carried her inside the house. Everyone got the pictures. After all, that was what Jayne wanted!

Jayne showed me her wedding ring for Mickey. It was a simple, plain gold band inscribed, "To My Husband on his Wedding Day. I Love You. 1-13-58." For her wedding gift to him, Jayne said, "I'm duplicating a gold tie clasp that Mickey lost, and it is inscribed: 'My husband from his wife.'" Jayne loved saying "My

Husband." She caressed each syllable.

"We are going to Florida for our honeymoon. We will return to Las Vegas for rehearsals on our own show—the 19th," she disclosed. "Mickey is helping me—and I'm going to have my own show in Las Vegas! Isn't that divoone!" she exclaimed. She was bubbling with excitement and anticipation. As she talked, she jumped up and down around the room. "Our act at the Tropicana is going to be my life story, about a little, wide-eyed girl from Texas, who knew she was born to be a movie star, and made it. Doesn't it sound interesting?"

"Mickey is a wonderful business man," Jayne disclosed, as we put the shower and wedding plans in abeyance for a couple of hours and drove to the Ambassador Hotel, where we were both scheduled to appear as guests of honor at a civic luncheon.

"When I was first offered a show in Las Vegas," Jayne disclosed, "at $12,500 a week, Mickey and I were visiting my parents in Texas. I was thrilled to be offered such big, big money. Even Marilyn Monroe has never been paid $12,500 a week!

"'I'll accept,' I said, 'and with great pleasure.' Mickey said, 'No, you should get more.' I told my agent what Mickey said. My agent was terribly upset. I told Mickey, 'You'll cost me my career! I don't have special acts. I'm not a nightclub star.' But Mickey said patiently, 'Then we'll get you an act, and you are a star wherever you appear.'

"Imagine the confidence he gives me. My agent said that the offer would never go higher. But it did—up to $18,500. Mickey said, 'It's not enough!! If they give you $25,000 a week for four weeks, then you take it.' It looked like I wouldn't get it. Two days later the contracts were signed. I will start at $25,000 a week!

"Mickey and I have made some wonderful plans," Jayne confided. She was driving her new, pink Cadillac de Ville along Wilshire, headed towards the Ambassador. People in cars were waving to her. Everyone recognized the platinum blonde in the pink car. Jayne waved back. "I love people. I love it when they love me—

recognize me—love me," she said.

"Mickey's completely devoted attitude towards me and my career is something I've never had. We also have plans for security for us and for the children we hope to have.

"Mickey's major occupation is not acting, you know. He plans many enterprises, like a chain of gas stations and a health and food club. And perhaps, a photo business.

"Movie money you can't keep," Jayne continued in a practical vein. "So you have to make a long range of plans. We are incorporating the Jayne Mansfield Enterprises. We have an apartment house already. And we are going to open a chain of pet stores and kennels. We have plans for a Hungarian restaurant but, of course," she said softly, "our main plan is to love each other the rest of our lives!"

Her next picture, she said, would be serious and dramatic. "I'm making a change of pace career-wise too."

Driving home, she flipped on the radio. Announcers of spot news on every program were giving the details of Jayne Mansfield's wedding to be and the shower I was giving her on the morrow!

"This is the little intimate wedding we planned," she sighed. "But," she concluded, "isn't it wonderful that everyone is so interested and wants to participate in the most important day of my life!"

At this time Reverend Knox was becoming anxious and worried. His church advisory board feared a typical la-de-da movie type of wedding at the glass chapel. They also feared the beautifully landscaped grounds would be trampled and ruined. By telephone, Jayne reassured them there would be no crowds. It would be small and simple, as agreed.

The day of the shower arrived. Jayne had agreed no publicity and no photographers. She walked in my front door accompanied by *Life Magazine* photographers! I almost collapsed with shock. This was to be a private affair, with no publicity! After all, this was my house. Jayne ignored my look of wonder!

; Jayne opened her pink, satin-bow-tied shower gifts. Maureen O'Hara's was an automatic skillet. Vera Ellen's, a white beaded wedding bag, and Marilyn Maxwell said, "Mine is practical!" It proved to be white bath towels with pink satin monograms.

Mickey and Jayne's step-father arrived at sundown in time to hear Donald Maloof, who was soloist of the Arthur Godfrey show, sing "Because" and "Ave Maria" which Jayne had asked him to sing later at her wedding.

I asked Mickey how he happened to come to America. "Did you see a picture of Jayne Mansfield?"

"No," he laughed. "That was ten years ago. I was eighteen and completing my course in psychology at the University of Budapest. I was to be drafted for the army and sent to Russia for four years. I escaped and was captured three different times. After many attempts, I finally reached America and two years later I became a citizen."

"My parents, Frank and Maria Hargitay, and my two brothers and my sister are still behind the iron curtain," he said.

At night, the men arrived for a buffet supper. It was a gala, happy party which went on from four in the afternoon until four the next morning. We numbered over a hundred.

Jayne received all sorts of gifts; perhaps well over a thousand dollars in presents were showered on her in my house that day.

Unbeknown to Reverend Knox or me, hundreds of pink cards authorized by Jayne and her press agent had been sent out to the press. Some were even dropped from a helicopter over Los Angeles. They were printed: "See Jayne Mansfield Married Under Glass at the Wayfarers Chapel, Palos Verdes, Monday Night." Hundreds of people besieged the chapel, tied up the roads and trampled the flowers, shrubs and lawns. Police and highway patrolmen attempted to handle the chaos.

Sybil Brand reported Jayne's dress was so tight she could hardly walk to the altar. After the service, Jayne and Mickey spent an hour posing for photographers, while more police were sent for in all directions, so the little glass church wouldn't be crushed by the milling mobs of spectators. There was no wedding cake or reception. People had a difficult time departing, due to the traffic jams that tied up traffic and the roads for miles.

The newspapers all over Europe and the United States referred to Jayne's wedding as "a publicity circus." "Our church membership was quite upset," Reverend Knox said. "An indignant minister wrote, saying that my parish must be hungry to have permitted such a wedding to take place in our chapel. My wife, who had no use for Jayne's publicity image in the first place, was upset. I asked Jayne about it later, and she told me that it was her publicity manager who made it such a spectacle. I had to justify myself to ministers all over the world. 'I take people as I find them,' I said."

From the night of the wedding Reverend Knox, like everyone close to Jayne, found himself in the position of defending Jayne Mansfield. "However, I still found her to be a very decent, sweet and spiritual young woman. I received Christmas cards from them, and for three years she and Mickey would return to the chapel on their wedding day. They would go through their wedding service again. Each time, Jayne would put on her pink lace wedding dress. And there would be no publicity and no pictures—it would be just for them.

"On one of these occasions, my wife became acquainted with Jayne. She relented and decided she liked and admired her for the sweet woman she really was. She felt Jayne was perhaps victimized by 'her image' and her publicity. It was regrettable that Jayne, herself, seemed to believe she had to react to that image and not be herself. She had so much going for her. Had she been her natural self, she could have been anything she wanted to be. I wonder about that many times."

Jayne and Mickey took the midnight plane to Dallas, where the press awaited them at the airport. After a press conference, they went to Jayne's parents' home, where the guest house was their honeymoon abode. Jayne hoped that her mother approved of her now, at long last. Later, she said, "I'm never sure of Momma. She just doesn't like the way I do things."

# CHAPTER X

"Jayne And Mickey Float To Dallas On A Pink Cloud," said a Dallas newspaper headline. Pictures of the bridal pair covered the front pages. The home town girl had come home to celebrate her nuptials. If Paul Mansfield, who had reportedly become the manager of a soft drink business, was about, he was all but forgotten.

Even though Jayne and Mickey arrived in the pre-dawn hours, the Dallas field was filled with waiting press and photographers. Dallas had never seen anything like it. Jayne kept holding her "ten carat diamond engagement ring" high to catch the flash of the lights. "It cost $25,000," she purred modestly. "Mickey has a fortune of his own you know!" That was to be questioned immediately in news stories in Philadelphia, where Mickey's acquaintances said they didn't believe it. They also, reportedly, believed Jayne's $25,000 diamond was not for real.

Counteracting these doubting Thomases and the press, Jayne's press agent had released a story to Associated Press writer, James Bacon, that Mickey had arrived in this country with ten dollars and had amassed a fortune. The new $150,000 house, it was said, was Mickey's wedding present to his bride. That was on top of the $25,000 diamond engagement ring. "You don't give gifts like that on money earned from weight lifting," commented Mr. Bacon in the *Herald Examiner.* The report continued that Mickey had $50,000 in the bank within his first three years in the U. S. Filling stations and physical culture gymnasiums, besides construction, had increased his wealth. "Wow," Mickey was reported saying, "When I hear people say that America is a land of opportunity, I say 'Wow!' Where else could a crazy Hungarian—all Hungarians are crazy—get wealthy and Jayne Mansfield too."

The doubting Thomases in Indianapolis told the press they refused to swallow this Horatio Alger story. The first Mrs. Mickey Hargitay asked for more support money, pointing to the newspaper reports of Mickey's alleged wealth.

Jayne learned from then on to be more conservative in statements to the press. She was careful that her imagination was restricted to facts in the future. "As a child, I had such an imagination, Momma had her hands full!" she now said. "Anyway, I wish Mickey could have been wealthy and could have done all of that. We just thought of it as publicity at the time. We didn't realize how it would backfire. We're sorry."

Jayne's mother might not have approved of her daughter's career; nevertheless, it was noted that the decor of her home was the highly publicized Jayne Mansfield pink. The newlyweds retired to a pink guest cottage at the rear of the Peers' house until the wedding reception.

Jayne and Mickey stood just outside the door sipping pink champagne. They greeted eighty invited guests. Between, and in free moments, they openly exchanged caresses. "Still the little exhibitionist," laughed the man who had hired Jayne for her first professional modeling job. That had been in Dallas, posing in the nude for life art classes.

Jayne explained why she was holding the reception in her home town "Mommy and Daddy live here," she purred. "We wanted to be with those we love." Jayne wore a tight fitting, pink jersey dress. Mickey drank pink champagne from one of her pink high-heeled slippers. Jayne called attention to the fact that she was speaking on a pink telephone and she selected the eggs for Mickey's breakfast from a pink refrigerator!

Any and every reporter and photographer, from major wire services to the neighborhood throwaway shopping guide and high school papers was welcomed. "I just love newspaper men," Jayne said. "I am thinking of sending Mickey to journalism school!"

Jayne's mother, Mrs. Peers, graciously reacted to all of the hullabaloo with, "I'm happy to say I played a key role in Jayne's life and I never cease to be amazed at what has happened to Jayne since." A biographer of the press reported, "Jayne Mansfield has made more personal appearances than a political candidate. Some she does for charity and most, at $10,000 per!"

On the morning of January 15, the newlyweds arrived back at the Dallas airport to fly to Miami. Thousands of home town people were there, cheering, "Our Jayne," as she departed in the air.

Elmer E. Palmer, Jayne's paternal grandfather, died January 2, 1957, leaving a large estate held in trust for Jayne. She had also been left over $36,340 in trust by her grandmother in 1945. Jayne and Mickey returned from their honeymoon to purchase the big, old mansion on Sunset Blvd. It was to become known as the Pink Palace. "Momma is angry with me again," Jayne sighed. "She thinks I should have given her part of my inheritance, since my real Daddy was her first husband. But this will be my first home. I've never had one before."

The palatial thirty-room house Jayne bought with her inheritance had been built years before by Rudy Vallee for his bride Fay Webb, the beautiful brunette daughter of a Santa Monica police chief. Neither had lived in it. It had been sold to a multi-millionaire. "The man we bought it from was living in this big place all alone," Jayne disclosed, "except for a staff of servants. We shall get by nicely with two servants." Later she said, "Everyone thinks we have thirty-six bathrooms. I think we can seat twelve."

"There's only one thing wrong with Mickey," Jayne said after the honeymoon. "He has no hair on his chest. Not a single hair. I'm a girl who always likes hairy men." Asked if she had known this fact before they married, Jayne replied, "No, I handn't noticed."

Jayne and Mickey moved into the big mansion which had been stripped of furnishings. "We are sleeping on cots and in sleeping bags," she announced. "We don't mind. We are very busy preparing my act for the Tropicana in Las Vegas. Then I have another picture to make for Fox almost immediately."

"We haven't so much money," Jayne and Mickey told the judge when asked why Mickey could not raise the support of his ex-wife and daughter from $250 a month. Not even a refrigerator graced the kitchen and Jayne and Mickey were cooking on a gas plate. Afterwards, Jayne had to admit, "We could buy furniture but we have no time now. We have to leave for my next film. We don't understand why Mickey's ex needs $415 a month to support his daughter, Tina. We spend about $71 a month on Jayne Marie." The judge raised the support payments to $300 a month.

Pictures of Jayne and Mickey and Jayne Marie and her assorted dogs and cats sleeping on the floor of the big house were freely distributed and duly appeared in the press. The police of Laguna Beach pooled a significant sum from their combined salaries to buy Jayne Mansfield, their pin-up favorite, a bed. They promptly dispatched the money to Hollywood and to Jayne. "What marvelous men—how understanding," Jayne exclaimed. "They are really noble to buy me a bed so another man, can sleep in it with me. Few men would be so generous. That proves they really love me. They care for my comfort."

Jayne opened at the Tropicana in Las Vegas in the spring of

1958. The Las Vegas Sun reported her act: "Jayne wiggles and waggles and warbles and does some acrobatic maneuvers with Mickey Hargitay. Mickey tosses her around his waist and grabs her arms and spins her in wide circles. She never touches the ground in this dangerous fete. There's her famous squeaking and squealing, and while she says she's playing Trixie Divoon—she's playing Jayne Mansfield, herself. She has a male chorus behind her. She dissolves her ample figure in sheer nylon with strategic spangles."

"I don't compete with the nudes here," Jayne said, speaking of the beauties in the strip shows. "They have been through a war, those poor German and French girls in the nude lines. And after all of that hardship, they are not as healthy as I am. I am covered and in good taste."

Jayne's photos in the lobby and about town in Las Vegas were stolen as quickly as press agents put them up. At five-minute intervals, hotel operators were paging, "Call for Miss Jayne Mansfield." This went on continuously and had several stars climbing the walls. "She's paid the switchboards girls to keep paging her," was the accusation. Another star headlining at a rival hotel complained to the management: "All you hear is Jayne Mansfield ringing in your ears day and night," he exploded. The hotel complained that she sat outside by the pool all day, signing autographs. They'd prefer the public pay to see her inside. However, "inside" was always sold out for all of Jayne's shows.

Jayne's new pictures, *The Wayward Bus* and *Will Success Spoil Rock Hunter,* were in release. The sisters of the press resented Jayne's munificence, but photographers and the male press were always eagerly on hand for any news of Jayne. Finally, Jayne insisted on exclusive press conferences. "It's the only way," she decided. "I can't possibly fill all of the requests individually." She'd keep ten or twelve bathing suits and bikinis for each press conference. By rotating and changing them for the different world wire services, they got their exclusives.

It was about this time that Jayne also discovered she was pregnant.

"I am so happy. I can't tell you how happy I am—how happy we are!" Jayne's low, soft voice with its breathless expectancy fairly bubbled over the wire from her telephone in London to mine in Hollywood. It was ten in the morning her time, and 2:00 A.M. my time.

"We just want a baby. We don't care whether it is a boy or a girl," Jayne enthused. "I knew I was going to have a baby before I left for England. On April 10th my doctor in Beverly Hills confirmed the wonderful news. The baby is due Dec. 5th.

"The United Nations invited me to make a week of personal appearances in the Gaza Strip in the Middle East. I'll also visit the refugee camps. I am so happy to be able to do this."

"I may make one picture before the baby—although it will have to be mostly closeups," she said. I have a picture scheduled to start the last of December.

"Having a baby is the most natural, normal thing in the world. It is the God given enrichment of our lives. Our baby is the glorious fulfillment of our marriage—of our belonging to each other.

"Jayne Marie is so excited. She didn't know until just yesterday when the news slipped out, and she saw the newspaper headlines over here. She ran to me, and kissed and hugged me, and then to Mickey, and kissed and hugged him. And she kept saying over and over, 'I just can't believe it is true. I want a baby brother!' She is so delighted."

The first Hollywood knew of the anticipated Hargitay heir was the banner, front page press headlines: "Jayne and Mickey Expecting Stork!" When Jayne was so ill before she left for London, I thought she had the flu. Jayne, I now remembered, told me then, "I want babies—three or four of them." "When?" "Well, right away! Mickey and I want a baby as soon as possible."

I called Jayne in London the next night. "Jayne, I'll give you a baby shower," I said, quite forgetful of my dismay that Jayne had invited over a hundred guests to the bridal shower I had given her earlier in the year.

"I'd love that," Jayne replied.

"We'll borrow a tremendous stork from the studio, and stand it in front of the door with streamers of pink and blue satin ribbons," I said excitedly.

We began planning the shower. An hour later, regretfully, we said goodbye since neither of us owned that many shares in the telephone company, especially transatlantic.

Jayne's film career had now become almost a sideline with Jayne. She devoted more time to the exploitation of the Mansfield Image. Mickey became the European type of husband—the head of the house. He worked around the clock attendant on the many duties of Jayne's career, as well as remodeling the entire house. He worked to the point of exhaustion, day and night, plastering, brick laying, painting, constructing—to keep his promise to give Jayne her mansion. Press and visitors always met Mickey pushing a wheelbarrow or laying a brick.

Jayne never touched a dish nor washed her tub. She was a movie star super style, and she maintained that image. There was hired help for all of that.

The theme of the house had become hearts. Jayne's personal bathtub was shaped like a pink heart. And so was the swimming pool, which was surrounded by miles of pink terrazo. The bottom of the pool was emblazoned with two-foot high tile letters, spelling "Jayne, love Mickey." Money was spent so lavishly on the mansion that James Bacon, the columnist, reported, "The Mansfield mansion has a nice view. overlooking the mortgage."

"You like the house?" Mickey asked me with genial interest. "We are doing the whole place over, except the really fine carved wood ceilings and doors. There's painting and papering and carpeting and furnishing.

"We have eight bedrooms and thirteen baths," Jayne laughed. "I think we're going to be the cleanest people in the world."

"We're putting in a new driveway and a new pool which will be heart-shaped and pink, to coincide with Jayne's dreams," Mickey said, giving his effervescent bride a kiss.

"We have old fashioned French phones—just darling, and we'll have them painted pink. There's a push button service for the upstairs maid, the downstairs maid, the butler, the cook, the houseboy, the gardener, and the chauffer. Imagine us ever having a chauffeur," Jayne smiled. "Don't think we have a staff like that," she added. "We just have the buttons to ring them."

"The pool will have twenty steps, twenty-feet wide, with an island in the center with splashing fountains. It will look like the Gardens of Versailles. And we will build a steam room and showers."

"Come, let me show you the house," she invited. "It has so many secret rooms, and sliding panels. It was built originally by Rudy Vallee."

We started on the grand tour of the really magnificent mansion, starting with the servants quarters, where Jayne and Mickey were sleeping and living out of their suitcases.

"Our bedroom will have all mirrored walls," Jayne said with delight. "We are keeping the pink-mirrored headboard that Mickey made for me, of course. And there's the big suite for Jayne Marie. And this big room and bath and sitting room is the nursery—for all of the babies we hope God will give us.

"And this, the next suite, we will do for our guests, including our parents. Someone gave us two Texas-size beds."

Pointing to a new portable sewing machine—sheathed in her favorite color, pink—she announced another inspired aspiration. "I want to start sewing, making myself some clothes and Jayne Marie's too."

"When will you ever find time to sew?" I asked incredulously.

"Oh, I'll manage," she returned lightly. "I always do."

"With our security and trust and God's goodness and our faith, how can we fail?

"It's that way," Jayne said snuggling on a red leather covered bench in the big recreation room downstairs. "My marriage means everything. It is no longer just Jayne Marie and I bucking the world, trying, working, striving, alone. We have the strength and protection of Mickey now. And his love and devotion."

# CHAPTER XI

When Jayne wasn't at the studio, she was cutting the ribbon on a supermarket opening or drugstore or such, for which she was usually paid $2500. Or she was riding in a parade for $1000. With the then Vice President Nixon, she lowered her parade price to $500, "out of patriotism" for her country she said. The money from her six weeks in Las Vegas was poured into the reconstruction of the pink palace.

Jayne continued to act out her own conception of a glamorous movie star. She drove a pink Jaguar, posed during press conferences taking pink champagne baths, walked on Hollywood Boulevard with a great dane and on ocelot on a leash, both wearing huge pink bows. She bought a new full-length white mink coat and wore it when it was 95 degrees in Hollywood because it made her look and feel like a movie star. She began garnering magazine covers all over the world.

She mapped out her career like a political campaign. "I realize now that I have the men on my side—that if I want to continue to be a super movie star I need the women too. I play it that way now with the P.T.A. I win both. I am going to make a pitch for the intellectuals, like presidents of the United States and kings. I will make it a point to go to every city and meet the mayor. Most of them will give me the key to the city, and lots of publicity, which is high class prestige for me. I will always take my children with me, which turns on the women."

Jayne also pursued astrology and various religions in due order. Sunday mornings she was up and attending church at the All Saints Episcopal Church in Beverly Hills. She thought of returning to college. "I need only one semester to get my B.A. degree."

Sunday afternoons would often find Jayne with Jayne Marie in tow visiting Forest Lawn Cemetery. She hunted the graves of the film famous. She declared that one day she would like "to find my final resting place here. I want a statue of me on my grave, so my fans can find me more quickly."

She was a frequent visitor to the city pounds and animal shelters. There she would adopt a few stray cats and dogs and take them home. Friends and studio acquaintances were no longer surprised to see Jayne taking a feline or pooch from her car and handing it to the first nice person as a gift from her. In that way, she found homes for her hundreds of strays. Who could refuse a pet from Jayne Mansfield?

Jayne owned ten dogs, three cats, many assorted fish, and four monkeys.

Pregnancy didn't bother Jayne. She blossomed and enjoyed vigorous health. A sad sack pregnancy wasn't necessary, according to Jayne. She proved it by remaining glamorous! She refused to become overweight and dowdy and she was happily making personal appearances right up to the minute her baby was born.

Hollywood's Annual Oscarette Awards this year found Jayne had been voted "The New Star of the Year." The Chairman of the awards committee, Dr. Ernst Katz and I arrived at 20th Century Fox Studios bearing the proclamation and an invitation. It was a most important and unusual one for Jayne, who by her unusual publicity had been trying to bring back "the old time glamour" to the movies.

"I'm sooooo honored," she said gratefully to Dr. Katz. And then she and Dr. Katz were discussing music crescendos, sharps and minor keys, and flats. Next, they were going over Jayne's music, and he was asking her, "Next year, Miss Mansfield, please be soloist at our concert!"

"Really," Jayne gasped in delight.

"We have had Dorothy Kirsten, Lauritz Melchior, Heifetz, and now you will bring this recognition to the film industry," he said.

Jayne was all sweetness and light—and appreciation. "May I bring Mickey, Mr. Hargitay, with me?" she asked.

Jayne, who had been Queen of the Artists and Models Ball, Gas Station Queen, Miss Standard Foods, Miss Roquefort Cheese, Miss Four Alarm, Miss Maple Syrup, to mention a few, now found herself being "Miss Mansfield, Extraordinary; Guest of Honor" at the Oscarette Award Celebration a position filled the previous year by no less than Miss Mary Pickford.

The big night arrived. Backstage there were many notables, but Jayne's arrival was electric. Mickey Hargitay came with her. The President of the Chamber of Commerce stopped them to talk before Jayne went on.

"Is it possible, all of the energy they say you have?" he asked, disbelievingly. "I was reading about how you worked at publicity day and night to get started in New York. It sounds incredible. Wasn't that publicity?"

"I was busy," Jayne admitted with a smile. "You see, I am young, and I can keep busy. In fact, I kept three press agents in New York busy. They used to work shifts in relays. But I worked all of the time. Those were wonderful days," she sighed happily.

"Give us a sample of your day here," she was asked.

"It is something like this," she said thoughtfully. "I am up at five in the morning. When I am making a picture I have to be on the set, 'ready for camera,' at 8:30. Otherwise, I see about the house, the shopping, and Jayne Marie. Then by nine, the telephone starts going crazy with reminders of appointments, and requests for other appointments. This can go on all morning. Then it's time for lunch. I never eat much because I want to keep my waist tiny. So next we start on interviews lined up. They had over a hundred requests waiting for me one week. Then I change clothes to go out into the country for some nature shots, only they don't go quite as far back to nature as they used to. Then I rush back for a radio or TV show, or an interview, or a home layout. For that I have to dress Jayne Marie, too, and fix her hair. By then, it is four o'clock, and I have to appear at a charity tea and a couple more benefits. Then there's a dinner party to attend, or a premiere, or a preview, or a personal appearance I have been asked to make for some worthy cause. I couldn't begin to recreate all of it. Except it is like resting, living in California, compared to what it was in New York. If we ever can, Mickey and I go to a movie, like any two people."

When Jayne walked on stage that night, with that swivel-hipped motion, the dignified audience broke into applause. She didn't change the Mansfield manner at all, nor the undulations. She stayed as she was, and they loved her. After she had accepted the honors and agreed to play as soloist next season at the symphony concert, Jayne walked off—only to be called back again and again. "Just have her walk back on the stage so we can look at her," someone in the audience called. Jayne accommodated and she brought Mickey with her. There were cheers of approval from this very elegant audience of Los Angeles' elite.

Asked if it were true that she made an entrance with Mickey at a ball, with him holding her horizontally aloft, she said, "Yes, that was for The Publicists Ball. It was for publicity." She made it clear that it wasn't her usual entrance to a party.

"Mickey has been a great help to me. He gives me what little ego I have," she admitted. "Actresses have to have ego. He tells me I'm a great actress and beautiful. Every woman wants to hear that kind of encouragement from a man who really means it."

Jayne said it was the luckiest year of her life. There were Jayne Mansfield dolls on the market. She had a red Lincoln and two mink coats and a pink mink stole. And she bathed in pink champagne. "I really do. It takes many bottles—just bottles and bottles, but I do it twice a week. It gives my morale a boost."

As Jayne left, she noticed a bystander who was trying to catch a ride. She generously offered him a lift. She and Mickey drove him direct to his destination. She was now a star, Grade A, but she was still Jayne, the naive girl whose goal was "Stardom or Bust!" She had made both famous.

# CHAPTER XII

In the three years since Jayne had made her debut on Broadway, she had become the most spectacular and controversial star in a decade. In 1960, she topped all press polls for more words in print about her than anyone else in the world. Her publicity exceeded Elizabeth Taylor's. She created instant news, daily—everything from dresses falling-off, clothes that burst at the seams strategically in the presence of cameras, to well-planned, fictional plots that would make headlines.

Jayne planned and plotted her peccadilloes as adroitly as any playwright. Some of them were successful. The more fantastic incidents didn't make it. Her claim that she was stolen away for love, even though sworn as truth by Mickey and a detective friend, was generally considered a hoax. It never made a headline or even a ripple in the press.

Jayne's story told of a man telephoning her, stating he was from the studio publicity department. He'd arrive shortly at her house, he said, for an important interview. Jayne opened the front door to be told by a handsome, tall stranger that she was being kidnapped! In her nightgown and at gun point, she was taken to Malibu where she was held captive a day and a night, until Mickey rescued her. Later, equally bizarre plots were laughed at and disbelieved, even when some were true!

Jayne accepted various offers for publicity if a nice check and all expenses for four people was attached. One came from a hotel in the Bahamas. Jayne and Mickey flew there for a weekend vacation of publicity and water skiing.

I was awakened early one morning by a pitiful call from Jayne Marie. She was crying. "The radio says my mama and Mickey are lost in the Bahamas somewhere," she sobbed. Trying to reassure the child that the radio was mistaken, I called the wire services. Indeed, Mickey and Jayne had disappeared while taking a trip in a boat. They had been missing now for 12 hours. It was believed to be another Mansfield publicity stunt. "She'll probably come out of the water like Amie Semple McPherson, saved by a miracle," said the AP Man. He added, "the hotel's press man was with them." Even so, by morning search parties were looking for all three.

Jayne and Mickey had been swimming off the boat after water skiing. "Jayne dove, hit her head on the side of the boat and disappeared," Mickey said later. Seeing only bubbles coming up, he dove down after her. The water was shark infested. While trying to hoist Jayne's unconscious form into the boat, the boat turned over. The hotel publicity man and Mickey, seeing sharks circling, decided their only chance to survive, for now it was dusk, was to swim to a tiny coral reef close by. They spent the entire night on this bug infested reef until a Coast Guard amphibian plane, aiding a 400-man air and sea rescue search squad, found them. Jayne was carried into the hospital, her eyes, face and entire body painfully swollen with mosquito bites. A newsman smirked, "A good publicity stunt Jayne and Mickey!" Mickey was ready to smack the reporter! Later he sat down and cried, emotionally spent from the terror they'd experienced. "My God," he wept, "we almost lost Jaynie!"

Jayne rode atop an elephant in Ringling Bros. and Barnum & Bailey's Circus. She rode a circus horse bareback—stood up to the cheers of the spectators even though she was secretly scared to death. She let an elephant put his foot on her face without weight. She dove into a Marineland water tank to flirt with a killer whale. In one day she drove to Mount Baldy and posed in a ski suit in the snow and four hours later, she was posing at Malibu in a bikini. No effort was too much for Jayne if it spelled her name right!

Bids for Jayne's appearance came from all parts of the world. Jayne accepted invitations to appear in Rio de Janeiro.

She caused a three-car collision when she appeared in her bikini on the beach. Jayne pooh-poohed the idea that the female figure had anything to do with sex. "It's all in the mind," she said. "It's what you have inside—the feelings that you transmit—that counts! The rest is all tinsel. Sex appeal has nothing to do with body proportions."

At a press conference Jayne wore a clinging, white gown with a low v-cut neckline and a pink stole. The fur was purely display, for her "image," as the temperature was 101 degrees. Mickey told the people that puny men have as much to offer a girl in bed as a big he-man. "Muscles are nice but not essential for love," he said. He also confided that being married to Jayne he had to be very broad-minded. Men overcome by her aura leaped at her to kiss her, to touch her. Mickey was cheerful about it all.

At the Copacabana Hotel in Brazil Jayne attended the Mardi Gras Ball. She wore red roses in the bosom of her dress. They were hand-picked off her and she revealed a black and blue chest of pinches. Mickey had to bodily lift her and carry her through the crowd, as her dress was being torn off of her by the impetuous guests. From a safe balcony above, Jayne reappeared to smile and receive their acclaim.

Some of her publicity was exactly the way she liked it. Some not!

A woman reporter wrote, "I have seen the Jayne Mansfield boobs up close. Who hasn't? They're not too big. The fact is she has a big rib cage from holding her stomach muscles in, and the boobs rest on that expanse of support beneath for self-push up." In another section of the same paper was a dignified article and photo of Jayne, speaking at her local P.T.A. meeting with Jayne Marie in hand. Simultaneously, a spread in the center fold of *Playboy* magazine revealed Jayne with all her charms—nude!

Jayne was extremely popular in Europe and in all the Latin American countries. In Rome, where she was making a film, Italian men pinched her so often, that it took Mickey and a security guard to flank her on all sides to protect her. She was bothered by the pinching, but she also reveled in it. Everyone wanted to touch her. Jayne now fully realized that her "sex goddess title" was for real.

During the filming in Rome, Jayne tried to hide the fact that she was pregnant for the second time with Mickey. She kept it secret, realizing that her studio would be unhappy with this event: two babies in less than two years! and she was a sex symbol? "I eat carrots and green string beans and vitamins, so I'll keep my shape," Jayne said. "I have to take plenty of vitamins to insure my baby's well-being."

Jayne made a small budget film for an Italian company with Mickey as her leading man. Her Hollywood studio wouldn't go for the co-starring idea she requested for her husband. Jayne's friend, Leona Goldring, wife of her business manager visiting in Rome, was amazed at Jayne's patience. Mickey was supposed to fight a lion for Jayne. The lion would only go lay down and to to sleep, being heavily tranquilized. They had to go over scenes repeatedly to get any action. Jayne never objected, no matter how many times she was required for retakes.

Jayne took Leona on a sight-seeing tour of Rome. Visiting a cloistered cathedral, Jayne saw with pleasure that the nuns stole out to look at her, even though most were shy. One reached out to touch Jayne's arm, admiring her skin.

"Mickey has me on such a health kick," Jayne revealed. "No more champagne for breakfast." Her skin was flawless pink and white. Her body was trim and curved. Jayne was gorgeous!

Jayne returned from Europe to have Zoltan, her second son, here. Leona Goldring gave Jayne the baby shower. I explained to Jayne that it would not be good taste to invite the same people over and over for showers at my house—not after a wedding shower and baby shower in less than two years. Jayne agreed, but she naively believed that people just loved to give her presents. She loved to receive them.

Jayne was constantly traveling. She made films in Europe for independents. At the West Berlin Film Festival, Jayne was challenged by actress Laya Raki, who wriggled to burst her skin-tight dress, a la Mansfield. Jayne was amused. Coyly, Jayne refused to hand over the spotlight to the younger actress. She did reply that the charge of pulling in her stomach, her bosom was placed to better advantage was okay.

A reporter wrote about it all, saying: "We get angry when career-seeking women and shady ladies and actresses of riper years use every opportunity to display their anatomy unasked." Jayne wisely refused to comment.

At the Cannes Film Festival, Jayne was revered as "The girl with 1,000 curves and every one of them enticing!"

It was a beautiful spring day. Jayne had invited me and a boy friend to swim. The previous day's magazine section of a Los Angeles paper had devoted a full-page spread on Jayne's happy marriage. Pictures showed Jayne and Mickey and their three children about the spacious pink palace. The reporter said Jayne had bought the house with an inheritance for $72,500. In the 1930's, Rudy Valle couldn't give it away for $30,000, although it had cost a quarter of a million to build. The article said further that Mickey was a good carpenter and bricklayer and had done wonders in remodeling the mansion. The story told about the heart-shaped decor of the house. Jayne said she had "wanted the toilet seats heart-shaped, but nature wouldn't cooperate." A biased reporter speculated that perhaps when Mickey laid the last brick for the pink mansion, Jayne would no longer need him. She might even get rid of him!

Jayne was so upset at this report that she marched into the editorial room the very next day! She demanded a retraction. Jayne's demands were not only met, but she was photographed provacatively sitting on an editor's desk, with her legs crossed high of course. The photo caption headlined: "Jayne's Marriage Happiest in World says She!"

On this particular afternoon, we went in the pool, all except Mickey. He explained he had to complete some masonry work on a statue.

Jayne was voluptuous in a pink bikini. Her voice was sexy and soft as she spoke of Mickey. When he joined us, a little frown of displeasure crossed her face, as though he distrubed her serenity. She had begun the afternoon so gaily, that I wondered what could possibly have gone wrong between her and Mickey. Now she moved slightly away from him, almost in distaste.

"Is anything wrong Jayne?" I asked before I left. "No," she said. "But I am tired of what I have been, and what I am. I am going to become a serious dramatic actress. That is my dream now. I have worked hard with my body, my mentality, my emotions and I have consistently practiced and studied. I feel that with my drive and energy and ambition, I have to accomplish more. I can't go along just being a sex symbol.

"I want good dramatic roles. If the studio won't give them to me, then I'll go on the stage. If I have to, I'll do my own plays with my own company!"

"That will take alot of money."

"I know," Jayne replied. "The house here is finished. We have poured all my earnings from Las Vegas the last four years—over $200,000 a year, into this place. With my picture work and appearances, I'm making over a million and a half dollars a year now. I'm going to put my money back into my career!

"I have the talent of a Bernhardt or a Duse. I really have! I wouldn't dare say that for publication for fear of being laughed at. But you will see. I will succeed!"

"I need stimulation," she sighed. "So far Mickey has been everything to me that I need. But now he is turning into just a husband!"

"He gets up early and wants to go to bed early. He forgets that I diet, starve myself to stay this slim. When I am between pictures, I have to go out and see and be seen or I'm dead. There's no incentive. He is so stubborn," she frowned. "Everyone thinks he is so romantic. Part of that is his 'image.' He needs a jolt to wake him up to be like he was when we first met. I don't want just a dull, unexciting man in my life. I want, and have to have a lover!"

"Are you ready Jayne for a big dramatic role? What if you fall on your face, opening in a big dramatic play?" I asked.

Jayne was aware of her shortcomings , and of her faith in herself.

"You must remember I am not a spoiled, pampered darling," she argued. "I've worked hard for everything. I figured everything very carefully. This is my next step." With that, Jayne sprang up, turned three rapid cartwheels across the lawn. "I was never an acrobat until last year. I can be anything I want to be," she said. "I have no inner satisfaction with where I am today. I have to be more. I'm going to form my own company—get the best director and the best play and open on Broadway," she announced.

"Be sure you're ready Jayne," I warned. "You don't want to be laughed off the stage. A play is a big investment. You don't want to lose all of your hard earned money overnight with a Broadway flop!"

"Even you," she accused. "Even you don't have faith in me?" Tears sprang to her eyes. She was suddenly very angry.

"No, just be cautious," I protested. "Cary Grant told me you have so much going for you!" I placated. "He said when you made your picture together, he wondered why you didn't drop the silly, dumb blonde image and be yourself. You have so much natural talent! Honest Jayne, that is what Cary Grant did say."

She was pleased. "I have to be deeply in love," she said, "and then you'll see. You'll see emotions like no one ever has expected of me."

I'd better talk to Mickey, I thought. He's got to play the lover, not the devoted husband, or he'll be losing Jayne. I didn't get that chance.

Two hours after I left Jayne, the radio blared: "Jayne sues Mickey for divorce." But how, why, where and when?

The very minute I had left her, Jayne had jumped into her car and drove to her lawyer's. They rushed to the court house, making it just before closing time, to file for divorce!

Mickey was baffled when reporters swarmed in front of the big gates of the pink palace. Mickey hadn't heard the news. He was still trimming the hedge.

"You are kidding," he said, in complete disbelief. The press boys asked what he was going to do about the divorce?

"It's not true!" he said. "Why Jayne's upstairs in our room resting." Pressed for proof, Mickey dashed inside the pink palace and ran up the stairs to find the door to their room firmly locked and bolted. All his pleading would not evict an answer from his wife. Defeated, crestfallen, visibly puzzled, he returned outside to face the reporters.

Mickey was saved explanations by the arrival of Jayne's press secretary. He promptly announced that Miss Mansfield had consented to a press conference. She would appear shortly.

Jayne arrived clad in gold lame, tight-fitting pants and a white sweater, scooped to her navel. The lens lads popped their flash bulbs. Jayne posed sultry and sexy. After two or three hundred photos were taken, sixty more press had arrived. Jayne spread her arms out with love and affection to all. All, but Mickey, who remained quietly in the background. Stepping up to an improvised microphone, Jayne, with a deep intake of breath, said in a low voice, "I am sorry that our marriage has ended. It is due to irreconcilable differences." Blowing a kiss of farewell towards Mickey's direction, she was immediately surrounded by her press secretary and two aids, and she was swept inside the pink palace. There she remained, unavailable for further comment!

Forty-eight hours later, Jayne and Mickey arrived at my home for dinner. With profuse kisses and hugs, Jayne rushed to the kitchen telephone. She called Louella Parsons. "Darling, I want you to be the first to know that Mickey and I have reconciled," she said. "You were right to tell Jayne Marie what you did. It was all a terrible misunderstanding. You see," she explained on the telephone, "I am going to Rome to make *Panic Button* with Maurice Chevalier. He will be my leading man. Naturally, I want to take the children. Mickey had insisted we leave the children home. You know, I never travel without my children. Well, Mickey has now agreed to take the children. So I have forgiven him."

No sooner had she hung up the receiver, than she dialed Hedda Hopper. "Darling," she said, "I want you to be the first to know." In almost the same words, she announced her reconciliation with Mickey to Hedda.

With a sigh of relief that that was over—since Louella and Hedda were rivals and both insisted on exclusive news first—Jayne admitted that carrying water on both shoulders was not easy. "But you've got to keep friends with both of them. They are so powerful!"

Mickey modestly said, "I'm a very happy man. I'm glad Jaynie has forgiven me." Aside to me he whispered, "I thought it would be good for Jaynie and I to be alone in Europe—give ourselves a second honeymoon. We have been working too hard without a minute's letup. But I was wrong, I guess. The children will always come first with Jaynie."

The following day they left for Rome with the three children and Jayne's two dogs.

# CHAPTER XIII

According to Louella Parsons' column, Jayne had spent the night in a hospital after filing for divorce from Mickey. Jayne Marie had called Louella, imploring her, "Please call Jayne! Please make some sense with my mama. I don't want her to divorce Mickey!"

According to Louella's report, this had all happened in forty-eight hours: the divorce filing, Jayne's press conference and then the revelation that her marriage to Mickey was on again. "It was my exclusive," Louella wrote. "Jayne called me first, before the press conference." (Yes, from my kitchen telephone, I thought.)

Jayne arrived in Rome to be mobbed by thousands of cheering Italians at the airport. Mickey, stuck with the three children and two dogs, couldn't protect her from the onslaught of fans. In desperation, he secured police to take the children while he endeavored to get his wife off the shoulders of admiring college boys, who were carrying her!

"Let me be," Jayne said to Mickey. She was enjoying the homage! She loved it. She had already lost both of her shoes, which had fallen off into the crowd. "This is divoone!" she exclaimed, rapturously spreading her arms out to embrace all Italy with her love. Flashbulbs popped at every step of the way. Jayne was the Queen, the beloved sex goddess! Italian gallants acted like school children, yelling "bravos, bravos, bellisimas" to their adored. They threw flowers at her, over the heads of the crowd. She was showered in red rose petals.

The Italian newspapers front-paged Jayne's arrival with pictures and flowery salutations. It was like heady wine to Jayne. Her hotel suite was crowded with flowers and bottles of champagne. Baskets of wine and fruit were arriving by the minute from her admirers. So were the invitations.

Rome's "dolce vita" proved hypnotic to Jayne. Every step was salutations of admiration from the Italians. What girl would turn her back on all this? Catching up with the spirit of the romantic, gay, free, swinging life she was seeing all about her, Jayne gave an interview that shocked her Parent Teachers Association group in Beverly Hills! It went wire service all over the world. Said Jayne: "I believe that sex is the most important human factor between two people. I love sex.

"I believe that in physical relationships, everything goes. The wildest form of love is beautiful. I don't see how you can make a floral arrangement out of it. It should be animalistic. It should be beautiful. It should be tender. It should be brutal, sadistic. It should, at times, even be masochistic."

The mother and happy wife image for the spectacular star was now out, as Jayne clasped Rome to her bosom, and Rome embraced her to its heart.

"There are few rules and moral conventions," Jayne marveled. "It is adventure, adventure every minute of the day and night.

"Perhaps I love the excitement so much because I feel the freedom. As a little girl, I was homely. In school, I was a bespecta-

cled nobody. I wasn't popular. I didn't win beauty contests. When
I became desirable at 14, I was married and even had a baby. I
have had responsibility on my shoulders all my life. Now I want to
be young and free—as I should have been as a teenager."

Mickey found himself more than disturbed with men so openly
paying their adoration to his wife. Consigned to taking care of the
children and dogs, Mickey more often spent his nights in the hotel
room as baby sitter. Jayne sallied forth without him for publicity
for her picture. She was a star making a new, big picture in Rome.
All Rome wanted Jayne. No one seemed to want Mickey; finally,
not even Jayne herself.

It was constant parties and excitement before filming began on
Panic Button. At all hours of the days and nights, parties were
going on. Jayne was toasted in champagne at every step. Everyone
wanted to honor Jayne, and Jayne was not going to turn down the
parties held in her honor. But she would not allow a strange
nursemaid to stay with the children. "The children would be
frightened in a strange city with a stranger." There had also been
kidnapping threats. For once, Jayne did not reveal any peril that
could endanger her children—even though it could have made
headlines. Mickey and she vowed that one of them would always
be with the children to secure their safety. The responsiblity fell to
Mickey who had no work pressing on him like Jayne.

Jayne and Mickey had arrived in Rome on the heels of their
reconciliation. Things had not been going well between them for a
long time. Jayne was restless and eager for fun. She thrived on
compliments. Jayne called me from Rome late one night. "It is so
exciting. Please fly over. The men will love you. They are so
turned on by blondes!" Then, "Can't you smell the aphrodisiac
perfume of the flowers and the scent of this fabulous city?" she
enthused. Not by long distance.

"You should meet my producer. He's Enrico Bomba—the most
exciting, suave, attractive man!" Jayne purred. "I just had to call
and tell you. It's love at first sight—me and Rome and Bomba."

Bomba was portly, middle-aged gentleman, who somewhat resembled Carlo Ponti.

Since a star of Jayne's stature has no privacy, it was soon being reported in the columns that Jayne and Bomba were inseperable. They were seen together all over Rome. He escorted her to all of the parties. The report said he was a married man with children.

The Italians spirit of pleasure for the moment enjulfed Jayne and she was the biggest moment Rome had ever known as a playmate. Men were charming, poetic and above all lovers, proud of their art of conquest.

A millionaire prince one of society's jet set, gave a party at his villa for Jayne. Bomba, of course, escorted her. Such affluents as Arri Onassis, Maria Callas, Gina Lollabridgida, Lawrence Olivier, the Rex Harrisons, an Indian prince and an Arab Sheik were among the guests. Jayne was bedazzled when they all raised silver cups to toast her beauty and her fame!

"I never want to go back to Hollywood," Jayne said. "I feel free—suddenly free and loved. I was confused and lonely before I came to Rome. I never want to be lonely again."

Bomba lavished her with praise and compliments. He was proud to escort her to the night life of Rome and all of the parties. Soon, pictures of Jayne and Bomba were appearing in the press.

Mickey, bitter and involved with household problems and the children, moved his family into a villa. He thought getting Jayne away from the Via Veneto would be good since she would not be so accessible for the parties and the gay life that hypnotized her. The plumbing didn't work. Jayne moved back to the Excelsior until the bathroom functioned. Mickey, with borrowed wrenches, in desperation, repaired the plumbing himself, after a long, futile wait for a plumber.

*Hoy* and all of the leading magazines carried pictures of Jayne and Bomba. Jayne began to take daily Italian lessons. She also announced that she was of Italian descent which proved quite a shocking surprise to her relatives back in the United States. Jayne, however, insisted she was of royal Italian lineage and was looking for her family's royal crest and insignia to use on all of her stationery and for a signet ring.

Bomba was now to Jayne as Carlo Ponti was to Sophia Loren, she said. "All of my life I have needed someone with experience and talent to guide my career. Bomba opens new vistas—a new career for me."

Bomba would make her a great dramatic star. Jayne began to order new clothes with high necklines. "I am serious about becoming a great actress. Bomba says I can be another Duse." Now Jayne talked openly about her dramatic talents which had, until now, been unexposed.

Mickey, infuriated with the Bomba press and Jayne's constantly leaving him behind as baby sitter, told Jayne unless she "stopped this nonsense of running around Rome like a single woman," he was going back to the States without her. Jayne momentarily recalled Paul Mansfield issuing her the ultimatum back in Hollywood years before. "It's all part of my career," she flashed back. "I can't be a movie star sitting home every night. The spotlight is out with the people!"

Jayne and Mickey now reached the silent treatment with each other. All communication between them stopped. Yet Mickey did not return to Hollywood. He hoped that Jayne would wake up and realize she still was his wife.

One late evening over coffee at Donate's, Jayne and Bomba gave an improptu press conference. Jayne announced that she was going to divorce Mickey. She was planning her own film company in partnership with Bomba. "I like cultural things. I study Italian and French. Mickey doesn't care for art and music and cultural development," she said. "For a long time I have been searching myself to understand why I was not a fulfilled woman. I am so incomplete. Now, I know what I need. I am sorry for Mickey, but there will be a divorce. He has begged me to wait until I return to Hollywood to be sure of my emotions. I'll wait until I reach home to let the law take its course."

Reaching over, she touched Bomba's hand lightly. "Don't worry darling. You know you are the man I love," she said softly to him. Bomba kissed her cheek and smiled. "My angel," he said. "My golden angel," he repeated in reverence.

Jayne's movies, including "The Wayward Bus," were marqueed in theaters all over Rome. Just as Jayne felt secure as an acclaimed Super Star with international popularity 20th Century Fox dropped her. Her five-year contract was not renewed. Said Jayne: "I feel free as a bird. I'm happy with my new picture, 'Panic Button.' I have offers from Germany's 'Elvis Presley' singing star to co-star with him in a movie and eight more offers as well."

Rome, indignant that Hollywood should drop Jayne, gave her its highest acting honors for 1962. The festivities were held at Fuiggi, fifty miles from Rome. "This is our Oscar to honor you as the great actress of Two Worlds," was the inscription on the plaque. As Jayne, reached for it a jealous Italian actress screamed, "Why does *she* get it? Why not me?" The voluptuous girl tried to take the trophy out of Jayne's hands. A hairpulling match was stopped when the Italian Oscar officials pulled the hysterical woman away.

When the picture was completed, Jayne and Mickey returned home with the children to the Pink Palace. Jayne filed for a Mexican divorce. Mickey moved out of the pink palace and into an apartment. Yet, at any household crisis Jayne would call, and Mickey would return to help where and when needed.

"It is so difficult to rely on help," Jayne said. "Mickey has always run the house and everything. I am now completely absorbed in my career."

The long distance calls came from Bomba nightly. Jayne called him on occasion. He sent big packets of press clippings showing their romance in the world press. In the American press, Jayne only referred to Bomba as her producer—not her fiance. "This," she told me, "was out of respect to Mickey."

"I don't want to live here any more. I intend to take a place in

Rome, and an apartment in Paris." She also changed agents and hired Elizabeth Taylor's agent, Kurt Frings. She requested that her image be entirely changed from sex symbol to great lady.

Bomba was coming to Hollywood to claim Jayne. Reporters asked Mickey what he was going to do about it? "If that wop sets foot in Los Angeles, he'll face me!" Asked why he hadn't flattened the Italian in Rome, Mickey said he had not wanted to make a scene with Jayne's producer but coming here on Mickey's home ground was too much.

"Many times I wanted to sock Bomba, and tell Jayne she had to stay home and be a dutiful wife. But what can you do with a girl like Jayne? She has a mind of her own. To force her would be to lose her. I thought she would get over that aging, fat Italian."

Mickey bought a house and began building. He was later to sell it for a reported $90,000. He told Jayne's lawyer he did not want anything from Jayne. She could have the Pink Palace. "I built it for her—for our love," he said.

Jayne parried by saying that she earned all of the money and also paid his child support and alimony payments.

Coming to Mickey's defense, I reminded Jayne that Mickey had worked very hard to remodel Jayne's Pink Palace, wash her cars, tend to her business, and help her in every way possible. He should be allowed a share of the money.

Things, however, now began looking up for Mickey. He had obtained a health and exercise show on a local T.V. station.

Jayne, left on her own, became indecisive. She needed Mickey's help. Almost every night they talked on the telephone. New men came into her life. Jayne began dating. Mickey began dating other girls. When the press asked Mickey if he was heatbroken over Jayne's reported coming marriage to Bomba, he replied, "I'll probably be married before Jaynie is."

Jayne wasn't happy living with Mickey, and she was not happy living without him. "If he would only be my manager and take care of things, and the responsibilities," she deplored. "But I can't turn

Mickey's love off. And in a way, I still love him. But I no longer am in love with Mickey. That's the big difference. To function as an actress, I have to be in love. I have to have that incentive to work."

The Christmas holidays approached. Jayne and I always spent holidays together whenever possible. Jayne called to tell me she was meeting Bomba in New York two days before Christmas. "We are going to fly back here to have Christmas. May I bring Bomba with me for Christmas night at your house?"

"You've got to meet my Italian. He's so wonderful," she said over and over. It was though Jayne was trying to sell herself on her enthusiasm, for it was lacking in many respects I thought.

Christmas Day arrived. Usually I would go to Jayne's house for an early Christmas dinner with the children. Then Christmas night we'd have a big open house at my home and a Christmas buffet. "That way," Jayne would laugh, "we have turkey twice on Christmas!"

I always invited anyone I knew who had no home to go to for Christmas. Mae Murray, the famous star of *The Merry Widow* and others, was living in a Hollywood apartment with a pension from the Motion Picture Relief Fund. Mae was still trim and dressed beautifully. I admired her courage. She held her head high, even as she climbed on a bus. She had had millions of dollars and custom-build chauffeured limousines with gold fittings. When people asked Mae if she was the former film star, she would coldly reply, "I am the film star, Mae Murry. Once a star, you are always a star!"

For two days I decorated my home for Christmas. On the eventful day, in the late afternoon, I was putting the final touches on the big turkey roasting in the oven, the monkey bread, the fruit salad, the pumpkin and mince pies and the plum pudding. It was now 7:30 and guests would soon be arriving. A fire burned cheerfully on the hearth. The big Christmas tree twinkled with lights. All of the big picture windows were wreathed with holly. There was an abundance of Christmas goodies. I was thinking, "Will

Bomba like this American Christmas? And what will he really be like?"

The telephone rang. It was Mae Murray, as temperamental as she had been in her M.G.M. days when she was queen at the box office. She wanted to know why the chauffeur I was sending for her was keeping her waiting? "Why Mae," I replied, "Dr. Ernst Katz, the conductor of the California Junior Philharmonic is the one who'll call for you. He should be there any minute!"

"I've already waited five minutes. How dare he keep me waiting," she said tartly. She was going into a fine show of histrionics befitting a tragedienne, when I finally said, "I've got to hang up or the Christmas dinner will be ruined! He'll be there for you!"

Mae arrived, looking every inch the glamorous film star. She had not a line in her face. And she was 72! The guests all paid homage to Mae Murray, befitting her stardom. Producers, directors and the various guests gathered around her. She was a super star again, seated on a white satin chair, like a queen, at one end of my living room. Then the doorbell rang!

Jayne, in a flurry of excitement and glamour, rushed in laughing and kissing me. She said, "I know I was supposed to bring Bomba, but I brought Mickey instead! Is he welcome?"

A red-faced and embarrased Mickey brought up the rear, carrying a suitcase. "I just got off the plane from New York," Jayne announced. "Mickey met me. My plane was late. I came right here," exclaimed Jayne.

Since her life was no private matter, for it would all be in the morning papers, Jayne announced, "I was having dinner with Bomba in New York. Earl and Rosemary Wilson were there with us at the Pavillion. Suddenly, I wanted to be home with Mickey and the children for Christmas. I told Bomba that even though he had flown from Rome to be with me for the Yule, I had changed my mind. I could never marry him at this time. It was Mickey I had to go back to. He was a great gentleman about it." Later, Jayne told me, "Bomba couldn't get a divorce; Catholic, you know. And I would never be a mistress! I always get married to a man I love! In that way, I'm very old fashioned! I have to also think of my children!"

Mickey smiled. "Jaynie called me at six this morning. I've always loved her. This is the happiest Christmas of my life that she has come back to me."

Jayne, up to her ears in white fox furs over white mink, and with her diamonds glistening, stole the attention completely, although not intentionally, away from Mae Murray. People thoughtlessly left Mae to hover over the glamorous, younger, today star. Mae sat there, silently watching, probably remembering when she was the current favorite, when she was young and the world loved her, and paid homage to her, when she had furs and diamonds, and people jumped for her every whim and when millionaires begged for her favors. Now, there she was, wearing hand-me-down clothes of movie stars, living on charity from the Motion Picture Relief Fund. What her thoughts must have been! She sat there so quietly. I took people back over to her. Soon Jayne was holding court at one end of the room and Mae Murray had resumed at the other.

Three months went by. Jayne and Mickey seemed to get along. But the old love and adoration, on Jayne's part, had gone. "Keep your T.V. show, be somebody," I warned Mickey. "Jayne will respect you more. Hire gardeners. Hire a man Friday for Jayne, but you keep being a personality, not a handy man!"

Jayne was extremely thrifty in small ways and so was Mickey. But soon, he was back in the same routine: gardener, houseman, man Friday for Jayne and her career. And Jayne became restless, tiring and longing for new adventure. "I love him in my way," she said. "But I miss the Italian moonlight, the Italian sunshine, and the people who are so romantic, so delightful. I want to go back."

# CHAPTER XIV

"My whole feeling about me and life has changed," Jayne said now that she was back on firm ground again, home in Hollywood. "I look at things so differently. It's as though I used to see everything in black and white. Since Rome, I see everything in technicolor. Now I want to exploit the real me—not just a glamour girl."

Announcing that her reconciliation with Mickey hadn't worked after all, she asked him to move out of the pink palace. He moved out. They reconciled. He moved back again.

She had an offer to make a film, "An Act of Violence," in Yugoslavia. Sporting a new short haircut, Italian style, Jayne took a great interest in chic clothes. "I'm going to win an Oscar for acting, not for my physical assets," she announced. "From now on, my clothes will be well sewn, and cover me up." Cover they did—but Jayne's curves proved more tantalizing fully clothed.

During a tour of nightclubs in the south, Jayne met Nelson Sardelli who was Italian, young, handsome, and very talented. He sang beautifully. Jayne become enthralled. He was, she thought, a younger edition of Bomba, whom she had now surrendered back to Rome. With all of the graces and gallantry and romanticism of a true Italian, Jayne and Nelson became inseparable on the tour. Pictures of Nelson kissing Jayne's ankle, pictures of Nelson drinking champagne from one of Jayne's high-heeled slippers, pictures of Nelson on his knees to Jayne appeared in the newspapers. Jayne said she had again filed for divorce from Mickey in Mexico. She also said she was not going to rush into another marriage immediately!

Jayne was making a film in Europe, but she had to return to Washington, D. C. to fulfill a night club engagement. This was one which had been booked for her and Mickey when they had last been together. Nelson, on his way from Milan to chaperone his future bride while she would be working with her ex-husband, was involved in an automobile accident. This prevented him from arriving in this country. While he was recovering his health, Mickey was on home territory recovering Jayne.

Meantime, there was much speculation as to whether or not Jayne was in love with Nelson, or Bomba, and where Mickey fit in all of this.

"I had Bomba join me in New York last Christmas to show the world I could have him, if I wanted him, after all of that publicity. Besides, he had me under contract for four pictures," Jayne confessed. "But the truth is, Bomba couldn't get a divorce according to Italian law and I am a girl who marries the man she loves."

The affair with Nelson Saidelli was shortlived too when Jayne heard he was married.

"Nelson Sardelli?" Jayne sighed. "We had such a beautiful romance. He is young and virile and sexy and wild in love, and sweet. I really believed we would be a big thing—but then I heard he was married all along. I called him long distance to ask him the truth." "But," she said sadly, "Nelson didn't even return my call."

At this period, the magazines and newspapers were giving Jayne a rough time during the affair with Nelson. One columnist wrote: "Last winter when she left the reluctant Bomba to go back to Mickey, everyone knew it wasn't for publicity because there was a newspaper strike on right then. This time it's very confusing: it might have been love or publicity, but then it might have been love or labor pains, because there have been rumors that Jayne is going to present Mickey with his fourth offspring. Jayne had already divorced Mickey in Mexico to marry Nelson Sardelli. Now poor Nelson is reduced to a solo act.

"As a fiddler upon the strings of one's heart, our Jayne can be classified as the world's most reliable performer. Anyway, Mickey's moved back into the pink palace."

The press openly debated its conjectures. Was Jayne pregnant. Was it Mickey's or Bomba's or Nelson's baby? For once Jayne remained silent. Every editor in New York was calling for facts! "I pray that Mickey won't hear too much of this," Jayne said.

In early August (1963) Jayne and Mickey and their three children arrived in Budapest. Jayne was to make a picture close by, and the other purpose of their journey was to bring Mickey's mother back with them from behind the Iron Curtain. "I want her to make her home with us in Hollywood," Jayne said.

Jayne caused a furor in Budapest. She was admired by hundreds of goggle-eyed women and men everywhere she went. Jayne was a sensation. "Like Venus come down from the heavens, this beautiful blonde woman—and her three children are with her. She is ecstasy. She is a real woman. She is also a mama—a good mother!" reported a Budapest paper. No American had ever been so rapturously received by the Hungarians before.

Mickey's mother lived in a modest little house. Jayne regaled her with the wonders of life in the Pink Palace—automatic washing machine, garbage disposal, everything electric. Mama Hargitay insisted that she didn't want to live in America. She had other children in Budapest and she expressed her desire only to pay a visit to Hollywood.

Through Jayne's popularity, a visa was granted for the mother to return with Jayne and Mickey.

Jayne told the press that although she and Mickey were divorced in Mexico, they were still married in California. Taking time to buy infant clothes in a Budapest store, Jayne announced that she and Mickey were expecting their fourth child. "We planned it all along. We were only separated two months," she said. Jayne made a film at the same time, and the Hungarian television, radio and news reporters and photographers followed her from morning until night. Such popularity had not been accorded even Khrushchev. After four weeks at the Dalmatian port, the Hargitay family flew back to the United States with Mickey's mother in tow.

In Hollywood, the press insisted on more explaining of Jayne's marital status. "There were reasons that impelled me to file for divorce," Jayne said. "But Mickey and I have ironed those out, and we hope to spend the rest of our lives together." Said Mickey, "The separations were not publicity. Jayne will never argue. She hates quarrels. When there is a difference of opinion, she states her feelings and retreats. Even to picking up and going away!"

With a smile Jayne said, "We wanted this baby. We had planned it. We are going to have a big family. I always said I wanted at-least ten children of my own."

Jayne was expecting her baby in February. "As soon as the baby arrives, I am to appear on the Jack Parr Show in New York. And then I am to report to Europe for my next film. It's *Jayne Mansfield Reports—Europe.* It will be similar to Elizabeth Taylor's tour of London on T.V. Elizabeth was unable to do this one and we have the same agent, you know. I am happy to make it. I'll be filming one picture after another, with only travel time in between," Jayne said. "Another film starts in March in Hollywood. That is *Promises, Promises,* for Tommy Noonan."

"Mickey's mother is cooking the dinner and we want you over to meet her," Jayne telephoned a few days after their return from Hungary.

Mama Hargitay (she has another name too difficult to pronounce or spell, so we all settled for the simpler) proved to be a delightful homespun, motherly woman with a twinkle in her eyes, clear skin, graying hair and a comfortable figure, somewhat like Mrs. Khrushchev's. She was wearing a new American dress and while she could not speak English, her eyes conveyed her thoughts. She was slightly overwhelmed at being in Hollywood and seeing, firsthand, the tremendous popularity of her daughter-in-law.

"Come into the kitchen," she beckoned "and see what I have made for dinner! " Mickey acted as immediate interpreter. She had cooked fantastic Hungarian food—stuffed cabbage, noodles, pastries, salads and hot bread. She offered spoons so we could all taste what was cooking. She was such a lovely, motherly woman, a little bewildered with the Pink Palace, the servants and the fast moving life that surrounds a film star. But she was proud of her own cooking, and rightly so. She felt at home in the kitchen.

Another Christmas came and we were together again, with the children. Bicycles, children's automobiles, and all sorts of toys from Jayne's fans and people who would like to have been closer to the star supplemented Santa's bundle. The Pink Palace looked like a toy shop!

Then February was coming, and Jayne was expecting her fourth child. There was still open speculation about who the father was and this bothered Jayne. "I wish the gossips would stop," she worried. "It isn't fair—it isn't fair. I've always thought I was like Isadora Duncan, but now I don't want scandal. It would be so nice if we had a baby shower at your house. And if you would invite Mayor Sam Yorty—he's so important. That would stop the gossip, wouldn't it? "

I had taken Jayne along to several big civic events honoring Los Angeles Mayor Sam Yorty, a dear friend, and whom we both greatly admired. I wondered if I should ask His Honor. Did he know about all of the gossip? Besides, it was just gossip. I said I would give the baby shower, even though by now I was beginning to feel like a professional party giver for Jayne Mansfield. Jayne was so thrilled that I immediately scolded myself for even hestitating or thinking about all the work and expense a Jayne Mansfield party entailed. There I was again, decorating my white living room with pretty baby shower things. This time, Jayne's baby had already arrived. She was just two weeks old when Jayne walked in with her.

Mama Hargitay took charge of little Mariska, who was named for her. Two-week old Mariska was very bright and alert, watching every incident, never crying and not sleeping for the eight hours of the party. I was perturbed. "Isn't this asking too much of a tiny baby?" I asked Jayne. Jayne laughed. "No, my children have to get used to being in public so they can always be with me."

The press made a big event of the shower, but handled it with dignity and prestige. We had turned the tide of gossip and public opinion. Jayne and Mariska were happily written about. One photo was captioned by the *Hollywood Citizen News,* Los Angeles: "Mayor Samuel Yorty, who's presidential material, turns baby sitter at May Mann's shower for Jayne." The picture showed the Mayor holding Mariska, while Mama Hargitay, Jayne, Jayne Marie and I smiled approval.

*Screen Life Magazine* gave a two-page spread of photos of the shower, entitled "The Mansfield Man-Filled BABY Shower." A report read: "A lot of showers for babies have come and gone out Hollywood way, but none like the one columnist May Mann threw for Jayne Mansfield's latest child, Mariska. No hen-party this. It was full up with men, all of them godfathers. One of them was Los Angeles Mayor Samuel Yorty (whom a lot of big wigs are talking of drafting for the presidential nomination). Another was Richard Schenck, exalted ruler of Los Angeles Elks Lodge; Mark Hansen, "Mr. Hollywood," million theater owner, Herbert Klein, and several more millionaires. And such a lot of celebrities were present from the distaff side including Baroness Lotta Von Strahl, Mrs. Gig Young, Mrs. Al Zugsmith, entertainer Patti Moore and Cara Williams, to name a few of the thirty-five ladies present, besides Jayne herself, baby, and hostess May Mann. Oh yes, and we almost forgot, Papa Mickey Hargitay was very much present too. What a pround papa he is. And they carted three station wagons filled with baby gifts home!"

# CHAPTER XV

In the first weeks after Mariska's birth, all was sweetness and light for Jayne in the columns.

Walter Winchell wrote: "Jayne Mansfield is as beautiful as Marilyn Monroe and effortlessly delivers the most devastating impression in years." After that, Jayne began inventing guips, a-la-Monroe. "I don't sleep in the nude, I put on Chanel No. 5. " When asked if she could cook, Jayne replied, "I love to cook turkey. They're so good when they're cooked." Another time she said, "When I go to the Girl Scout meetings in Beverly Hills, I plan to wear a simple cloth coat. But I change to mink finally. I don't want to look conspicuous."

The world press awarded Jayne the title of the "World's No. 1 Sex Symbol." The walls of her home were decorated with 500 framed magazine covers. (Two were *Life Magazine*.) "Here I am," Jayne chortled, "on the covers of magazines in London, Paris and

Rome and look, I'm even very big in Istanbul."

At this time Linda Murdick became Jayne's personal maid and housekeeper. Jayne loved Linda and so did I. This wonderful black woman, with the marvelous sense of humor and a certain flair of style, had complete loyalty. "She's a lookalike for Pearl Bailey," I told Jayne. "Don't tell Linda that," Jayne said "or she'll go into the movies and leave me."

Linda was to become Jayne's confidante. "Linda's like I wish my mother had been," Jayne often said. "She understands me and loves me as I am." Linda was with Jayne to the very end.

Jayne had never been invited to the elite, jet set parties. My friend Cobina Wright Sr., a local society orbitor, who didn't approve of Jayne or my friendship with her, called me one day. "I think it would be interesting to invite Jayne and Mickey to my party this week," she said. "What do you think?"

I gave her Jayne's telephone number. Arthur Cameron, the millionaire, was paying for the party. It was extravagant with a dance band and beautifully appointed tables on Cobina's back garden patio.

Jayne and Mickey's behavior was no different at Cobina's house than at mine. They sat, arms entwined, whispering sweet nothings with constant kisses.

"They were amusing and Jayne is really a very sweet girl," Cobina said afterwards. "If only someone would take her in hand and teach her how to dress! Anyway, I'm going to invite them again for Saturday night. I have friends here from New York and the men are crazy to meet Jayne!"

When Cobina called Jayne, she accepted but said that perhaps she'd be bringing a new escort. "Why?" gasped Cobina, "you and Mickey seemed so madly in love!" "That was last week," purred Jayne.

Three weeks after Mariska's birth, I was appearing as femcee of the program for the annual Ida Mayer Cummings Jewish Home For the Aged Charity Ball, to be held in the Beverly Hilton Hotel

Ballroom. Ida, who was the sister of the late Louis B. Mayer, asked me to please invite Jayne Mansfield to take a bow. Jayne had to tape a Johnny Carson Show first that night, but she agreed that she would be there by 10:00.

Joe Pasternak, the eminent producer, was in charge of the show. I had already done my part in a skit with George Hamilton and was now off stage for the evening. Jayne had arrived back stage. "I have been waiting for an hour to go on," she said. "My legs and back hurt so badly in these high heels. I am hemorraging. Do you think I could go on so I can get home. I'm really quite ill."

I sent word to Mr. Pasternak, who was out front. He sent word back that he had not asked Jayne on his show. She could go home. She was not going on!

How could I tell that to Jayne. She had been publicized in the trades as a star of the Ball. Of course, Ida had asked me to invite her! I was terribly embarrassed. I didn't want Jayne embarrassed. Bob Hope arrived. Jayne said, "Could I go on with Bob? We have a bit we did together on one of his tours." Mr. Pasternak sent word back. No. I asked Bob, who is a prince among men, what to do. He was naturally disturbed but at that point, someone said Mr. Pasternak had relented, and Jayne was to go on stage. I wrote Mr. Pasternak a powerful letter. I had no reply but an evening later at the Cocoanut Grove, Mr. Pasternak stopped by my table to say he was sorry.

The following year at the Ball, Bob Hope who always appeared was on stage. Marie Wilson and Pat Wymore, two luscious, sexy actresses with plenty of curves of their own, were on stage with Bob. Jayne was called up to be a third. Since Marie was holding Bob's left arm and Pat his right—this left Jayne standing on the side. Jayne would never be second when it came to her career. She maneuvered naively and innocently to the mike and said, "Would you like to hear Bob and I sing a song that we sang together for our boys in the service in Alaska?" The audience heartily applauded. Naturally, Bob had to relinquish Marie and Pat to sing at the mike with Jayne. Pat and Marie stood back, completely upstaged. Without smiling, they walked off. There was little else they could do. Needless to say, they were not Jayne Mansfield fans after that. Meanwhile, Jayne prettily took her bows with Bob Hope to thunderous applause!

One day shortly after the Charity Ball, Jayne added a new twist to her already complex life. The hottest sex symbol of the era, whose rise in the past six years to headline stardom had been both controversial and impressive, quietly announced that she was embracing the Catholic faith. "I am taking instruction," she said simply. However, every move Jayne made was not "simple" even when she intended it to be.

The religion that she had chosen was a demanding one. Equally demanding was Jayne's career, founded and centered on her voluptuous body! The big problem Jayne faced was: could she remain the world sex symbol, and still become a Catholic? Must she sacrifice all she had worked to obtain for the deep religious faith that impelled her to seek Catholicism?

"Yes," Jayne admitted a few moments later. "I may have to sacrifice some of my career—anyway a little" she admitted. "Father Sullivan, my instructor, has explained to me that being in the spotlight, I will have to be exemplary.

"I have always considered my career-self and my personal self as two different and separate people. There's Jayne Mansfield at home, a wife and devoted mother, and there's Jayne the sex symbol which is my career. I have always kept them completely apart and separate.

"In Catholicism I have found everything I have dreamed a religion should be. In Rome I saw wild romances between men and women, women and women and men and men. I was surrounded with people with unreal standards. One can become confused. What's right and what is wrong?

"Fortunately I only observed. I never partook. I saw intelligent people living all sorts of ways.

"Italian men began explaining their way of life and their religion, and what it would mean to be devout and give up everything to marry me.

"My eyes were opened and I wanted to learn. Suddenly I knew where to turn—to God and the truth.

"My career will be toned down but it will continue, I believe, to become even better. I have always believed you can accomplish anything by giving just that extra effort. I will make it."

Jayne admitted that it would not be easy to turn aside the roles and the big money offered to her as a sex symbol. When Jayne appeared in a parade or at the opening of a new building or super market, she was Jayne Mansfield, super-star movie queen. She was not paid large sums for being the sweet girl she really was, who loved her home and her children. People wanted to see her to "oh" and "ah" at her curves, her body and her glamour.

"I know with faith that I will work it out. I have starved and worked night and day for this career. I don't feel the Church would want me to give it up. I believe with all of my faith that God will have something better for me, as I give up some of it. Perhaps I can lighten it some and play down the sex image."

"I need God. I suddenly found myself with all of this success, big success I had never dreamed possible—picture contracts being flung at me from every side," Jayne continued. "Everything was for Jayne Mansfield, but actually I was being pressed on all sides and I became confused—lost. Mickey and I separated, and it seemed the more success came, the more lost I became.

"I came to the full realization of this in Rome. I loved Mickey, but everything seemed against us continuing our lives together. Bomba, as I said, began telling me about the Catholic religion and how wonderful it is to turn to God, to believe and to let him take over your problems and give you help.

"I began to realize that you have to have spiritual principles for guidance. And that they are faith and trust in God—implicit trust. Only then, when you can say let it be God's will not mine, can you relax. This can not be realized by theories and principles but by actual test in everyday living."

"I found," Jayne disclosed, "that whatever problem you have and no matter how difficult it is, and mine were, God can help you. When I thought it was too late to change anything, I began to pray. Not until I gave myself to God's power, unconditionally and completely, did my life work out to the happiness and security I feel now.

"Even before I began to realize that stardom and everything I had worked so hard to obtain, were not enough, I did not have sufficient power within myself to be happy. Achievement, stardom and success, without the spiritual success, is empty.

"The key to any successful life structure is the right foundation. Do I want a good, lasting, happy life? Yes. I do.

"It is an effort, a big effort to become a good Catholic. I am taking the time every day and every night for what may be the most valuable and the most rewarding part of my life.

"I was born a Catholic in Pennyslvania, and later raised an Episcopal. Later, in the frantic hectic rush that is Hollywood, to make a career my life became like a song—an ever-playing record of career demands for myself. I didn't go to church and keep up with it.

"Not until I reached Rome—and necessity opened my eyes did my separation from Mickey became the turning point. I had to know where I was going. I realized that I was drifting. My life badly needed something. And that something was what I am finding in my religion today.

"When I first came to Hollywood, I had no idea of becoming a sex symbol. It just happened."

"If I give up the sex symbol image to become a Catholic, it will be God's way," Jayne concluded. "I know he will have something better in store for me. Something like becoming a fine dramatic actress."

The proof was that Jayne could be a person separate from her sexpot symbol. It was her tongue-in-cheek attitude to her 'sexiness' that was her security—no matter the path she followed!

# CHAPTER XVI

Jayne was summoned by telegram to meet with one of Hollywood's foremost producers. Since he was an Oscar winner, Jayne was impressed. Now that she had decided to become a serious dramatic actress, she quickly made an appointment.

She was ushered into the plush inner office by a secretary, where the producer sat behind his massive desk openly admiring her. Wearing a white wool Dior with white foxes casually caught on her shoulder, a perky matching hat on her head, her hair short and chic, she made the right impression.

"My child," the man said, rising and extending his hand to greet her. "You are more beautiful than I have seen you on the screen. I first saw you in New York, when you were appearing in that Rock Hunter play."

Jayne smiled appreciatively and sat down on the chair he indicated near his desk.

"I have in mind several pictures to make with you," he said. "I have waited on purpose, before making you an offer, until you had your family settled and could give your full attention to your career!"

Jayne's long lashes swept down on her cheeks, which were heightened with sudden color at this remark. "I have always given full concentration to my career," she defended gently. "My family has never interfered. I have never been late, never been unprepared. I am completely professional."

"I know all of that," he smiled now, slightly apologetic. "Please don't misunderstand me. I mean I want to intensify your glamorous position in this business with a big publicity campaign. You have never had the right press agent or any, I understand, in recent years to handle you as you should be. You have long deserved better management. Your potential as an international star has great scope, as yet untapped!"

"I don't need a press agent," Jayne replied with a little smile. "My telephone rings all the time with press requests. I hire a press secretary just to keep up with it."

"I know," he placated. "But I have something in mind. I only want your full cooperation and just one assurance: that you now have your family—four children, I am told—and there will be no more for many years! I don't want to start a campaign which is going to run into big money, and then have you do something, no matter how innocently, and have all of my meticulous, long-range planning go down the drain!"

"What do you mean?" Jayne asked, clearly puzzled.

"I mean," he said emphatically " that at least for the next five years, you will assure me no more babies. I want your body to be perfect at all times—no pregnancies. You must be ready to be photographed at all times. I want the 'mother image' out, and the 'Jayne Mansfield, exciting, ravishing, glamorous super-star image intact! That is very easy to assure, is it not?"

"I can't reply exactly. I don't know," Jayne said honestly, her face disturbed. "How can I guarantee I won't have children? I am married, you know."

"Come now," he smiled. "You are surely more sophisticated than that! There's always means and ways to not have babies that are not wanted, that are inconvenient at the time." He added, with assurance, "I have a reputable doctor who can take care of any such emergency."

"You mean abortion?" Jayne gasped. Her eyes widened with surprise!

"That's common, isn't it?" he replied. "Hundreds are done every day. Why do you look so surprised? You are in your middle twenties and a sophisticated young lady, from all of the romances I have been reading in the papers this past year that you are having." He spoke pleasantly and not unrespectfully.

"Abortion is murder!" Jayne replied evenly. "I would never consider one, never!"

He didn't hide his surprise, even shock, at Jayne's attitude.

"Come now, there may never be a need for one," he laughed. "We're putting the cart before the horse. However, the campaign I plan for you, and the pictures I have in mind call for a perfect figure and an exciting woman. In expert hands, you will become one of the most successful and famous stars of our day."

"I am all for that, but never an abortion," Jayne said evenly. "I have to be completely honest with you. Pregnancy comes too easy for me. I could not make a guarantee."

"You ruined your career at Fox, Jayne, I must remind you," he said.

"First you are sitting on top of the world. Fox pays a hundred thousand to spring you from that Broadway play, and, disregarding all advice, you marry that muscle man and have children every year. If you are that unmanageable, what is going to happen to your career?"

"Elizabeth Taylor has children, and they are with her all of the time!" Jayne replied. "It hasn't hurt her career!"

"Elizabeth Taylor became a star as a child. She has years of M.G.M. promotion and publicity and public acclaim behind her. You have not and although you are relatively new you, by circumstances you, yourself, have made, have been badly mishandled!"

Jayne rose to her feet, as she always did when making dicisions. Walking back and forth in front of his desk, finally she said quietly, "Did you know that an embryo is completely formed as a separate entity, with its own cellular structure, and it is a complete breathing baby only six days after inception?"

He sat there astonished at Jayne's intelligence and knowledge which until now he had never suspected.

"Did you know that in twelve weeks it has a distinct heart beat? It is breathing, has brain activity, a nervous system and a digestive body which is functioning? I would never murder a baby—would you? Could you?"

He was speechless.

"How do you know all of this?" he asked. "Abortion is common. No one ever thinks of it as murder!"

"A baby-in-utero is a human being, like you or me!" Jayne said. "I would never be a murderer!"

"I see your point," he replied, visibly shaken. "But you can surely take utmost precautions otherwise against pregnancy."

"I have many times," she admitted. "Too often they never work satisfactorily. The proof is that I have four children," Jayne concluded, in all honesty.

He frowned, rising to his feet. Jayne rose with a sigh. "If you have any offers with which I can comply," she said, "you can let me know."

Crossing from behind the desk, he shook her hand, still at a loss for words. Jayne walked out of the office.

Back at the pink palace, she reached for her pink jeweled telephone and orally committed an agreement to star in *Promises Promises* for Tommy Noonan.

"It isn't the kind of a picture I want," she said to me. "But I've got to keep the money coming in. All of these people, my family, depend on my pay check as you know. The expenses are so high with the children, the house, Mickey, the servants, our travels, everything. I have to make a thousand a day to survive it. I must."

*Promises Promises* went into production. Marie MacDonald had second lead. Marie, known as "The Body," and Jayne and Tommy combined their respective talents to make a picture about the mad marital mixup of husbands and wives and babies, which they hoped would be great box office. It was a mild forerunner of the swinging sex films to follow five years later.

Jayne had a scene in her bubble bath and in bed. She was filmed on a private closed set. When the stills came through, it was decided that her nude scenes would be the big promotion gimmick of the film. Jayne held her breasts in her hands, as modest as possible, but the ads were to say, "This Is The First Time That I Have Ever Appeared Completely au Naturel, Says Jayne." She couldn't bring herself to say "Nude."

*Playboy Magazine*, who had photographed Jayne for its centerfold when she was first under contract to 20th Century Fox, had made her repeated offers of $20,000 to again appear in the center fold. As persistently, she had refused.

"Globe Photos had asked me to pose almost in the nude but not quite that first time and the studio okayed it," she recalled. "I posed in many reclining poses in some leopard leotards. They came out sexy, but the studio press agent and the photographer insisted they were art." No set of pictures in *Playboy* had stirred up such interest.

"*Playboy* offered me big money for another centerfold. I refused. I have never done anything knowingly that would be in bad taste. It just wouldn't match me now, as a mother."

Tommy Noonan persisted that *Playboy* would give the picture tremendous publicity if the bath scenes of Jayne could be used as centerfold. Finally, Jayne agreed, if it would help sell the picture. "I was a bit off, wasn't I?" she said. "I could have been paid

$20,000 for a centerfold." By now several major stars had contributed their charms to the centerfold. But Jayne's appearance this time brought her slaps from the P.T.A. and some clergymen. Had she forgotten her 'mother image?'

There were tears and travails, and Jayne decided to go on the road and do summer stock. "Gentlemen Prefer Blondes" was a natural, she felt. "I'll take the children, of course, and Mickey," she said.

The entire family departed in a huge white land camper with Jayne's name emblazoned on the sides. The tour gained momentum and great success enroute. Mickey played "Curley," a second lead in the play. Linda remained to take care of the pink palace. "It was lonely. Mama Hargitay stayed on too, and half the time I couldn't find her," said Linda. "She didn't like my cooking, and I didn't like her Hungarian cooking. We each ate our own food. Mama Hargitay spent most of her time upstairs in her suite."

In New York Jayne gave numerous interviews that found the press her admiring coterie. Jayne explained that while she had wanted to do dramatic cover-up movies and plays, the public seemed to want her as the sex symbol.

"What can I do?" she said. "I have to think of my children's needs and their education. By fall, when I return to Hollywood, I have picture offers which will give me the chance to prove that I am an actress. Meanwhile, I am letting the critics make their own evaluations of me on stage. And my children are seeing America—a wonderful education for them. We visit all the historical landmarks, just as we have in Europe. They should get straight A's in history and geography in school this fall!"

The critics were kind, which encouraged Sammy Lewis, to make Jayne an offer to open in *Gentlemen Prefer Blondes* at his theater in Anaheim, California for a three-week run. Jayne agreed. However, she wanted Mickey to have co-star marquee billing. Sammy refused. Mickey, he said, was not a theatrical star, and Sammy was an important veteran producer. He would be laughed out of the business if he put Mickey in big lights as star at a Melodyland production. After further negotiations Jayne finally agreed to solo star billing, and Mickey was to be handsomely paid as a member of the cast. He had scenes with Jayne and that was sufficient.

Jayne spoke of her life up to this point in an interview in New York. "I am always grateful to my mother for rearing me strictly to be a lady. There are times when I fall off of it, under some bad influence. Perhaps I had too much champagne to color my world differently. But most of the time it stays with me. It holds inside of me.

"I dislike intensely dirty stories. Vulgar language and obscenities embarrass me. Sexy talk with a detached natural innocence, since it concerns a force in life as vital as breathing, I find amusing. Sometimes I shock my maid Linda when she comes in with my breakfast tray. I'll say softly, 'Linda, did you ball David (her boyfriend) last night?' She gets so embarrassed. Sometimes I feel the need to shock people. A little ballsy talk is as far as I ever go.

"I always relate automatically to whomever I am with. I would never try to shock May Mann with talk about balling. I've too much respect for her although she is a sexy girl too. As close as we've always been, I can't quite figure her out. She's not a swinger and she's not a square either.

"With May I love to be the young woman of elegance, good taste, correct clothes, sables, minks, real jewels, elegant dinner parties with fabulous crystal and silver, china, flowers and candles, and intelligent conversation with cultured people. I like mingling with the people I find at her parties, people with respect for themselves and each other. And for me. I meet some of the most famous people in the world at her home. They are never publicized. I secretly wish my career would permit such exclusive small circles at the pink palace. But people call and ask to come over, and I never have the heart to say no, for most of these people help make my career!

"Evaluating my life sometimes, I realize that I have always had a little girl's attitude of expecting miracles, of happiness every tomorrow morning, every day of the year. I thrill when anyone sends me a present, even if it is only a handkerchief or a tiny bottle of perfume. The fact that it is a present is as exciting to me now, when I can have everything money can buy, as when I was just starting. For each gift says, 'I love you. I went out of my way to think of you—to please you!'

"I am not conceited. I don't really think I am the most beautiful woman in the world at all. If I can create some illusion to that effect, and it seems I have, then that is what spells success for me. I am one girl who wanted one thing, and I believed there is only one road to Rome. I took it and I went after it. I got everything I wanted except lasting love. I could never count on that with anyone. Sometimes not even from my mother or my daughter."

"Was she happy now with Mickey?" Jayne avoided speaking of him which surprised everyone, for he was still appearing nightly in her play.

"I love sex. Since it is one of God's gifts to everyone, there should be no shame in saying so. It gives me a glow of happiness all day, being in love, being loved. I don't care for sex in any way less than with love and spontaneity. When it is honest it enchants, it captivates, it amuses, it fascinates. It arouses within you the desire to protect and shelter. I have experienced all of it but I have not yet found ultimate protection and shelter from any one man. As always, just when I think I have it, I discover I am alone and on my own.

"When times were the most difficult for me in Hollywood, after Paul had left, I met a very important director. My ancient Jaguar had stalled on Sunset Boulevard. Nothing I could do would move it. I had neglected to get my automobile club insurance renewed, since I was so low on funds. I had no way to move it. A big black Cadillac pulled up along side of me. A very famous director, whose name I won't reveal, since I would not want to hurt his wife and family, stepped out. Seeing my trouble, he offered to take me in his car to the nearest service station and get help. Enroute, he discovered I was trying to get into pictures. He suggested we go to his beach house for dinner, and he'd show me how he could help me. He intimated he and his family were spending the summer there.

"This man is well-publicized in the magazines and papers. I automatically thought his wife and family would be there. I was happy to accept. When we arrived, there was only his Filipino servant. After the first course, he maneuvered me towards a divan, threw me back and jumped right on top of me. I fought and to his dismay, I resisted! When he saw I was absolutely serious and would not give in, he started to curse in my ear. My fingernails tore into his face and ripped open his cheeks before he let go. He told me he would have me blackballed at every studio in town.

"Later on, when I was a success, I made a picture at his studio. When we would perchance to meet he was always cold and reserved. Someone told me the stories he had told about me. Among other things, he said I had visited his Malibu Beach house and had tried to rape him, offering my body to get a part in his picture. He said he threw me out because I had a disease and was on dope! It was such a lie. All of it, such a lie.

"In my own way of thinking, given the chance, I can be a warm, sweet, womanly Grace Kelly type. I admire Jacqueline Kennedy more than anyone else. I used to buy clothes from Oleg Cassini because I liked her covered-up look. Except on me, they never look demure.

"I relate sometimes with Elizabeth Taylor, with whom I share many similar situations. I tried so hard in the beginning to become the Sex Symbol. I have tried so hard recently to switch my image to the real me, without success. But I keep hoping."

# CHAPTER XVII

Strange rumors that Jayne had fallen in love with her director in summer stock began drifting back to Hollywood before the news broke in the press. Mickey and the children were still with her. It became a matter of open conjecture. Then a columnist reported "Jayne and her director, Matt Ottaviano Cimber, were observed dancing until the wee hours in a night club. Where was Mickey? Home, baby sitting of course."

It all began at the Yonkers Playhouse when Jayne arrived to play *Bus Stop.* Matt was the director. After the opening night with applause ringing in her ears, Jayne suggested to Mickey that they go to a night club to celebrate. Mickey said no. He was tired and he was going to bed and so was she. The next night, Jayne lamented to Matt that she had wanted to join the company to celebrate, but Mickey wouldn't escort her.

Then Jayne and Mickey were at a small club and when Mickey

began playing a marble machine, Jayne accepted Matt's invitation to dance. From that moment on Jayne and Matt became inseparable. When Jayne arrived in California with her company to play Melodyland, she called me.

"You're coming out to my opening?" Jayne said on the telephone. "I've got lots to tell you. Bring your boy friend and we'll make a foursome and celebrate after the show."

Jayne was gorgeous—but what were those black and blue marks doing on her legs and arms, plainly visible from the stage? Sammy Lewis was worried, but smiling at the large house that Jayne's name on the marquee attracted. Mickey and Jayne seemed emotionally strained in their scenes which were few.

After the show, I told Sammy I was going backstage to see Jayne. I was told that not even Sammy could go into Jayne's dressing room. It was heavily bodyguarded.

At the star's door was a huge Italian, at least 6'3" and 250 pounds. He was immaculate in a tux with a white carnation in his lapel. "No one can see Miss Mansfield," he said curtly.

"Tell her May Mann, her best friend, is here," I replied equally curt. The man disappeared inside. I heard Jayne's voice calling, "Of course she can come in—can't she Matt? May is my best friend."

The door opened slightly and in I went. Jayne rushed to my arms and we hugged and kissed. Who had rushed in behind me but Mickey. I turned and hugged and kissed him and congratulated him on his stage performance. Mickey looked ill at ease. He was shortly evicted by two bodyguards. In surprise, I turned to Jayne with a "What's happened?" look on my face, as she turned to introduce me to Matt Cimber!

Jayne then took me aside and whispered that she had been restless and unhappy for a long time. "I can't stay home every night and eat and get fat and blow my career," she said. "Mickey today is not the same man I married. He doesn't want to share my life of pleasure. He expects me to work and stay home or sit in a hotel room and watch TV. I love meeting people. He knew that before we were married. I've done everything to make him feel important, bue he's got a complex about being 'Mr. Jayne Mansfield' or something. I've actually been very lonely! Too lonely, until I met Matt!"

Matt Cimber proved to be charming and attractive. "He's a year younger than I am," Jayne laughed. "Isn't he beautiful!"

Jayne and Matt talked freely to me of their romance, at that time swearing me to secrecy. Since I have always liked Mickey Hargitay I felt sorry for him. He had told Jayne, "I love you! You are so beautiful. I can't lose you!" But obviously some things had happened which had turned off the love they once had for each other.

Jayne explained how she and Matt happened to fall in love.

"Last April I reported to the Yonkers Playhouse for *Bus Stop*, and Matt was the director," Jayne said. "He was Italian and handsome and I thought he looked like a Greek God. But he didn't really turn me on until he began to direct me, to talk to me. He is absolutely brilliant, a real intellect. I was amazed. I had never had anyone work with me this way before. He anticipated my every move, mood, shading and feeling of the words, and action, in the play. It was like one mind directing and reacting. It was beautiful

"To have a great talent helping me, working with me for the first time, was so great, I can't tell you. At last I had someone in show business who knew the business far better than I did. Until now, I had started in a hit-and-miss fashion to become an actress. Here was a man, who at 28, is a master director-producer with an I.Q. of 165. He has a Masters degree in Theater Arts from Syracuse University, and the director's workshop of the Actors Studio Theater East. He also taught at Marymount when he was barely 20. The fact that we fell in love is one thing. But the fact that our interests are so mutual, and he loves me so much that he will develop my career and make me a great serious actress—well," Jayne sighed, "It's something like Sophia Loren and Carlo Ponti in a way. Being part of a team, instead of alone out front or before the cameras—such support is the greatest thing that has ever happened to me."

Matt sat quietly, smiling at Jayne's enthusiasm. "We want to do great things together, more serious things in the Fellini, DeSica vein," Jayne continued while taking off her makeup. "We are reading scripts and plays constantly to find the right roles for me. I lean on Matt's every word, like one starved and thirsty for knowledge.

"The second day I met him, he turned me on. We are always going to be together, work together, and never be apart. Matt and I have vowed this. That is why he is willing to leave his own work in New York to wait in dressing rooms for me while I do this play at Melodyland. We both have to make sacrifices for this togetherness which is so important to both of us."

Matt, dressed in white slacks spotless with an open white silk shirt, needlessly apologized for his informality. He said he was first attracted to Jayne naturally by her blonde beauty. "I first saw her starring on Broadway in *Will Success Spoil Rock Hunter*, he said. "It never occurred to me to go backstage and meet her then. I have always admired her beauty, and her appeal. I have also studied her on television and on the screen. I've thought, 'why are they wasting her talents?' I could see her potential. If I didn't, I wouldn't give up my own work for her career. I fell in love with her, I think, when I saw what a wonderful mother she is. I love her children and they love me. Her first concern is always for them. This a real woman, as an Italian understands a real woman. Her family is first. And how Jayne has been able to manage a career and her family is amazing!

"I take Mariska, out in her stroller, and everyone stops me to look at her, she's so beautiful. And they don't know she's Jayne's baby. But all of her children are beautiful and so beautifully mannered.

"I never thought that we would fall in love, that I should be so lucky. Working with her in a play I soon realized, and my heart was all for Jayne.

"I confess when I first saw her way back I had the impression that she was nothing more than a 'sex symbol'. But all you have to do is to meet Jayne to discover that here is a highly intelligent and an unusually sweet girl. And with a huge reservoir of talent waiting to be properly introduced. I think Jayne is pure talent, and in many respects she is still a little girl waiting to be shown the way—the right way.

"Jayne is also a wonderful pal, a buddy, as well as an exciting woman."

After the show that night, Jayne invited me and my friend to accompany her and Matt to his cousin's house for a midnight snack. Instead of going to a big glamorous night club on Sunset Strip where she would be seen, we drove for an hour to find his aunt's house. It was a neat, little attractive house on a strip somewhere near Long Beach.

The people were Italian and delightfully hospitable. There was the father and mother and the son and his wife and a child. Jayne instantly took the little child in her lap and held him most of the evening. Matt and Jayne might just as well have been the most common ordinary folk, instead of extraordinary people who were about to burst into romantic headlines all over the world.

Only one thing worried me. Seated in the back of Jayne's Cadillac convertible, I asked point blank, "Jayne, how did you get all of those horrible black and blue bruises on your arms and legs and your neck. Even on your cheek?"

Jayne replied, "Oh Matt beats me. But I love it." With that she cuddled closer to Matt who was driving and put her arms around his neck. Matt didn't say a word. My boy friend, who was also Italian, looked at me in shock. I was speechless. Jayne didn't remark further!

Three nights later, we four met for supper after Jayne's show. Matt was furious at Mickey and would have liked him out of the show. Jayne was highly indignant too. I've never seen her so upset, although with the genuine professionalism of the actress it had not shown on stage.

"You should hear what Mickey did—and on my opening night! He kidnapped Maria, my baby! He said I could get her back when I dropped Matt and came back to him! Imagine that!" "We call Mariska, Maria, because Maria is Italian for Mariska," Jayne explained.

Linda had answered the door at the pink palace to find Mickey and two men. They said they wanted to come in and see Mama Hargitay. "I asked them if they'd like some sandwiches and coffee. They said they would. I made them and was going to take the food to them, when there they were, running out the door with Maria.

"I went upstairs to find Mama Hargitay unconscious on the floor. She had had Maria with her. The doctor came and he said someone had plunged a knockout needle in Mama Hargitay's arm so they could kidnap the baby. She was a long time coming out of it."

Even after Maria had been returned, Jayne's anger towards Mickey didn't completly vanish.

"I had always believed Mickey's sincerity and that he loved me. I loved him, even though I was out of love with him. But now my indignation makes me incapable of any affection for him whatsoever.

"Usually anger doesn't stay with me. But after what he has done, my hate is inescapable. I hate him. How dare he!" Jayne had never hated anyone before but even this was not to stay with her more than a few days.

The following week Jayne said tenderly and with regret, "I like Mickey. In spite of what he has done to me, I feel sorry for him. I hope only the best for him. It seems like he's gone off emotionally somehow. To think that on my opening night he kidnapped my baby Maria , and I had to go on almost out of my mind with worry. He said I would only see her again when I came back to him.

"I can understand a man irrationally in love trying to get back the woman he loves. But to kidnap my baby! And to have no professional concern for my opening night, when I had to be at my best for Hollywood and the critics! It was unforgivable. In the middle of dress rehearsal I had to get Matt to get a detective to find my baby, and put my children on a plane to my parents in Texas.

"Matt has promised me he will never let Maria out of his sight. She is always now with one of us or my mother or Matt's mother in New York. My children are now with Matt's mother, enjoying the wholesome, good Italian life, and Jayne Marie is going to a Catholic boarding school in New York. Our headquarters will be in New York and we are buying a town house there so I can have my children with me, although most of our time may be spent in Europe with my film commitments."

Mickey now made a statement to the press: "I don't want to fight Jayne. If she wants to marry her new manager, God bless her, and I hope she is happy all the rest of her life."

Jayne played to rave notices as "Lorelie," a role cut to order for her blonde, sexy innocence. Matt stated that they had plans to make Jayne a great dramatic star in the theater. "She has the talent and the potential. All she needs is the roles and the direction," he said. "I hope to give her my full support, in fact my entire life making her dreams come true."

"It's just too, too wonderful, almost unbelievable but it's all real. It's not a dream, and I won't wake up sobbing in my pillow," Jayne said three seconds after exchanging wedding vows with her 28-year-old Italian director.

"Matt Cimber, besides being a genius, epitomizes my great dream which will now materialize," said Jayne.

Unlike the usual fanfare that had accompanied Jayne's every move since the start of her career, the nuptials were kept entirely secret. Absolutely no one but two people closest to her knew and they kept it secret, no matter how the columnists and the press pried.

"It's so sacred," Jayne said. "I've been taking instruction in the

Catholic Church. Matt is a born Catholic. We are going to be remarried in the Church as soon as I'm given permission. That's why we kept it so quiet."

After the wedding, Jayne and Matt flew to Italy where she was to complete the second part of her picture originally titled *Jayne Mansfield Reports* then changed to *Primitive Love*.

"I may make a picture for M.G.M. in Italy this winter," Jayne said. "I have one problem. I open at the Pabst Theater in Milwaukee in a play October 27th. In spite of the rumors, I have no intention of selling my beautiful home in Hollywood. Never. Nor will I rent it. Even if my work keeps me from it fifty weeks a year, I'll treasure the two weeks I get to spend there. I have had many offers to rent it, but I wouldn't even consider it."

The forty-room palatial Pink Palace, filled with priceless antiques, and the lavish garden and the pool with its waterfall and all-glass bath house was Jayne's one dream become a reality.

# CHAPTER XVIII

Dr. J. Lewis Bruce, a prominent doctor in Hollywood and the Hargitay family physician, had gone to San Diego to see Jayne and Mickey in "Gentlemen Prefer Blondes."

"I found Mickey all broken up, still in love with Jayne, and unable to see her except during their few moments on stage," said the doctor. "'I can't talk to her, reason with her, and I love her,' Mickey wept. I asked Jayne if she would come and talk with Mickey and me after the show. She said yes, but later said no. I felt the kidnapping of Maria before the opening night of her play at Melodyland was very wrong. She refused to forgive Mickey for that. He was beside himself with his frustrated efforts to hold on to her as his wife.

"I went to talk to Jayne without Mickey. Matt Cimber handed me a bottle of coke. I tasted it and exclaimed, 'This isn't plain coke!' 'Oh no,' he said. 'It's Jayne's.' It was a coke bottle filled with alcohol. She was drinking perhaps the same wine Judy Garland drank that looked like water. I realized Jayne was not as happy as she insisted, or why was she drinking? She had kept good health rules for so many years, and now?"

Maria was restored to Jayne and the shelter of the Pink Palace. Jayne and Matt and Marty, his bodyguard, moved in. Mama Hargitay quietly departed for Hungary. She said goodbye to Linda, called a taxi and vanished, bewildered and shocked, and wondering if all movie stars lived like this!

Jayne and Matt listed the furnishings they wanted from the pink palace to be shipped to New York. The children's toys filled a van. Linda was left in charge of the house. Jayne and Matt and the children flew to New York to make their home temporarily with Matt's parents on Long Island.

Matt told the press in New York, "Life with Jayne is gulping pizzas and hamburgers and living with four active kids and eighteen animals. It's smuggling her three chihuahuas onto airplanes. It's good because we accept the fact that we will fight one minute and love the next."

Jayne murmured, "He's the star—such a great director. I'm the wife. I'm his lackey. He rules everything."

Jayne called me long distance. "I'm having a cocktail reception for my marriage to Matt," she said. "Can't you fly in for it? I've invited all of the stars on Broadway and everyone of importance in New York."

I would join Jayne for the Christmas holidays in New York, I said, but now was impossible.

The reception proved a disaster. The important stars, and even those who had loved Jayne before, ignored her now. Very few of the press showed. Those who did took pictures of Jayne with one eye swollen shut and covered with heavy makeup. One picture was captioned, "The Marriage Least Likely To Succeed." Reports from Hollywood said Mickey would fight the marriage. Then he said he wouldn't. He wanted the children to be happy. Jayne said she had paid Mickey plenty of cash for her freedom.

"We are buying a town house," Jayne telephoned me around Thanksgiving. "We have taken a marvelous, three-story town house, and we'll be moving in a week after Christmas." "I'll keep the pink palace for vacations," she sighed.

"I can manage the expense of two homes," she said. "I'm doing a lot of T.V. here in New York. I have pictures to make in Europe. I have as many club dates as I want. And I'll play the Latin Quarter at $11,000 a week for a month."

"I want a good social life now in New York," she disclosed. "Now that I am Italian, I'm going to have a family crest on my stationary and everything elegant."

Jayne firmly believed that if you said it's so, it's so! Her mother and relatives were astounded to read that Jayne was of Italian origin. That didn't bother Jayne. "Believe and it's so. That's the power of positive thinking!"

It was now Christmas week. I telephoned Jayne that I had arrived in New York. "Come out right away. Matt's mother is going to cook you the most fantastic Italian dinner you ever ate," she said excitedly.

It seemed more practical to take the train to Floral Park, which saved almost an hour of travel time by taxi. Jayne was disturbed. "You should have come in a chauffeured car," she disapproved. "I would have sent my new Bentley for you, if I had known. You're too important to take a train, May. Remember who you are! I'd never take a train!"

She was sweet, gracious and very pretty, I thought, happy and obviously enthralled with Matt.

Matt's mother, Fanny, and his father, Tom, greeted us with warm Italian hospitality. The whole family including a sister and brother-in-law who sang opera, some nephews and nieces, an aunt and a cousin and some neighbors and friends were there.

Everyone toasted the newlyweds! Jayne Marie, now fourteen, and Mickey Jr., six, and Zoltan, four, bowed and kissed my hand as they had been taught to do by their French governess back in Hollywood. Maria had a cold and was next door at a neighbor's.

"Want to hear my new record?" Jayne asked excitedly. She put it on a small player. It was good, I thought, sweet and sexy. Then she autographed one to me: "The sweetest, dearest, prettiest friend I have," and she gave it to me. Next, she put on a Tony Bennett record. "He's now my cousin-in-law," she exclaimed.

Three news photographers arrived. Jayne sat on Matt's lap and kissed him while the cameras clicked. "You want the usual?" she asked. The lens men nodded. "Excuse me," she said. "I'll change." She returned, wearing a very low-cut blue dress with matching boots. This was a few years before boots became the rage. Jayne was always ahead of the fashions. A little nephew stared at her cleavage. Then he ran to her and she hugged him and kissed him.

"He's only seven," she smiled. "It's amazing how early things happen!" Fanny, ignoring the sex implication, injected, "Jayne has a wonderful way with children. They forget their troubles when they are in Jayne's motherly arms." We all smiled.

Jayne Marie sat watching her mother, her face a blank, but with a fourteen-year-old's thoughts. Matt seemed a little embarrassed posing. When it was over, Jayne volunteered to change again so "the boys can get the shots they want." She was still the star and she loved being on! She returned, wearing a bathing suit. "It's topless but I always put a top on it," she smiled. She lay down on the couch and posed provocatively. Everyone stared. Jayne next brought out a new fur coat. "Did you want some outside shots?" she offered.

We all went outside into the cold, rainy late afternoon. Jayne tried to get atop the hood of the Bentley, but she didn't quite make it. "I need Mickey Hargitay to hoist me up," she smiled. Then she cautioned, "Don't let Matt hear that. He's very jealous, you know."

The photographers wanted a fully family picture. Everyone came outside in the drizzle and posed. Jayne insisted that Maria be brought out. "But she has a high fever!" Fanny implored. Matt added, "We should not take her out on a rainy night like this, Jayne." Jayne turned to Matt. "Bring her out and then take her right back inside."

Everyone posed with big smiles. Jayne turned to Miklos and Zoltan, "Bacci Poppa," she said. They kissed Matt. When the pictures were taken, we shivered and went inside to eat a marvelous Italian feast.

After dinner the family considerately disappeared, leaving Jayne and Matt and me and my friend to talk in the living room. Jayne said, "I can't even crawl out of bed without his permission." Then she added, "I always dreamed about falling in love, but I didn't think love like this really existed. I had always heard that a girl should have a real friend in a loved one or a husband, someone you can tell your troubles. After Matt kissed me, I didn't believe I had ever been kissed before. I felt like I had been a virgin all of my life."

This was little too much for Matt. "A mental virgin," Matt interposed with a grin, affectionately amused.

"Matt is so well read. He's teaching me about authors and books and plays. He will be for me what Carlo Ponti is for Sophia Loren," Jayne said. "We will work together. Until now, I have always been out there alone with all of the work and responsibility. Now I have someone—we are a team!"

Jayne had stopped drinking and everything was evidently settling into a happy time.

Jayne was ecstatic about moving into the town house on Park Avenue. "Already we are receiving so many invitations from the top social people," she told me. "This is the way I was meant to live."

The long hallways of the first floor were crowded with toy automobiles and bicycles and toys. There were still large packing boxes everywhere. Jayne, in a tight leopard jumpsuit, her hair in a long loose bob, and diamonds flashing on her arms and fingers, took me on a tour of the house, with its three floors, mirrored walls, real wood carvings and all. The kitchen was still old-fashioned. She said, "I am going to have this kitchen all pulled out and made very ultra modern, like we did in the Pink Palace." Later when Jayne discovered the cost, she was shocked. Mickey had always been able to remodel, pull out and make new at only the cost of materials. Matt was a director —not a carpenter or plasterer—and he had no interest in becoming either.

Jayne and I went out shopping for Matt's birthday gifts. Jayne, walking along Fifth and Park and Madison Avenues, going into the small shops, caused a furor. Everyone seemed to love her. She stopped repeatedly to sign autographs or to return a hello. She was so gracious and kind, everyone said.

With arms filled with packages containing birthday hats, favors, napkins, table cloths, confetti, and eight birthday-wrapped gifts for Matt, we returned to the town house on Park Avenue, which sat next door to the Italian Embassy.

Matt's father, cooked chicken Italian style. Jayne set the table with all of the birthday trim. We sat down and toasted Matt——Jayne with a soft drink. Matt seemed uneasy at Jayne's overtures of affection. "I love him more than he loves me," she complained fondly.

The next day Jayne called that she and Matt were invited to Dorothy Kilgallen's formal dinner party. "Can I ask her to invite you, May?" she said. I told her no.

"She'll have so many important people there," Jayne worried, suddenly timid. "I do want to make the right impression. I wish you'd check on what I will wear." I suggested that Jayne wear a chic black chiffon Oleg Cassini with her real diamonds. "And my real pearls?" she asked. I agreed. Jayne and Matt were a success and a slew of social invitations followed.

New Year's Eve was here and what should we do? How should we spend it? I had been invited to several parties, but had sprained my wrist in Greenwich Village the night before. I told Jayne I would have to do whatever was the easiest, as I was still in quite a bit of pain. Jayne had to guest star on the Johnny Carson Show. She said she would meet me immediately after it. We agreed to attend just one party at the home of song writer Gladys Shelly. Connie Stevens and Jim Stacy, newly married, were also in town for the holidays.

I asked if it would be all right if four of my Hollywood friends came to the party. I didn't mention who the friends were.

Peter Brandon, socialite and Vice President of Mr. Johns, Inc., was my date that night. We arrived at the party around eleven. We went into the library to watch the Johnny Carson Show. There was Jayne, on the show, wearing the exact copy of the dress I was wearing. It was a black velvet Dior with luscious black fox trim. Jayne had had my dress copied. After I got over this surprise, I heard her say to Johnny Carson, "You'll have to excuse me if I don't stay for the finale of the show. I promised to meet May Mann at the stroke of midnight. It's a custom of ours each New Year's." Johnny looked his surprise, and Jayne, sweetly throwing kisses to the viewers and the studio audience, walked off camera.

Those in the drawing room were flabbergasted to see Jayne Mansfield arrive, with Matt and her entire family of children, her chihuahuas, and Morty, their bodyguard who also acted as their chauffeur. Jayne and I both laughed over our identical dresses. She also brought a big German star, "the Elvis Presley of Germany," to the party to meet me. Jayne had just completed a big musical in Germany with him. He was all exclamation points over the glamorous Jayne. I could see why, when we attended the premiere of their film a few nights later. Jayne, with big production numbers and excellent direction, was a delight to see on film.

After the guests had recovered from the surprise of Jayne, in walked Connie Stevens and Jim Stacy. It was a memorable night.

I had no sooner left New York and returned to Hollywood than the newspapers exploded with front-page pictures showing Matt and Mickey trading punches on a New York street corner while

Jayne looked on horrified and the children were crying. The news report said that Mickey had arrived in New York to see his children, Micklos and Zoltan. It had been agreed that Jayne and Matt would bring the two boys to a corner of 72nd and Fifth Avenue.

It seems that Mickey was embracing his two small sons, when words flew and there was a tussel between the two men. Mickey said, "Zoltan leaped into my arms and Matt Cimber swung at me. I told him, 'If I swing at you, you'll be sorry!' A friend of mine persuaded me to walk away from it."

"Jayne's solid gold but her husband is zero," Matt said. "I'm not scared of that muscleman. I come from Brooklyn. I can knock his capped teeth off. He belongs in a tree." Jayne, with her newly acquired Manhattan Park Avenue social position, was horrified.

When Jayne completed her tour of plays in the East, she decided to return to California after all. The pink palace had a strong hold on her. The furnishings that had been shipped east were loaded in vans and shipped back to Hollywood.

Buying the town house in New York, however, proved to be a good investment. Jayne disclosed, "We sold it for a big profit." Matt, more realistic, said that while Jayne made a T.V. appearance almost daily as a guest star all of the time she was in New York, it was actually no money. Jayne received $300 for an appearance but paid a hundred dollars for a chauffeured limousine and two hundred more for a new dress so there was no profit.

Then Jayne and Matt, his parents, a grandmother, a cousin and a bodyguard all moved in to the Pink Palace. Jayne was hoping to make a movie soon. Except she announced happily, "I'm expecting Matt's baby in a few months!"

# CHAPTER XIX

The Pink Palace, elaborately furnished as a glamorous movie star's abode, where you expect butlers and maids and formal attire for dinner, presented quite a different picture now.

Fanny had taken over as housekeeper. Linda, Jayne's maid, was still there. The family—nice Italian people, lounged around the house in their shirt sleeves, relaxed as people who are not movie stars should be at home. But the press, photographing the present days in the Pink Palace, said it was startling, like a look into the Beverly Hillbillies T.V. Show.

Matt was unusually kind and considerate of Jayne in her delicate condition. Still, Jayne would say, "May, he doesn't really love me. I'm in love with Matt and he isn't in love with me, not the way he should be." She worried about it. She never took a drink now. The physical condition of her child to be born was of upmost consideration. She loved her mother-in-law, Fanny and Matt's cousin, Kitty

Burke, a beautician who had taken over Jayne's coiffures. Jayne never looked prettier. Pregnancy always gave her an extra glow.

I had newly acquired an unusual pussycat; a pink point white Siamese named "Princess." She was as glamorous and regal as her name. She originated from the Palace of the King and Queen of Thailand. Since there are very few pink point white Siamese, Jayne was very impressed. Whenever she came to my house, she snuggled Princess on her lap for the entire time. "Please try to find me one like her," she pled. "I'll pay any price." We tried, but kittens were out of season and there were none like Princess to be found.

Finally, I discovered a lady who had two tiny, white pink-nosed angora kittens. I tried to get one for Jayne. To my surprise, the woman declined. "I know Jayne is wonderful, but she travels too much to take proper care of a kitten." Jayne was disconsolate. She promised she would have the kitten sleep on her bed if necessary, and she would take it with her if she had to travel. The lady was adamant and said no.

One evening, Jayne arrived in a beautiful black velvet evening gown. We were going to a premiere. Jayne, as usual, clasped Princess to her and hugged the pussycat for some time before our departure. To my horror, when we stepped in front of the blaze of lights for the television cameras, Jayne's black dress was white with kitten fur. "Oh," I exclaimed, trying to brush it off. "Never mind," Jayne said into the camera, "That is Princess and I love her. Now May, never explain, and never complain!" The crowds laughed. "Besides, I am Princess' godmother!" she announced.

On a Merv Griffin broadcast later, Jayne recalled how we had all been in a Christmas parade. Jayne was queen on a float with her children. I shared a float with the famous silent film star, Fifi Dorsey, who was to regain the spotlight on Broadway in 1971. Our names were bannered on both sides of the car. Since Jayne always had a chihuahua tucked under her arm, I thought children would love to see a pretty white kitten in the parade at Christmas time. I took Princess, and Princess stole the parade. Everyone cheered and asked about the white pussycat. Children yelled and pointed. The T.V. cameras focused on Princess.

At the cocktail party for the celebrities following the parade, Eleanor Chambers the Deputy Mayor of Los Angeles, held Princess for the photographers. Then Jayne took Princess, announcing, "I'm Princess' godmother." Eleanor replied, "*I'm* Princess' godmother." After that, Jayne was even more devoted to Princess. In all her letters when she was away she'd send her love to Princess. Princess purred her response to this affection from both notable women.

"Look Matt," Jayne said. "Look at how gorgeous Princess is. She would be wonderful in my new picture. She's all pink and white. I could have my wardrobe in pink and white to match her. Princess would be so unusual in a motion picture. So different than carrying a dog."

Matt agreed, and asked if Princess would like to play Jayne's pal in *Las Vegas Hillbillies*. It had never occurred to me to make a movie star out of Princess. But Princess purred and Jayne said, "You see, she wants to."

There we were on location, Princess in her pink-jeweled collar and pink satin bow and Jayne in a pink satin gown under a white coat. Jayne was playing a night club star in Las Vegas. She drove by the camera in a long white Lincoln with Princess sitting beside her, both profiles whizzing by in the breeze.

It was a proud moment to see my pussycat, not quite a year old, actually co-staring in a movie with Jayne Mansfield. The director marveled that Princess would take such marvelous direction. "Of course, she understands every word you say," said Jayne. The next scene showed Jayne and Princess getting out of the car at a gas station. Jayne was very careful to see that Princess got all of the camera angles, rather than herself.

Jayne and Princess were talking to a handsome station attendant, and as the mike boom moved down to catch their dialogue, Princess meowed. It was left in the final print. "You're a real scene stealer!" Jayne exclaimed, hugging Princess who purred, enjoying it all. They had a few more scenes and it was a long, long day. Princess, as long as she was with Jayne, acted her scenes to perfection. When Matt stepped forward to take Princess, she responded with a scratch. Nothing doing, she was a star now and only Jayne was her equal!

Jayne and Matt started Princess' salary at $150 an hour. Which was promptly raised to $250 an hour, and Princess donated her earnings to poor, starving, homeless cats. The film was completed by Christmas time. On the last day's shooting, I had been invited to a luncheon, honoring Jerry Lewis' son Gary, who was to receive his first gold record for "Diamond Ring." In the middle of the luncheon, I was paged. The studio needed Princess for more close-ups. Ah, the stage mama bit. Unfortunately, I couldn't leave at that critical moment, out of devotion to Patti and Gary, or I would have missed the presentation.

"So poor little Princess missed her final close-up," said Jayne, very upset. "That's very unprofessional. I'd have seen she got them—she's so gorgeous and such a perfect actress," soothed Jayne when she saw Princess.

It was revealing, said the film editor, to see a glamorous star actually give her scenes to a pussycat. Jayne actually went out of her way to place Princess to the best camera advantage. That was Jayne when she loved!

Jayne and Matt arrived for one of my fun parties. We had about twenty guests. My living room is forty feet long and quite apropos to play the game of movie star improvisations. Starting with a script and a narrator, the guests drew their roles from a basket. Everyone improvised the role they had drawn. It was hilarious. Jayne was almost shy in a situation like this, when I was present. She played her role of "Little BoPeep who'd lost her sheep" admirably. George Hamilton played Prince Charming. We took snapshots and had a lot of laughs. About eleven-thirty, Jayne exclaimed, in that naive, little girl voice, "Oooh, can we turn on television? I'm on the twelve o'clock news." That disrupted the whole party. We all marched into the bedroom, where a large T.V. screen enabled all twenty of us to watch. Some sprawled on the king size bed, others sat on the floor, and we were all ready to applaud Jayne. For thirty minutes Jayne didn't appear on the screen. Her face became pink with embarrassment, and we all began to tease. When her image finally flashed on, she breathed a sigh of deep relief. "I was so embarrassed," she said. "I would have died if I hadn't showed."

At my party Jayne met the Mustos, who had come with Herbert Klein, a builder and sometimes movie producer. Musto immediately asked Jayne if she would be interested in making a movie for him. Jayne said she would agree if Matt liked the script, and if Matt would be the director. Matt had never directed a motion picture. In the chance of getting Jayne at any cost, Musto was agreeable. This would have to wait, of course, until after the arrival of her baby.

"Jayne," I said, "I would like to but I just can't give you another baby shower. It wouldn't be right to invite all of those same people again to bring presents. We've had them all here three times already, and in such a short time. I'd like to, but I just can't." Jayne smiled, but I knew she would have loved another baby shower. I had a baby blanket custom made and embossed with some royal lace inherited from my great-grandmother, who was a Princess in Kaiser Wilhelm's Court in Berlin. Jayne was very impressed that I would give it to her baby. Little Antonio Otaviano (Matt's real name) was born in October. Matt was thrilled. So was Jayne. And Fanny was wild with joy. Indeed, Little Tony was like a tiny royal princeling in the pink palace.

Two hours after Jayne's delivery at the hospital, she sent for Kitty Burke to dress her hair. Donning a robe, Jayne was discovered a half hour later attending a class on child care in the hospital. Natural childbirth had Jayne up and on her feet almost immediately. She insisted that Kitty come each day to dress her hair. To the consternation of the hospital authorities, the newspapers showed pictures of Jayne and her hour-old baby in bed. Photographers were hidden in the closet, and they'd come out with their cameras when the nurse was out of the room.

Two weeks after giving birth, Jayne was trim and slim and going again at full steam. Plans to start production of Musto's *Single Room Furnished* were on schedule. Jayne played three roles, giving her a wide dramatic range. The film proved unsalable for lack of proper distribution. The few critics who saw it declared Jayne a magnificent actress. The picture was not completed until after Jane's death. Strangely, the last scene showed Jayne looking in a mirror which shattered in her face as you heard a terrible crash of cars, it was almost like a warning of Jayne's own death to come. Nothing more was heard of Jayne's last movie in Hollywood.

"I've decided to give a housewarming and a top drawer social event for the christening of our baby," Jayne told me on the telephone. "I want it to be the biggest and most successful party. You know, I've never given a big party. I am depending on your help. I plan to spend at least ten thousand."

"But Jayne, I'll be in New York for two weeks. It is impossible for me to be there," I told her.

Jayne was dismayed. "I won't know what to do," she pled. "please, can't you change your plans?"

"I can't," I told her, regretfully, "I just can't. My trip east is business! I have to go." Jayne was disheartened.

Jayne's press secretary read off the guest list. Jayne had invited almost every top star in Hollywood who had children. The list began with Debbie Reynolds and included Elizabeth Taylor and Richard Burton, who were living across the street in a leased house, taken for six months during their stay here.

Secretly, I wondered if all of these stars would show at Jayne's party. I hoped they would. I knew that they would not want to play secondary roles to Jayne, who would, as usual, invite all of the press photographers. Jayne, of course, would star as she always did.

When I returned, I heard the party had turned out badly for Jayne. Strolling musicians played around the pool. The setting was perhaps the most beautiful in Hollywood, with the pink terrace, spacious grounds, the heart-shaped pool and splashing fountains and the glass pool and guest houses. Buffet tables were heavy with delicious food. Champagne flowed like water. But Gypsy Rose Lee, who took endless snapshots with her camera for future use on her T. V. show, was the only important star who accepted and came to the party. While there were many guests, most of them were not celebrities.

To hide her disappointment, Jayne gathered her children, even before the last party stragglers left, and took them "trick or treating" in the neighborhood. Jayne would never admit defeat or cry unless she was all alone.

Matt and Musto agreed to the idea of giving Jayne a big birthday party in my garden. We tied all of the garden furniture in pink satin bows. To top it all, we had a real pink elephant.

Princess gave Jayne a pink bag. My gift was a sexy pink chiffon nightie. Musto's wife made dainty sandwiches and Jayne was like a little girl cutting the big birthday cake. The photographers were Jayne's best friends, and I invited them all. Everyone, especially Jayne was delighted with the pink elephant. The birthday party helped make up for the disappointment Jayne had felt at her own party.

It was now holiday time and Jayne called, asking what shall we do that will be elegant for Christmas and New Year's. My cousins, the Martin VonDehns who were among the social elite of Bel Air were having a party. Since I had always been their favorite relative, and they had long insisted that I live with them as their daughter, I asked if I might invite Jayne and Matt for Christmas.

I have never seen Jayne more beautiful than she was on that night we went to the VonDehns. Her blonde hair had been wound in a braid around her head and she looked like a princess herself. Mr. VonDehn was charmed. So was everyone. We had a delightful evening and Jayne said later, "I enjoy society and the social world." She instructed Matt to have more stationary printed with their Italian coat-of-arms, which had been done in New York with their town house address. "We need it now out here for the pink palace," she said.

We enjoyed Christmas dinner at Jayne's house, Christmas night at the VonDehns. I held my Yule open house the following Sunday, when Jayne said, "Please May, come over and let's spend a late afternoon before the year ends." "I have lots to say." I agreed.

When I arrived, Jayne was bathing in her pink, heart-shaped tub. We began discusing a most unkind T.V. reporter's description of Jayne. She made her sound almost immoral, which Jayne was not. "Consider the source," Jayne laughed. "She's evil, poor woman—jealous, frustrated. She's never known a man's love probably, nor ever had a date she didn't ask for."

In a talkative mood, Jayne discussed her thoughts of the moment. I lay relaxing on the thick, pink wool fluff carpeting, a little tired from the Christmas merry-go-round, and a willing listener.

"To be loved and cherished is my goal and my complete motivation in life. It always has been. And you know something, when I am pregnant I am happier than at any other time.

"After Maria was born in 1964, my mother arrived from Dallas. She told me, 'Don't have any more children Jayne. You, and only you, have to raise and educate them you know. . .Children are not playthings you can deposit with other people. And certainly not me.' When I'd had three, she told me I should stop. And whenever I've sent my children to her for a visit, she asks for a big check for their expenses and governesses. I've always known I could never count on my mother and yet, I am always trying to get her approval. I don't know—." Jayne slid down into the tub to chin level. A photographer should see this, I thought—Jayne, with her curls pinned on top of her head and tied with a pink satin ribbon. "You look like September Morn," I laughed.

"My dream has always been my children," Jayne continued, wriggling her toes in the water. "They are a part of me and part of the man I love, as nature intended. My emotions are very basic as a woman. And as a woman, I constantly seek fulfillment and happiness," she analyzed.

"Perhaps I have a greater need for love. I see too many beautiful women who live by the side of happiness, but are strangers to its beauty and reality.

"When Jayne Marie was placed in my arms—my first baby, I thought this is the ultimate achievement of a woman. She was so tiny, so precious, so dependent on me for love, for her very life. I wondered why all women didn't have babies every year. After all, you can have them free. You don't have to be rich. I was only fifteen, and I knew I would have to work twice as hard when I had Jayne Marie. But I was willing.

"When Miklos was born, it was a mutual love affair from the start. I adore him. Then came Zoltan, quiet and intensively brilliant, and I was so proud. He is like my father. And all of these years, I have wanted my father. Realizing this, I have never deprived my children, not one of them, in spite of the differences I have had with their respective fathers—of being with their fathers. They need a father's devotion just as I always longed for it—as well as a mother's. I have had to go to court to insure their equal rights with their parents. But always, I have taken the financial responsibility of raising them. And I am happy to do it. When you have five children that is a considerable investment.

"I have always said I want at least ten children. I have my five, Jayne Marie 16, Miklos 8, Zoltan 7, Maria 3, and Antonio 18 months. If God is willing, I will have five more.

"Many of our great stars were afraid to take the chance. Isn't that strange," she thought out loud. "I have read of Jean Harlow and

Marilyn Monroe, and then there is Mae West. My predecessors, all international sex symbols, each forfeited their divine, god-given right to bear children. I feel sorry that they denied themselves this great joy. They were afraid, I guess, that it would detract from their 'image,' My children enhance mine.

"I know people often condemn me for the way I have lived, which has not always been conventional. They should not condemn me. The true circumstances will show that I have been victimized.

"I have never had an abortion. Very few of our top glamour queens can say that. I have never deprived a little baby of mine from being born. I have always had a father for each one, to give him or her their rightful place in the world of conventionality."

"Jayne," I said, "you are giving quite a discourse!"

She laughed. "I don't hate the people who condem me. I feel sorry for them. It's their frustrations and jealousy talking. I live as I see best, regardless of critics.

"A girl can have a baby every year, and grow more beautiful with each newborn. And she can have a better figure and a lovelier skin! I am actually the living proof of my theory!

"Two weeks after the birth of Tony, I was back to my size eight dress. My curves were perfect and symmetrical, and my skin was young looking and absolutely flawless. I was on stage and working. I exercised daily like I had done during my entire pregnancy."

Jayne, relaxing in the scented bubbles, was in beautiful shape just like she said, except there was more of her in the bust department. There were no sags, no wrinkles, nothing hanging over, just a solid roundness where it should be.

"I love children," she said. "I'm the mother type. Besides, I know how to have them. Lots of them!"

I wondered if she was so unique in that, as it is assumed most expectant mothers also know how to have babies. Before I could inquire into such a delicate process, Jayne exuberated; "It's just a matter of self-control—having babies!

"Each one of my babies is a joyous affair. It is wanted."

"I'm the mother type," she purred softly stepping out of the tub and putting on a flame chiffon clinging robe with cascading white fox fur, and pulling it tight around her! This made her look like anything but the mother type!

"I turned off the telephone so we could talk," Jayne said. "I wanted to get a clear perspective of me. I like me—do you? The real me?"

"Oh Jayne," I laughed. "Of course I do."

"Okay," she replied blithely. "I just wanted to hear you say it. For you're the only one who knows how I'm victimized by love and fate. Too much, too much—" she sighed.

"I am sorry to say, when I get in with the swingers during long night club engagements away from home, I have been a swinger too," she confessed, stretched out in comfort on the heart-shaped pink bed. "That's the long hours, the loneliness, the booze. That isn't the real me.

"I have been called an immoral girl, a broad of easy virtue. I am accustomed to such criticism, and the many things that are not true. I am always proud though when people know the real me. I could never have an affair of the moment, nor for money. Not even for my career. I couldn't take the casting couch routine. A human being must have dignity and self-respect to survive in this business. Or you smother out with sleeping pills.

"My compulsive search for real, lasting love has kept me in the throes of romance, marriage and remarriage. Each coming up before I was out of the preceding one.

"I have never been really free in my adult life. I was under parental supervision until I married at fourteen. There has been no let-up, except those few brief months on Broadway after my divorce from Paul. Even as that ended, Mickey Hargitay came on the scene and we married the day my divorce was final. That has been the constant, repetitious pattern," she declared, her tone turning a bit angry.

"And the christening party you missed—," she recalled. "The

people I wanted didn't come. Debbie Reynolds didn't even have the courtesy to acknowledge my wired invitation. I spent thousands of dollars entertaining people I hardly knew—who just came anyway. I'm through with the social scene," she said.

"So many film stars indulge in amours and flaunt their unmarried, illegal status all over the world," Jayne said, her mood changing. "Elizabeth Taylor and I are unique in the fact that we believe in old-fashioned marriage. And children with marriage—that love and marriage come together. While we are pictured as flamboyant, we actually adhere to moral convention. We are both, foremost, good mothers and family women, as strange as that may sound. But it is a fact.

"Elizabeth and I have generous curves, and we both share a problem keeping them. I have long accustomed myself to eat for health. But I love goodies, like chili—Elizabeth's favorite. But I don't eat everything," she repeated, "because I have to have a perfect figure! Elizabeth, too, diets strenuously at times.

"Elizabeth has won her Oscar. I am hoping one day to have one." Jayne had thrown off the negligee and was dressing; no bra or underthings. Selecting a dress, a yellow jersey high-necked shift, and matching shoes, was "dressing."

"Elizabeth seems to be a highly intelligent girl. I hope some day we become friends. I know I'd enjoy knowing her," Jayne observed. "Besides our children, we do have much in common— the headlines, our careers and our love for jewels, furs and status symbol custom cars. And much more I am sure. But she's the luckier one, with her mother and father so devoted, and always there to help when she needs them.

"If I were to envy Elizabeth Taylor, I'd envy her the devotion and love of her parents and the security it gives her. Not her Oscar. I have hundreds of trophies and awards, but I've really never had the other.

"I've faced the shadows to give birth to all five of my children. But no one, except the real me, knows the insecurity and the terrible hurting heartache and aloneness I have deep inside of me."

Jayne was in a most talkative mood, and I enjoyed listening.

"Elizabeth Taylor and Richard Burton, with great secrecy, leased that hideaway mansion across the street," Jayne said, after we had stepped out on a little balcony on the north side of the pink palace. "You can see their house and pool from this balcony.

"I am far too busy to be interested in anyone else's affairs except my own. But during my lavish christening party three weeks ago, my butler discovered that some of the guests were wandering upstairs and lingering a long time.

"To my astonishment and annoyance, I found a free peep show was going on from the balcony," Jayne disclosed. "Several people stood there, looking down at Elizabeth and Richard Burton and their own group sitting around their pool on this weekend afternoon. In fact, Richard was playing croquet. Elizabeth, relaxing on a pool chaise lounge, was giving instructions to Liza and Maria. 'Let daddy alone, so he can play!' And the Burtons' pooch was misunderstanding the whole thing to chase the ball, much to Richard's annoyance.

"I said, 'Please!' quite dramatically to my guests. 'Do not look at the Burtons. It isn't the thing to do. It isn't nice.'

"'But it's a show to watch them,' was the reply. I literally ordered my guests to depart and return to the pool side, and leave Elizabeth and Richard to their own respective peace."

Dressed, Jayne suggested that we go into the library and shut the door for further privacy. The children's voices shrieked at play, outside by the pool. Frangrant odors of dinner cooking drifted up the stairway. Jayne turned on a T.V. set, checked the news reports and then settled down again to talk. This was unusual, for neither of us had this kind of time for girl talk!

Jayne had recently made a film in Florida with Jordan Christopher (Sybil Burton's new husband).

"The press photographers really tried to make something of it with us. When they visited our set, they kept trying to edge Christopher and me into romantic poses. But he was a perfect gentleman. He finally said to the photographers 'I am a very happily married man. My wife isn't able to join me yet on this location. And Miss Mansfield has been more than gracious. So please, don't try to make anything of it. No scandals, please!' He was not ambitious for publicity at all.

"It is strange how things have happened with Elizabeth and myself," she mused. "In our respective ways we are sex symbols. And the paths and patterns of our lives have crossed many times. They continue to do so.

"I first met Elizabeth at a party at Romanoff's long ago. Then at the baby shower you gave for me, Elizabeth sent a silver piggy bank. I like her. We both had the same agent and the same press agents.

"There were big, controversial headlines when Sharon Hugeny left the Frings stable, because she said 'all of the *big roles* were offered to the *big stars*, Jayne Mansfield and Elizabeth Taylor.' Imagine naming me ahead of Elizabeth Taylor!

"The worst thing that happened was when Elizabeth was in Rome making *Cleopatra*," Jayne divulged. "The first big scandals of Elizabeth Taylor and Richard Burton were breaking in papers around the world. A reporter asked me to comment on it. He wanted me to put Elizabeth down for what she was doing to her children. I refused to comment on Elizabeth Taylor or her private life, except to say she is a very fine mother, for she always has her children with her, as I do. No matter where we go, we always have our families with us.

"The news service ignored my refusal and went ahead and carried a big story that I had put Elizabeth down for her immoral actions. This distressed me terribly. I sent her a telegram, telling her I didn't say it. I guess she understood because stars are always being misquoted by sensationalists.

"I always say people are so anxious to point a finger. They forget to recognize that Elizabeth is a very good mother. She adopted a little crippled girl and has, with her money, patience, devotion and love, made the child whole. She is giving her a wonderful, normal life. Whatever people used to say, I knew Elizabeth would get over this, and again be a favorite with acclaim and respect—which she now has.

"Here's a press clipping that links us." Jayne handed it to me from a box filled with loose ones. It read: "Elizabeth the brunette and Jayne the blonde both visit the top fashion houses on two continents. Often the designers will say to Jayne, 'Elizabeth wanted this number, but we didn't sell it to her; it's for you.' It is likely to presume that Elizabeth gets the same sales pitch, especially in gowns that cost from $500 to $3000. And both Jayne and Elizabeth maintain tremendous wardrobes of such clothes."

"Now that we are neighbors there have been all sorts of mix-ups," she remarked. "Flowers have been delivered to my house for Elizabeth Burton. And flowers and packages for me have been delivered to Elizabeth's house.

"When I planned the christening party, I sent Jayne Marie across the street with an invitation by hand to the Burtons. Jayne Marie was amazed to discover that the Burtons had no electrically controlled gates surrounding their house, like the ones surrounding ours.

"'You just walk right in and ring the front doorbell,' Jayne Marie said. 'Mr. Richard Burton came to the door himself and said, "Hello, what can I do for you?" He was very friendly and nice. I told him I had an invitation for him and his wife. He called over his shoulder to someone, "Is Liz up yet?" Then he said, "She's still asleep. But here, I'll take it." It was a very informal household.'

"The more happiness you get, the more sadness you get, I've found. One balances the other. Elizabeth has found this to be doubly true."

# CHAPTER XX

The Beatles arrived in Hollywood on their first American tour. "The one movie star we want to see is Jayne Mansfield," said John Lennon. Jayne was pleased and kept a rendezvous with the boys at the Whiskey Go-Go on the Sunset Strip. Matt went right along of course, which proved a disappointment to the English quartet. "I just wanted to be alone with Jayne. I've dreamed about it," John said.

Jayne began trying to undo all of the sensationalism and wild, way-out publicity which had first attracted public interest and named her the "Queen of Sex," but which now was destroying her. At the same time it seemed financially impossible to turn her back on her established trade-mark to start over again. No one wanted to hire her as a dramatic actress, which had become her goal and obsession.

"I've outgrown all of that sex goddess stuff" Jayne was telling a

London reporter one afternoon by the pool. "No one was taking me seriously, and I have to prove that I am serious.

"And to think I worked so hard to join the ranks of Brigette Bardot, Marilyn Monroe and Jane Russell," she acknowledged.

"But you have far surpassed them. You are the world's established Queen of Sex!" the reporter said gallantly. "Marilyn Monroe has put her career aside too many times to be the international sex symbol she once was. Today it's Jayne Mansfield."

Jayne smiled. "Marilyn and I are entirely different. We've really never been in competition," she explained, in a soft voice. "I admire Marilyn and she's told me she admires me. Marilyn voluntarily stopped her career for two years and again for another year or so to demand her chance for dramatic roles . But I can't think of just what I want. I have to keep working because I have so many mouths to feed, so many people dependent on me. And my children's welfare has to be first!"

People who happened to meet Jayne were always very surprised. Their immediate reaction was, "Why, she's a sweet girl and not like her public image at all!" The London reporter told me he had expected Jayne to be a seasoned burlesque type with a vocabulary of four-letter words and off-color jokes. Once in her company, he discovered he had been dead wrong. Jayne was refined, spoke, not only good English, but Italian and French as well. She avoided all types of slang. Those who met her always wound up not only becoming her admirers but loyal friends.

Preparing for a tour in a play, Jayne went immediately into rehearsal. Often I would find her seated on the floor of her stall shower, fiercely studying and memorizing her lines. Sometimes Jayne Marie would cue her. Jayne prided herself on always being letter perfect and she worked hard at it.

The night before leaving on the tour with her new play for Seattle and Portland, Jayne confided how disappointed she was that she would not be able to play "Harlow" in the movie then being cast.

"I have thousands of letters here, from people all over the world, saying I am the perfect Harlow. I even naturally have her mannerisms of caressing my body and my arms in a way. But no, they can't see me playing the dramatic side of Harlow's life. This sex image is destroying my happiness and my marriage with Matt. I can't seem to drop it. After the play's run, I am booked in night clubs for months ahead. I wouldn't take the bookings but we need the money to keep this place going. I'm supporting thirteen people living here in the pink palace. I have to keep the money coming in. Miklos can't understand why I keep working away from home. The other day he said, 'I hate this pink palace Mama because it takes you away all of the time!' But what can I do?" Jayne seemed suddenly weary and discouraged, something she rarely showed.

A full page story on "Jayne, the Glamorous Sex Symbol," in a Sunday supplement was lying with her mail by her bed. The article began, "Jayne Mansfield is more often described as a little girl in a woman's body, play-acting with sex. But today she has grown up to consider the fun things and the sexy quips more seriously. Most of them are true, she admits. Like she said, 'I never went to bed with a man I didn't love,' and, 'Once he's happy in the bedroom, the kitchen and the living room are a cinch!' Today, Jayne says, 'Any intelligent girl knows that!'"

"I guess it's my looks," Jayne sighed a little fretfully. "I assumed everyone knew that I was laughing when I said things like that. They are true but they are only meant to amuse. I am equally frank about being a devoted mother to my children. The only trouble is people can't seem to differentiate between the public image of Jayne Mansfield they know, and me as I am."

"Better days Jayne," I comforted. "You're in big demand and that's what really counts with a career, isn't it?"

"I don't ever want to grow old," she mused. "I don't want to become a has-been, an old biddy with scrapbooks of press clippings. Once I start to slip, I'm going to stay home and be a wife and mother full-time. I want to have at least ten children. I mean that, sincerely," she added. Foremost in her mind, however, was the present decline of her career.

"It seems strange the public can't accept me as a serious actress. If *Single Room Furnished* ever gets released, that will be a surprise, I am sure. It should bring me a whole new career. I didn't study acting, singing, dancing and go to college just to look good in bikinis."

Jayne said she had received some good reviews for her work on her national theater tour the previous year. And in several television segments she'd played strong dramatic roles without makeup or glamour and the critics had been laudatory. "Hollywood producers don't remember them because the name 'Jayne Mansfield' is all wound up in sex," she said ruefully.

"There's an old adage," she recalled. "'Be careful of what you wish or it will surely come true.' My dream was to become a glamorous film star, and now I find it isn't worth it.

"I used to dream day and night of becoming a glamorous star like Lana Turner, and I'd live in a big pink house with pink hearts all about me." "Now," she sighed, slipping into another mood of wistful nostalgia, "it all seems so long ago. Here it is, all of it, and I'm not happy with it. I want something more worthwhile."

"Look Jayne," I said, "don't belittle yourself and your career." I had been glancing through pages of a press clipping book as Jayne talked and I read: "Jayne Mansfield began her career posing for male magazines at $60 a week. Twentieth Century Fox values her at 20 million." I read the item to Jayne. She smiled.

"All I really want is the respect that is due me, not to be passed off in Hollywood as a yeh-yeh-rah-busty play girl in the girly business whose every move appears to be sensuous. Even when I say something serious people think it's extremely funny and they laugh. I've gone through enough in the last few months to know what being scared to death and terrible anxiety, heartbreak, threats, complete disillusions and all—really are! It's a terrible price to pay for my career. Without that career, none of these horrible nightmares of the last few months would have happened. Most of it was blackmail over the money I've made!"

Jayne and Matt returned home from the play's tour for a few weeks. Jayne soon became restless. Matt, she discovered, preferred to stay at home and rest, read, or play poker. Jayne, who had to diet severely to keep her figure, needed to go out and be seen to keep from eating. She became morose and then happily turned her talents to writting.

A new comedy skit for her night club act was her first effort. She also wrote a play, entitled "Hedy De Vine," The cast included Gabby Dunn, Hedy's agent, Cecil Trumpetski, a movie director, Sandara Stiles, a bitch, Gregory LeGrand, a producer. The setting, was the pink palace and Colossal Studios. The comedy script was a shooting script, and those who saw it were amazed at the technical knowledge Jayne displayed in writing a working film script.

Jayne left for New York where she starred for eight weeks at the Latin Quarter. The critics gave the Sex Goddess rave reviews. The box office tingled happily and she was held over. Again, she was the darling of Broadway with billboards and posters bigger-than-life of Jayne Mansfield. Except this time, Matt held tight rein. She was not permitted to go out on the dazzling bright white way to the smart night clubs after the show. Matt insisted it was a light supper and to bed. Jayne complained, but she had put her career into his hands and there was nothing she could do about it. Then came a successive tour of night clubs and a tour in Venezuela. By this time, the bird had been caged too long and she and Matt quarreled. She found herself in Venezuela alone.

Front page headlines in the American and world press told of Jayne's difficulties in the South American country. She had been stopped at the airport and her passport revoked temporarily for some error of local taxes to be paid in that country. For several days, we frantically tried to call Jayne in Venezuela to help iron out her difficulties. Finally, she came home. With her came a boy who spoke only Spanish. He was twenty years old and madly in love with Jayne. He moved into the pink palace and Matt and his family moved out. Jayne Marie developed a tremendous crush on the new young man, Douglas Olivares, who was her mother's sweetheart but only four years older than herself.

The pink palace was full of people coming and going when I arrived the night of Jayne's return. There were always agents and promoters, trying to inveigle Jayne into some money making schemes. Now, for the first time in the ten years of her career, the money was slowing up. The bills of growing children, the upkeep of the pink palace and the expenses of her tours were mounting. With Jayne Marie, Miklos and Zoltan all now in school, Jayne could no longer take them with her, except during summer vacations. And there were governesses for the younger Maria and baby Tony. She had to maintain a staff of servants in the pink palace to keep it going as a home for them. She was worried now also, for she had not been paid in Venezuela.

She confided to me that she was worried. "Most girls would jump at the chance to marry the first millionaire to take over. I would never have to worry about money again if I married Jorge Guinlee of Brazil or Harold Dassen of Virginia. They are multimillionaires. Not to mention the ones in Europe." "But," she said proudly, "I'm not a gold digger. I never was. I have never been a taker—always a giver."

It was Sunday night. I stopped in on my way to church in Westwood. Matt was in the library completing negotiations for Jayne's four week engagement at the Freemont in Las Vegas. Jayne refused to speak to him. I ran back and forth, trying to patch things up between Matt and Jayne without any results. Jayne felt Matt had deserted her when she needed help in Venezuela. "He did not come, even when I called and begged him to come and help me," she said. "Now I'm through with him. Absolutely through.

"I always felt he never loved me. Now I know. It was my image of Jayne Mansfield." Matt told me differently in the library, but

Jayne wouldn't listen.

"I won't prostitute myself just to marry a man who can pay my bills," she said. "I work for the material things in my life—my $28,000 Bentley, Cadillac, Jaguar and other cars, furs and jewels which are a part of my career. First," she said in that disarming little girl voice, "first and foremost comes love! Love for my children, and for and from the man I am in love with, which I always hope and believe will be forever! I can't live without a man loving me.

"Life does not give you what you want 'forever.' That's the lesson I have been learning almost continually lately. My babies, I realize, will grow up. They will not leave me but they will have families of their own. My marriages, all three, have not turned out successfully. But somehow, I am not bitter. I still believe in love and loving. It is as necessary to me as breathing. As necessary as life itself. I could never live, or work so hard without the incentive and the inspiration of love, from both a man and my children." Jayne sipped a coke amd smiled at a handsome, obviously very young man who walked into the room. He was tall, with great dark eyes, smooth dark hair, pale for his olive skin and slender. "Douglas!" Jayne called softly. He crossed the room and sat at her feet, kissing her toes showing through her slippers, and reverently whispered, "I love you—my darling wife." His words were in Spanish—but I understood Spanish!

"Jayne!" I gasped. "Be careful. Does Douglas speak English?" "Not a word," she said, reaching down to kiss the boy from Venezuela on the forehead. "He's precious—and so in love. I'm his first love. He won't be 21 for two and a half months yet. So we have to be careful—very careful!"

"At the moment," she admitted, speaking of all the men in her life, "I am confused—terribly confused. Here is Douglas Olivares, this handsome, Arabic Italian boy I met in Venezuela. He is a university student who is so completely and madly in love with me. He flew back here with me; 'Didn't you Bel Bambino?'" she said in Spanish, giving the handsome, six foot young man at her feet a look of adoration. He reached up to kiss and caress her arm. Clearly, he worshipped her.

"I don't understand, however, and I can't after all of this time—why men can be so wonderful before marriage and then afterwards, change so much. My husbands became completely different people. I live in beauty and love and kindness. Anything less is not for me—for it would be unnatural.

# CHAPTER XXI

Hollywood was scandalized at Jayne's South American boy lover. Douglas never let her out of his sight. He even sat in front of her bedroom door nights, guarding her, as he had done in his own country.

"I was so helpless, so lost, down there all alone," Jayne told me. "Douglas was the only one who offered me security. There I was, in a strange city, in a strange hotel, with men knocking on my door all hours of the day and night. I was terribly frightened. I'd lock myself in the bathroom all night I was so scared. Sometimes I'd hear keys turning the lock of the door and someone would enter. They would be men who'd tipped some hotel man to get into Jayne Mansfield's room, with rape in mind.

"Of course it's been the same in the States when I haven't had a husband along to protect me. I bitterly complained to the management. They kept moving me from room to room.

"Douglas, is a college student, of a fine family. He was working as bus boy in the club where I appeared. When Douglas heard my plight, he quit his job to become my bodyguard. He's sworn a sacred oath that he will never, never leave me."

Jayne and I were sitting in the glass poolhouse, sipping tall glasses of iced milk. Her masseur had just left. She was stretched out on a fluffy, white spread on a couch. Suddenly, she began watching something outside first with astonishment, and then with intent interest. I looked. Douglas had just stepped out of the pool Jayne Marie walked over to him. Suddenly she put her arms around his neck. Imitating her mother's screen image, she provocatively drew her body close to his, looking up into his eyes with a tantalizing expression. Douglas froze at first, then nature began taking over, visibly.

Jayne jumped up and ran to the door calling, "Jayne Marie!" The girl sprang away. A bulge in Douglas' wet swim trunks revealed the teenager's appeal.

"I'm shocked!" screamed Jayne. Douglas ran into the house to cover his embarrassment. Jayne Marie defiantly stood her ground. "You're shocked?" she screamed back. "Look at you standing there naked, Mother. I'm shocked! Besides, he's my age. You're too old for him!"

Bursting into tears, Jayne Marie ran into the playhouse. Grabbing a robe, Jayne ran after her.

I sat there waiting. Linda, Jayne's maid, had already told me of Jayne Marie's crush on Douglas, who was only four years older than herself. She had confided to Linda already, "Mama's too old for him. I'm going to have him." Jayne's daughter had become a woman—and a rival.

Minutes later Jayne returned, poised and confident, as though I had not witnessed this traumatic spectacle.

"Jayne," I said, "are you becoming like the immortal Isadora Duncan, the famous dancer who lived for love? With each great love affair, she reportedly was said to have had a child. Be careful."

"Except," Jayne now laughed "I always get married. My children are always legitimate and raised with conventional dignity, and more importantly, with great love and understanding."

"I hope," Jayne said, almost to herself thinking out loud, "that my experience with Douglas doesn't color or affect my children's lives, especially Jayne Marie's, now that she is a teenager.

"I just told Jayne Marie that she has to do as 'Mama' says, not as 'Mama' does, until some day she grows up and becomes a mama. Then she can do as she pleases. I am strict with my children and I am proud that everyone who sees us together remarks how affectionate and how close we are. And how well-mannered they are. I give them everything in life that is good for them—and more, because I love them so much." Jayne made no reference to Douglas and Jayne Marie now. Douglas was hers. Jayne Marie had been put in her place.

"He is so young, and he is so old and mature and intellectual. He is my type really—handsome with dark eyes and dark hair and tall." Jayne said, "He is the boy I used to dream of when I was a little girl. I guess the age difference seems a little shocking —twelve years! I have worked and had responsibility since I can remember, and now it is fun to be young. I really never was a teenager, you know. Some people try to recapture their youth when they have worked hard all of their lives, when they get old. Me, I'll enjoy mine now, while I am young. It's an interval—a special dividend."

Douglas returned, somewhat sheepishly. We all sat by the pink, heart-shaped pool. Douglas sat at Jayne's feet, caressing her legs and her toes, kissing them, looking up at her with love-filled eyes. "Isn't he handsome?" Jayne exclaimed, "like a statue of a young lithe Greek god," she observed with measured admiration. How many times Jayne had described the physique of first Mickey, and then Matt, as Greek gods, I thought.

"I drink in her beauty," Douglas said to me in Spanish. It was all so real and so unreal—like a dream in technicolor—Jayne and her new love.

"At the moment I am wearing his rings, but I don't think I'll make any decision to marry again for a long time." She sighed, fingering the South American diamonds set in silver.

"In South America, the last three weeks, a manager who had booked my night club tour ran off with all of the money. I was stopped at the plane, as I was departing, for not paying taxes which I knew nothing about. Some people were put in jail over it. Because I was innocent, the people in Caracas were wonderful to me. They put me in the luxurious presidential suite of the leading hotel. I lived like a queen while they took legal steps to straighten out my affairs. Douglas was devoted. He was all I really had down there to lean on.

"In some ways, after Douglas took over my safety, I began having such a wonderful time that I could have stayed on forever. They want me to return to make several pictures." "But I am worried about my jewels," she allowed. "They were kept for safety and have not been returned—by a private individual, an Arabic man, Jose Attara Tahan. I hope they don't become an international crisis. I have no insurance, since my $200,000 robbery in New York." (Jayne's jewels, valued at $250,000, were never returned.)

"I'll always have guards posted at my hotel doors at night. I am afraid to go to sleep alone," she sighed. "I'm afraid someone, even a bellhop for a fee, will put a drug in a drink for me—and I'll wake up being raped. It's as bad as that. You know, when I'm single, I sometimes hire my secretary to sleep on the floor to protect me. Sometimes I go to sleep in a clothes closet and lock the door to be safe. You can't imagine what men, even highly respectable men, will do to try to go to bed with me. My sex symbol image has gotten way out of hand! I seem to be an international challenge. That's why, from the first, I always was glad to have a husband and my children along—to protect me." "Maybe," she reasoned "that's why I'm always getting married.

"I tried so hard to be a housewife, I mean a home-maker, and merge myself with domesticity and my children. With each husband I was very domestic and completely faithful. And everything, all of the millions of dollars I have made and am making, goes for my home and my family. I made every effort. But somehow, no matter how hard I tried, it has never worked for me.

"With all of these men calling me, sending me flowers, gifts, at least twelve that I know of are sincere. They keep offering to give me the moon and the sun and the stars if necessary, so I will find happiness again. It is all like the romantic dreams every pretty girl in her teens dreams. I guess actually, all through her life, a girl dreams of romance. To be so wanted; so loved!"

Women, during this last year of Jayne's life, resented and distrusted Jayne. Jayne Mansfield, with her ever changing, swiftly moving life, had suddenly become the focal point of a certain shocking fascination and the symbol of escape from the routine drudgery that most mothers with five children have to endure.

Whether Jayne was motivated by psychological drives or inner dammed-up emotion, a leading psychiatrist from London flew to Hollywood to make her acquaintance and to learn. He revealed in a widely read article that he was utterly amazed to find an alomst naive young woman, one who has just never quite grown up to conventional adult standards. She places her faith completely in love, and has discovered, to her dismay, she has unwisely misplaced it. With her abiding trust in the world, she always believes that she will find the sun shining for her the next morning no matter what took place the night before.

"She is blameless for all of the marital misfortune that has befallen her," he said in a report, after a long, lengthy discourse with Jayne. "Only one woman in a generation is born to be like her. She pays a high price—too high. Her whole motivation in life is to love and to be loved. She showers love on her children. You always see her with a half dozen dogs or cats in her arms. Always, some thing or some one has to be in her arms. Because she gives so much love, she requires more love than an average woman. Without love, she cannot breathe; she cannot live. The men who love her, who know her, must know this all important fact or they will kill her. She will suffocate emotionally.

"It stems from her childhood, with her longing for father love. Her father was a prominent man, a noted attorney in the east, who always said one day he would become president of the United States.

"Unfortunately, Jayne's father died when she was three. Her mother remarried, and Jayne herself married when she was fourteen. Almost immediately, she became a mother. She was delighted to have a baby in her arms, and she always kept her baby with her as she attended Texas State College, changing her baby's diapers between classes as though all of this was the natural thing. To her it was.

"This invincible fortitude that she possesses again denotes her full womanhood which does not offset her ambition to succeed as a woman and as a personality. She was born with that inner excitement, the magic quality that makes a Valentino and a Monroe— one that makes a personality light up a room by mere presence. Call it sex appeal or what you will, Jayne has it.

"She has a fine mind. I only hope she does not become victimized by this game of romance. Each man who pursues her further deepens her in the arms of amour.

"Whether Jayne herself recognizes true love is a point of conjecture. For she is in love with love itself."

When Jayne showed me a copy of his report, she smiled proudly. "He is so right," she said. "And just think, it is going into a medical book on psychology! About Me! There now, that's something I've contributed to society—that will live after me!"

# CHAPTER XXII

"Jayne Mansfield starring nightly at the Fremont in the Fiesta Room" twinkled on billboards all over Las Vegas. It was September 1, 1966, and Jayne's opening night at the hotel. Matt had made the date, but he did not accompany her. Jayne wouldn't permit it. Instead Douglas was by her side. Victor Huston, a wonderful friend and now her road manager, was in full charge of her month's engagement.

The week before Jayne said, "I am going to give you a big birthday party in Las Vegas." "My birthday is on your opening night," I protested. "You can't do both!" "Yes I can," Jayne retorted. "And I will."

In a whirl, she sent word that she wanted the party for her second show. "I won't tell you what's happening behind the scenes," she called, "because I want your birthday to be just perfect."

A special front table for me and friends who had flown up with me for the party was reserved. Jayne publicly announced my festive day from the stage. Then she went into her "Diamonds Are a Girl's Best Friend" and other numbers that had given her top reviews at her recent four weeks at the Latin Quarter in New York. During her act, she walked off stage into the audience and sat on a patron's lap. She'd sing to him. Usually, she would select an old man and it was all great fun for the audience.

As soon as her show was over, Victor Huston arrived to say the party was going to be held in the coffee shop. This seemed a little odd, for no tables were made up and nothing was really going on. Jayne arrived and after we were all seated, she exclaimed , "This is no way to give a birthday party. We'll hold it in my suite upstairs." In her flower-filled suite, there was a big, luscious birthday cake, decorated with the words, "To May, Happy Birthday, My love always, Jayne."

Jayne was nervous, I noted, but she was going to be a hostess in the grand manner or die in the attempt. She looked so little-girl like and so very thin. Steak dinners were ordered but Jayne did not touch the food. "We don't eat—we just drink to stay skinny, skinny!" she chanted, laughing with Douglas. Tony Bennet arrived to sing Happy Birthday. Later, we went up to the starlight roof to dance to George Liberace's wonderful music. Jayne and Douglas, very much in love, danced the night away. In fact, we danced until the sun sprang up over the purple hills of the desert. Then we went to the coffee shop for breakfast, where Jayne announced that my birthday celebration would be continued that afternoon at four o'clock around the pool. Etta Cortez joined us there.

The next day Jayne told me what had worried her so much. "Before I went on opening night, I received a message that I was going to have acid thrown in my face," she said. "I was so scared, not knowing any minute what could happen. Why do these things always come up to try to spoil my opening nights? Matt has kidnapped my baby Tony, and now there's the begging and legal battles ahead of me to get my child back. Before, it was Mickey who kidnapped Maria. And before that, Paul who was asking custody of Jayne Marie. Always I have to be smiling and go on stage and face an audience or a camera and be perfect in my lines. 'Oh God, how can I go on this way?' I thought last night. But you know something, God does know my heart and he sees me through. With God and faith, I find I can always do everything I have to do. He always comes to my aid."

Jayne was also upset because her salary, which had been $35,000 a week in Las Vegas had been dropped to $50,000 for four weeks at the Fremont.

"Matt has my Bentley," she said. "I guess he's going to cause me a lot of trouble. He has a lot of my money tied up as well. My husbands always turn out this way, taking my money and forcing me to go to court to get my children back."

"But why not leave Tony with Matt, while you're here these four weeks Jayne," I persisted. "Matt's mother loves the child so much and she is so good to him, Tony will be better off with her than left at home with a governess."

"If I let Tony stay, it could become a habit. I want all of my children with me at all times," she said. "No, I'm calling Greg Bautzer, my lawyer, to start legal proceedings to get him back."

"You're surely not going to marry Douglas," I implored. "He isn't even of legal age." "No," Jayne smiled. "I don't know what to do about Douglas. I'll try to help him get a career going or something. He is such a darling. He will be twenty-one in two months. He's so dazzled with all of this, and he's such a comfort to me," she said. "I feel like a teenager. I'm so weary of all the problems. I want to be free and have fun for a change. I've been weighted down with responsibilities since I was fourteen."

I was no sooner back in Los Angeles than Jayne happily reported she was dating Bobby Darin. "We met at a television station. Bobby asked if he could drive me home. Imagine, it was on his Honda! We're having a ball!"

"Douglas is very jealous," she admitted, "but he has to know that I can't confine myself to any one man right now."

A week later Jayne called. "May, I want you to meet my new attorney. His name is Sam Brody and he is brilliant. He's going to take over all of my affairs and get Tony back for me. And he's not going to charge me one penny. Imagine that? You should see all of the stuffed animals he's bought me. I have a regular zoo. Here, talk to Sam!" She put him on the wire.

"I'm crazy about her. Jayne's the most wonderful girl in the world. I'm going to marry her some day, even though she still keeps telling me no."

"Listen," I interjected. "Jayne is already married, and she can't go on getting married and unmarried and leaping into another marriage before the ink's dry on a divorce from the previous one. Please, if you are a good lawyer and you care anything about her, don't get her involved in a lot of court cases. She works hard for her money, and she can get things straightened out with Matt by sitting down and talking sense."

Sam laughed. "Jayne has been used too much. I'm going to get her where she belongs." Sam was to use her more than anyone, but how could anyone know that now?

"Oh May, I think I'm falling in love with him," Jayne called me secretly from Las Vegas the next night. "The only trouble is he is short—a little man. Douglas is fit to be tied. Sam insists that I send Douglas back to Venezuela, but I can't do that to the boy. I can't hurt him. Sam lost twenty thousand gambling last night. He didn't even care. He's very rich."

Jayne arrived from Las Vegas with a station wagon filled with huge stuffed toy animals that immediately graced her formal drawing room. Sam Brody moved into the Pink Palace and Jayne's home was never the same after that. On Douglas' twenty-first birthday, he was given a couple of hundred dollars, a ticket and put on a plane back to Venezuela. "And to think he was sent home on his twenty-first birthday. It was so unkind," Jayne worried. "My poor

Bambino."

Sam, determined to rule Jayne. "Sometimes I hate him," Jayne confided. "I have no intention of ever marrying him. But he's got all of my business papers—everything in his brief case. He won't give them back. He has a terrible picture he'll blackmail me with too."

The children had all been moved, from their own rooms upstairs next to Jayne's, to downstairs rooms. Linda, Jayne's maid, called. "Miss Mansfield's so worried at times. That Sam Brody just moved in and took over! Sometimes I go upstairs when Miss Mansfield calls me in the morning, and she's screaming, 'Don't put that needle in me.' It is something he threatens her with to make her sleep, or rather, unconscious. I'm so worried. We've had the police here twice and they throw him out and he comes right back. Miss Mansfield lets him. I don't know what to do."

Sam turned on real charm from gray blue steel eyes set in a smooth face, with a rugged jaw and sparse light hair. He had a trim, athletic build in spite of his short stature. He walked with the air of a Napoleon, and Jayne suddenly switched from her usual four inch spikes to wearing flat heels. "The little man doesn't want me to tower over him," she said in a whisper.

"I'm going to do a lot for Jayne," Sam snapped at our first meeting. "Matt has Tony, and he is suing Jayne as an unfit mother. I'm going to prove she is the best mother in the world and in court!"

"Sam was a trial lawyer. He assisted Melvin Belli in the Jack Ruby case," Jayne said. I sensed her tone of resentment, even indignation. Sam went on, his voice now silky smooth, "I want to meet some of Jayne's more influential friends."

"Yes, people I've met at your house," Jayne said. "Sam wants to subpoena Mayor Yorty to appear in court for me as a character witness."

"Jayne, don't you dare," I warned. "Don't you dare. The Mayor has no personal knowledge of your private life. You've only met him. Don't you dare make a grandstand play like that and use the Mayor of Los Angeles!"

"It's Sam's idea."

"It would make marvelous press for Jayne," Sam argued.

"If you do, I'll never speak to either one of you again," I said icily.

"Okay, that's out," Sam conceded. "How about Ida Mayer Cummings, President of the Jewish Auxiliary Home for the Aged?"

"Ida's an elderly woman. You shouldn't bother her," I interceded.

"Jayne's appeared for them plenty of times. We only need her as a character witness."

"I'll see how she feels about it first," I said.

"Don't bother," Sam's tone was changing to firm control. "I'll call her myself!"

Ida called me two days later. "Sam Brody was here to tea with us. What a perfect gentleman," she said. "He right off handed me a check for $500, as a contribution to our home. He's a nice Jewish boy. He's going to give us lots more, too. I'm going to make a match with him and one of my secretaries. He also took a character deposition. I was happy to give it."

Jayne Marie and the children resented Sam. Their little faces showed what controlled manners held in check.

"Sam's accompanying me to the San Francisco Film Festival. Why don't you come," Jayne suggested. "They have sent me four plane tickets and all hotel accommodations."

"Not with Sam going with you."

"At least come to the party we're giving Martha Raye at Sam's Malibu beach house," Jayne invited. "Marth's just back from Vietnam and I'll be going there in January to entertain our boys." I agreed.

Something came up that I did not go. When I called to apologize, Jayne's hippy secretary said sleepily, "Glad you weren't there. Jayne's parents arrived from Dallas. Her mother can't stand

Sam. Sam got Jayne drunk before the party even began, and took
her into a bedroom and locked the door. They didn't even make an
appearance for Martha Raye when she arrived. Jayne's parents had
one big arguement with Sam and left immediately for their home
in Dallas."

Jayne received big headlines at the San Francisco Film Festival
two days later. She was given a royal reception. People stood in
lines on the streets, wherever she was scheduled, just to glimpse
the sex goddess. The second night, a press agent invited Jayne to
visit San Francisco's Church of Satan, where Anton Lavey claimed
to be the representative of Satan, with supreme evil forces and
powers at his command.

Soon after their meeting, headlines declared Jayne the High
Priestess of Lavey and the Devil's Black Magic Cult. It was neither
confirmed nor denied by Jayne.

"It was all for laughs. We drove up there, Sam and I and Victor,"
Jayne said. "Mr. Lavey was dressed in black, wearing a cape and a
black cap with horns. He has black magnetic eyes. He said he had
the call from the Devil. He read the Bible too, except from the
Devil's side. He said the Devil controlled one-third of the hosts of
heaven, as it says in the Bible. And that the Devil has supreme
power on this earth. If you want anything here, the Devil can give
it to you if you join him, he told us. We didn't take him seriously.

"He showed us through his home, which is the First Satanic
Church of the Devil. There were some candles on the altar. He
said they were death candles and would curse anyone who touched
them.

"Sam scoffed. He was instantly jealous of Lavey's attentions to
me. Sam said he didn't believe in any of it. Mr. Lavey took me into
another room to show me the black magic charms from the Devil
and he presented me with one. He said I was now the high
priestess of his church. Someone is always giving me some honor
or title. I didn't want to insult him, so I accepted the emblem on a
leather string, which he placed around my neck. He said some

witchcraft words I didn't understand.

"When we returned to the altar room, Sam was angry and more jealous. To spite Mr. Lavey, Sam had lighted the forbidden candles on the altar, which only the Devil himself has the authority to light.

"Mr. Lavey was furious with Sam," Jayne said. "He proclaimed, 'You are cursed by the Devil. You will be killed within a year!' He was very serious. Sam laughed, believing it all amusing.

"Mr. Lavey called me into a back room. There, he told me, 'The Devil has placed a curse on Sam Brody. There is a heavy black cloud over him. Get rid of him at once or you will share this curse from the Devil. No one laughs at the Devil! He'll be killed in a car crash—not one but a succession of them. Anyone with him will be killed. Get rid of him at once!'

"It was our first day of the film festival. Everything was going so well. I had been headlined and photographed and then televised. I was given the key to the city. Mr. Lavey was very obstinate about the fact that I would be under the Devil's curse too if I continued on with Sam. It made me wonder in a way. Sam, who said he didn't believe and wasn't superstitious, laughed again and picked up the forbidden two skulls and silver chalice. That was adding insult onto insult.

"Sam was in plain defiance of the Devil, himself. Mr. Lavey was outraged. He said outright, 'You will both be killed in a tragic car accident within a year. When it happens, it will be very sudden!' But the Devil told me if I got rid of Sam, I wouldn't have to worry. I think Mr. Lavey would have liked me to marry him. He had a wife, but when I was there I seemed to turn him on. He was very attractive, and so intelligent." Jayne, who always accepted male admiration without comment, seemed to be elated as though her own ego were suffering suddenly, or was it Sam's insane jealousy?

The next morning's San Francisco papers headlined, "Jayne Asked To Leave Film Festival." The disgrace and embarrassment was countered by Jayne in her hotel suite saying she was amazed and couldn't understand why. This caused a film festival executive's rebuttal to the press, that Jayne had appeared in a half-naked gown at their banquet. "It was open all down the sides, exposing her body." It was considered a great affront to the Festival's dignity. It was a stage dress she had worn in a strip segment of her act at the Latin Quarter and in Vegas. It was never intended for use in her private life.

Actually, in a fit of insane rage over Lavey, Sam had poured Scotch over her new evening dresses—leaving Jayne nothing to wear except her show wardrobe, securely packed. This had happened within minutes of the banquet. Jayne felt rather than not appear, she'd make her white satin dress do and keep her furs close to her. But someone had stolen her chinchilla stole. Jayne had tried valiantly to make the best of it, as all the stores had long been closed. Besides, there was no time.

Jayne laughed it off to the press and announced she was on her way "with my barrister and my road manager on a tour of night club engagements", at a night club outside Sacramento. Jayne had now turned hippy in her dress, at least three years in advance of the times. She wore boots and mini skirts and her hair long. Her secretary, a hippy with long hair, encouraged her "new image."

"I've split to teenage. I look it." She was now 32 and "with it." At least she was acting it. Instead of the fabulous glamorous clothes she had worn, she now bought ten dollar dresses off the rack in department stores. These she threw away after a couple of wearings.

By October 28th, she and Sam had suffered two major car crashes. It seemed the Devil's curse was hitting at them. The scandal in San Francisco, the headlines and now two car crashes.

Victor Huston said Sam had dragged Jayne bodily into the bathroom one night and, in a fit of insane anger, had stuck her head in the toilet. Victor and hotel employees had broken down the door to rescue Jayne. Sam now had flashes of maniacal rebellion because Jayne would not deliver herself to him "lock, stock and barrel," and promise to marry him.

There were terrible fights. Jayne's maid, Linda, told me of one that had taken place three weeks earlier in the Pink Palace. The usual argument over "other men" and "lost money" had begun between the two of them. Sam had been furious. Jayne had called the police for the sixth time that year only the night before and had had Sam forcibly evicted from her house The next day he returned. He made his way past Linda in the kitchen and ran up the stairs. Jayne was sleeping.

Sam walked into her room and crossed to the bed. He pulled the sheets off of her, fell on top of her, and grabbed her arms spread eagle. He kissed her fully on the mouth. She struggled but he held her down with arms of steel.

"Get out!" she finally managed, trying to release herself. "I mean it! I swear it! I don't want you here anymore. I don't need you. I never want to see you again! I hate you!"

"You have no choice, Baby," he said running his hands over her smooth, warm flesh. "I'm yours for keeps. I'm for always—remember? You'll never get rid of me like the rest of those sissies in your life. Never!"

"This is my house! Get out!" Jayne screamed. With a sudden lunge, she turned and lurched and Sam lost his grip, falling to the floor.

Beside herself with rage, Jayne grabbed a shoe and threw it at him. The shoe missed and crashed into the mirrored wall. The glass shattered, scattering pieces of glass onto the soft, thick, pink carpeting.

Sam sprang to his feet. He stood there appraising her mockingly. He laughed a high falsetto laugh, goading her with sadistic delight.

"You pig!" he scoffed. "You whore! You goddamn—bitch!"

"Don't you dare speak like that to me," Jayne screamed. "I won't have four letter words used in my presence or in my house. I won't stand for it. I am a lady!"

"A kept lady is better," he mocked, stretching his slight, wiry body taller. "You've got a nerve ordering me out of this house. And calling the cops! I paid. I've got $17,000 invested in the plumbing and the carpeting here already. Remember? This is my house as much as it is yours. And what about all of the thousands of dollars you owe me for my legal fees? How about $100,000 on the line right now?"

Jayne picked up an empty champagne bottle from the night table. She threw it at his head. He ducked. The bottled crashed into the mirrored wall.

"Go ahead and break the goddamned mirrors. It's your luck," he jeered. "But I'll never leave. And you know it. No matter how many times you call the police, I'll always be back. I'm a lawyer—one of the best in the business! Remember?"

Jayne fell back on the bed crying with indignation and frustration and pulled the sheets back over her beautifully curved body with its bulging breasts. "How I despise you," she sobbed.

"It's you and me to the death, Baby. Make your choice," Sam said quietly. He enjoyed the threat and her tears. In some crazy way it made him feel the master. Everything else in his life was out of control. But goddamnit—he'd control Jayne Mansfield or kill her!

"You really turn me on, Baby when you get helpless like a woman should be," he said, "and let your man take over." He was coming towards her again—taking his clothes off and letting them fall to the floor.

"I will call the police!" she screamed, jumping up from the bed, again revealing her nudity. She picked up a pink chiffon negligee from the floor and clasped it to her modestly. At the same time she reached for the telephone on the heart-shaped mirrored night table. "I'm calling the police!"

Sam sprang at her and knocked the receiver out of her hand. "Don't pull that again," he warned. "Or I'll have to really take care of you!"

"You don't scare me," Jayne hissed. "I *am* calling the police. I've had enough of this! Can't you understand I am sick of you!" She reached for the telephone again. Sam struck her across the mouth, his ring cutting her lip open. Blood trickled down her chin. At the sight of blood Sam reacted like an enraged bull. He sprang at her, knocked her down on the bed and beat her body and her head unmercifully with his fists.

She cowered into the sheets in self-protection, screaming with pain. He suddenly stopped. He stood up, looking down at her in disbelief and shock. "What have I done?" he gasped in horror. "Oh no!" he cried. "Not again! Why, Jayne? Why do you make me do this to you? I love you! You know I love you. You are the only thing in the world I love. I've made my will out to you to prove it! I've made my life insurance out to you. I love you so. . ."

He prostrated himself by the bed—kissing her hair, her head, wiping the blood from her mouth. "You are my baby! You are my beautiful baby," he moaned. "Forgive me, Jayne."

For several minutes he cried like a child. "I don't know why I do it. You are driving me insane with your beauty—with my need!

"I must be insane," he reasoned half to himself. "It's the thought of losing you that makes me so angry. You won't give in. That's it! You won't give in and say you are all mine and that you'll marry me! That's the trouble. That's why I do it. I love you so much, I'll kill you before I'll lose you!

"Why won't you sign those divorce papers from Cimber? Damn you! Sign them—I tell you!" He was in a rage again.

"Sign them and give me some peace, so I can make plans for us."

Jayne was crying uncontrollably. "I am so tired of being beaten, of hurting, always hurting all over," she wept. "You just moved in, and took over," she accused. "You had no right!"

"You always said you wanted a masterful man," he replied. He was contrite again. "I'm that man. Don't ever forget it, baby. No one ever loved you like I do!"

He rang Linda and told her to bring up some ice. "I've got to fix your eyes, Baby," he said softly. "They are swelling up big! Don't ever make me angry again," he admonished. "I'm not responsible for what I do when I get mad!"

A half hour later Sam showered, shaved, dressed and ran downstairs for a quick breakfast. He was whistling and happy with the world. He left on some business.

Upstairs, Jayne called Jayne Marie, on the intercom. "Please come up and bring your camera. I want you to take a picture of me."

When Jayne Marie walked in with her flash and Brownie, her eyes widened in sheer horror. Her mother's face was black and blue. Her eyes were swollen shut from Sam's beating.

"Take the picture," Jayne instructed her daughter. "Get it printed and don't let anyone see it. Hide it. I'll get him out of here yet.

"You see," she explained later between sobs and pain. "Sam has all of my papers, all of my law cases and all my business. He's got me pushed into a corner—trapped! He's got my money—everything tied up in every direction. He's a lawyer, a clever one. But God will help me, somehow, to get us out of this! Or I'll be dead. I can't take anymore. I can't. The pain is killing me! "

Half of the time now Jayne's photos in the press showed a swollen face and black eyes, covered with heavy makeup in an attempted camouflage. Sam's rages continued and were repeated throughout the entire Canadian tour. Something would snap in Sam, his self control would crumble and he'd start punching Jayne with hands so violent, that had not Victor or a secretary or a hotel staff member pulled him off, he would have killed her. After he'd been restrained, he'd suddenly turn white, and his eyes uncomprehending would react like a man coming out of a trance. "Oh no," he'd start sobbing, "I didn't do it again. No—not again!"

Everyone was horrified. Sam would call a doctor. They'd patch up Jayne and he refused to leave her, smothering her with affection and remorse.

Jayne said, "Sam got me drunk one night and took pictures of me naked with a strange man I never saw before nor since. I think he put knockout drops in my drink. I was framed. I didn't even know what was happening to me. I never knew until Sam showed me the pictures. He says he will give them to the judge and release them to the press and the scandal magazines to prove I am an unfit mother. He'll take my children from me." That was the big fear of Jayne's life. "The Devil's curse will get him first, if I can only stick it out a little longer," she said, swearing me to strictest confidence.

Jayne played it cool to the press who were constantly making inquiries. How many husbands, how many lovers? "Let's put it this way," she replied to a Portland paper, "if I had had one husband who really loved me for me, I would have always remained faithful. With me, it's like it was with Catherine the Great of Russia, my heart can not rest one hour without love. . . ."

# CHAPTER XXIII

News of Jayne's Canadian tour filtered back on postcards from Jayne. Victor sent some of the newspaper clippings. The first was almost a half page picture in the Victoria Daily News, October 31, 1966, of Jayne hugging a little boy.

"She's Just Playne Jayne Terribly Misunderstood" headlined the story. "Sex Symbol Jayne Mansfield, the perpetual dumb blond of the screen. . . Slinky Jayne of the low cut gowns and the heart shaped swimming pools . . . Provocative Jayne whose Playboy pictures in the altogether set a new mark in published nudity . . . .came to Victoria Sunday to indicate we've had her all wrong. She's really a simple girl who loves children. She's really a responsible adult with an intelligent interest in society's handling of children. She's really a sympathetic person who loves animals. Why, she came to Victoria to visit our orphanage children. Even if she was two hours late, she was polite and motherly. And those two lovable chichuahuas she carried. She had them dressed up in knitted suits with pom-poms so they wouldn't be cold didn't she? She showered the kids with hugs and kisses and said she'd like to take them all home with her. And all those rib-poking teenage boys outside the solarium with their whistles didn't throw her a bit. Matter of fact, trailing after Jayne, you might get the idea that her next picture will be *Anne of Green Gables.* It's a good thing Jayne came to Victoria to let us see how wholesome she is. Those darn movie parts and publicity shots can be awfully misleading."

In italics, also page one, a later edition read, "Mayor Alfred Toone finally stood up movie star Jayne Mansfield today because she was more than an hour late for her city hall appointment and the Mayor, after waiting, said he had other things to do. A crowd of spectators awaited her 10:30 visit until 11:35. Jayne said a mix up occurred in her schedule. A spokesman for her hotel said she's been unwell and had required medical attention. "

Victor reported Sam had beaten Jayne again and it had taken a doctor and lots of makeup to cover up her bruised face. "Why Jayne didn't have him arrested and thrown in jail for good is beyond me! I'll never go on a tour with Jayne again if Sam is along."

Sam didn't care if the constant lateness and broken appointments ruined Jayne's carrer. "I want her to quit anyway and stay home and be my wife."

Sam now shared the world spotlight with Jayne. His name, Sam Brody, was now known. That was all he needed, he said. He was a good trial lawyer. All he wanted to do was get back to Beverly Hills and re-open his practice. His law offices had long since been closed. "I'm afraid to let Jayne out of my sight, or some other man will steal her away," was his explanation.

Jayne made the headlines front page every day she was in Canada. Some of it was not good at all. One story, November, in the Canadian press read, "DOGGONE IT JAYNE. Miss Mansfield held a trial charging her dog with sexual misconduct. Miss

Mansfield's lawyer helped conduct the mock trial. Alderman Hugh Stephen said, 'I am mad. The whole dignity of the British justice and municipal institutions has been brought into flagrant disrepute. And you can say this kind of exhibition is an insult to all the people of Greater Victoria, Canada.'"

Just when everything in Vancouver was going well, the Vancouver Sun headlined Jayne a disaster. "Indians Upset Over Jayne. Chaos, Confusion Reign at Musquean Ceremony." Jayne Mansfield had one of those days and not even a press agent would have believed it. She cut her thumb. Before the episode was over, two doctors attended her, the Georgia Hotel lost ten blankets, and 100 irate Indians waited almost five hours to make Jayne a Musqueam princess.

The actress was to appear at the Musqueam reserve community at six P.M. She would be the first white person to be initiated into the band, and the subject of the last public performance of a centuries old naming ritual.

At five P.M. people had gathered. At six, no Jayne. At seven P.M. a press agent telephoned that Jayne and six others of her entourage were wandering around the hotel trying to find ten blankets —Jayne's contribution to the Indian ritual. While Victor Huston sought a car to replace Jayne's Bentley, which had been smashed in an accident, Sam Brody took ten blankets from their rooms and stole out the back way with them in suitcases.

Jayne finally arrived with bandages hours late. "I cut my thumb," she said. "I can't stop if from bleeding." The Indians after much persuasion finally put their costumes back on. Someone sent for a bottle of cognac. Jayne tried some of it and disappeared into a wash room. The Indians clamored up and down the corridor. Sam Brody announced, "Jayne would like to have the ceremony tomorrow night, same time, same place."

The angry Indians said, "It's all over. Not later tonight or tomorrow." The chief said Jayne was offered the honor after an hour long talk the week before. And she was supposed to believe in the same standards of human rights and justice as the Indians believe in.

After a series of three more car crashes Jayne, Sam and Victor arrived back at the Pink Palace.

"How was Canada?" "Lovely," purred Jayne.

"You can't come and see Jayne for at least a week," Sam telephoned. "She bumped her head on the windshield and it gave her two black eyes." Linda said Sam gave them to her.

Jayne and I had both been invited several times to visit Jungleland, and see the baby lions and tigers. When it was nearing Christmas time, Jungleland decided to give a Christmas Parade to start the Yule season. Jayne and I were asked to participate with Jayne as Queen of the parade.

"I'll drive my car," Jayne said. "We'll take Zoltan and Miklos and Maria with us." As we were about to leave, Sam drove up in a Masseratti and announced that he was going too.

Jayne seemed troubled at this announcement. Turning to me, she said, "May, do you mind taking your car and the children with you?"

"Yes I would," I flared back. "What is this? You ask me to go with you in your car. And now Sam. . . . . ?"

"It's that Sam drives so fast," she said. "I worry about the children being with us when Sam is driving." At this time I had yet to hear about the Devil's curse on Sam. "I'll either go with you, or I'll go alone," I replied. At that, Jayne asked a visitor from the east if he would drive my car and bring the children to Jungleland in it. It was agreed.

Sam soon had the Masseratti up to a hundred miles an hour. Jayne didn't demur. I hung on. Soon we were all at Jungleland two hours late for the parade. "We had to have it without you," the owner said. "We couldn't keep the crowds waiting any longer."

We rode atop the elephant and had hot dogs and popcorn and pop and were having a wonderful time at Jungleland, seeing all the animals. We were invited into a compound where several movie animals were chained to trees. This was quite remarkable since they weren't in cages and could run about ten feet at the end of their chains.

Since we all loved animals, we were pleased but Jayne was apprehensive. A sixth sense seemed to tell her to watch out. She kept holding onto the children even though her house guest was there to see to them. He was a professor of psychology.

Jayne and I were looking at the big male lion, which she said she would like to take home for a pet, when people asked us to move in close for a picture. All the people visiting Jungleland were out behind the rope on the outside with their cameras. And they were all taking pictures. Jayne and I moved in close but the lion tossed his head and growled, in a way that frightened us. We moved away fast, but the Jungleland people told us not to be afraid. Jayne went back by the lion's right side and I was just behind the lion, leaning in, when he suddenly roared, lurched up and back, knocking me down an incline flat on my back. I hit my head severely and in a split second, the lion was turning on me. I froze in shock,. The trainer managed to pull him away with the chain. Jayne grabbed Miklos and called to Maria and Zoltan and said, "Let's get out of here. This is dangerous." It took me minutes to get up. Everyone was afraid to cross in front of the lion to help me. I rolled over and over and finally managed to get to my feet. A lump, the size of an egg, swelled at the base of my neck. I was dizzy and everything seemed unreal.

I heard a scream. The same lion now had Zoltan in his mouth by the neck and head, biting and shaking him.

My heart stood still. Jayne began screaming, "Run, save my baby!" I held Jayne back with all of my strength, while the Jungleland people, the owner and two trainers, who know how and what to do, made the lion open his mouth and let go of Zoltan. Jayne rushed to the child, who was still conscious and moaning, and covered with scratches, bites and blood. By this time all the animals in the compound were roaring in panic, and we were rushed out over a back fence, or we might all have been attacked.

Jayne was screaming and then praying in the same breath. We ran after Roy Kebat, who had Zoltan in his arms to a car to rush to a hospital. In the car, Sam held on to Jayne while Mr. Kebat held Zoltan and we drove at panic speed to the hospital.

Zoltan was rushed into emergency and we didn't see him again for nine hours. We all prayed that we would see him alive. We prayed and prayed. There was no other way to go.

Jayne and I went into a small room to wait the longest wait of our lives. The tears wouldn't come. My mind refused to believe that Zoltan might not pull through. I kept clenching my fists. Jayne said, "I would kill the lion if I had any weapon, no matter whether he turned on me, and killed me." She'd become humble, then angry, and grateful and fearful.

Sam was a great strength. He took over and began calling specialists to be flown in from Los Angeles. He never stopped calling, demanding the best in the world. Miklos and Maria had been sent home. They were too young to be fully aware of what had happened.

All of those long hours we waited, trying to comfort Jayne, holding her hands, her arms, reassuring her. At six that night I was called outside. I was told Zoltan wasn't expected to live. I came back only telling Jayne to keep praying. From time to time I, a Mormon, Jayne, a Catholic convert, and Sam, a Jew, knelt down praying, each in our own way, but each to the same God who watches over all of us.

Telephone calls began tying up the switchboard. The press, T.V., radio, were outside. The news wire people, national and worldwide, wanted to see Jayne. I couldn't face anyone, but Jayne knew they all had a job to do. So for ten minutes she spoke to them, praying for self-control. Then it was just Jayne and me again and most importantly, God—waiting, waiting, waiting. The minutes, the hours, were ticking away. Finally, the doctors began coming in, in relays, each reporting what they, as a team, had been able to do, until the next team of specialists took over to do what they could.

Zoltan had suffered a terrible gash on his face, and a worse one on the back of his neck. A bone had been broken and chipped, and was resting on his brain area and another on his spinal cord. Miraculously, he was whole, and while he had deep scratch marks and lacerations under his eyes, his features and little body were intact.

"Your little son," said one doctor after another, "is the most remarkable child we've ever seen. He has never complained nor whined nor objected to anything we have had to do . That includes the tracheotomy we had to perform in which we slit his throat open to insert a tube so he can keep on breathing. He has also never lost consciousness. The miracle is that he has no paralysis and his reflexes are intact!"

Jayne was overwhelmed with gratitude to God for sparing Zoltan as He had. The lung specialists revealed he had a lung punctured, three ribs broken internal injuries and more.

For the next six and a half hours ten doctors worked in relays, using all the skills they possessed. At midnight they returned to announce that while they hadn't expected Zoltan to live, he was doing satisfactorily. "Your little boy has the most remarkable courage and spunk we've ever seen in a child so young," they told us. "You have been a fine mother, for he reflects a good sound bringing up," another doctor said, which made Jayne very proud.

Again we all knelt in prayer and thanksgiving to God for his goodness and mercy to this courageous little man.

Jayne had Mickey called in Rome where he was filming a picture. He came on the first plane possible.

When Zoltan saw his father, you could tell by his eyes that Mickey's presence was a tremendous moral boost. His father being there meant a great deal. From time to time, I would see a little tear fall from his eyes. His head, swathed in bandages and the big tube sticking out of his throat made it difficult for him to communicate. But not once did he complain; only a single tear would drop now and then.

The strained day and night was lightened by the encouragement that each day he was still alive and holding his own. On the third day, however, he had become so anemic the doctors scheduled another operation. Again the decisions were up to Jayne, who was praying around the clock.

"The picture I was to have begun filming on Monday at 20th Century Fox seemed like something in another world," Jayne disclosed. "The career that has enabled me to support my children seems very unimportant now. Being a mother is my only thought."

White roses with white orchids came from Elizabeth Taylor and Richard Burton, bearing the card, "Our thoughts and prayers are with you." Flowers, candy-grams, dolly-grams, and thousands of telegrams, cards and letters poured into the little Valley hospital, for Jayne Mansfield and her six-year-old son Zoltan. Calls from all parts of the world tied up the switchboard and the reception personnel.

Jayne was with Mickey and although divorced, their child and their mutual concern banished all past differences as they united in prayer asking God to save their little son.

"God is the only one we can trust, to whom we can turn," Jayne said. "I never stop praying.

Zoltan responded and came through and then on the seventh day, suddenly his temperature began to climb alarmingly!

Without sleep or rest, Jayne came down with a severe cold. Mickey took over the vigil and she was ordered home and not to see the child, for fear of transmitting cold germs.

On the way home Jayne stopped at my house to see how I was recovering. She was no sooner there than the hospital called. The doctor was asking permission to take a spinal tap. Again, we all froze with fear.

The tests revealed Zoltan had spinal meningitis and a virus. Jayne was told again she must not see him. She must stay away, for fear of further endangering him with her own virus. The next day

Jayne had viral pneumonia.

"I feel I can't endure any more, but God makes you strong. And a mother and a father both rise to the occasion when the strength is needed for a child, for the child you carried in your own body and gave birth to and have reared the very best you know how, with God's help," said Jayne.

# CHAPTER XXIV

It was almost Christmas. While we didn't have the traditional flurry of snowflakes whitening our window ledges, nights in California were frosty cold. The spirit of the Yule season was everywhere, with holly and Christmas trees in the stores and vacant lots and Santa Clauses. Jayne and I went on a wild shopping spree for her children.

Zoltan was still seriously ill in the hospital. There had been many complications including pneumonia. Jayne grew restless with fatigue and the long hospital vigils and the worry.

My ears still felt like I was coming down in a plane and couldn't swallow back the pressures. I was under specialists, care for years for pulled neck tendons.

Jayne worried about me. Sam filed several law suits against Jungleland, including one for Jayne's shock over her child. She became more and more involved in law suits and depositions.

From day to day we were never sure about Zoltan, then age seven. Mickey continued his vigil by the child's bedside. Scandal pursued Jayne. Sam Brody had been ordered out of the hospital due to his conduct and the hysteria Jayne's presence created with the constant press and photographers. There was awful gossip all over Thousand Oaks. Jayne, in pink pajamas, had been chased through the hospital corridors in the middle of the night by Sam Brody, threatening to kill her. He had pulled the telephone off the wall in another jealous fit and beaten her.

"We're going to the Bistro tonight for dinner," Jayne said.

"Oh no you're not, Jayne," I replied testily. "You have a child dying in the hospital and the whole world is worrying for you, and you are going to be seen at the Bistro??? Are you crazy? Do you want to destroy the sympathy, prayers and concern of millions of people for you and Zoltan?"

"I can't just sit home night after night," she said. "I cant't!"

"I'll tell you what," I said. "I'll cook a turkey and you come to my house and we'll have dinner—just the four of us, and sit by the fire. You can't go to gay, fashionable restaurants and night clubs while Zoltan is still so seriously ill. It will go against you—pictures of you having a good time!" I warned.

It was raining that night, and Jayne arrived at the back service porch door, wearing a white vinyl raincoat with white boots and white umbrella, her hair long and pale gold. With her was Sam and two strange men. "I am mindful of your white carpeting," she laughed, as they came in the back way. I was astounded.

"Who are these men?" I asked Jayne quietly. "Oh, some business men," she answered carelessly. I was furious. Jayne knew I never cooked for strangers and to bring two strange men along to dinner without so much as asking!

I tried to be gracious and we all sat around the fire. For the first time, Jayne ate heartily. She always ate so skimpily for fear of gaining weight. But home roasted turkey and dressing were her favorite. She ate one full plate and then went back to the kitchen and returned with another full plate. Later, she went back to the kitchen to pick on the turkey bones. This delighted me for she was enjoying eating all she wanted for the first time, since she had had a career.

The telephone rang. It was the Thousand Oaks hospital calling. To save Zoltan's life, they would have to remove his spleen with immediate surgery. We discussed the pros and cons. We called Dr. Wendell Henricks, a close family friend, and Dr. J. Lewis Bruce, Mickey's long-time physician. Since there was no alternative, Jayne gave consent. It saddened us to think this little boy had to suffer so much.

On a gayer note, Jayne called a week later that Zoltan would be brought home to the pink palace Christmas morning. He was still seriously ill but he could now come home. "Christmas will be the happiest we've ever known. You come to dinner at four and then we'll have Christmas at your house at night, same as always."

At Jayne's I was horrified to see Zoltan pale and wan, his head and face still swathed in bandages, sitting on the drawing room floor wearing an Indian headdress, propped up against a teepee. Maria and Miklos were throwing a ball and it hit Zoltan square in the head. The child seemed in a semi-conscious state. No adult was watching out for him. He was at the mercy of the children at play. The dogs, as usual, were littering the floor.

"Jayne, what are you thinking of?" I gasped. Another set of photographers had arrived. Jayne was caught up in more pictures with Zoltan which, of course, made front pages around the world. Linda had cooked dinner and left earlier. I asked Jayne Marie how long Zoltan had been sitting on the floor posing for pictures. "Oh, since noon," she said. Over four hours!

The child seemed, through weakness and weariness, not quite aware of what was going on. Jayne certainly was not. Grabbing Sam Brody, I said, "Please, let's take Zoltan upstairs to bed. If the hospital saw him this condition, you'd all be arrested!" Sam got the message quick, and Zoltan was put to bed with his prescribed medicines.

"Look at what Santa brought me!" Jayne squealed. It was a ten thousand dollar diamond bracelet to match the ten carat diamond ring Sam had already given her!

"Now you can see my intentions are serious," Sam announced jovially.

Just as we were about to sit down to the dinner table, the telephone rang. Jayne's mother was calling from Dallas. "Get on the extension, May and listen!" Jayne suggested. I did for a moment to hear her mother saying, "Jayne, your children are not toy playthings! They are little human beings. You should have a nurse there full-time to take care of Zoltan." I hung up. Her mother must have used stronger words, for Jayne suddenly angered.

"Mother, you may as well know that Samuel and I are announcing our engagement," she trilled. "I know you don't approve of a Jew in our family, but he's just given me a ten-thousand-dollar diamond bracelet for Christmas. You can prepare for some nice Jewish grandchildren soon!"

She hung up, defiance written all over her face!

"Jayne, that's no way to talk to your mother, and especially on Christmas Day! She must love you or she wouldn't be telephoning you!"

"Oh that," Jayne said. "She always calls collect. And today she called because already the front pages of the newspaper in Dallas have pictures of me playing Indian on the floor with Zoltan. She thinks that is terrible!"

"So do I," I seconded. Then suddenly, realizing that lately I was starting to scold Jayne, I shut up. I must make the best of it or our friendship would end. But that little fellow upstairs who had been so close to death and was still so vulnerable! I worried!

Dinner was delicious, even if served rather haphazardly. People kept pouring in, and Jayne kept asking them "to pull up a chair and get a plate in the kitchen and join us lap style.

"Wait until you see what Christmas is at May's tonight. She decorates her whole house and garden so beautifully," Jayne said. There she was, building me up, and I had scolded her—and on Christmas day!

Jayne seemed so scatterbrained these days. In fact, I worried so much about her, that I called Dr. J. Lewis Bruce, asking him for help, since he had been her physician when she was married to Mickey.

"I'm so afraid," I said. "It seems like Jayne is on a fast express toboggan and no stops. There is nothing I can do to stop her. I'm so afraid of tragedy! I feel it for her!"

He shook his head. "You're wasting your time," he replied. "No one can help her except herself. And she won't or can't."

Twice that week I tried to talk to Jayne seriously. She'd agree to everything I said, and do just the opposite. Since she never criticized me, and was always complimenting everything I did, I felt so guilty reprimanding her all of a sudden almost every time we were together. I had no right to do so. But I loved her like a sister and I couldn't stand by, seeing her destroyed before my eyes!

"Won't you have a date with Mickey," she asked one afternoon. "I'd like to see you two get together."

"Absolutely not! What's the matter with you? You're over matchmaking," I laughed. "I only think of Mickey as your former husband. I'm embarrassed at the suggestion."

"Oh May, you're so square," Jayne sighed. "You're so pretty and so sexy looking. I just can't figure you out sometimes!"

Pouting prettily she said, "I know that you permitted Matt Cimber to drive you and three other people to Palm Springs for Linda Kaye Hennings' opening. I was so shocked. I said they were lying when I was told. Then you told me yourself that it was true or I'd never have believed!"

"I explained that already. I was not with Matt. Herbert Klein asked me, as a columnist, to go up for the opening. He was going to drive me, but his wife had to go a day earlier. To my surprise, he asked Matt and his friends, who were going, to pick me up too. That was all there was to it. And you know it!"

"Well," Jayne pouted, "with Matt and I in court soon with his charges of my being a bad mother, it was quite a thing for you to do to be seen with him anywhere."

"Matt had his girl friend along Jayne, and it was nothing," I replied. That was close as Jayne and I ever came to quarreling. We dropped the subject then and there.

Martin Von Dehn, approaching his 93rd birthday, and a very lonely, ill man, asked me if I would bring Jayne to dinner at his Bel Air estate. "It would cheer me up considerably," he said.

Mickey called to see Zoltan that evening as we were leaving. I invited him to come along as he seemed so unhappy. One of my actor friends was with me, and Sam drove Jayne's Bentley.

"Faster!" Jayne kept saying, as we spun around curves on the winding roads of Bel Air. When Sam didn't drive faster, Jayne would press her foot on top of his on the accelerator, and the car would leap forward to a hundred miles an hour!

"Jayne," I screamed, "this is suicide. Stop this crazy speed." Sam was challenging, "Want to go faster, Baby? All right, Baby!" and he'd push the throttle down all of the way! The speedometer went up to 150 with Jayne screaming, "Faster! Faster!"

It was like she was on a carousel, and Jayne wanted the music played faster and faster to spin to orbit, and she'd shout out like a child. We arrived all shaken, with Jayne excited and thrilled. I announced I would call a taxi to go home unless they promised to drive safely. They promised.

Upstairs, Martin was excited seeing Jayne, who was wearing a tight silver lame pants suit, her long pale gold hair almost to her waist in back.

"You deserve a big kiss," Jayne said. Throwing herself full length down on top of him, she started kissing him. This delighted the elderly man and shocked me! Pulling her off I exclaimed, "Jayne, that's no way for a lady to act!"

"But I'm a sex goddess!" she retorted sweetly.

"You're a lady when you're in my company," I reprimanded.

"I'm sorry," Jayne said plaintively. "He's so near death, I just thought he'd like one more thrill before he passes on." (He did, three months later, and he often chuckled about how "Jayne Mansfield came here and hugged and kissed me. Made me want to get out of bed. I felt thirty years old again and in my prime—even if for only a few moments!")

When we departed Sam said, "May's right. You should watch your behavior!"

Jayne said, "Okay." We weren't reaching her I knew. Jayne had turned into a wild, swinging, wacky girl. At the same time, she was warm, sincere and lovable. 'She'll get over this,' I thought.

"Come in for a night cap," she insisted when we arrived back at the pink palace. "May doesn't drink but I squeezed fresh orange juice for her myself before we left tonight."

Inside, the telephone was ringing. Jayne picked up the receiver. "Oh yes," she purred. "I just got in. You're coming out for New Years. Wonderful. Where are you calling from? Rio? Yes, I'll meet you at the plane darling," she said. Sam glowered. Mickey looked at Jayne dumbfounded.

"That was Jorge Guinlee. He wants me to marry him as soon as possible," she squealed gleefully. "He's bringing me a diamond twice as big as this one!" she laughed.

The telephone was ringing again. It was about ten o'clock. Jayne whispered, "The call's from my millionaire airplane man in San Francisco!"

Jayne purred back on the telephone, fully aware that she was playing a scene to make Sam jealous. "I can't marry all of you," she was saying over the long distance, while playing with her new diamond bracelet while the huge diamond on her finger shimmered under the lights of the chandelier overhead. By now Sam's eyes were flint, his jaw taut!

'Oh Jayne,' I thought, 'Can't you see you're enraging him!'

"He wants to marry you too, does he, Baby?" Sam's voice was silky, looking at Jayne as though he would strangle her.

"Yes," Jayne said, hanging on to the receiver. "I just may marry him. I assure you I'm not marrying you, little man! You'll never make me!" Too much champagne had made her defiant.

Mickey quickly excused himself. My date insisted we depart too. Poor Jayne—what would happen to her? I wanted to stay to protect her. But no one would stay. "Jayne, go to bed right now!" I suggested. "Hang up the telephone, please!"

Jayne ignored me.

I didn't have to wonder. Linda called me the next morning. Another beating. "I hate that Sam Brody," Linda said. "I took my shoe and went after him this morning and hit him good, I did."

"What are we doing New Year's?" Jayne called me. My one boy friend of long standing had returned. He was digusted with the whole scene of Jayne and Sam. "No New Year's with those two," he'd warned. But I couldn't let Jayne down. We'd spent ten New Year's Eves together!

As we always did, we put our invitations together. "First I want to go to the Rabbi Max Nussbaum's open house," Jayne mur- murred. "He's the famous rabbi who married Elizabeth Taylor and Eddie Fisher. He also converted Sammy Davis, Jr. to the Jewish faith. He's having me read instructions, just in case I decide to marry Samuel."

"Jayne, you're studying to become a Catholic, are you not?" I reminded.

"Well, " Jayne sighed, "if I marry Samuel after all, it doesn't hurt to know a lot of religions. Rabbi Nussbaum is such a learned and intelligent man! Let's wear something real wild New Year's Eve and really celebrate! You know, I leave for Vietnam in a week."

My date and I were late getting to Jayne's house by about forty-five minutes on New Year's Eve. Unexpectedly, I had seen a designer dress of shocking pink sequins and chiffon that looked bubbly like New Year's Eve that very morning. I'd had to wait to get shoes dyed to match. Jayne scolded, "Well, you're being like me, keeping everyone waiting!" Then she kissed and hugged me.

Jayne was wearing a daring white satin slinky gown, opened down both sides from top to bottom, exposing her full body, and held together with two-inch bands at strategic points. It had no back and was cut almost to the tail bone. It was her most daring stage dress. It was too, too much!

I shuddered inwardly at the thought of going to a Rabbi's house with anyone in this outfit. Wearing no coat, Jayne carried a white feather ostrich boa and when her skin touched the cold black leather seat of the car, I exclaimed, "Jayne, aren't you freezing?"

"No, I'm fine," she insisted.

The Nussbaums, with superb poise, didn't change expression, but welcomed Jayne and her nudity with warm affection. 'How kind they are,' I thought. Mrs. Nussbaum was wearing a comfortable dress with high neck and long sleeves. Their house guests from out of state were also middle-aged people dressed conservatively. Jayne immediately sat on Rabbi Nussbaum's lap and laughed that her gown pulled down and revealed her tail bone. She seemed to think it funny and pulled the dress up to cover it. Rabbi Nussbaum kept his cool. I am sure I blushed.

People kept arriving. Among them was a kind faced, middle-aged man. "Jayne Mansfield," he exclaimed. "I am going to tell you where I first met you!" Everyone listened.

He recited their meeting, which had taken place in 1955, at a photographer's nude model agency on Santa Monica Blvd. "It was a sleezy place where any man with ten dollars could go in and take pictures of a nude girl," he said. "When they pulled the curtain back, there stood Jayne in a wrapper. The owner told her to drop it! 'You are hired for nude photographs!' Jayne instead began to cry, when we were left alone. She said, 'I just can't do it. I didn't know I had to strip all nude. I thought I could wear a bikini.'

"You told me you were doing it," he turned to Jayne, "because there was no food in your house, and you had a four-year-old child to feed and you were desperate! She was obviously a lovely girl, not a street walker. Her language was refined and I knew she was telling me the truth! I told her to get dressed. I paid the ten dollar fee, took her to the nearest supermarket, and bought her a fifteen-dollar bag of groceries and sent her home in her little, beat-up car to her child."

"That's right," Jayne squealed with delight. "That's the truth! That was my lowest point in Hollywood, when I was trying to get work. Paul Mansfield had left us, and there wasn't a thing to eat in the house. I saw these model photo places and I went in. You were so very kind and such a gentleman," she said.

Arriving at actress Olga Velez' house warming New Year's Eve party Jayne took one look at me and then at our hostess. Olga was wearing an exact copy of my dress, except hers was mauve green. There were many stars and producers present. In our mutual embarrassment we didn't say anything about Jayne's dress and now our identical dresses.

"And to think my dress was to be the talk of New Year's Eve, May," Jayne giggled. "If I could go home and get back in time, I'd change." I apologized to Olga. This relieved the tension and we all laughed.

"Ooooh!" said Jayne. "You see, you have the most talked about dress in town to start the New Year."

Jayne decided to do something about that. Turning to my friend, she whispered, "Pretend you are trying to pull up the zipper on my dress—only pull it down!"

"But that would expose your bottom!" he remonstrated, pulling the zipper up instead.

Jayne flared, "You blew it! You could have made us a sensation by mistakenly pulling the zipper down, as though you misunderstood.

"Your tail bone would show," he argued.

"That was the idea—but you blew it," she repeated. "Where's

your sense of comedy timing!"

Throwing up his hands in disgust he walked away.

Now Sam was quarreling with Jayne openly. She sat on Jose Jass' lap, a long time friend of hers from the West Indies. You could see the resentment building up in Sam. There would have been exploding fireworks between them had not my boy friend intervened. Finally we said, "We are going." It was three A.M.

"I haven't eaten," said Jayne. We waited. She wouldn't eat. "Champagne again!" she called out. Jayne was acting in a strange, desperate way for attention.

'What's the matter with her? Something's so terribly wrong,' I worried.

Someone brought up the name of Anton Lavey, the Devil in San Francisco. "He says you are his new high priestess. It said so in the newspaper yesterday!" she was told. "What is all of this?"

"Oh, that's so silly," Jayne replied. "He's a former circus lion tamer or something. He's a good showman. His idea is that Satan represents indulgence instead of abstinence! He insists that Satan represents vital existence instead of spiritual pup dreams. Satan, he says, represents undefiled wisdom instead of hypocritical self-deceit!"

"Are you reciting the satanic rules of his church?" she was asked.

"I have a photo flash memory," Jayne replied. "His precepts have their points," she went on. "Satan represents kindness to those who deserve it instead of love wasted on ingrates. He believes in vegence instead of turning the other cheek. Satan represents all of the so-called sins as they all apply to physical enjoyment or emotional gratification."

"You know something," Jayne laughed, mockingly, "Satan has been the best friend the church, I mean conventional religions, ever had for he's kept them in business all of these years!"

Sam, angry by now at the spectacle Jayne was making of herself, grabbed her arm and began pulling her out of the house. I quickly stepped forward. "Sam, you're hurting her wrist," I said. He let go. "Come on Jayne," I countered. "Let's get in the car and go home. It's coming dawn already."

"I won't go home with him!" Jayne flared. "How I hate you, Sam Brody." He said nothing. We drove quietly to the Pink Palace. It hadn't been the best start for 1967. Not at all!

# CHAPTER XXV

Jayne was to leave in two days for Vietnam to entertain our service men. "At least nothing can go wrong this time," she declared matter-of-factly, "because Sam is not going!"

"I never told you but Anton Lavey telephoned while Zoltan was on the operating table. He offered to fly down with a magic healing potion for the Devil. I declined."

"I'd hope so," I seconded.

"That lion gave warning, you know," Jayne said, remembering out loud. "We were such fools to go in there.

"I don't know what's wrong—so wrong with everything I start these days. With my little son hovering between life and death, Sam's wife Beverly Brody served us with divorce papers in the hospital charging me with adultery. She was making a play for publicity. She calls all hours of the night with horrible things to say." "Poor woman," Jayne added, "she's in a wheel chair with polio and she is trying to get Sam back. I wish she'd take him and keep him from bothering me. I have such wonderful plans if I can ever be rid of him."

Jayne kept talking as we munched celery, sweet pickles and cheese and drank cokes. "The nurses said Zoltan was such a little man in the hospital. He's an introvert, thinks deep inside of himself.

"Even though we had to send money to Mickey for him to come, Zoltan's reaction was tremendous. Mickey has always loved me." "Here," she said, handing me two or three love letters from Mickey written in Rome, "see, he says he will walk behind me in my shadow the rest of his life if I'll remarry him. Mickey did some terrible things to me, but I can forget them I guess," she confided. "I have grown to love him again but not sexually. Just as a good friend. Mickey's slimmed down and is terribly chic, don't you think? He looks like Steve McQueen. He's changed.

"Thomas Hagethy, a socialite millionaire, wants to marry me in San Francisco. He'll buy me a mansion and a yacht but he doesn't turn me on. I've concluded that the social register, which I once considered so important, is really a shallow thing. I can always swing with the jet set, but I want more. I keep thinking of my father if he had only lived. His parents came from Europe, developed big slate quarrys and became very wealthy. I've always had that striving for elegance and acceptance and what's proper."

Miklos, now eight years old, came running into the library. "Look mother, a garden snake," he said, holding a wiggling long green thing in his fist. The snake and Jayne eyed each other with mutual distrust. Jayne remained cool. "Did that kangaroo rat get loose?" "No," Miklos said. "Well," Jayne replied, "it's just ten minutes until your French lesson. Get cleaned and dressed for your lesson. Put the snake wherever you put snakes." She called after the handsome, blue-eyed, golden headed child, "You have to spend two hours on the scrapbooks tonight, remember, after dinner and after you get your lessons prepared for school tomorrow."

"Yes Mother," Miklos flung over his shoulder, his heels clicking through halls and a door slammed in the back, denoting he had left.

"I want all of my children to take piano and dancing, and the boys polo lessons," Jayne said. "Little Maria is doing very well with her French and Italian lessons already.

"I could live in West Palm Beach and be the wife of socialite Frank Osgood Butler," she smiled. "He doesn't turn me on either. I wish I could make an arrangement that we might marry and remain platonic, like the kings and queens of old Europe. I'd organize his house, hostess his parties and lend my popularity to his name. He could have his loves on the side and I'd have mine."

"Jayne!" I gasped. "How you talk!"

"I was just thinking in a practical manner" she giggled. "But it's true."

Sam telephoned. Jayne took the call. "Listen May, pick up the extension."

Sam was saying, "I like trouble. The more, the better. I can always conquer. I always do and I always can."

"Sam's promised to start his law practice while I'm in Vietnam," Jayne said hanging up the receiver. "When he can prove to me that he is serious about his law practice, I may consider him a little more. Meanwhile, I've invited my mother to tour with me in Vietnam. I'm going to try to make up to her for all of our disagreements and trouble. She hasn't spoken to me since Christmas on the telephone, you know."

"You shouldn't agitate her so," I said.

"She shouldn't agitate me so," Jayne mimicked. "Anyway, I'm taking my mother and paying all of her expenses. I'd like us to be close. We never have been. I have to go to court January 14th for Mrs. Brody's action. Mickey's ex-wife is threatening to arrest him for back alimony. Sam knows Mickey still loves me and wants to remarry me, but he's taking care of that action for Mickey. Sam has to support his wife and two children and his parents, about $3,000

a month. It's up to me to get going and be bread-winner as usual."
"Besides," she laughed, "it's adventure—you never know what's around the corner. It might be love!

"I've always pictured a wonderful husband, the Vic Mature type, wildly wealthy, noble, tall with blue-black hair, Roman features, aesthetic, tender, adoring, physically beautiful with black hair on his chest, virile, brave, ballsy, daring, who drives a sports car 180 miles an hour, very educated and very elegant, and who will let me continue my career and help it. At the same time, I'll be a great lady. The closest one who comes to that here is George Hamilton. He is my type but he's never tumbled at all in my direction. I know he's escorted you to premieres and you're great friends. Can't you arrange a date for me sometime? I think it is exciting to be a lady and be sexy too.

"If I lived in San Francisco, I'd have beautiful gowns and jewels and furs and go to the opera, and I'd entertain on my estate. The pink palace is too theatrical for my tastes now." "I've matured so much," she smiled, "don't you think!"

"If you'll stop that champagne kick you're on Jayne," I said boldly.

"I know," she sighed. "I got on it due to all of my troubles. I've always been so afraid I'd turn out like my mother. I've got to stop.

"It gets hold of me at night, when I've had a really horrible day. When I'm pregnant I never take a drink, as you well know, because it would not be good for the baby." "I'll have to get married and get pregnant fast," she said, "and then I'll stop and all will be good in my life again."

Sam arrived, swung into the library as though he were Jayne's husband already. Planting a kiss on Jayne's lips, he turned to me and said, "I love her the most. I'm so jealous, that's the only trouble we have. When Jayne marries me, our life will be perfect!"

"It would be better Sam if you moved out of Jayne's house until you marry her; that is, if she will."

"This is my house," he replied, not offended as I thought he'd be. "I've put $17,000 worth of new carpeting in the halls and some of the rooms and taken care of extensive plumbing bills. I now own part of this house as well as Jayne does!" Jayne's face paled. She made no remark.

Jayne's mother arrived from Dallas. Another quarrel. Mrs. Peers flew back to Dallas almost immediately. Jayne left for Vietnam with her new hippy secretary. Sam went along as usual.

Newspaper headlines almost daily reported Jayne's Vietnam Tour. At first it began gloriously. The men loved the sex symbol star. Then came a report that Sam Brody, after a fight, had flown back to Los Angeles. He was going to his wife Berverly. The next news report said he had flown back to meet Jayne in Japan. Another dispatch said Jayne's hippy secretary had been caught with marijuana. Jayne had finally been requested to leave. An inside source said Sam had had a big fight with Jayne. She had been pushed back against a sink with such violence that her back had all but been broken. Jayne's unhappy escapades were driving the military up a wall. She had to leave.

"I know," Jayne said, once again back in her library, "the men loved me. I brought back hundreds of telephone numbers. I'm spending all day on the telephone calling wives, sweethearts, girl friends and parents of the men and delivering their messages. I did my best. But when Sam's around everything becomes hectic—like some terrible cloud that keeps pouring down on me.

"I've forgiven Sam again. He has promised to back my pictures for our own producing company. He has excellent ways of raising money for the company. I'll star in the pictures I want to make. We'll be like Sophia Loren and Carlo Ponti."

"Jayne," I said, "you had better sit down and think very carefully why you are getting such terrible press! It is ruining you."

"It's because everyone is playing my life like Faust," she replied.

"Think of the headlines, the law suits and the legal tangles you are now involved in! You are a nice girl and a sweet woman, and you are getting a terrible image!"

"I know," she sighed. "I'm going to get a press agent to make a new image of me, the real lady.

"It's too ridiculous, but I can't help but wonder about that Devil's threats and curses on Sam in San Francisco! He warned me as long as I was with Sam, it would pour down on my head too. We've had so much trouble. Yet it is so ridiculous to think he has the powers of Satan. I went to his black castle because it seemed a fun thing to do.

"How can I undo all of this mess?" Jayne flashed with sudden anger. "I'm certainly not pregnant, as reported on a T.V. gossip show. I'll sue them. I am not married, and I am in the middle of getting a divorce. How can people be so cruel and so wicked? I have never done anything to hurt anyone!

"Being a member of the Devil's cult was just a laugh to me—until now I begin realizing it is being take seriously.

"Anton Lavey is a very handsome and interesting man. He has this big black house on a hill with a 500-pound lion. He drives a black hearse. He is highly intelligent. He told me he had fallen in love with me and wanted to join my life with his. It was a laugh.

"He showed us some ointments that he said were supernatural, and could heal or kill, or do anything. He showed us a skull and said if you touched it you would be cursed. Sam wasn't superstitious and picked it up. Mr. Lavey, who prefers to be called 'The Devil,' declared, 'You will die in a year. You will see what it means to laugh and scorn the Devil!'

"I did not wear the Devil's symbols and the charms he gave me. I was too polite to refuse, however. As a good catholic I went to my priest, Mon. O'Sullivan. I asked him if it were true that Anton Lavey had evil powers. He told me, 'Yes.' He said the fallen angel Lucifer did possess evil powers.

"I didn't think too much about it until the very next day. There were those headlines asking me to leave the Film Festival; that I had not been invited. This was absolutely crazy. The Festival people had not only sent me letters of invitation, they had paid for four airplane tickets and my hotel reservations at the Festival. They charged that I wore a topless dress and held my two latest chihuahuas to cover my breasts. This was such a ridiculous charge—it was unbelievable!

"Speak of the Devil, it suddenly occurred to me! I began to wonder—but I thought it isn't possible. I am not his subject.

"I no sooner returned home than came Jungleland. My little Zoltan attacked and mauled by a lion. Again, I thought, was this evil curse by the Devil possible? I refused to believe it."

"It is all incredible," exploded Jayne with righteous indignation."

"But playing with fire," I interceded, "you have been burned!" Had the evil powers been attracted to her in an attempt to destroy her in a diabolical scheme, I wondered to myself.

Jayne admitted she did wonder if the evil powers had been attracted to her because of her friendship with Anton Lavey. "I find it hard to believe," she said in the next breath.

Jayne had suffered severe loss by theft. "I came home to find a grand piano had apparently walked out of the playroom downstairs. Later, a small piano was taken from the library. Not to mention paintings, television sets, silver, dishes, books and typewriters. I gave an attorney over two hundred and fifty thousand dollars in jewelry to hold for me in Venezuela. The attorney disappeared with my jewelry.

"I am tired of continuously being robbed of things, right here in my own house. This morning the servants walked out when I questioned them about a large sum of money that had disappeared from my room since last night. Not to mention," she added ruefully, "the thousands of dollars unaccounted for on my many tours. I admit I am good-hearted, and let my entourage traveling with me charge room service, meals, notels, etc. but not cash sums for clothes and whatever they fancy and long distance telephone calls.

It is amazing how my kindness has been taken advantage of.

"And my mother has always been jealous of me, and never liked Hollywood. I think it's because she was well-known as a public speaker at clubs and things. And then when I began going ahead of her, well—as you know, we haven't really spoken as friends for months and months. She means well. I love her, despite everything . . . even if I can never please her. I was sorry she didn't accompany me to Vietnam. Had she, Sam wouldn't have gone."

On a happier note Jayne smiled. "It hasn't all been bad. There is always ultimate victory! Zoltan has recovered from the lion mauling although there are still scars on his face and neck. And one of his eyes isn't quite right. I have received all of these beautiful jewels from a new admirer." She revealed a gorgeous new $100,000 diamond bracelet and an even more expensive diamond ring. Just that day to help her smile again, diamond earrings came from Sam Brody.

# CHAPTER XXVI

Jayne had to have "a new image," a better one. Several ace public relations men were called in to salvage her from the damage that alarmingly was taking place almost daily. Some stories originated in Hollywood, but the dispatches were also coming in from all parts of the world, wherever she and Sam would be on her night club and theatrical engagements.

I was giving a birthday party for Joe E. Brown, the famed comedian. Martin Von Dehn, George Dareos, the noted psychic of Hollywood's superstars, Ida Mayer Cummings, Baroness Lotta Von Strahl, and Mayor Sam Yorty were some of the celebrated guests coming to the birthday party. It was to be an exclusive and beautiful party for which I made great preparations. I also had a new pale pink hostess gown made for the occasion. Jayne's gown was ladylike and lovely and we were both very excited about the party. This was also to re-establish Jayne as a young woman of taste.

Cholly Angelino, Dean of society editors in the United States, said he would use the party and pictures as an exclusive for his page in the Herald Examiner.

"This will give you the proper setting to let people see you as you really are—a charming, lovely young woman," I told Jayne. She agreed. As a finale of my party, Jayne agreed to sing "Diamonds Are A Girl's Best Friend" from her night club act—"in a subdued, ladylike manner."

"I'll have to have an accompanist," she said, "and one rehearsal." This, I discovered, would cost me fifty dollars. Andre Villon, the French singing star from Paris and a longtime friend, said he'd take care of it. Emanuel Lakow, a Russian concert pianist who had just appeared on the Ed Sullivan show, said he would be delighted to accompany Jayne, as well as entertain my guests after dinner.

The white rooms of my home were beautiful, with vases filled with a profusion of long stemmed pink roses. The menu was perfection. Dinner was served promptly at seven-thirty to thirty guests. There was no crowding. Everyone wore formal dinner clothes. It all looked more like a movie set, with the glamorous gowns and the beautiful people against the white satin background.

"All's going well," I thought happily. Emanuel had telephoned from Jayne's house that he had rehearsed with Jayne. "She's a dream—walking in her beautiful white gown, her real diamonds and her long pale gold hair!" He went into Russian ecstasies on the telephone. "Miss Mansfield asked me to wait while she goes upstairs to freshen her lipstick. Mr. Sam Brody went up with her. She said to tell you we'll be right over," Emanuel reassured me. "It will be a matter of minutes before we arrive!"

Jayne was timed to sing at nine-thirty. Mya, a marvelous entertainer from Brazil, who reportedly wrote the popular song "Brazilia," was going to start the entertainment with Emanuel accompanying her. The exuberant, flamboyant Brazilian was almost too much for our more restrained American culture, so we prevailed on her to remain in a back room until she was introduced to perform. Otherwise, she would be kissing everyone and taking over as she had done before. But she was a talent. "If you want to be a real star tonight, you can't come out until you perform," Andre told her. "You have to make an entrance."

Dinner went smoothly. Dessert had been served. It was now eight-thirty. Jayne had not arrived. Emanuel, who was to be first with a repeat of his Ed Sullivan show act, hadn't arrived either. I was perturbed. Surely, any second Jayne and Emanuel would be walking in. They'd already missed dinner. The irrepressible Mya was hard to hold back. She wanted to be out front with the guests. Nine o'clock came, no Jayne. No Emanuel. Nine-thirty and then ten o'clock came and no Jayne and no Emanual. Andre was trying to pacify Mya, who was now demanding she go on without accompaniment. "Just a few more minutes," we pacified. She had eaten her dinner, she wept, without being with the movie stars. "That's the price of stardom in America," we sympathized. "A star," she was repeatedly told, "comes out for a performance, otherwise you spoil your entrance." More concern, however, was to keep Mya's gentleman friend she had surprised us with under wraps as well. "He looks like a Mafia gunman," worried Linda, borrowed for the occasion. "If your celebrated guests saw him, they'd all leave!"

A society photographer came in the back way, and now Mya was fit to be tied. "I must be in there getting photographed," she insisted, "with Joe E. Brown and Mayor Yorty and Mary Pickford and Buddy Rogers." She rattled off names in semi-Spanish. We tried to explain that the photographer was society. Mya now revealed her gentleman friend was owner of a bar in some rather unfashionable neighborhood. Now I had to not only worry about where Jayne and Emanuel were, but I could visualize Mya getting her picture with my guests for her friend's eastside bar!

The Prince of Thailand was photographed with Princess, my pinkpoint white Siamese, and said she was the finest specimen from the Royal Palace of the King and Queen. Martin Von Dehn, Mary Pickford, Buddy Rogers and Joe E. Brown were being photographed around the huge birthday cake. Joe E. Brown told hilarious stories of his career in his own inimitable way, and still no Jayne. Since Jayne had my accompanist, nothing could start.

By now I was furious. We put in a call every few minutes to the pink palace. Obviously, the telephones had been turned off for the night. By eleven-thirty, Andre answered my kitchen telephone to hear Emanuel say, "I've been sitting here since eight o'clock, and Miss Mansfield has never come downstairs yet. What shall I do?"

"Go upstairs and knock on her door," I said icily, trying to control my indignation. "Tell Miss Mansfield that she is ruining my whole party and to call me immediately and tell me what is wrong. You, Emanuel, are to come over here right away!"

"But I took a taxi here. I have no car," Emanuel said. "Charge a taxi to me!" I demanded.

Ten minutes later Sam was on the wire, with an apology. "Jayne is drinking coffee like mad," he said smoothly. "As soon as she can get herself together, we'll all be over."

"Coffee? What for? I demanded angrily.

"Well," Sam clued me, "we had a glass of champagne to celebrate your party—and before we knew it, we had drank the whole bottle and another one and we fell asleep."

"Sam Brody," I gasped with chagrin, "you have ruined my whole party. I shall never forgive you."

"We'll be right over," he insisted.

I banged down the receiver.

Mya could be contained no longer. Grabbing her guitar, she swept into the living room, took a bow, and announced, "I'll sing for you without the piano." She did. Andre then sang "I'll Search For You" in French and several other love songs. Still no Jayne and no Emanuel. The society photographer was departing when Mya grabbed him with a strangle hold insisting, "I have to be photographed with Joe E. Brown! And the stars!" She was, and as we had feared, the pictures, blown up life-size, were put on display in her friend's bar. This shows what a twenty dollar tip will do to a photographer, society or not!

It was one A.M. The guests were telling me they had such a wonderful time. Someone asked out loud, "Wasn't Jayne Mansfield coming to sing?"

At this point the telephone rang. Andre took it in the kitchen. It was Emanuel. "We are in the Beverly Hills police station arrested!" he said. "What shall I do?"

"Arrested?" Someone picked up an extension in my bedroom. Andre's voice, in excitable French-accented English, boomed from the wire! "Arrested? You and Jayne Mansfield? What are you in jail for?" he demanded.

"Keep your voice down Andre," I implored, ushering my frankly curious guests, one and all, back to the living room.

I picked up the extension to hear Emanuel saying, "Miss Jayne Mansfield and Mr. Brody got into a fight. The police stopped us on Beverly Blvd. when she threw the car keys out onto the street. They took us all to the station house," he explained in a conglomeration of highly excited, accented Russian. "Do I get bail? Can you bail me out? I am an innocent man. This will ruin my career." The poor man began to sob.

"Don't let anyone hear this," I said, rushing to the kitchen. "Keep quiet Andre, everyone can hear you from the kitchen. Tell Emanuel to call a bondsman. Or better still, use my name and call a bondsman and tell Emanuel to take a taxi here and I'll pay all costs."

Back in my living room, I was saying goodnights to some of the guests when Emanuel arrived in his impeccable tux.

"Please, I want to perform!" he announced.

"Where's Jayne Mansfield?" someone asked him.

"In the police station," he said . . . . . . . !

"Ooooops," I rushed to Emanuel, "Come on quick, and give Joe E. Brown a musical play on the piano of his personality."

Emanuel complied, and everyone's thoughts were quickly, I hoped, removed from the current status of Jayne.

Later Jayne telephoned, all tearful. "I ruined your party. Oh May, I'd never do that to you."

"You only hurt yourself Jayne," I said as kindly as possible. Sam got on the wire.

"It is never Jayne's fault. She's a lady. It's all my fault."

"Then why do you keep ruining her life?" I asked tartly.

"I'll never do anything to harm her," he said, his voice breaking down. I hung up.

Jayne planned for her British Isles theatrical tour with happy aspects. The English adored her. Sam would definitely not be going. Victor Huston made that a condition of his managing the tour. "If Sam goes, I will not!"

As late as midnight before the morning's departure, Jayne called Victor's mother and promised Mrs. Huston, "Sam Brody will definitely not be on this tour!" She was taking baby Tony only as her other children were in school. "It is a court ruling that I can have Tony with me until July and this dreadful law suit Matt Cimber has against me is over," Jayne said.

It was a good feeling that crisp morning, when Jayne and her little entourage boarded a plane at Los Angeles International Airport. Her troubles were over; she breathed a sigh of relief to Victor. In the next breath she squealed, "Oooh!" with surprise. There was Sam Brody boarding the plane. "Sweetheart, you know I couldn't let you go without me to protect you," he smiled.

Jayne arrived at Heathrow Airport on March 24th, 1967. It was Good Friday. The English press were out full force to welcome her like no star had ever been honored. Adjectives flowed in printer's ink for Super Star Jayne Mansfield.

"Not even the Queen of England," one British paper reported "has ever had such a royal welcome by the press."

With Sam Brody along, there had to be an immediate incident. He tried to carry Jayne's two chihuahuas, Popsicle and Momsicle, through customs with Jayne's leopard skin coat over his shoulders, concealing the pooches in his pockets. Sam was stopped and smuggling charges hit headlines. Jayne said, "He did it without asking me." The dogs went into England's required six-month quarantine.

Jayne's refusal to wear a see-through dress for publicity for her British agent Don Arden, who was also co-owner of a dress shop on Carnaby Street, brought headlines the next day. "It's a see-through. I don't wear that kind on the street," Jayne said. "It would be an affront to the Queen. I met her you know, when I was presented at her Command Performance. She's a lovely woman."

Later Jayne said, "I love all those people with the long hair on Carnaby street. They're so kind to me." Jayne was always political.

Ensconced in the Savoy Hotel, flowers poured in for Jayne while crowds milled outside the hotel to catch a glimpse of Miss Jayne Mansfield! The English bobbies had to break up the lines chanting, "We Want Jayne!" outside the hotel at all hours!

Rehearsals began. A disagreement brought on by Sam Brody and Jayne's late show-ups at rehearsal, caused Don Arden to terminate her $8,400-a-week contract.

Meanwhile, Jayne visited the public gallery of the House of Commons, and was hosted for lunch by Timothy Kitson, the Tory MP for Richmond, Yorkshire. Jayne's physical attributes impressed the press more than what was going on in the house. Jayne said she thought Edward Heath was a superb looking man, and that she was quite free and almost single again.

Jayne sent me cards describing the green, lush beauty of the English countryside. Victor Huston sent me letters that he was having a hectic time. "Never again will I ever go any place with Jayne when Sam is along," he wrote. "The dogs messed the carpets of Jayne's hotel suite and we had to pay for new ones. Tony is left part of the time with a hotel maid and I am doubling as baby sitter. But Englanders love Jayne."

Within days, Jayne was signed by new British agents Frank

Taylor and Bernard Hinchcliffe. Her new tour was set. She would now open in Manchester for a schedule of night club engagements.

Victor wrote me that after Blackpool, they drove through Ireland where the roads were lined with people four deep to pay homage to Jayne passing by in her car. "It was like she was the Queen. They loved her."

It was in Ireland that Jayne ran into scandal headlines that reverberated around the world. Victor wrote, "It is as though the Devil's curse is working 100%. Jayne is always trying to cover body bruises. She begs Sam not to beat her face. If we can only get rid of Sam!"

Sam's openly admitting they were not married, but were traveling together, brought frowns from Irish church fathers. Jayne was scheduled to appear at the Mont Brandon Hotel in Tralee, Ireland on April 13th. She visited the parish church and lit a chandle with Sam. She also had a photographer along to show she was a deeply religious woman.

The church fathers were furious to have their own church and altar thus used. The Dean of Kerry, Monsignor John Lane said in the press, "A woman is brought here to give a show for which she is being paid 2,800 pounds. This woman boasts that her New York critics said of her: 'She sold sex better than any performer in the world.' I appeal to the men and women, to the boys and girls of Tralee to dissociate themselves from this attempt to besmirch the name of our town for the sake of filthy gain."

The hotel management cancelled Jayne's engagement on the heels of the church pronouncements. Said Jayne sweetly to the press, "I'm a good Catholic. I said I am a sexy entertainer. I give as much to the church as the Bible says—much more in fact. I think the Bishop, who is nearly ninety-nine, must be a sweet old man. He's got his job to do and people see things differently in different parts of the world. But the people like me. Women come up crying and kissing my skirt, and they line the roads to say hello."

British-born Victor Huston was quoted in the Irish press saying,

"Oh baby, if Jayne had put in her salary to the church there wouldn't have been a problem. We got the most fantastic receptions for Jayne everywhere in Ireland! I've had to hire extra bodyguards to keep the crowds back when Jayne gets out of her car to keep her from being squashed to death."

Jayne posed for pictures and then happily went on to her next engagement at the luxurious Webbington Country Club, near Weston Super Mare, owned by handsome, tall, young, personable Alan Wells. "This is the happiest time of my life," Jayne told the press. She was not aware that only six more weeks of life was left for her to live.

# CHAPTER XXVII

. Alan Wells immediately flipped over Jayne Mansfield. "What a living, breathing doll," he exclaimed for the whole world to know. "Jayne's the loveliest woman I've ever met." Everything Jayne did was perfection to Alan. Sam sulked but Jayne welcomed Alan's happy disposition.

Alan became Jayne's best press agent as well as an ardent admirer. "She's most cooperative" he said. She even let them take her measurements. When her famous 44–18–36 turned out by British tape measures to be a 46 inch bust, why all Jayne said was, 'Ooh, isn't that wonderful! I don't know how it happened but I guess it must be the five babies I've had. I'm a big girl now!'"

Alan leased a Silver Cloud Rolls for Jayne. He later offered to give it to her, she said, if she would marry him. "Alan is so kind and so unlike Sam, with his moods and terrible temper."

The press was continuously agog over Jayne. One paper read,

"The shrapnel from Jayne Mansfield's explosive tour in England will take months, maybe years, to simmer down. She arrived with her American barrister, a promotor and chauffeur, hairdresser, maid and a boyfriend. In the middle of it, she changed her vital statistics, her promotor, impresarios, chauffeurs and she's acquired a handsome British boyfriend."

It was party time nightly after Jayne's show at Alan Wells' cabaret. Always there were words, harassment and flares of jealousy from Sam. Alan ignored Sam's threats. After all, he was owner of the club, wasn't he? He had the say.

Now that she had met Alan, Jayne purred, "I've changed my mind about English men. I thought they were so cold. Alan Wells has proved quite differnt. I love Englishmen now and Alan in particular."

Jayne's act was always the same and always hours late. Whether she played the plush clubs or the more salty ones frequented mostly by men, the impatient audiences had to be pacified by the management. But once Jayne was on she was idolized by rich and poor alike. No one ever asked for their money back.

Jayne wore the backless, low-cut, white satin gown, that she had worn New Year's Eve in Hollywood. She sang "Strangers in the Night," "What Now My Love," and then "Diamonds Are A Girl's Best Friend." She'd slither among the customers, sit on knees, kiss blushing, often weather-worn cheeks and bald heads, and she'd wiggle!

She sold sex and everyone bought it, even women! One reporter summed up her tour of England with, "Jayne Mansfield has vamped and crooned her way through England from working men's clubs in Greasborough, Yorkshire to the elegant variety club in Batley with tiered seating for 1500 people. She is always a delight. She must have tweaked, stroked and kissed a thousand men in the northern provinces."

"What I sell is not pure sex, but laughs at it, a satire," she explained. "I always ask the wives present if I can play with their husbands for a minute, and I only kiss a few bald heads. Everyone seems to enjoy it, as they are all part of it. But one night a gentleman too deep in his cups threw me over a table and tried to rape me. They pulled him off. I was most upset. Usually they don't get that carried away."

Sam's brooding jealousy was held in check as long as Alan Wells was on the scene. Jayne blossomed and her beauty was back with no more black eyes. Alan had warned Sam, "If you so much as lay a finger on her, I'll beat you up within an inch of your life!" Sam behaved.

It was on the last night of Jayne's engagement at Alan's club, at a celebration party that Sam's good behavior ended in an explosion. Pictures were taken of Jayne in Alan's embrace with Sam at her knee. Sam lost his cool. There was also a huge chocolate cake with the inscription, "Farewell Jayne, Love Alan."

About three A.M. Sam and Alan got into a bitter argument. In the scuffle someone's face was pushed through Jayne's farewell cake! Fists, champagne, and glasses went flying. A table was overturned. Jayne ran sobbing from the room to her suite. The whole party came to an abrupt end.

Sam took the next plane to America—a beaten man. Alan announced that he would accompany Jayne on the remainder of her tour in England.

At one of the hotels a plump Diana Dors, England's Sex Symbol, and Jayne were brought together. The two sex queens had much in common mainly a love of attention. Jayne clearly overshadowed Diana, who left the party. Jayne was declared winner.

Asked if she had any ambitions left in life, Jayne told a press conference, "I'd like ten more babies and ten more chihuahuas and a few Academy Awards. My critics tell me I have the potential as a dramatic actress. That is if I live that long. Meanwhile, I enjoy being a sex symbol and making people happy."

No sooner was Sam back in the United States than he was on the telephone to Jayne. "He still is begging me to marry him. Maybe I will," she said. "But now that I have met Englebert Humperdinck and Alan Wells, I don't know. Maybe I prefer Englishmen."

Englebert was observed nightly with Jayne. Jayne said that she was turned on only by a man with mental aspects as well as physical. "My IQ is 163 you know."

Jayne now continued her European tour with Alan. Finally, after all of his lavish attentions and presents, which included chartering private planes to show Jayne the English countryside, he had to go back to running his club.

Sam Brody then flew back from the States to be with her in Stockholm. There, Jayne broke all existing records, including Sammy Davis, Jr.'s. With Sam came the scandal headlines again and black eyes and bruises for Jayne. A front page headline in a Stockholm newspaper for May 28, 1967 showed Jayne on the floor knocked over in a melee with Sam and a black patron of the club. "Fists flew and the mini-skirted Jayne was knocked sprawling. Police were called to restore order and Jayne, weeping, was whisked away in a taxi."

Victor Huston vowed he'd return immediately to the States. He could not endure Sam Brody's outbursts on the tour. Jayne decided to return also to see her children. "I've been away from them too long—almost two months," she said.

Jayne came home to the Pink Palace reunited with her two chihuahuas, who had been in quarantine during her stay in Britain, her two new chihuahuas and her two new great dane puppies from Alan Wells. Sam Brody moved back into the pink palace as though he owned it. It was now early June 1967.

"I will be going back to England to star in a play on the West End," Jayne purred happily on the telephone to me.

"Jayne," I said, "get rid of Sam."

"I'm trying to," she replied. "I'm honestly trying to. Please come over for dinner," she said, in the next breath. "I'm having a kosher dinner cooked for Sam."

"You don't make sense Jayne," I sighed. "You just don't!"

"What's next?" I asked Jayne, as we sat curled up before the fire in her drawing room.

"I don't know," she replied thoughtfully. "Don't worry about all of that scandal in the press. I really had a marvelous time on my European tour."

"Really, I've had a wonderful thirteen years in Hollywood," she said. "I've been able to get everything I've always wanted, except real, lasting, unselfish love from a man. The Chinese, you know, wish you seven happinesses, but they only name six of them: gentle birth, pleasant childhood, good marriage, many children, prosperous business and quick death. The seventh, they tell you, is up to you. You've got to figure it out and find it for yourself.

"I feel sorry for Sam. He is such an unhappy man. But that too will soon end. A lot has happened, good and bad, but all things considered, I like people and animals and myself," she laughed. "Not necessarily in that order. I think most people like me and I know the animals do. And I like myself. I've enjoyed life pretty much. As for the future, it is always a surprise."

Jayne picked up some magazines, each one an entire issue on Jayne Mansfield. "Look at this one in Spanish," she mused. "Mother gave an interview for it when I first started. She was shocked all through the story, she wrote, that I wore bikinis. She kept repeating her daughter would never wear a bikini to a party. Mother and I never got along. But then she is my mother," she signed.

"I'm glad I have a stronger rapport with my children. Except Miklos tried to burn the Pink Palace while I was gone. He's almost nine years old and he's getting very rebellious. He hates Sam. The children all do. Miklos took an old mattress and set it on fire underneath the house. 'It's this house that keeps you working and away from us,' he told me. I have to spend more time with Miklos and my children. I can't ever leave them alone so long again. And I never will," she said.

She never did.

# CHAPTER XXVIII

Jayne had been home a few days when Anton Lavey arrived from San Francisco at the Pink Palace. Jayne was gracious, but secretly terrified of the so-called Devil.

"You may or may not believe in mystic powers of the Devil and his earthly emissaries, or even voodoo or witchcraft," she told Linda, "but how else can you account for all of this continuous string of horrible things that keep happening to me and Sam."

"I dare not refuse to see Lavey," she said. "I've got to be nice to him. Linda, you have to admit him. He's telephoned from the airport. Victor has gone to drive him here."

"If you don't leave Sam Brody immediately, you will get it too, Jayne! The curse is on him and this house! Anyone who places himself under the same cloud will get it!" said the tall, dark man in the Devil's cape and cap with horns, as he walked through the Pink Palace from room to room.

Jayne followed along, alternately laughing and crying and at last pleading. "Please take the curse off of Sam and the house," she begged. "Please!"

"I cannot!" The man was adamant. "Once it is given, no power on earth, not even I, can remove it!"

., He turned to Linda who was making sandwiches in the kitchen. "See this ring, this black ring?" he said to her. "You will see the Devil's face in it!"

Linda turned away. "I won't look," she half screamed. "No sir, I won't have nothing to do with you or it. Go away. Leave me be!"

"Every hair on my head stood on end," Linda said. "If there was ever a Devil, he was it! He went around the house with Sam Brody walking behind him, and Sam laughed mockingly all the time. Poor little Jayne was so worried and troubled. Then she'd try to make a joke of it. But she was scared inside. She kept telling me so—when she wasn't telling herself she didn't believe it."

Lavey had come from his Devil's Church in San Francisco to ask Jayne to pose for some publicity pictures with him. When I learned of it, I told Jayne she must be out of her mind. But Jayne said, "Oh May, it's just for publicity." However, she confided to Linda, "I'm so scared. Everything has gone wrong since we met him in San Francisco and he cursed Sam because Sam laughed at him.

"'I' was asked to leave the film festival, where I was an honored guest. Then, on the way to Canada, we had two terrific car crashes, and barely escaped with our lives. In London, we had two more severe car crashes. Sam was so jealous, he broke up my engagements and publicly brawled with the managers of the theaters and night clubs. In Vietnam I almost broke my back, from being pushed against a sink in one of Sam's tempers. Then Zoltan and May were attacked by that lion and both of them almost got killed at Jungleland. Of course, Sam was with us when he wasn't supposed to be! We've had three bad car accidents since then and the main water pipes and plumbing have broken twice and flooded part of the house, almost ruining it. I don't know what can happen next.

"Maybe if I pose for the pictures with Anton Lavey, he'll take the curse off Sam and the house even though he says he can't."

"Anyway," Jayne said, "we are going to take Anton Lavey to dinner at La Scala. There I pray we can talk him out of this terrible curse that persists. I didn't believe it for a long time, Linda, but you can't get away from the facts!"

As she went swinging out the door in her orange mini-skirt suit and her matching orange leather knee-high boots, she said, "See if I don't charm the Devil, himself!" She laughed. She was confident. She was beautiful, desirable. She was Jayne Mansfield, whose name was known throughout the world. She had night club and T.V. series offers and movies in Europe. She had five beautiful children. She was only thirty-four—she still had good years ahead. She had never been unkind, nor hurt anyone in her life. She could free herself of Sam, get the curse removed from him, and go on her own sweet happy way! The future was rosy.

Whether you believe in curses or black magic the factual evidence of the curse placed on Sam Brody and its effect on Jayne made the very few who knew the facts wonder. The evidence was terrible, frightening, and unrelenting.

Jayne did not return home that night in the gay, confident mood in which she had left. Jayne and Sam left Lavey off after a sumptuous dinner and on the way back to the Pink Palace in the Masserati they crashed into another car. Both were badly shaken, but miraculously escaped with their lives. The new car was completely demolished.

Jayne called me the next day. "May, I'm so tired of hurting all over from so many car crashes. The Devil Anton's curse seems to be working all of the time. I can't get rid of Sam. I don't know what to do!"

"Get the police to get him out of your house," I suggested.

"I have, five times," Jayne replied. "The police take him, and he always comes back!"

"Why, Jayne?" I implored. "Why be in such a mess?"

"Oh May, I'm so confused, so tired, so tired of hurting all of the time," she moaned. "So tired of so much trouble!"

"Cheer up, Jaynie," I replied. "Tomorrow you are going to forget Sam and go with me to the charity luncheon at the Cocoanut Grove. We will have a marvelous time, as we always do. We'll play movie star!"

"I hope so," Jayne replied forlornly. "Anyway, I'll be at your house promptly at twelve noon."

Except Jayne did not arrive the next noon at my house!

Instead, a call came that Sam Brody had called and insisted that he pick Jayne up and drive her to my house. As he rounded the corner on Sunset to Jayne's Pink Palace, he suddenly lost control of his car and ran up a tree. The Mercedez-Benz was smashed beyond repair. Sam was pulled out, miraculously still alive. He was taken to the UCLA Medical Center with a broken hip and leg and internal injuries. Jayne rushed to the hospital. As Linda helped her dress, she wept. "Linda, how can this keep up? What else can happen to me and this cursed house?"

The late afternoon sun set enveloped in a gray gloom of cloud and fog coming off shore to unite with the smog engulfing the city. A faint glimmer of hope probed the awesome dank cold with a pink hue of promise lying out there on the horizon. Suddenly, the capricious Santa Ana winds started blowing through the canyons sweeping the chilling bleakness, and the smell of dead fish, human debris and weary people, as weary as the weather. It was as though it were giving the hope of release from this morbid, vacuous usurpation that came and went with the shoosh-shoosh-shoosh-shoosh of the breakers.

A few people, as tired as the day, moved in silhouette—aimless and disconsolate along the walk. Among them was a young woman with a small girl and boy struggling forward against the winds. Hugging a tiny dog encased inside her coat to give the animal her body warmth, she too moved against the penetrating cold. The children hugged their coat collars tight to their necks. She seemed almost unmindful of them; almost unaware of the cold. Her eyes seemed unseeing as she trod forlornly, yet resolutely, along the water's edge. Wearing a blue woolen coat over a matching mini skirt and sweater, her shapely legs were encased in matching blue suede boots. Her long pale yellow hair whipped back in ripples with the wind.

"Mommy, let's go back to the car," the little girl whined. "It's soo cold!" The little boy echoed the other child's complaint. The young woman, her mind intent and apparently consumed with thoughts in her own obviously troubled world, did not immediately respond. Anxiety lined her beautiful, really lovely, yet lonely face. She walked as though she were reaching out for help, somewhere. Somewhere—she did not know where. There was a sort of quiet desperation in her, and occasionally people turned to stare after her.

As the three reached the old pier, which had once been Santa Monica beach's famed amusement park, the little girl began to cry softly. "I want a hot dog," she sobbed child-like. She did not know how to voice her fear and pain in the chill damp that was whipping through her tiny body. The woman suddenly turned on to the need of her children, turned off her reverie, and stopping at the one small coffee stand on the sand, went in. "I'd like two hot milks and two hot dogs for my children," she ordered.

The counter boy took a double look. "Hi!" he exclaimed in surprise. "You're Jayne Mansfield the movie star! Aren't you! Don't try to say you aren't lady," his face beamed in a broad smile. "I know you are! You are gorgeous!" he aftermathed.

She smiled acknowledgment but the smile was fleeting, for the anxieties pressing into her refused to release her.

"What're you doing here on this god forsaken place on this lousy day?" the young man ventured as he prepared the hot dogs.

"I don't know," replied the distracted Jayne with a deep sigh. "I just don't know. I am so confused. I don't even remember driving down here." Then she added with a shrug of her shoulders, "I just came, that's all." She hugged the little Chihuahua closer to her, visibly shaking with the chill.

"I can't help noticing, Man, your legs are blue. You must be cold all the way through," the young man said. "Here, take this cup of coffee on the house and warm up!"

Staring ahead at something she seemed to be seeing, she half sat down. Mechanically, she began sipping the hot coffee. The children were chomping their hot dogs, which shifted her preoccupation to them, and her own whereabouts. "This is really a hippy joint," she said, looking around. "That's right lady," the young man replied. "How come a big movie star like you is down here alone? Look at those rocks on you! Someone will twist your arm off for those before you make it back to your car Jayne. I'd better close up and body-guard you."

"I'll make it okay," she said.

"Yuh?! That's what you think. Maybe like as not you've already been followed. A lot of heads got the word. There's more than hippies and flower children down here you know. Looks like a lot of nothingness—! Except it's a human crap game, with everyone from cops to hopheads looking to bust someone. No, I'm going to take you back to your car, and see you get out of here safely!"

"Let me ask you why you came here?" he said, as he walked her and the two children the mile back to her Rolls parked on a pavement facing the beach. A few seagulls were hovering on the top, miserable in the wind. "I don't know," she replied. "I just had to get away, to get my head clear. I have so many problems, sometimes I don't know where to turn." Her eyes painfully reflected the worry and a deep inner sadness which turned to bewilderment and hopelessness in turn. "I just don't know," she repeated. "I just don't know what to do!"

He helped her and her children inside the luxurious car. "Here's five bucks," he said, handing her five one-dollar bills from his wallet. "Will this help?"

"Oh," she laughed now, refusing his offer. "It isn't money. I wish it were only money. It's—so unbearable, so awful," she sighed. Resolutely, she turned the ignition and with a brave smile and a thank you, she backed out from the curb.

Curiosity forced him to run over to her and stop her. "Jayne," he said in a respectful tone, "a doll like you in a Rolls can't have it all that bad. How many Rolls' you got anyway?"

"I have a new one I'm taking delivery on—custom ordered—in July," she brightened for a second at the thought.

"You know something," she said, now turning confidential, "I'd give anything—everything I have—if I could just keep my children and my career, and be free of all of the horrible problems besetting me. Honest, I could earn more money—if God will just keep my children and me safe!"

"Someone threatening you?"

"Oh, it's much more," she acknowledged. Then, with a shake of her windblown hair, she disclosed, "When everything gets too much for me, I always come down here and walk in the sand. Or I go to Forest Lawn and walk and walk and look at the graves, and think how lucky I am to be alive and have my children. I get my head back on straight that way. That is most always!"

Her voice drifted off and again there came that look in her eyes of sudden vague nothingness, of bewilderment, of despair. The young man puzzled that a super movie star like Jayne Mansfield would be seeing something out of the nothingness, that was the beach with its awesome dark dankness, now drawing a curtain of black down on the last ray of light, as the sun had now fallen below the horizon into the sea.

"A big movie star, a gorgeous looker with a Pink Palace and a Rolls—and everything? Why would she look so desperate? Why would she come here?" he pondered. "Don't mind me," she said. "I've always been a very lonely person." He shrugged his shoulders and returned to reopen his hot dog stand. Lots of queer,

queer things happen, he thought. No, he decided, there was no idea that she wanted to commit suicide. But he could not erase that terrible sadness, even almost tragic look in her eyes—he had seen—that he had felt so deeply.

When Jayne pulled up the drive of the Pink Palace, that look was long gone. She was again her resolute, sparkling, brave, beautiful self. No one ever guessed the inner loneliness of the girl—she continuously fought within herself.

Later, Sam returned to the Pink Palace, his leg in a cast up to his waist. Jayne was too kindhearted to refuse to let him stay. Besides, she was leaving the next morning for Biloxi for a night club engagement.

Linda was beside herself with worry. "We can't get that Sam Brody out of this house no way," she phoned me. "There is nothing but trouble, tears, fights, and more trouble in this house. I want to get out of here. It's only those three little unhappy children here that keeps me on."

I admitted that I, too, felt a very horrible feeling in that house. The children were so unhappy. Jayne Marie, unable to stand it, had run away and brought long months of humiliation and court action to her mother—to escape it.

"Surely, Jayne, you won't let Sam go to Biloxi with you!" I said. "Why, why! When there's been nothing but tragedy ever since he came into your life, and that Devil's curse was put on him just a month later?"

"I don't know," Jayne began to cry. "Anyway, he will be killed if the curse goes on as it has so far. That's the only way he says I'll ever be free! I'm so tired, so confused. I'm virtually a prisoner," she whispered, with tears streaming down her face. "Sam can be so kind, and so horrible. I don't know what comes over him. He beats me. I'm so tired of hurting all over!"

# CHAPTER XXIX

Jayne and Sam Brody called me early in the morning a few days later in great anxiety. "It will be in the next edition of the newspapers," they chorused over a double extension wire.

Sam continued, "Jayne Marie has left home and appeared at the West Los Angeles Police Station, asking for protective custody. She told them she had been beaten by her mother's boy friend, me."

"This is terrible," Sam muttered on the telephone. "Jayne Marie has been a terrible girl. She has become completely delinquent. She had been punished as she should have been. And now she's filing terrible charges against Jayne."

"The court is to designate where the child shall remain for the following three weeks—until a hearing and a legal decision is rendered," he said. "Right now we don't know where she is. She is hiding somewhere!"

Actually, Jayne Marie had called her Uncle Bill Pigue, who was a relative of Jayne's first husband, Paul Mansfield. Bill, a *Herald Examiner* editor, and his wife Mary had always taken a close interest in Jayne Marie since she was a baby.

Jayne Marie had asked Bill Pigue to take her away from the pink palace. She was taken secretly to the home of a trusted press agent friend, Shirley Carroll. Mrs. Carroll, a lovely woman, told me later, "when they brought Jayne Marie here, she was like a little flower, sweet quiet and needing love more than any child I have ever seen. It didn't seem like she was sixteen—but more like she was younger than my fourteen-year-old son. I put her to bed and I tucked her in and kissed her and put my arms around her. She was frightened and shivering. She had no clothes with her—nothing but a pair of gold earings. I suppose the court will send her to juvenile hall, such a pity—but right now her uncle is trying to avoid that."

As far as Jayne knew, her child was in hiding, and even with a detective she was unable to locate her. "I feel so helpless," Jayne said wearily. "If only I could get her back to talk to her, to reason with her." Jayne was on the telephone to me intermittently all day. Sam was always on the extension.

Now Sam's voice interrupted. "If Jayne ever needed help, she does now. I don't mind for me. But my God, to do it to Jayne! These charges can ruin her career!"

Before I could say anything, Sam said, "you know Paul Caruso. Call him! Tell him to do everything he can to help! He'd have respect for you—more than me."

"You call him. You are also an attorney. You two know each other professionally! My calling him wouldn't be important."

"I have already called him," Sam said. "But a call from you could help," he added. He then asked me to also call a Los Angeles city official for help. I did.

The city official interrupted before I could even say hello. "I know what you are calling about," he said. "We know the case. The child has to be protected. Tell Mr. Brody to get an attorney. He had better not try to defend the case himself at the hearing."

"He has Mr. Paul Caruso."

"That's good," was the reply. "If anyone can do anything, Mr. Caruso can. I feel sorry for Jayne and the child."

I called Jayne back that night to find her still crying. "Oh May, I don't know," she sobbed. "How can my very own—my own flesh and blood, do this to me, her own mother?"

Sam's voice chimed in, "You should have heard what Jayne Marie called her mother! The vile name!"

Jayne said, "I wanted her spanked. I was at my wit's end to know what to do. She has been doing things, I don't even want to tell you, May. I will protect her, by withholding the real truth. But drastic action had to be taken. She's my first baby. How could she?"

I consoled Jayne as best I could. "Jayne Marie has always been devoted to you, Jayne," I comforted. "But you should realize that Jayne Marie is sixteen years old—a young woman. You can no longer treat her like a child. She is not going to let Sam Brody, of all people, spank her! You would rebel yourself under the same circumstances." Then I added diplomatically, "I don't think the Pink Palace has been a good home for her for a long time."

Sam had called Paul Caruso at dawn with urgency and desperation cracking his voice. "I need your help desperately, Paul," he said, actually sobbing with fear. "Paul, Jayne and I found a boy in the closet of Jayne's sixteen-year-old-daughter Jayne Marie. Jayne Marie was in a baby doll nightie. She was reprimanded. She was spanked."

"There's much more, I won't go into on the telephone," Sam said. "But I am gravely concerned, Paul. Jayne Marie has run away to the police. She has filed criminal child beating charges against Jayne and me. I don't mind for myself, but My God! This will ruin Jayne's career! Please do something! We are desperate!"

Paul Caruso got to work on the case immediately. He had once respected Sam Brody for his legal abilities. Now, he was puzzled at Sam's wanton life style. The following morning he met Jayne Mansfield for the first time. She was wearing orange shorts and a revealing sexy bra, and anxiously flashing her television set from channel to channel to catch the latest news reports on Jayne Marie's child beating complaint. Sam was lying on her bed in her pink bedroom with a broken leg in a cast from the recent accident in the Mercedez.

Unlike most confidential law conferences, Paul Caruso found this one most unusual. For it was held in the bedroom in front of three other people and maids coming and going. Jayne gave Mr. Caruso the impression she was hooked on publicity. During the entire conference, she restlessly returned to switching the TV tube and the radio simultaneously to hear the latest news reports.

After discussing the fine points of law on the criminal child beating charges, Jayne ran into the next room and brought her children in to be introduced to Paul.

After the children had departed Paul said, "Sam, it is not respectful to have you living here with five children under these conditions. You are in a divorce. Jayne's divorce isn't final. You are not married. It is not right, especially for these children. After all, Jayne is their mother!"

"Rest assured," Sam replied, "that all is very circumspect. I cannot leave Jayne here without me. I will never leave her now that I have found her. I'll marry her any minute she tells me she will!"

Paul, a father of five children, shook his head sadly and departed. He had to reschedule a trial, and work all night to make the necessary preparation for court. He admonished Jayne and Sam to be in court the next morning no later than eight thirty A.M. He advised Jayne to dress conservatively and modestly befitting the mother of a sixteen-year-old runaway daughter.

To Paul Caruso's dismay, he paced the courtroom corridor from eight A.M. to ten A.M. when he received a call from Sam Brody.

"We are going to be a little late," Sam explained, not apologizing.

Jayne and Sam finally arrived at eleven thirty. Jayne wore heavy makeup, a long pony tail tied with blue ribbons, a tight mini skirt and boots. "She looked," said Paul Caruso, "like anything in the world except a member of the P.T.A."

According to the court transcript, highlights of Jayne's and Jayne Marie's day in court revealed many pertinent and sensational facts.

Mr. and Mrs. William Pigue (an uncle of Paul Mansfield, who was stated to be the natural father of Jayne Marie), their attorneys, Jayne Marie, Jayne Mansfield, Sam Brody (who in spite of warnings insisted on being the lawyer with Paul Caruso as co-counsel), and court attaches, some fifteen, met for the hearing.

The Pigues petitioned for custody of Jayne Marie. Jayne naturally opposed it. The witnesses were duly sworn in and the interrogation followed. Since court was so late in starting the proceedings were rushed to get started before the lunch hour break. Jayne's outbursts and indignation were tempered from time to time by Sam. But at times she became semi-hysterical as the hearings progressed.

Paul Caruso asked Bill Pigue on the witness stand, "Do you know as a matter of fact, do you not, sir, that Mr. Paul Mansfield has never paid for the support of this child? Has he?"

Mr. Pigue then related his association with Jayne and Jayne Marie since their first arrival in Hollywood with his nephew some twelve years before.

He then recalled he had last tried to talk to Jayne Marie a few months before on the telephone. When the child's birthday approached in the fall, he called the Mansfield residence and asked to speak to Jayne Marie. Instead Jayne herself came on the wire. He said he and his wife would like to take Jayne Marie for a birthday dinner. Jayne said she was punishing Jayne Marie, and she was not allowed to leave the house. Jayne told him, "You know I am a very strict mother, and Jayne Marie has been a very naughty girl. She is not being allowed privileges. She is presently confined to the house."

"Further," she said, "Jayne Marie wants to wear long eyelashes, heavy makeup and stay out late at night. She has been so naughty that I may put her in Juvenile Court care."

When he called the following day he was told, "Miss Mansfield had left for Europe and would be out of the country for some time." He was still not allowed to speak to Jayne Marie.

During the lunch hour recess Paul assured Jayne and Sam that Mack McDonald, Chief Deputy of the Santa Monica Office, had not filed criminal charges yet. If they were not filed by the deputy attorney and if none were filed by city attorney E. Davenport's office, Paul reassured them, it was possible that Jayne and Sam would be cleared. It would be a miracle however!

Sam and Jayne were both so highly nervous they did not even attempt to eat lunch. They both kept repeating over and over that if Jayne Marie's charges were actually filed, then they were both ruined. "It is so unfair, so terribly unfair," Jayne would flare with rage and cry with heartbreak and frustration by turn. Her changing moods, hopes, fears and anger were making her a veritable emotional powder keg!

Paul Caruso opened the afternoon's session. "The child has made disturbingly serious charges which have been contradictory in nature to other statements made. I believe our suggestion that she not be placed with anyone during this period would be fair to all parties.

Sam Brody declared, "I might add, your Honor, that there is testimony at the trial in contradiction to a declaration she (Jayne Marie) signed, wherein Judge Lynch made the statement (Page 245, line 7,) 'As I indicated to counsel in chambers, I cannot believe testimony of this young lady on any statement made by her on the witness stand or in her affidavit, because they are absolutely contradictory. She has lied either to the court today or she has lied in making the affidavit. So her testimony is absolutely of no value at all.' Judge Lynch wanted to send her to juvenile hall. And only under insistence of the mother, we kept her out from going to Juvenile. We are asking that the girl be placed in a third party home."

Jayne took the witness stand. She said she was the natural mother of Jayne Marie Mansfield. She also said, "Miss Jayne Marie Mansfield knows that Paul Mansfield is not her natural father!"

This bombshell was taken apparently in stride by even Jayne Marie, for Jayne had recently given this fact in several magazines and newspaper interviews in England and on the Continent during her tours earlier in the year.

"Although I am very broad-minded, I don't approve of four letter words being used by friends of mine, but most assuredly not by my children," Jayne continued on the witness stand. "I don't believe in smoking marijuana or getting joints from friends before you get to a party, or finding naked boys in a closet of the child; specifically one naked boy that the child says is perfect for her mother.

"I don't approve of diet pills and sleeping pills being taken by a child. Yes, I am strict because I have four beautiful babies that I want to protect. I have never had marijuana on my property in my life. I will never have it. An I will never endanger the lives of four very perfect and wonderful children because of Jayne Marie's quotation in a letter, 'I am stoned out of my mind twenty four hours a day, every day.'"

The court asked Jayne "What reasons you can think of that your daughter Jayne Marie should not reside with her great uncle and aunt, Mr. and Mrs. Pigue?"

Jayne replied readily, "Your Honor, the child is not the blood relative of the Pigue's."

Jayne was then asked, "Would you be kind enough to tell this court who the father of this child is?"

Jayne replied, "Ian Parrish. The child knows about this. I was raped at fourteen years of age." Jayne said she did not know his address or whereabouts now. "I was raped. My mother knows about this, if you care to ask her."

The court then asked, "Whose name appears on the birth certificate (as father)?"

Jayne replied, "The husband, Paul Mansfield."

In explaining her home for her children, Jayne said, "I have a very large home. Forty bedrooms, not one bedroom. I have quite a few servants, three who stay on the place all of the time. Four or five who come in. My reputation as a sex symbol actress I know is far and wide. But I am very square as a mother. My children are the most important things to me in life. I have five now. I want five or six more. But I want them to be good. And I will protect them as long as I live. I feel that this child, because of her jealousy of me, should not go back to the house. I don't appreciate the fact that the child tried to imitate me, dropping the 'Marie' from her name. When asked her name she says, 'I'm Jayne Mansfield!' "

"People imagine sex symbols being on a couch with practically nothing on. And I try to protray that role in pictures. But when it comes to my children, I am completely the opposite."

By this time Jayne was 'coming undone' as she called it. "I'm very conservative. I really am," she said. Then the tears began to spill down her cheeks. Wiping them away, she concluded, "Should I sit over here? I'm sorry. I am never this emotional except when I know what is true. And what is right. And I tell the truth!"

Sam took the floor to cross-examine Jayne. "Now with regard to Jayne Marie. Have you had a discipline problem with her?"

"Yes, I have," Jayne replied. "She wants to wear makeup, long eyelashes, wants to be me, wants to—the whole thing. What I do as a motion picture star. I don't do these things. I don't smoke marijuana, never have. To me the most important thing is my children much more than my career. And the reason she has been disciplined is because I don't want my child smoking marijuana and drinking booze until five in the morning. Call the maid and ask what she does in my bedroom when I'm out of town!! I am sorry. I am a mother talking. I say it is not possible to have the child back here.

"But when a child tries to say, 'Mama, you should meet my boyfriend. He's beautiful. I know he's just turned sixteen, but you would really dig him!'"

Jayne Marie avoided her mother's eyes, although Jayne looked directly at her daughter when she spoke.

Jayne Marie was called to the witness stand.

"When was it finally decided you were going to leave home?" she was asked. Jayne Marie replied, "Last Thursday night."

"And did something unusual happen without going into detail, did something unusual happen between you and Mr. Brody the night that caused you to decide to leave home?"

"Well, as far as I can recall, Mr. Brody had never touched me or struck me in any way," Jayne Marie said, "but that night he literally beat me."

"Was that the night that you contacted your uncle?"

"No, I contacted him the next morning. The last time that I recall talking to him was in Vifginia. I was in Virginia around March and April and maybe the beginning of May, 1967."

"And how did you happen to go to Virginia?"

"My mother sent me there to stay with some friends, Mr. and Mrs. Boyles."

# CHAPTER XXX

Jayne called me at six o'clock that night. "We're out of court. We won our case. Paul Caruso was marvelous. Please come right over. I'm leaving at seven in the morning for Biloxi."

"I can't Jayne. It's the opening at the Huntington Hartford tonight. I'll see you when you get back."

"Please! I've got some things to go over with you for my book that can't wait."

Reluctantly, I arrived a helf hour later to find Sam hobbling around with the cast on his leg. Obviously he was in pain. Was it the king size ego of a small man, or the frustration of not being able to make Jayne say she'd marry him or was it following in Jayne's shadow, with no practice to bolster him, that was making Sam's inner demons destroy him? You sensed something unbalanced in his quick, calculated smiles that made you uneasy to be around him. Two ex-convicts he'd sprung out of the penitentiary were always around him to do his bidding.

An entourage of advertising executives, accompanied by a secretary with a dictation machine, arrived at the Pink Palace minutes after me. Sam showed them into the drawing room.

"A nice place Miss Mansfield has here," observed the president of the company. He was there to negotiate with Jayne for a series of appearances at super markets in connection with a new brand of ham.

Sam courteously asked their preference in drinks and left to shortly reappear with a tray holding scotch, vodka, bourbon, ice and a mix.

"Are you the houseman?"

Sam's blue-gray eyes flinched. "No," he replied.

The group turned in unison to look Sam over. "I'm her attorney," he added.

"Oh!" said one in surprise. Abruptly they turned their attention back to each other and more important matters, leaving Sam serving the drinks.

"He is a brilliant attorney," I interrupted, feeling sorry for Sam. Until his insane infatuation with Jayne, he had been, at least locally, in the legal limelight.

"Oh," said one of the men with indifference. "What kind of an attorney?" His query was an afterthought.

"I'm a trial attorney," Sam replied lamely.

"A good one," I insisted.

"Thank you May," Sam acknowledged with humble and genuine appreciation. He was fully cognizant of his appearance and his own state of affairs. Less than a year before his name was on the front page of the newspapers across the world as Melvin Belli's associate in the Jack Ruby trials. For one day his name, Samuel Brody, had been news. Now he seemed insignificant, forgotten. He was willing, for the time being, to remain in this graceless state until he solved the problem of Jayne; to conquer her and force her to become a submissive female who would be all his. Then he would have the last laugh. All of this scum surrounding him and adding to his humiliation would be brushed out of the pink palace forever.

After a carefully calculated time, Jayne made an entrance. She was wearing a stunning shocking pink jumpsuit, which set off every curve. Her hair was tied with matching ribbons. High heeled thongs graced her bare feet. In them, she towered over Sam, who hopefully persuaded her to wear flat heels whenever possible. As the gentlemen arose, she walked by Sam actually preening, stretching her height to be even taller. His face smiled, but the eyes were sad, bewildered, and then his anger flared growing with a desperate fury.

If he left her, even for a day, he knew other men would be there after her. He had now given up going anywhere unless Jayne would go with him. They slept late, arose by noon, and proceeded with Jayne's schedule until after dinner. When Jayne was in the mood, he'd take her to a cafe. Sometimes he'd attempt to grind out some work in the library. At all times he carried a brief case stuffed with legal documents. The brief case was his crutch.

Sam was reputed to be a good lover. Women had always tumbled for him like ripe plums from a tree. All except Jayne. His wife, he said, hadn't minded if he went amiss. She knew he was highly sexed. If he came home at night with lipstick prints on his face, she'd still welcome him with open arms. Women should be like that, if they loved you. He couldn't understand Jayne. Why wasn't she like all of the rest? Well, patience. He'd win in the end.

Jayne had a way of her own with men. Even the ones who loved her. She'd say, "I love you. You're beautiful." In the next second, she'd be saying, with a wide-eyes innocence that exasperated Sam, "Donald wants to marry me. Here's this long letter from him. He wants me to call him collect. He complains, the darling, that he can't get through to me on the telephone Samuel!" With that, Jayne would dial long distance and call Donald, or whichever one of her admirers she felt so inclined towards. Sam would sometimes sit for an hour or two listening to Jayne talking to another man, with such stirring phrases as, "Yes Baby, I think it would be wonderful to marry you. You want to love me tonight, you say?" She'd repeat every word so Sam could get the sum total of the conversation. "Oh, that would be beautiful. Fly out! . . . I'll love going to Paris with you. You will open all of those charge accounts for me? And we'll be married where? Oh, that would be lovely. I love you too, Baby, I really do. You are a gorgeous man. I can see you. Honest I can, as you talk."

Jayne would talk breathlessly and sexily into the telephone. "Yes, here's a kiss for you too, Sweetheart," she'd continue in seductive, sweet, gentle tones. "I feel you holding me. Yes I do. Do you feel me too? Is it good?"

This would go on and on. How many evenings I watched this scene in the pink palace—the same moods, the same dialogue and the mounting disaster between them.

"Please Jayne, Sam will kill you in a jealous rage," I warned.

"I'm showing that 'little man' he doesn't own me. I'm a free woman," Jayne would reply. So it continued. You sensed how tragically it had to end.

Sam would sit simmering, with the fury of being made a fool goading him inside into a fevered pitch.

Jayne would sweetly hang up from the calls, and observe innocently (if he were Donald), "He's the most wonderful man. He has millions and a yacht anchored on the Green Isles. He is a friend of Elizabeth and Richard Burton and Ari Onassis. He wants to charter a plane and fly over and marry me. We'll honeymoon over there. I am thinking it over," she'd add.

It was the same this last night in the Pink Palace Everyone sat still as spectators enjoying the scene. Sam's face, turned white with rage, tensed. "So you want to marry that guy, do you Baby?"

"I don't know Samuel, I really don't." Jayne pouted like a child. "I am thinking about it. He has so much to offer me. He's so tall and strong and handsome—just gorgeous! But then there's Charles in Louisiana!

"Oh May," she turned to me, "you should meet Charles. He is soo divine. Six feet four. A girl can wear four inch heels and still look up to him as a man to protect her. He's so handsome and such a wonderful lover." She added, "Charles and I haven't had each other yet, but————!" She ignored the group of advertising men, as though her drawing room were a theater and she was on stage.

Now Sam was seething and nearly bursting with jealousy.

"You want to go to bed with Charles, do you Baby?" he said in a desperate, quiet voice. "You want to go to bed with Charles, do you Baby?"

"Well," Jayne smiled, pleased, knowing she was goading him on, "He is coming out here next week, and if I feel like it. Who knows what may happen."

"You see," she turned to all of us now, "I am truthful about sex. Sex is the most beautiful and natural thing in the world when two people are attracted to each other. It is when you stifle it, suppress it, deny what nature has given to you—that is when it is wrong. That is the big sin with me, not to do what nature intends you to do."

Sam's hands gripped a copy of *Life Magazine* and choked it with rage—as though it were Jayne's neck.

"I have this beautiful body to enjoy," Jayne added, smiling child-like. She stretched herself like a kitten and lay full length on the sofa.

"Some day Jayne, I'm going to kill you," Sam said with a quiet desperation. "So help me God!"

Sam strode out of the room.

Jayne giggled. "Now he's really turned on. He thinks he can put me under his thumb like all of the rest of the women he's had! Well, he can't!"

Jayne giggled "Jayne, why do you egg him on, enrage him on purpose?" I admonished her again, fearing for her safety.

"Because he thinks he can own me. And he can't. He never

will!" she repeated. She was adamant.

"You don't know the half of it,"she said in a ladylike manner, turning to the others. "He thinks, he, Sam Brody, can own me! It's a laugh. Sometimes I hate the little man. Besides, I want to be free. I want to be rid of him forever!"

"We've got things to do," she said now. The group of strangers swigging Jayne's champagne remained content. It was all free, wasn't it?

As we turned on the stairs, a new group of business men arrived. They were from C.B.S. T.V. Jayne took a deep breath, posed on the steps for a second-to enable everyone to take in the effect ofthe Jayne Mansfield sexuality. "Go in and have some champagne," she invited. "I'm busy at the moment."

"I just gave an interview," she laughed. "Esquire asked me if I had a new love," she recounted. "Would you expect me to stay home every night with a book?" I replied. "Let's go into the library, May."

Jayne sat behind the big desk. "I hate going to Biloxi. That's where I met Nelson Sardelli," she said. "Some day he's got to see Maria!" she observed as an afterthought. "Maria's so talented. She'll be a big star one day!"

"I have no intention of going on with Samuel," she said."The more I insult him, the more he sticks with me. He's like smallpox-you can't get rid of it-just weather it out. One happy day, it's over with."

Jayne went to a file in a small closet. She pulled out pictures and began carefully making selections."These are pictures that tell my story. They have never been published. They are personal," she said. "They are for your book about me."

She stood transfixed, staring at something straight ahead. She seemed to be seeing something startling happening.I broke in with, "What are you looking at all of this time, Jayne? You look hypnotized!"

"Ohhh—," she brought herself back slowly, as though it were

hard to break away from the distraction claiming her. "I don't know. I'm so confused. Maybe Sam and I ...." She didn't finish. She seemed in shock or reverie, like she couldn't pull herself away from what she saw.

"Jayne!!!" I grabbed her and pulled her back into the center of the room "What's the matter with you. What's come over you?"

Slowly, as though she'd been brought back from somewhere else, she became conscious of me. She shook her head, but a puzzled look glazed her eyes. It was minutes before she began to talk to me.

"May, I want you to write down all of my jewelry," she exclaimed suddenly, as though this were now urgent.

"Not now Jayne. It's late. Wait until you come back from Biloxi. I want to go home."

"Please now. There's no one else who knows what I have. This morning I fired my Mexican couple. I hadn't been to the bank. I'd put $2700 under the matress. It was gone. This afternoon, Sam admitted he was short and he'd taken it. Now he's confessed he's had no money. except my earnings, since he lost that $20,000 gambling in Las Vegas the first night we met. He's been taking my money all along. He's never sent any of my checks in to my business manager, Charles Goldring. like he said. He got my power of attorney when he took over my affairs last September. He's been cashing my checks and using the money. The $7500 paid on this diamond ring was even my money. I don't know—I guess it's been my earnings paying for everything," she sighed. "Poor little man.

"And there's a blackmail picture he took—a snapshot of me nude with one of his men nude standing looking at me. Oh yes, Sam did such a thing, trying to get me in his power. He'd put a needle in my arm to make me unconscious. I didn't even know about the picture until it was too late. It's hidden in the doorcase of the library here. The south door—you see. And Sam's made out his will to me. It's upstairs, hidden in a shoe in my shoe closet.

"And my jewels. Sam bought them all with my earnings. My bracelet, my charm bracelet and those from Marvin Hine. Sam stole my diamond earrings to hock them too."

"You write it all down when you get back from Biloxi, Jayne."

"One more thing," she ignored or didn't hear my plea to leave. "Here's these pictures of me with Anton Lavey."

"Were you crazy to do such a thing?" I scolded.

"I did it because I thought he'd remove the curse. He said he couldn't. But here are the pictures. The photographer said he'd get $500 for them and they would only be used in Germany, not in this country."

"And," she continued breathlessly, as though in fear I'd leave before she could finish, "here's my life story which ran in a London paper. They paid me $50,000 for it."

Jayne and I left the library. Several agents, T.V. and advertising men were still in the drawing room sipping champagne.

"I'm not going in there. There's nothing they propose I'd want to do. If anything, I'll have a T.V. show of my own with all of my children—right here at home. Jayne Marie, my teenager, will be coming home to me, now that her charges were dismissed in court. I'm sure she's sorry. I have all ages, even to Tony. What a wonderful show it will make."

As she pushed the electric gate buttons, she began to sob. I put my arms around her. "I feel so alone, May. No one really cares now—except you."

I comforted her—feeling so sorry for this distraught girl—whom I loved.

"Sometimes I wonder," she said sadly. "I dream of the day when I can stay home and be with my children. Just be a woman and not a breadwinner."

"Be a wife and a mother and enjoy my home and family and have close friends in. Not always be packing to go to the next place, the next engagement. Perhaps just make pictures, one or two year. Just be me," sighed Jayne.

"The most rewarding experience I've ever had was my USO tour in Vietnam. I visited the hospitals and talked with the men there, and I love them all. And, I think they all love me, too." she said hopefully. Then, pulling her shoulders back resolutely, she managed a smile.

"My world is really beautiful—this lovely home, my new Rolls, my Masserati, Ferrari, and my Bentley in the garage, the man I love—when," she now laughed, "I decide which one. There are so many asking me to marry them. I wish my family and I were free of all these troubles. There's a beautiful saying "The rain has to stop some day, and the sun will shine." It will shine for me. That promise makes it all endurable.

"There isn't anyone—no matter who or what they have done to me—that I don't love," she concluded as she walked me out to my car.

As she kissed me an affectionate goodbye, she said, "I'll call you from New Orleans."

The next morning Jayne left the Pink Palace for Biloxi. Linda had arrived at her regular early hour. "Miss Mansfield had been up all night, going through things, checking out things—like she was putting everything in order before she left.

"As she walked down the stairs to the car, she turned and said, 'Linda, if anything comes up, call May Mann. She will know just what to do. She is my dearest and closest friend. You know you can depend on her. She was here last night until early this morning. She is the only one who knows everything. So call her if you need to.' She smiled and I walked to the gate with her. Jayne was the sweetest woman I ever knew in my life. She said, 'I didn't wake up baby Tony to say goodbye. But I know you'll take good care of him for me!' Then she was gone."

# CHAPTER XXXI

A call came at 3:30 in the morning. Sleepily, I picked up the telephone. "Jayne Mansfield has been killed in a car crash outside New Orleans" was the message. A half-hour later, another call: "Jayne Mansfield was decapitated!"

My telephone never stopped ringing. Reporters, T.V., the world press descended on me. Jayne's death was headlined all over the world! Front page headlines continued daily for over a week! Vivian Leigh, an Academy Oscar winner and star of GONE WITH THE WIND, received a modest inside piece at the time of her death shortly thereafter.

Sam Brody and the chauffeur had also been killed in the car crash, while Jayne's three children suffered injuries.

In shock and heartbreak I refused to see anyone. The next day a letter arrived from Jayne, postmarked Biloxi, mail stamped 12:30 a.m. She'd mailed it that night on the way to New Orleans.

Enclosed was a carefully okayed chapter for the book.

In Jayne's inimitable handwriting, with all "i"'s dotted with hearts, it read:

June 28th, 1967

Dear May,

A great story! Once again you've proven yourself as not only a great writer but a wonderful friend!

Doing record business down here. I'm wearing the two new ribbon sets you presented to me!

Samuel sends his love. He can't swim because of his broken leg, but I've been making the silver and gold lame bikini scene by the pool. We have Miklos, Zoltan, and Maria with us + four chihuahuas.

Love You and Princess,

Jayne

Anything Jayne might have done couldn't have shocked Hollywood more than the news that her remains were not be be returned home for a funeral. Mickey, who had just arrived in Hollywood from New York, flew immediately to New Orleans to take charge of the children in a hospital there, Jayne's mother and stepfather, Vera and Harry Peers, flew from Dallas to take charge of the body.

Jayne's mother and Mickey had agreed to bury Jayne in Argyle, a small mining town in Pennsylvania. She would be laid to rest in an obscure grave, but happily, next to her father.

The fact that Jayne had fought to make her own special niche in Hollywood; that her home and children were in Hollywood; that she had often visited Hollywood's world-famous cemetery, Forest Lawn, "where all the movie stars are buried" and had often expressed the desire to be buried there was completely ignored. Jayne's friends in filmland strongly protested. Her mother had voiced disapproval of Hollywood and that was it. What was Mickey thinking of to agree to it? Who had the right to make these decisions! Legally, only Matt Cimber. Jayne's divorce from Matt would not finalize for two more weeks. Matt insisted that Jayne's

body be returned to Hollywood. He was ignored. I argued ......
Jayne's children, Jayne's friends and thousands of her fans would
want to visit her grave and take flowers through the years to
come.It was not fair to bury her so far away. She'd earned her
place in the Hollywood she loved. It was a great wrong not to
return her. My pleas, too, were ignored.

Jayne had left a financial will with Charles Goldring, her
business manager of fourteen years. She had not signed it.

Mickey identified the body. "I held her little hand, and it was so
cold," he said. Several T.V. and radio commentators speculated
ghoulishly whether the head had been sewed back on. There were
other equally sickening world-wide reports and comments.

Jayne Marie, accompanied by her temporary guardian Mrs.
William Pique, flew to Argyle, Pennsylvania for the funeral. So did
Mr. and Mrs. Charles Goldring. They found Jayne's maternal
relatives who lived there to be nice, average, middle-class Ameri-
cans. An uncle, Bert Milkeem, played the organ including three
hymns and a ballad, "More." The latter was one of Jayne's favorite
songs. An aunt was blonde and beautiful like Jayne, while a cousin
was said to have equally as good a figure although not quite Jayne's
spectacular measurements. The family was deeply moved at the
tragedy. According to the first news reports, the Reverend who
was to officiate said he was not going "to whitewash Jayne." Rather,
he would speak of her as the little girl who had once lived there.

Masses of pink flowers from all over the world filled the room. A
blanket of pink roses from her children covered the closed bronze
casket. A huge heart of pink roses was lettered in gold, "To My
Beloved Wife, Matteo." Mickey's tribute was thirteen red roses
with a gold sash, worded, "Forever and Ever, I Love You Jayne,
Mickey." "This has always been our unspoken love message," he
said. "Today it means nothing."

Those listening were disappointed if they expected to hear a
eulogy about Jayne. Instead, passages from the scriptures were
given. There was a prayer and it was over. It was as though her

family wanted it over—to hide her and forget her, said Jayne's fans.

Thousands of telegrams and letters from Jayne Mansfield fan clubs came to me, since everyone seemed to know of our friendship. Most were bewildered and indignant that she was not laid to rest in her beloved Hollywood. Matt spoke of having her body brought back after the Pennsylvania internment to rest at Forest Lawn. He had the legal right to do so. But he shuddered at the thought of more headlines for Jayne.

Three hundred local and state police held back the crowds of curiousity seekers and fans who pushed forward around the chapel and lined the roads in Argyle. At the cemetery, literally thousands had gathered since early morning to witness the burial. Flowers were heaped around the opening after the casket was lovered. The mourners had barely departed when the souvenir seekers had taken them all. And there was Jayne, left in peace, far away from home and the glamorous world which she had been a part of.

Hundreds of calls continued coming to me, asking when and where services for Jayne would be held. Would Hollywood let one of its brightest stars, known the world over, pass on without a word? What about all of her friends and the studios who would want to pay their last respects?

It seemed if it were to be done, it was up to me, just like it had always been with Jayne's bridal and baby showers and birthdays.

The task seemed monumental! And then impossible, for it was the Fourth of July holiday week.

It had to be done somehow, kept forming in my mind. But can I do it? Will I have the strength? Can I afford the money? I prayed, humbly and sincerely, and I knew I would have both. I had to have both. This was the last thing I could do for Jayne.

I wanted to ask permission from someone although it was not necessary. But there was no one to call. Jayne Marie was in Pennsylvania. I called Jayne's mother and left word, but there was no reply. I tried to reach Mickey in vain. Matt Cimber, emotionally overwrought, agreed it should be done. I talked to Jayne Marie's guardian, Mr. William Pigue. I talked to Fanny Ottaviano, Matt Cimber's mother. The Goldrings were in Pennsylvania for the funeral. There was no one else to call.

All here agreed that Jayne would want funeral services at home. It was up to me to give her a memorial, which conventionally had to be done within the week of death.

Although Jayne had said she was a Catholic, we discovered she had only taken instruction. She was not baptized. A memorial, therefore, could not be held in the Catholic Church. I remembered she had often attended the All Saints Church in Beverly Hills. Fanny Ottaviano offered to help me. She called all day Saturday, and then Sunday, to reach the Reverend Dr. J. Herbert Smith, to ask if we could hold a memorial in his church. Fanny finally gave up. The task was mine. I was able to get an appointment for an interview on Sunday at 5:00 to see Dr. Smith.

I had attended Sam Brody's funeral in Inglewood. I had seen his widow, Beverly, in a wheel chair and his small children. The Rabbi told what a brilliant man and what a kind, good man Sam had been known to be. He had fostered and given large sums of money to help teenage boys. They spoke of the good Sam Brody had done. The chapel was filled with people who respected and loved him.

Now I was to meet Dr. Smith! I found him to be a tall, quiet man of stature and dignity. He spoke with me at length, while my heart was in my mouth. Suppose he refused the church? I had too much pride to go church-shopping for Jayne. It would be too undignified. If I had to, I would have those who loved Jayne attend a completely private eulogy for her in my garden. But we had to have the church. I prayed constantly as Dr. Smith discussed it with me.

The memorial should be held, I thought, the day after Jayne's children were returned from New Orleans, and Jayne Marie from Pennsylvania. I wanted them to have a beautiful, dignified memo-

ry of final tribute and respect given their mother. This, they could
hold in their hearts forever.

Dr. Smith was wonderfully kind. He said the church was the
house of God, and Jayne often came there. "Of course," he agreed,
"we will do everything we can." He made suggestions and we
discussed what I had in mind. I wanted beautiful organ music and
if possible, Frank Sinatra, a friend of Jayne's to sing. Dr. Smith
concurred. Who was to give the eulogy? Everyone said I should
because I was the only one that close to her. However, I hoped this
honor would go to Bob Hope. He was in Puerto Rico filming on
location, and was unable to be in California. Pride forbade me to
go shopping for a eulogy for Jayne. I could hear Jayne saying, as
she often had, "Oh May, you do everything so wonderfully. I love
you for it." That, too, was up to me.

Even though the church was donated and the Reverend was
offering his services, there were still expenses. I happily volunteered to pay the few hundred dollars involved. 20th Century Fox
said they would help financialy.

I called Sybil Brand, a wonderful woman whose civic work had
won her the honor of having the Los Angeles County Jail named
the "Sybil Brand Institute for Women." Sybil not only willingly
offered tohelp, but she asked to share some of the expenses. Her
help was invaluable, as was Patti Moore's. With the studios closed
for the long Friday to Wednesday July Fourth holiday, it required
unending telephone calls to locate people, especially those with
unlisted telephone numbers. I was determined to have a star sing
for Jayne's memorial. She was a star, and she would have wanted a
star. Frank Sinatra was away on a series of one-nighter's in the East
and could not be located in time. Vic Damone was opening in Las
Vegas the night of the service. Ironically, Mrs. Damone observed
that they were close friends of Mrs. Sam Brody, although she
agreed that at a time like this it would not stop Vic..

Patti Moore called. "Peter Palmer has the most gorgeous voice.
Ask him." Peter was starring in "Custers." a T.V. series at 20th

Century Fox. Again, the hectic calls to get someone who had his home telephone number, as the studios were closed tight for the long holiday weekend, which lasted until Wednesday.

Peter was relaxing at home. It was 9:00 p.m. He was having dinner when I announced who I was. "Jayne symbolized Hollywood itself," Peter agreed. "Everyone was talking about it at the studio and on location when the news report said she'd be buried in Pennsylvania," he remarked. "It seemed so strange—so far away."

Peter said he would be honored to sing at the memorial, greatly honored. "I had the pleasure of meeting her twice," he recalled. "We appeared on two television shows together. Earlier this year my wife, Aniko, and I followed Jayne's tour in Vietnam by a week. The men kept showing us snapshots they had taken with her. They adored her!"

"There's only one problem," Peter said. "I would have to get a clearance from the studio for that hour. Truthfully, I don't see how they could possibly let me off. It would mean four hours of production time budgeted roughly at $20,000 an hour. That could cost the studio $80,000 to spring me."

I was polite, sweet, and persistent. "I don't know how to get hold of the producer. The studio is closed down until the day you plan for the funeral—I mean the memorial," he ammended. "It seems impossible. Can you get the permission from someone for me? I'll get the sheet music and learn 'The Shadow of Your Smile' that you want me to sing. Thank you for the honor," he added and said goodbye.

Sybil, Harry Brand and 20th Century Fox performed the miracle. Peter was cleared and he would be off at four in the afternoon. A studio car would drive him back in time!

Four hundred people filled the church in Beverly Hills. Television cameras, reporters, and news media arrived in advance. An hour earlier, I had quietly gone inside the church where I remained an hour afterwards, to avoid any publicity that might be directed to me. This was to be all and only for Jayne.

The studio furnished a secretary who admitted those invited. A Jewish mortuary sent a beautiful white leather book for the names of those attending. The ushers included Jerry Dunphy, President of the Greater Los Angeles Press Club, Herbert Luft, President of the Foreign Press Association, Ceasar Romero, Harry Brand, James Denton, Frank Neill Jet Fore and officials of 20th Century Fox Studios.

A hush fell in the church as Peter's magnificent voice rose and fell with the words of "Ave Maria'.." Even the television cameras outside turned off in respect.

When he sang "The Shadow Of Your Smile...when you are gone...will color all my dreams...and light the dawn," tears rolled down the faces of the listeners. "All the lovely things you are... to me a wistful little star, was far too high..." the words came with true beauty and meaning. Fate had introduced Peter Palmer with a great voice at sunset for Jayne's memorial.

"Jayne Mansfield has been eulogized in headlines the world over. She was many things to many people," said the Honorable Deputy Mayor of Los Angeles, Joseph Quinn, representing Mayor Sam Yorty.

My eulogy said, "Jayne was like a ray of sunshine when she walked into a room. That last night when we talked, she said, I really love everyone. There isn't anyone I don't care for in this whole wide world!'"

Mickey Hargitay sat in the front row left. Matt Cimber sat in the front row right.

There was only one dissenting note. Mickey's lawyer stood up shouting "That's a lie!" when I said, "Jayne loved everyone." Those of us in the Rostrum were shocked! I had knelt and prayed before this with Dr. Smith that it would be perfect. The words flowed and I didn't stop in spite of the heckler.

None of Jayne's children including Jayne Marie attended. This was a great disappointment. I had wanted Jayne's children especially to have this memory of dignity, prestige and love to remember. Mickey didn't bring Miklos, Maria and Zoltan. Baby Tony was perhaps too young to remember. Jayne Marie said she "couldn't go through it again."

Mrs. Charles Goldring clasped my hand and remarked, "If you never do another thing in this world—you have done something so wonderful here today. Jayne would have loved it. It was absolutely perfect."

# CHAPTER XXXII

Eight-year-old Miklos, with blue eyes, wavy golden blond hair, who as an infant looked like a cherub off of a calendar, "too beautiful to be real, and he still holds his baby looks," Jayne always said, was in a wheel chair, His leg, broken in two places, and his broken arm were in casts. Zoltan, who had almost met death with the lion at Jungleland only seven months before, had miraculously escaped unhurt. Three-year-old Maria, dark-eyed with dark brown curls, had received skull, head and face injuries that required plastic surgery.

The children's eyes told the horror. They had been asked repeated questions in New Orleans. They were still bewildered and confused, except Miklos. His large eyes had been sad, serious and rebellious by turn for the past several months; eyes that were never laughing or happy since Sam Brody took over the control and discipline of the Pink Palace were now stunned with reality.

Linda had been devoted to the children. She remained the closest to them and tried to protect them. Often she had called me when they needed clothes and they were being made fun of by schoolmates for worn-out shoes. She loved the children like a mother.

Linda had told Jayne, "I can't take this Mr. Brody spanking the children, and you all being gone so much. I've got to quit. These children are so scared and so unhappy with Mr. Brody here." Jayne had replied, "Linda, you can't quit. I can't do without you, you know that. The little man won't be here much longer. You must stay!" Linda, for the children's sake, had remained.

A week following Anton Lavey's visit to the Pink Palace, as Linda left to go home, she was struck by another car. Her car was demolished, and she was seriously injured. She could not return to take care of the children.

In pain and agony she called me. "I feel so bad," she said. "I want to be there with the children. Something is so wrong with that place. I've been infected too. That devil man!"

The night after the memorial I took the largest flower displays to the now three different homes of the children The children, whom Jayne had always kept so close together, were now living under three different roofs. To Jayne Marie I took the huge basket of pink gladiolas, carnations and roses sent by Ida Mayer Cummings and the Junior Auxiliary of the Jewish Home for the Aged.

Jayne Marie was legally adopted by the Bill Pigues as their daughter within three weeks. Jayne Marie went to summer school and received a B+ the first semester, to the delight of, and justifying the faith of her new parents, Mr. and Mrs. Bill Pigue. She then went to Catholic school in Santa Barbara, going home to spend the weekends with the Pigues.

By October, four months later, Jayne Marie was posing and imitating her sex symbol mother, in front of some of the famed Mansfield sexiest portraits. Only now—Jayne Marie called herself 'Jayne Mansfield.'

A large star of yellow roses, I saved for the baby, Tony. He was now staying with his father, Matt Cimber, and being cared for by his grandmother, Fanny. Matt quietly came to my house and got it, along with a special picture Jayne had given me of the baby and herself in Sweden.

The pink heart of orchids I took to the three children at the Pink Palace. "This is from your Mamma," I said. I was not sure how much or how little they knew. "You can always keep the pink satin heart part," I told Maria, who stared at me with questioning wide eyes. Miklos and Zoltan just looked. I put my arms around them and hugged and kissed them, as I had done exactly the same night one week before, when their mother was there.

The children watched television. Every station was channeled on Jayne's memorial and the latest details of the tragedy. They must have heard and seen much of it.

The next day Miklos asked Linda, who arrived each morning at seven and departed each afternoon at three-thirty, as she had been doing for those three years she worked for Jayne, "My mother is dead, isn't she, Linda?" he asked with quiet resignation. He had waited until the other children were out of the room. "I know," he said manfully, "I know Linda, because I saw her!" Linda pulled the child's face to her bosom and held him. "Now, now, Miklos," she consoled. But Miklos wanted Linda to know.

"Zoldie and Maria, they don't know," he said. "I've kept it to myself because I'm the oldest, like Mommy said, and I have to be the man. They are just babies."

"When people ask," he continued spilling out all he had held in so long, "I just tell them what I want to tell them. I tell them the truth though," he quickly clarified. "I always tell the truth Linda."

"I know you do," Linda comforted him, stroking his blond waving hair that was his mother's pride.

"Mommy said when we got in the car, 'Now you three go to sleep, because we've got a long two-hour ride.'

"Zoldie and Maria and I were in front. At a gas station, she said she and Sam would move up front, so we could go back and sleep on the back seat. I know my Mommy was tired too. I said, 'You go to sleep too, Mommy!' She said, 'I will.'

"The next thing I knew," Miklos said, " was something terrible crushed us. The front seat was on top of us! A lady with blond hair, I thought she was Mommy, was trying to get us out. We were suffocating. We couldn't breathe," he said.

"I said, 'Mommy, are you hurt?' and she said, "Hush child!" I knew then she wasn't Mommy. She wasn't Mommy at all! When they pulled me out, I saw Mommy's head coming out of the windshield in front. People put their hands in front of my face. Every time I looked they kept turning my head away so I couldn't see. I saw my mother laying on the ground with a sheet or something over where her head was supposed to be. "I said, 'Is Mommy hurt bad?' They said, 'That isn't your Mommy. She is in the hospital.' But I knew better because I saw Mommy's blue boots sticking out and I knew them. I kept trying to look back at the windshield, because I saw her whole head there, but they kept putting their hands over my eyes.

"There were a lot of people! And then a siren from a long ways off came. And they took us to the hospital. You see Linda, I know my Mommy's in heaven and I'll never see her again! Did they sew her head back on? Did God put it back, now that she is an angel?"

For the first time since he had returned to the Pink Palace, Miklos buried his head in Linda's lap and cried his heart out.

The children clung frantically to Linda. Ellen, Mickey Hargitay's girl friend, had left after that first day. Linda said Ellen had assumed she could use Jayne's room and sleep in Jayne's heart-shaped bed. "I wouldn't have it," Linda said. "I wouldn't have it at all. I told her, 'That is Miss Mansfield's room and nobody is going to sleep in there.'

"I couldn't stand being there any more," Linda said. "I hadn't felt right being there since that Devil person had come to see Miss Mansfield, but I couldn't leave those children."

The courts impounded the Pink Palace until the fourway legal battle for it and the children's custody was settled. Guards and a couple of strangers, appointed by the court, were in charge now. Even I couldn't see the children without special permission. Linda had been dismissed by court order. Her departure was a second heartbreak for the children.

"When will our little brother Tony come to see us?" they asked. "Where is Jayne Marie?"

The baby Tony was brought to visit them. Jayne Marie came to see them. Everyone asked in whispers, "Have the children been told? Do they know?"

Ellen, Mickey's girl friend, said she had told them. Only Miklos knew for sure they'd never see their mother again, except on television. Linda kept hearing Miklos talking to someone in his room. When she entered he said, "I've been talking to Mommy. She often comes to visit me." Linda heard him talking many times. "I know Jayne came from the spirit world," she said.

The diamonds and jewels Sam Brody lavished on Jayne were claimed by his widow. Through neglect, Mickey Hargitay's name had not been removed from her $200,000 insurance policy, which would otherwise have been left to all of her children. The whereabouts of her cars, including a Bentley, were unknown. There was no one in charge and everyone tried to be. Since her death had occurred two weeks before her divorce from Matt Cimber finalized, all concerned chose sides and lawyers, and went to court.

The million-dollar Pink Palace was put up for sale, while attorneys and former husbands fought over the estate, which was still in litigation on the second anniversary of her death. Frightening events continued. Mickey Hargitay, driving out of the gate of the Pink Palace, had a severe car crash. Linda suffered another severe car smashup. Matt Cimber's closest friend, Marty, who had lived with them in the Pink Palace during their marriage, was killed. Matt's father suffered a heart attack. Matt, himself, ran into the law over his new night club.

The three Hargitay children, were left in the Pink Palace for over a year after their mother's death. New caretakers came into the house and ran into all sorts of problems. Waterpipes burst, ruining some of the extravagant, plush rooms of Jayne's movie mansion. Rats moved in.

While everyone wanted to see the house through curiosity, and proclaimed themselves prospective buyers, people were afraid to buy the elegant estate. The price was lowered by hundreds of thousands of dollars before it was finally sold.

Those who went through the house reported their astonishment. In Jayne's plushy, pink bedroom was a framed certificate from Anton Lavey's Church of the Devil, which proclaimed Jayne Mansfield a pledged member. Someone had placed it there, along with a picture of herself and Sam Brody. No one had taken it down. I saw it there the day the house was finally sold to people who bought it with Jayne's few remaining clothes and personal effects.

It took months to repair the damages to the house. No sooner had the new owners arrived, than "accidents" started all over again. Servants refused to stay on. In desperation, Linda was called, asking her if she would return, because it was too difficult to keep help in the mansion. People were hired but came and then left shortly without saying why. The new owners' son was killed in a motorcycle accident going outside the gate.

Linda said, "Not me. I never want to go in that house again." Workmen, there for months trying to repair all of the water damage from burst pipes, reported they were often plain scared. They said objects moved. A painter said someone touched him on the shoulder in Jayne's room. He could feel someone there and see no one. He went over to see who it was. He could find no one on that floor. Strange wailing sounds came from nowhere.

Linda said the so-called Devil called her after Jayne's death and said, "You are a nice girl. I don't want anything to happen to you. I would like to come and see you."

"Not me," said Linda. "He gave me shivers, just as he gave

Jayne. But somehow she didn't get rid of him, or she was just too sweet and polite, and even she didn't understand the strange hold he had over her!"

A lot of things went on that Linda and Jayne's road manager, Victor Huston, and I knew which we didn't talk about. Victor Huston, a comparatively young man, suddenly died a year later. Maria and Miklos, who had finally recovered from their physical injuries in that fatal car crash, were playing in a toy electric car in the playground of the Pink Palace when Maria, who was in the back seat, leaned back. Her long, beautiful, black hair got caught in the wheels, and she was all but scalped. The whole back of her head of hair was pulled out by the roots.

It was one thing after another, continuously! I had said to Jayne, scolding her soundly that last night I saw her, "Jayne, when this man proclaims himself the Devil, no good can come of seeing him. Besides, the terrible feeling there is in this house!"

"Yes, I know, " Jayne replied. "I was only seeing him in trying to get him to remove the curse from Sam and the house. When I get back from Biloxi, I will. "

I told Jayne, "I don't even like to come here, Jayne. There's such a terrible feeling here.

"Look at Maria tonight—terrified, and the children's faces —so tragically unhappy; and Linda is so worried. She's only staying on because of her devotion to you and the children."

"Things will be different. Everything will be changed when I get back from Biloxi," Jayne said. "That will be in ten more days, and by then, I'll be free, by the grace of God."

Only, Jayne never came back.

Or did she—to Miklos, Linda, Princess and to me?